THE
DEVIL YOU
KNOW

THE
DEVIL YOU
KNOW

❋ A STONEFACE FINNEGAN WESTERN ❋

WILLIAM W.
JOHNSTONE
AND J.A. JOHNSTONE

PINNACLE BOOKS
Kensington Publishing Corp.
www.kensingtonbooks.com

PINNACLE BOOKS are published by

Kensington Publishing Corp.
119 West 40th Street
New York, NY 10018

PUBLISHER'S NOTE:
Following the death of William W. Johnstone, the Johnstone family is working with a carefully selected writer to organize and complete Mr. Johnstone's outlines and many unfinished manuscripts to create additional novels in all of his series like The Last Gunfighter, Mountain Man, and Eagles, among others. This novel was inspired by Mr. Johnstone's superb storytelling.

All Kensington titles, imprints, and distributed lines are available at special quantity discounts for bulk purchases for sales promotion, premiums, fundraising, educational, or institutional use.

Special book excerpts or customized printings can also be created to fit specific needs. For details, write or phone the office of the Kensington Sales Manager: Attn.: Sales Department. Kensington Publishing Corp., 119 West 40th Street, New York, NY 10018. Phone: 1-800-221-2647.

PINNACLE BOOKS, the Pinnacle logo, and the WWJ steer head logo are Reg. U.S. Pat. & TM Off.

First Printing: July 2021
ISBN-13: 978-0-7860-4607-2
ISBN-10: 0-7860-4607-4

ISBN-13: 978-0-7860-4608-9 (eBook)
ISBN-10: 0-7860-4608-2 (eBook)

10 9 8 7 6 5 4 3 2 1

Printed in the United States of America

Chapter 1

The sigh, long and low, leaked out of the big man's mouth. It could have come about because he had gulped a long-needed drink of cool water or because he'd won the biggest hand of the night at the baize tables. But neither would be true. For this man wore spatters of blood on his face and chest, and on the twitching lids of his closed eyes. Runnels of gore dripped from his long fingers as he stood over two flopped bodies, people whose heads had been all-but-separated from their neck stalks.

Those necks bore tell-tale marks—wide, purple hand-prints that choked life from the pair in that effortless squeeze that brought the big man such sweet, pleasing release. That pleasure was only topped by the final act of slicing the throats and feeling the warm gush of blood.

In the glow of his reverie, the big man thought he heard a tinkling bell. How nice, how soothing.

"Miss Tillis? Mr. Tillis? Yoo hoo . . . anybody here?"

The voice snapped his eyes open. It was not soothing. It was foul, the worst of interruptions, a harsh jag of light in an otherwise serene, shadowed moment.

More tinkling bell sounds, then bootsteps as the nosey woman made her way through the store out front.

The big man let out a quick breath of disgust and, with a last glance down at his latest accomplishment that, had it not been for the interruption, he might have considered one of his finest performances, he stepped toward the back door, eased it open, and slipped outside once more.

He set to his next tasks with measured motions, walking with long, sure strides across the rear loading deck of Tillis Mercantile, then down the six steps, his oversize, soft-sole brogans making no sound save for a shuffling whisper. He crossed the graveled yard and ducked low between the sagged rails of a weather-grayed fence and into the neighboring paddock, home of a sway-bellied pony.

"Good morning, sir," he whispered to the old beast, who had not yet committed to waking from its nighttime doze.

He crossed to the pony's water trough, which he knew from his foray through this way but hours before to be half-full. The man also knew that at any moment he would hear a scream that would likely rise to shriek pitch— women loved to draw attention to newly discovered horrors—and then haste would be required, lest he be caught by the screamer's goodly neighbors while rinsing blood from his hands.

He set to the task with vigor, a smile tugging up the right side of his wide mouth. Since it was still early dawn and gray light was all he had to work with, he didn't worry about the scrim of blood he knew would be under his nails, coloring the creases of his palms and fingers.

Satisfied his hands were clean enough, he once more

bent low over the trough and splashed two handfuls of water on his face and throat, rubbing any flecks of blood that might still be there.

He unbuttoned the large, spattered shirt, peeled it off, and laid it on the ground, arms wide as if to welcome the rest of his ensemble.

He'd nudged his brown trousers down to his knees when the screams began. Despite his dicey situation, the big man could not help but smile. Standing on the shirt, he scuffed out of the large brogans and finished peeling off the trousers.

Beneath these clothes he wore black silk sleepwear, shirt and trousers, and black close-fitting house slippers. He bent over the soiled clothes, tied the sleeves and tails and collar into a tight bundle, and carried them with him as he bent low and left the still-drowsy pony's paddock.

The big man resisted the urge to whistle and instead hummed a nearly silent, low tune of sheer joy that only came to him when he'd completed a performance. They had been quite the couple, he mused. No, no, not yet. Don't give in to thoughts of the past few hours yet. Time a-plenty for that. First, he must pass behind four back yards to return to the rear of the Starr Town Hotel and Rooming House, where he'd propped open the back door with a slender wedge of wood.

Halfway to the hotel, he heard commotion as people in other homes and businesses were roused by the screaming woman's unceasing cries.

"Ah," he said to himself. "The thrill of discovery."

He measured his steps, eyeing the outhouses and sagging sheds tucked at the rear of properties until he saw the one he required, though not for the usual reasons. This one, but one building from the rear of the hotel, had a widening hole behind it where earth had slumped beneath the privy. It exuded a pungent tang and he held his breath as he dropped the bundle and toed it into the reeking pit. It fetched up, so he squatted and poked a quick hand at it, lest something foul begrime him. It was enough, and the bundle toppled into the drop and out of his sight.

And sight was something he knew would work against him soon as more people woke to greet their day and to figure out who was screaming and why. What he had not counted on was being interrupted by that woman.

Why had the front door of the store been unlocked? Unless the woman had a key to the door. Perhaps she is an employee of the Tillis couple. Correct that, former employee. He indulged in a low chuckle and walked to the hotel's back door. It was still barely propped ajar by his trusty shim. He palmed the sliver of wood, swung the door open, and stepped inside.

A steep staircase rose to his right, the same set of stairs he'd used earlier to descend from the second floor where his room awaited him. He was about to ascend when he heard footsteps on the squeaking floorboards above and then approach the stairs. A light sleeper, no doubt, roused by the muffled shouts from down the street.

He had to give that intruding woman credit, even five buildings away, he could still make out her screams. Hers was a dogged personality.

The big man stepped back from the stairs, saw no alternative, but in true thespian fashion, he rose to the role thrust upon him by the moment. He glided down the hall that led to the front of the house, turned halfway down, and tucking his hands under his arms as if he were chilled, he hunched and faced the person on the stairs.

A woman, and she carried with her a lamp. He squinted as she raised it and peered down the hall. "Oh, Mr. Bardo, you startled me."

"And I by you, madam. Tell me, am I hearing shouts?"

She fell silent, and they both cocked an ear. "Yes, as I thought. That's what roused me, as well. It's early. Something must be wrong somewhere."

"Oh dear," he said, working up a shiver. "I sleep lightly and came down to investigate. You'll forgive me, madam, but I was afraid it might have been you I heard, and I could not forgive myself had I not investigated."

His words produced the effect he expected—she half-smiled and looked askew and worked her face this way and that in a blushing moment. "Oh, Mr. Bardo, you are a thoughtful man. But no, I, too, sleep lightly—something else we have in common, eh, Mr. Bardo?—and had to find out what might be happening. Besides, my day should begin about now anyway. Those biscuits won't bake themselves."

"Ah, yes, your lovely cooking. But I wonder if you will excuse me just now? I fear I will catch a chill should I stand about in my sleepwear and little else for much longer."

"Oh, Mr. Bardo, please don't let me detain you. I will have a nice warm pot of coffee brewing in no time."

"Very good, madam. I look forward to it."

He moved to scoot by her, but she stepped to the side half the distance he'd wished, close enough that he had to brush her as he mounted the steps. Unfortunately, he thought as he climbed the steps, she is watching me. He sighed inward and had to admit that Mr. Bardo was perhaps not one of his better roles. He listened once more after he closed his room's door. The screaming had stopped, but he heard new voices, several, perhaps more, rising and falling like a barnyard of flustered geese.

"Let them flap and cackle," he said. "They will talk about this performance for years to come." Yes, he thought. I have done this tiny town of Wilmotville a generous favor. I have brought world-class artistry to their dreary lives, and they shall not soon forget it.

Ah well, he thought as he slipped out of his silk clothes. Not every role can be memorable. But they are all rewarding and, as he looked at his blood-crusted fingernails and smiled, he decided that frequently they were spectacular, too.

He splashed cold water into his wash basin and stripped down. The frigid water raised goosebumps up and down his body. He smiled even as his teeth rattled slightly. Nothing like it, he thought. A pure, clean feeling gripping him and forcing his eyes wide open.

He scrubbed and scrubbed and allowed himself to indulge in the briefest of memories of the encounter that led him to this moment, to this feeling. He'd chosen the town almost without thought, one of any such annoying little bumps of settled humanity along the tracks of Western Lodestar's southwest run. It had been easy after that to fall in love with a woman on first sight, something he'd never had trouble with.

Their comeliness and interest and availability were always secondary matters. Fortunately for him Mrs. Tillis of Tillis Mercantile had been not only handsome and flattered by his flirtatious attentions of the previous afternoon, but she'd been a little more than willing to return his devilish darings by sliding her tongue across her lips, winking, and blushing fetchingly.

Her husband had caught sight once of her straying eyes and suitably reddened. The big man suspected this was not a first for the woman who, he noted, was obviously some years her spouse's junior. Mr. Tillis was a flea at best, someone undeserving of a pretty woman's devotions.

Now I, thought the big man, I am one who deserves them all. Was I not carved of marble myself, a god among men? Have women not regarded me as such my entire life? I, I alone am worthy. Also, it is my obligation, too, to return the lustful looks . . . and more, whenever possible.

But Mr. Tillis did not scold his wife forcefully, at least not in front of this stranger, a man who obviously had ample money, if his fine raiments and perfect black moustaches and oiled hair and bejeweled fingers were of any indication. Even that black patch covering his left eye lent the man an air of daring that hinted at a treachery . . . and yet it also made him appear much more vulnerable and handsome to women, if his flirtatious wife was any indication.

And if that weren't enough, was not this stranger drawn to the most expensive two items in the store? A gold watch in a green velvet display case, and a nickel-plate revolver with bone handles etched with aces on each grip, and nested in an overly tooled black leather holster and belt studded with silver conchos.

And so the game unrolled for much of an hour late in

the day. When the stranger had rubbed his perfect square jaw and smoothed his black moustaches and regarded the items with his one good eye as if deciding something, only to suck in a breath through white, square teeth, Mr. Tillis had faltered, begun to reveal his frustration with the stranger and the situation.

That was when he had told the man he would sleep on the decisions. It was not a matter of money, oh heavens no, he'd said with a chuckle and a smile, but of having to carry the items, gifts are what they would be, yes, all the way eastward on his journey, though he suspected he would make the purchases. He rarely in life refused to indulge himself in such matters. After all, he'd said with a shrug, why have money?

Knowing chuckles were exchanged between the two men. He would decide and tell the man on the morrow, before he left on the train. Would that be fair?

Oh yes, yes, Mr. Tillis had fawned. The big man had turned to leave the store, turned back, and bowed at the waist to Madam Tillis. Without taking his eyes from hers, he uttered one word . . . simply, "Enchanted."

He turned and left the store, the tinkling of a bell and the memory of her fair blush carrying him down the street to a dining establishment. But return he did, though sooner than the pair had expected. In fact, it was well into the small hours when the big man turned up again at the mercantile, though this time through the back door.

He intentionally clunked into items in the store, making enough noise that, as he suspected, Mr. Tillis made his wary way downstairs from their living quarters, a shotgun barred across his chest. One quick knock to the head and the store-keeper was rendered unconscious. The wife, on hearing no response to her pleas, followed her husband's route and soon succumbed to the stranger's unforgiving intentions.

All he'd been after had been the blood, really. No, not even that, more the feeling of their lives letting go beneath his hands, though that took some hours of playfulness on his part. He'd dragged out the performance and then, with a flourish, had used a keen-edged shiny new blade from the store's display case to deliver the encore.

He scrubbed carefully above and below his false moustache—the theatrical glue worked well but its residue was a devil of a thing. He would deal with it once he returned home. The eye patch was a simpler prop to remove, and so he did, admiring himself in the mirror of the washing stand as he did each morning. Indeed, several times daily.

While he was pleased with having chosen the false moustache and eye patch as basic, useful items, in a simple yet straightforward theatrical ruse for this final fling before his grand outing, it did seem a true shame to dim the light of his own natural radiance and beauty with props and makeup and costumery. He sighed and patted dry his face. Ah well, such are the tribulations I must endure.

But well worth the trouble. Consider it a final rehearsal before opening night, he told himself. In fact, all of them through the years had been but rehearsals for his greatest show yet, the effort he would expend in seeking out, then rendering dead the greatest foe of his life, one Rollie "Stoneface" Finnegan. The very beast responsible for every single bad thing that has ever happened to him, for robbing him of the happiness due him in life.

The big, handsome man glanced once more at his

naked self in the mirror and laid out his clothes for the day. He couldn't wait to hear the chatter at the breakfast table, and then up and down the street. The town would be abuzz with whispers of intrigue and thoughts of delicious terror. He giggled as he dressed himself.

Chapter Two

The first bullet chewed a hole in the privy door, right beside the crescent moon. A second shot chased it. On his knees inside, with his trousers around his boots, Rollie "Stoneface" Finnegan looked up at the new ventilation and decided they looked like stars around the moon. High shots, not aimed to kill, but to scare. A third joined them. Not like the thunder pit couldn't use more airflow, but there had to be a better way of going about it. He checked the wheel in his Schofield and thumbed back the hammer.

"Stoneface Finnegan! Come on out and I'll make this painless."

Rollie sighed. Here we go again. All he wanted to do was spend a night away from town, holed up with a bottle and his thoughts. It was the cabin and claim he and his business partner, Jubal "Pops" Tennyson, had taken in trade for a sizable bar tab from a back-East furniture maker who decided he was not cut out for life in the diggings.

They'd not had time to do much with either the cabin or claim yet, but each had used it off and on in the couple of months since owning it. It was an ideal spot to clear away the cobwebs and give each other a break from living cheek-to-jowl in the cramped quarters of the tent. At least they had a tent, propped as it was just behind where their saloon, The Last Drop, had stood, torched low by arsons looking for Rollie's head.

They were nearing the end of rebuilding the bar, and Rollie finally felt like he could take a day and a night off. But instead of peace and quiet, what did he get? Another moron looking to cash in on a bounty. It seemed they would never stop seeking him out, would never learn. He guessed it was the indomitable human spirit at play—never believing you might not succeed. Until you don't.

Rollie and Pops had laid low a sizable stack of men in the past few months. He figured he was about to add to that pile. On the other hand, it was as true that his luck would one day run out. Everybody's did eventually. Was it this day?

Rollie tugged up his trousers as he eyed through plank gaps in the front wall beside the door. His attacker, so far he'd detected only the one, stood behind a wide ponderosa pine facing the outhouse. He looked out every few seconds, like a cuckoo clock. If he could time it right, he might be able to drill the bastard in the forehead.

"Oh, come on and answer me already. I saw you go in there. Heard tell there's a bounty on your head, Finnegan!" A ratty beard parted and a cackle burst out between two chaw-dripping lips.

"Where'd you hear that?"

"Now that's more like it!"

"I asked where you heard that."

"You saying it ain't true?"

"No."

"Well, I'll oblige you. I heard it from a fella on the trail, oh, Utah or somewheres . . ."

Rollie groaned. He didn't doubt the news was that widespread. What he didn't like was that he was still the target of undeserving hate by people he'd never met or wronged. It seemed that half the folks who'd come after him for being a Pinkerton agent once upon a time were just in it for the money. At least the other misguided souls had what they believed was reason enough to attack him. They were folks—or their vengeance-seeking relations—he'd sent to prison for various misdeeds over the years.

What was this fool's excuse? Had to be the money.

"Look. All I need's your head. The rest of you can stay put."

Rollie shook that wanted head. He had to give the man credit, at least he was forthright. Doesn't mean I won't kill him, though, thought Rollie. But first things first, I am pinned down in the outhouse and that cannot stand.

Getting out, he'd have to raise a ruckus, and no way was he exiting through the hole below. Kick out a side wall? He'd have to do it fast, because the man would reposition himself. It was a risk, especially if the crusty hick wasn't alone.

Or . . . Rollie eyed the man again through the gap in the planks. Wait, wait . . . and there he was, peering around the tree once more. As quiet as he could, Rollie jimmied the tip of the Schofield's barrel between the planks and eyed down the sights.

"Come on, man!" said the ambusher. "I ain't got all day!"

"Hold on a second, I'm fixing my trousers—you caught me unawares . . ." That ought to buy time enough to watch the man give a couple more peeks around the tree. And he did.

Amazingly enough the rascal performed his funny little head maneuver as if he were timed. One more and . . . Rollie squeezed a shot. The rough red bark of the tree burst in a ragged cloud. The man's screams told Rollie he'd not killed him, for a shot to the forehead would have snuffed any ability the man had to carry on so.

Within seconds the invader spun into view, holding his head and whipping in a dervish dance. He slammed into a knee-height granite boulder and flipped over it, collapsing on his back and flailing his legs.

By then Rollie had kicked open the privy door and stomped dead-on at the mewling man. The hot-nerved pulses always with him from too many old wounds prevented Rollie from a full-bore run.

He stood over him, though out of grabbing range, his revolver aimed down at the man's head. As he suspected, given the man's howls, his shot had blasted the tree and sent bark and jagged shards of wood into the man's leering face. From between his grubby, bloody hands poured gore, bubbling about the mouth as the man screamed.

Rollie glanced quickly up at the tree the man had been hiding behind. It was a huge ponderosa and now sported a furrow of raw, honey-color wood chiseled up by the bullet into a ragged wound.

Rollie kicked him hard in the thigh. "Shut up."

Another two kicks and it worked, the man's noises tamped down to gasps and chesty sobs. "I . . . I can't see! Oh God, I can't see!"

"Take your hands away from your face, fool," said Rollie.

When the man did, it revealed the reason.

"I can't go through this life blind!"

"Aw, you won't be blind for long."

"Huh? You reckon? I don't understand."

Rollie shrugged. "Simple. You aimed to kill me. I figure that favor deserves one in kind."

"You're a devil! I heard about you . . . you're a devil!"

Rollie nodded. "Yep, and next time you decide to dance with one, you best be prepared for things to go against you."

"But . . . no!"

"Yep. Now, it's your choice. I can string you up here or I can drag you back to Boar Gulch. I was planning on spending the day up here doing nothing much at all, but you've ruined that for me. Thank you very much."

"What? What are you talking about? I don't understand."

"You were going to kill me, right?"

The blubbering man didn't answer.

"Right?"

"Yeah, yes, I guess . . ."

"So it's my turn."

"No!" The man howled again and snatched up a slender-bladed skinning knife from a sheath at his waist. Before Rollie could figure out what the fool intended to do with it, the man had driven it once, twice into his own gut high, jamming the blade upward.

He got the two stabs in but lost steam. His hand, looking like a red-black glove of silk, trembled and released its shaky grip on the wood-handled knife. The hand dropped to the man's side, but the knife remained lodged in his breadbasket. Blood pumped and welled, pumped and welled from the fresh wounds.

Rollie wasn't certain the man had landed a heart wound, but he hadn't done himself any good. They were mortal wounds, to be sure. Rollie scratched his chin and looked down at the gurgling mess at his feet.

He couldn't recall ever seeing a man stab his own self to death. No, wait, there was that time in Alameda when he'd walked into that cabin to find that feral half-breed slicing on his own arms and legs for no earthly reason other than he'd been tetched. This fool didn't have that excuse. Well, maybe a little.

Rollie didn't like to all-but execute a man. This was rough. But the man was suffering mighty, his breathing was gaspy and ragged, blood bubbles rose and popped in succession up out of a mouth nested somewhere in the man's soaked, gore-matted beard.

Rollie crouched low, his knees popping, and held the revolver at the man's head, in case he decided to surprise them both and attack. Not likely, though.

"I'll not shoot you to ease your passing, as you've done yourself in, mister. Your foolhardy ways are about over with. Any last words?"

"Da . . . da . . . devil!"

Rollie breathed deeply, pushed out the breath at about the same time the man's skinny frame shuddered, then seemed to collapse in on itself. That final, momentous act was a mystery Rollie had witnessed many times but never understood. Maybe one day he'd find out, but not today.

"I expect you'll meet the King of Devils himself, soon. Give ol' Scratch my best."

But the man would hear nothing ever again.

Rollie stood, knees popping once more, and looked around the clearing. Behind him, in the lean-to attached to the cabin, he heard Cap, short for Captain, his gray gelding, whicker.

"How in the hell did my day get off to such a start, Cap?" He turned to face the horse. "What next? What next for Rollie Finnegan?"

He heard no reply but a mountain jay and a far-off breeze through the tall trees. But something told Rollie he wouldn't have long to wait to find out the answer to his question.

Chapter Three

A day later found Rollie "Stoneface" Finnegan at his accustomed spot behind the bar in his own establishment, listening to his steadiest customer, Wolfbait. Rollie was majority stake holder of The Last Drop, the best, or so he liked to believe, of the two drinking establishments in the grubby little mine camp known as Boar Gulch.

"I had my doubts, I don't mind saying." The gimpy old miner with the tangled, chaw-stained beard shook his head and drained his beer glass.

"Okay, Wolfbait," said Rollie to his old friend, crusty barfly and too-tough-to-die supply-run shotgun rider. "I give up—what did you have doubts about?"

Rollie didn't really care what the old man thought at any time of the day or night. But he knew Wolfbait wouldn't give up being annoying about it until he asked and at least feigned interest.

The famed ex-Pinkerton agent had threaded his way to the tiny but promising mountain town mere months before, in part to hole up and heal up after he was knifed and left for dead in an alley in Denver City. His intent on reaching Boar Gulch was to mine the miners while he convalesced.

What he ended up doing was buying what at the time was the town's only saloon, taking on ex-slave, Jubal "Pops" Tennyson, as a partner, and doling out a whole lot of hard justice to the hordes of vengeance-seeking brutes from his past. These men and women felt his treatment of them from back in his Pinkerton days had been the cause of all their life's woes, no matter the fact that they were all guilty of chicanery, deceit, treachery—and murder.

Once they found out Stoneface was still alive, they showed up with blood in mind, and were jerked to a halt at the end of a rope from Boar Gulch's answer to lawmen—Stoneface and Pops. The pards agreed they had no use for the law, but justice, now that was something they could get behind.

"Doubts?" said Wolfbait. "Oh, yeah, well, look at this place." He swept an old claw-tipped arm about himself at the newer, improved version of The Last Drop. "Never would have thought after those bums burned you fellas out that you'd rebuild, and in such grand fashion."

Rollie had to admit that after the fire he had been tempted to pull up stakes and call it a day, hit the trail while he still had his life and a few dollars in his pocket. But the fire—in which they'd nearly lost their lives—had been a boon. Sure, they'd spent the past weeks holed up in a drafty tent, the front of which served as a makeshift saloon, but the new version of The Last Drop was taking shape nicely. It had space for more tables, a longer bar, and better storage and living quarters out back for him and Pops.

"I'll admit, only this once, mind you, that I am in agreement with you, Wolfbait."

Just then Pops walked in through the back door lugging a wad of nails in one hand and a hammer in the other. "Hold on now, you saying you and this old tumbleweed are joining forces and ganging up on me and Nosey?" Pops' low chuckle had a way of spreading among the men.

"Not hardly," said Rollie. "I was merely taking a moment to admire our handiwork. It's not just anyone who could build a saloon from the ground up while serving liquor in it at the same time."

"Speaking of liquor, how's the stock doing?" Pops glanced over his shoulder at Rollie, who was fitting a seat on a bar stool. The ex-Pinkerton man had shown an impressive ability to cobble together serviceable furniture out of raw lumber and a hand saw.

Rollie shrugged. "Ask Nosey."

"The inventory's nearly done." On cue, Nosey Parker stepped out of the back room, peering over the top of his half-moon spectacles pinched on the end of his nose, which had healed crooked after he'd taken a mighty blow to the face in a fracas weeks before.

"Be done a whole lot faster if you weren't reading that dime novel." Pops stuffed a few nails in his mouth and resumed work on planking the front door's trim.

"I am studying the form, the nuances, the techniques of the author to see how I might render my own experiences in such a form."

"Why not start a newspaper up here, Nosey?" said Rollie, knuckling his waxed moustache, the man's one vanity. "This town's growing like I never imagined it would and folks are folks, no matter where they congregate. They have an urge to know what's going on in their town."

"This town's so small all they have to do is look out their front door and they can see what's going on." Nosey shook his head. "No, no, when I left the crime-riddled mess that is Boston, I left behind the journalistic arts. I am now a novelist." He stood tall, his slight frame and dented bowler, complete with bullet hole, tilted at a jaunty angle atop his head.

"Okay, Mr. Novelist," said Pops. "But don't forget you're also an employee of The Last Drop." He chuckled and shook his head as he drove in another nail.

The weather, for an early September day in the mountains of Idaho's Sawtooth Range, was deceptively smooth. Overhead rode a porcelain-blue sky with enough high-up streaks of white to give it humility. Now and again a light breeze carried with it a blend of pine tang from the sunsoaked ponderosas, and a crisp edge, too, as if reminding them of the coming season of brutal cold.

Despite such lovely, long days, Rollie knew they were battling time itself. He wanted the saloon to be complete, buttoned up tight. He also wanted enough firewood laid in out back before what he knew was going to be a long, hard winter ahead drove over them from all directions.

He and Pops and the boys weren't the only ones working long days and nights, though. The rest of the Gulch's denizens were hard at it improving their own lots, building new shops and homes, and still repairing damage done by notorious mercenary Cleve Danziger and his gang of cutthroats.

The residue of their attack of weeks before still tainted

the little mine camp, from hundreds of bullet holes pocking buildings to still-healing wounds in flesh. From the mounds of fresh graves in the farthest corners of Boot Hill to the memories of the fiendish townwide assault, in the form of nightmares, no one in Boar Gulch was left untouched by that attack.

And because he felt he owed it to them all, for that reason alone, Rollie gave up on his notion of leaving the town in hopes of drawing the vermin who hunted him away from the innocent miners. The townsfolk would have none of it anyway, as they wanted him and Pops to continue to render their brand of justice, to stay on and keep them safe, even if it meant more vermin seeking to lay Stoneface low. It had been a long few months, and would be longer still, given the outhouse attack of the day before by yet another bounty-seeking fool.

"Hey, Wolfbait," said Pops. "You going to drink all the beer or are you going to help me finish this door sometime this year?"

"I told you, you whelp, I woke up this morning with a case of the rheumatics! Only thing to ease 'em is a dose of liquor, steady like."

From under his impressive winglike eyebrows, the old buck's eyes roved over to Rollie, who stood closest to the newly lined up bottles along the barback display. They were still waiting on a special order of a mirror they hoped to pick up on their next supply run down the mountain to Bella Springs. Until then the layers of bottles looked just fine to Wolfbait.

Rollie took the hint . . . with a sigh. He poured the old man a solid shot of Preacherman's One-Eye Rye, a favorite of Wolfbait. Rollie had tried it once and still shuddered at the memory. It was not even an acquired taste. You had to have scar tissue for innards to drink the stuff. But he and Pops owed Wolfbait and Nosey more than free booze could ever repay. They'd risked all, time after time, in previous months to help the men.

"You're a gent and I won't hear anyone say otherwise." Wolfbait raised the glass and winked at Rollie, then let the caustic liquor slide down his old throat. "Hoo-aaah!" He slapped the bartop. "That did the trick. Okay now, what was it you were whining about, Pops? Oh yeah, you need my expertise, I reckon."

"Yeah," said Pops. "That's just what I need. Oh, and a smack upside the head."

"Happy to oblige," said Wolfbait, hefting a fresh pine plank.

"Be nice, boys," said Rollie, looking out the side window. "There isn't enough time between now and snow to keep you all simmered and civil." Rollie eyed down the dusty street to the hills beyond.

"What do you see, Rollie?" said Nosey, tying on an apron in preparation for the late afternoon crowd he knew would soon arrive.

"Nothing and nobody I don't want to . . . yet." Rollie's left hand slid down to his holstered Schofield out of long habit. His fingertips danced and tapped on the worn grips. The gun was nearly the first thing he strapped on each morning and the last he checked each night.

"You have any fresh ideas yet who hired Danziger and his army of killers?" Pops stood, rubbing his back. He, too, wore a revolver, though his preferred weapon was his double-barrel sawed-off Greener, Lil' Miss Mess Maker, leaning in whatever corner was closest to where he was working.

Rollie shook his head, but they all knew what was behind the question. Since they'd dispatched most of Danziger's crew, word would have surely reached whoever had hired him that Cleve had failed. Rollie expected a renewed, harsher effort to kill him any day now. But by who? And why? The outhouse incident, he was fairly certain, was little more than the feeble attempt of a desperate lone wolf seeking cash, a man who was not likely to have heard of Danziger's failure.

Rollie had raked over and over in his mind his old cases, and while there were plenty of devils lurking, few that he knew of had the ability to hire a high-priced mercenary like Danziger. There had been some, of course, such as Teasdale, the railroad tycoon who felt the sting of the law when Rollie had gone undercover and infiltrated his band of hired thugs bent on disrupting his biggest competitor's operations. It had not ended well for Teasdale. Or his bulky bank accounts.

So yes, he could be a possibility, but somehow Rollie doubted it. As greedy and as angry as the man had been, still was, he didn't doubt that, as Rollie's endeavors had cost him one whopping pile of cash, the old rich devil was not one to carry that torch of retribution for fifteen years. Seems like he would have done something about it well before then.

"Hey, Rollie."

He looked up to see Pops eyeing him.

"You okay?"

The barkeep nodded. "Yep, just thinking."

Pops chuckled. "Thought I smelled something smoking."

Rollie smiled and turned his eyes to the front door. The first gaggle of sweat-stained miners clomped up the steps, each babbling louder than the next about how he felt certain his claim was the one that would soon break the town wide open.

If Rollie had a dollar for every time he'd heard a rockhound sharing what he planned to do with his earnings once he struck a pure vein of gold, he'd be a whole lot wealthier than any of them ever would be. In fact, his plan to mine the miners, despite the fact that most of them were a good, friendly sort, had worked out just fine.

He was convinced that the true money in a mine camp, and Boar Gulch was as typical a boomtown mine camp as one could hope to stumble into, lay in selling the miners the things they needed, be it food, equipment, or liquor. He had a corner on the liquor sales in town, and he liked that just fine.

A married couple, the Pulaskis, had moved in after he arrived and set up their own saloon, the Lucky Strike. Though they were affable and offered gaming, too, somehow it was The Last Drop that attracted the lion's share of the town's thirsty patrons.

Still, Rollie and the Pulaskis were on friendly terms, and he reckoned that maxim he'd always heard about competition being healthy must be true, though he was at a loss as to figure out how. He was thriving and they weren't.

"I'm going to take a walk," he said to Pops as he passed by on his way to the door.

"Okay, Rollie," said his partner, nibbling his lip. He knew Rollie well enough to know when the man's instinct was getting rattled. The man's inner voice was a razorlike thing honed by long years as a Pinkerton man. Maybe their vacation was over with, thought Pops. And he knew, even as he thought it, that it was.

Truth be told, he'd had enough of it, too. Walking around waiting for badness to rise up from wherever it dwelt. Might as well get on with it. If it's going to come, let it come. He cast his glance at his beloved Greener and scooped it up. He noted out the window which direction Rollie walked—southward. Pops made for the back door. "Nosey," he said quietly. "You and Wolfbait are it. I'm taking a stroll up the north end, see what's doing."

Nosey nodded and set two glasses on the counter. "You need help, just whistle." He smiled. "Wolfbait will come running."

"I heard that, you whelp!" The old curmudgeon smacked a hand on the bar. "Just for that round of verbal abuse, I'll request a beer and a slug chaser. Then you want to see some runnin', by jove, you'll see it! You'll see it!"

Rollie slowly stalked the long dirt lane southward, thumbing a lucifer alight and setting fire to a stub of cigar he'd saved from earlier. As he puffed, he eyed the south end of the main street and the hillside beyond. He squinted at the darker folds where shadows dwelt. That's where they'd be hiding, scanning the town for a sign of him, just as he eyed the hillside.

He pushed out a blue cloud, but didn't take his eyes from the treed slope. The days and nights had been peaceful, quiet, pleasant. Too much so. He didn't trust it for a second. And yet . . . it was lulling him into false security, despite prickling his attitude and the back of his neck.

Too smooth and too deceptive. Something was going to happen. Had to, stood to reason. He'd rarely gone this long in his life without some part of the ground beneath his boots falling away. The trick was to know when it was about to happen, then jump. Simple as that, Rollie, he told himself, and smiled.

The scraggly clot of men outside Horkins' Assay Office was only topped by those at Geoff the Scot's eatery, still more tent and outdoor chow space than a proper sit-down diner, but the big, burly Scotsman had sputtered for months about making it a more permanent structure before winter hit.

Rollie knew the man was as tight with his money as the hide on a Texas steer, plus Rollie noted the man had only hired one set of hands to help him—a scrawny, young, sunken-eyed thing who appeared to not have slept in weeks. He also noted they were serving in shifts, and from the pile-up of grumbling miners drooling and staring without shame at the steaming mounds of food ferried from the Scot's kitchen, they were eating in double, maybe triple shifts.

Horkins' Hardware, owned by the assayer's older brother, had its doors propped open with a stack of new tin buckets on one side and a gleaming mattock wedged against the other. Young men, and a few older ones, with a glint in their eyes and a quicker step than they'd have in a week or two—once they'd spent time grubbing in a gravel bank for fickle gold—passed in and out of the shop.

All this activity told Rollie business in Boar Gulch was

good, which he knew. They were in the midst of a boom time. Whether it would last was something nobody could foretell. But like the rest of the merchants of the main street, he was happy to ride this pony until it threw him.

As the Gulch's de facto lawmen, though the notion that's what he'd become still rankled Rollie, he and Pops had grown accustomed to making more frequent tours of the little burg of late. Strange faces were everywhere, and the hills surrounding the town were crawling with hordes of hopefuls.

As if cued to his thoughts, the distinct ringing of steel on steel from Pieder Tomsen's blacksmith shop carried down the hill from the smithy's clearing to the west above the town. Despite the shot-up shoulder he received helping Rollie and Pops when Danziger rode into town, it sounded as if Pieder was busier than ever. Rollie wouldn't doubt he'd soon hear the man's hammer blows back to their old routine of filling the skies hereabouts from sun-up to sundown. He'd mentioned in one of their brief recent conversations that he was considering taking on an apprentice. Made sense, as he was so far the only blacksmith in town and the population showed no signs of slowing.

Rollie wondered if the fact that Camp Sal, now just Sal, moving in with the sturdy, quiet Norwegian had anything to do with the possibility of the blacksmith slowing his pace. Rollie chuckled. Yeah, likely a whole lot. She'd helped tend all the wounded, but it was Tomsen who received her most ardent ministrations. As Rollie recalled, for a man who was the silent, brooding loner, Pieder had not seemed to mind one bit when Sal cooed and clucked and fussed over him.

He might just wander on up that way and pay the man a visit. Rumor had it Sal was one heck of a cook, too. The other men in town with whom she'd shacked up in the past all confirmed this. They also had nothing bad to say about the woman. She sounded like one of those souls who lives to help others. Maybe with Pieder she'd found someone with whom she could stick for longer than a few weeks, as she had in the past with other Gulch men.

At the end of the street, Rollie turned and began walking back toward the north end, anchored by Wheeler's Mercantile. To the left of that business, along the west side of the main street, sat the hulking, half-finished hotel and theater that the self-appointed mayor, Chauncey Wheeler, had built. Now that was a building that showed little chance of being roofed and sided before the north winds came calling.

Rollie poked along, kicking a gray rock in front of him, puffing his cigar, and considering the events that brought him here and those demons that followed him. Then he saw his partner, Pops, emerge from the half-sheathed front entrance of the hotel, shaking his head and puffing up a cloud on his corncob pipe. He said something to someone hidden inside the building. So he was chatting with the workers again, and Rollie was glad of it. It riled Chauncey, because he was paying those men to build the hotel, and they were far behind schedule.

Even from this distance, he could hear Pops chuckle. He was a social man, loved to fraternize with the bar's patrons, and tell jokes and stories. Good thing, too, as

Rollie didn't earn the nickname he wasn't particularly fond of, "Stoneface," by being chatty.

He'd not even been aware of his trait of silence as a Pinkerton agent, especially once he'd taken his quarry into custody. But somehow word had gotten out that he was not inclined to hold a conversation or even speak more than a grunt, and then only when necessity required it.

He believed that people, as a rule, talk too much, and that long stretches of silence would do most everybody a bit of good. But those who'd felt the tight clench of his manacles had disagreed, and one of the wiseacres years ago called him Stoneface. And it had stuck.

In truth, it wasn't so bad. After all, it lent him an aura of mysterious menace that he didn't mind. He had the reputation as a no-nonsense man out to do the job he was hired to tend to, no more no less. But Pops, now there was a man could talk the ears off a rabbit, as Wolfbait said.

And Pops had done just that not moments before to the men working on what half the Gulch was calling "Chauncey's Folly." He waited for a two-mule team to rumble by before crossing the street to the store. While he was out, Pops figured he might pick up a sack of tobacco and another of boiled sweets.

While there was similarity in a number of goods between Chauncey Wheeler's Mercantile and Horkins' Hardware—picks, shovels, rope—Wheeler had a cornered market on the goods most folks needed more frequently. And the man loved to make money, loved it more than eating, and that was saying something, thought Pops, considering the mayor was a porky fellow.

That's why he was surprised to see the hand-lettered "Closed" sign hung on the outside of the plank front door. Just then the door opened and the chubby man himself bustled out and pulled the door closed behind him, hanging the steel lock in the hasp and clicking it tight with a key from his pocket.

"Must be pretty important for you to close up shop during business hours, Mr. Mayor." Pops shifted the Greener from one arm to cradle in the crook of the other. He rocked back on his heels and offered the surprised man a smile.

"Oh, it's you . . . yes," said Chauncey, doing little to disguise his dislike of the fact that he had to talk with a black man, even if this man had saved his hide in the not-too-distant past in helping clean up the death of a whore that Wheeler may or may not have had a hand in ushering along to her final reward.

"I . . . ah I don't have anyone to watch the place and sell my goods while I tend to my other business, not that it's any of your business."

"I'm sure you could ask Nosey Parker to lend a hand now and again. If not for his work at The Last Drop, I don't know how that boy survives. Sure ain't from working his claim."

"Yes, well . . ."

Rollie walked up. "Afternoon, mayor." He gestured with the last of his cigar. "Little early to not be selling flour and hard tack."

"And tobacco," Pops added, remembering he was almost out and he did like a pipe of a morning and an afternoon and an evening.

Rollie looked the mayor up and down. "You okay, Chauncey?"

"Why?" The chunky man tugged on his vest and smoothed his worn lapels. "Why do you say that?"

Rollie shrugged. "You look tired."

Uncharacteristically, the mayor's face lost its tight look and he nodded. And that in turn led him to lean against the store's doorframe and sag. "Yes, it's true. I'm a . . . I'm a wreck."

Pops pulled his pipe from his mouth. "Anything we can do?"

"It's the hotel and theater." He pronounced it "theeayter" and raised a smirk on Rollie's face. "It's going to be wonderful when it's done, something this part of the known world is desperate for."

"But?" said Rollie.

"But . . . I'm not sleeping well these days. The hotel and theater is behind schedule, I've sunk more money into it than I care to admit, what with the fittings and fixtures. It will be world class or I will not have it built. And yet I recognize I am in an enviable position."

"How's that?" said Pops.

"Why" —the man puffed up—"I am the proprietor of the only general store in town, and for miles around, I might add. I also still own parcels of land I would be willing to sell for a fair price. But if I don't keep my shelves stocked with goods, it won't be long before someone else seizes the opportunity and in short order there will be a rival where none existed before."

Both men looked at him as if he just told them the sky was blue.

"I should think it's obvious, gentlemen. I cannot have that. No, cannot have that."

Rollie let out a long breath. "Seems to me we're back where we started, with you closing up shop during business hours, the only such shop in these parts. That sounds like just the thing you said you didn't want to do."

"Yes, well, I have business to attend to. Not surprisingly, given the number of newcomers flooding into town, there is interest in some of the prime holdings I still retain in these parts."

"You mean house lots," said Pops.

"Yes, yes, if you must call them that. Though I would not be so crude in my assessment." He pulled in a big breath. "My holdings are vast and of great importance."

"Never doubted it, mayor," said Pops, lighting his pipe.

"I happen to be rather nerved up of late." He leaned close to Rollie. "High finance will do that to a man."

Rollie nodded. "Well, come by later, Chauncey. I'll stand you a whiskey to calm your nerves."

"That's very kind of you, Rollie. I . . . I believe I just might take you up on your offer." He tugged at his vest once more, though it rode up onto his belly immediately. "Now, if you'll excuse me, I have to meet someone." He clicked open his pocketwatch and said, "And I'm late. Good day, gentlemen." At that word, he looked Pops up and down as if he doubted the word applied. Pops ignored him.

They watched the man waddle away. Pops said, "I'm thinking his coin purse is so light he can't afford to keep his shelves stocked much longer. Must be a sore spot for him to keep selling off his remaining parcels of land."

Rollie nodded. "He and his partner founded this place, even platted it out and sunk their wad into claiming as much as they could." He looked up and down the main street. "But that didn't include too much of the surrounding area. I can't imagine he has all that much land left."

Pops shrugged, and they began their walk back to the saloon. "Hard saying. The mayor has surprised us before."

"Yeah," said Rollie. "But he's never been this uptight."

Chapter Four

Giacomo Valucci sighed and leaned back in his chair in the lobby of the St. Charlebois Hotel smack in the midst of bustling, downtown San Francisco, California. He lifted the foul letter once more, sneering as he read it.

This mess was the fault of one Cleve Danziger, a mercenary Giacomo had hired, along with the man's own small, private army of craven killers. Danziger had vowed to track down and lay low Valucci's nemesis, Rollie "Stoneface" Finnegan. But it hadn't happened that way, as the letter made plain. Not only had Danziger and his men failed, most of them had died in the attempt, Cleve included.

And now Giacomo had to travel to Boar Gulch—what a name—somewhere in the wilds of Idaho Territory to deal with the situation himself, and soon. Trouble was, he had little interest in trekking to God knows . . . where was this town? He dropped the letter to his lap and stifled a groan. He sipped from the cup of tea at his elbow, where it rested on the polished mahogany table.

A soft rustle of fabric by his left shoulder pulled his gaze up from once more perusing the annoying letter.

"Sir, more tea?"

"What? Oh, yes, thank you . . . James, was it?"

"Sir." The waiter nodded, blushing slightly at being remembered by the guest. No matter that his name was Jules. The last thing he would consider doing was correcting the patron. Not only would he lose his job, he would lose face before the wealthy man. He aspired to one day be as wealthy and as important as Mr. Valucci.

"Tell me, James," said the man seated before him as he lit another cigarette. "How do you feel about travel?"

"Travel, sir?" The young man reddened a deeper shade.

"Steady on, there," smiled Valucci. "You blush anymore and you'll be positively purple." He laughed a quick, sharp bark. "I only ask because I have this infernal trip I may be forced to plan, a business trip, mind you, but if I decide to arrange and then embark on the trek, I would need to assemble a small but dependable retinue of traveling companions, preferably people I know and who would not let me down. And certainly not abandon me should we fall upon hard times on the trail."

"Hard times, sir?"

"Yes, hard times. Surely you know of such things." Valucci waved a hand weakly in the air. He suddenly felt wearier than he had in the long months since this madness had begun. He thought back on that time, on that middle morning when his father had died suddenly, violently at the long, polished table at which his family had taken meals for years.

His parents had come to California by way of sea at the urging of Giacomo's mother, a sultry beauty with smoke for eyes and black fire for hair. She was also to blame for

Giacomo being the way he was, a natural thespian. At least that's what his dear mama had always called him.

Then there was the father, hard as a steel boot to the face. But the old man could make money. His parents had arrived in California, along with countless others, in time to pillage and plunder the landscape. Few of them ever came up with gold, but his father did, and what's more he bought a valley's worth of promising land and hired displaced Cornish miners desperate to feed themselves and their pock-faced families.

Yes, from the old man Giacomo learned the value of keeping the poor as poor, and the necessity of keeping the wealthy as wealthy, all the while becoming wealthier, even at the expense of what his father had called "the rough and stupid" classes.

Along the way Giacomo caused his father frustration, almost as much as did his mother. She was a pretty thing, and the money, for a time, made her even prettier. Then she came to realize that Mr. Valucci the elder had become satisfied with his pile and preferred to spend his days rattling around the mansion overlooking the sea, entertaining friends. She began to spend her time elsewhere on the town, and before long found herself in the arms— and beds—of men who, though her husband's financial lessers, surpassed him in matters of amour.

Her diligent dalliances ceased abruptly one cold winter morning with the discovery of her body facedown in an alley, her silk opera dress a soiled blue ruin. It seems she'd been trampled by a fast-moving barouche, not unlike that driven by her husband on nights when he could not sleep and so spent them patrolling the streets and quays questing for his strayed love.

The man she'd been dallying with in the alleyway, a dandy named Oscar Deyton, escaped the scene with little more than a throbbing, down low, of denial, and a bruised arm and shoulder where the barouche's fender had whipped wide. He was laid up in bed for three days, whistling at his good fortune when, on the evening of the fourth day, he ventured once more into the city night to see if he might replicate with a different woman the evening that had been unfolding before the unfortunate accident.

Alas, he would not see the gray of the next day's dawn. Not with living eyes, anyway.

A morning, not long afterward, at the breakfast table, burned into Giacomo's memory as if branded, smoking and sizzling.

"You have impressed me, Giacomo," said Father. "I had given up all hope of ever seeing you again, much less of sharing my considerable business acumen with you as a potential junior partner in your own birth right, the company I founded so many years ago."

He wiped his mouth and smiled. "But now here you are, once more at the family breakfast table. Reading the day's news and sipping coffee as if none of those horrible, wasted years had happened." The old man chuckled. "Honestly, a thespian? My son? I don't doubt you were good at it—too much like your mother not to be. But son, as I have said many times before, and I promise to never say again after this morning: You are a Valucci, and Valuccis do not act. They work."

The old man's hard eyes glinted like onyx chips. "For generations they did so with their backs and their arms. But now, with our good fortune, the Valucci line will work with our minds. We shall make one mighty business partnership, my son." He shifted his gaze to the scene of the long blue ocean straight out the window.

"Would that your philandering minx of a mother were here to see this." The old man fell into a musing sort of reverie and didn't much pay attention as Giacomo stood from his place at the breakfast table and moved to the sideboard as if to load up his silver plate with more fish and eggs.

He wadded three of the freshly laundered serviettes laid out beside the unused plates and stepped behind his musing, smiling father, who said, "God, but your mother was a beautiful woman."

The youngish Giacomo said, "Yes, father," and stuffed the napkins into his sire's half-opened mouth, forcing it wider, snapping off a tooth in the process. The old man's eyes bulged and his hands flailed and scratched and clawed and his nose snotted and his nostrils flexed open and closed and then he sagged, limp, eyes wide.

"Cook! Cook! Help! Father, oh father! No, don't leave me an orphan, dearest father!" Even as Giacomo shouted this, he tugged the serviettes free of the old man's mouth and smiled, at least until Cook thundered into the room and covered her mouth with her pudgy hands at the tragic scene before her.

She beheld young Giacomo weeping, cradling his father's bulged, purple face and weeping, weeping as if he were in the midst of the most horrific scene of a stage play before a packed house.

Oh, he imagined Cook thinking, this is all so unbelievable! But alas it was all too true, she knew, because, after all, it was common knowledge that the old man had a weak heart.

"Mr. Valucci, sir. Are you . . . are you all right, sir?"

Giacomo shook his head, looked around, then up at the concerned face of the hotel waiter, bent close and peering at him.

"Yes, yes, James, yes. I am, as they say in *The Fiddle and the Rock*, right as a spring rain."

He regarded the knitted brows of the young man and sighed. "It is a theatrical reference. Now where was I? Oh yes, I am about to embark on a trek that will take me and my select traveling group, my troupe, as it were, on a tour."

He waited for the young waiter to appear awed, perhaps prompt him to go on, but the waiter merely stared at him with eyes wide.

Giacomo sighed once more and plunged onward. "I am a world-renown actor, a thespian by birthright and by assiduous training. Why, I have trod the boards throughout Europe, playing sold-out shows to filled houses packed so tight they could only stand and clap. That, dear boy, is a sound one never grows weary of."

"Yes, sir."

"As to the trip, I have need of a sort of jack of all trades, a footman. The pay is a guaranteed handsome sum, payable half before, half once we complete our journey." He regarded the young man, who still stood staring at him, as if catching up on the flurry of words Giacomo had just unleashed.

"Well? What is your answer?"

"My answer, sir? Oh, you mean me? You have need of my services? Oh, but I have this job."

Giacomo snorted. "What are they paying you? I'll double it. Wait, what are your skills? Can you cook? Launder when need be? Ride a horse? Shoot vermin with a firearm? Tell me true."

"Yes, sir, I . . . I can do all that, sure. Only, where are you going?"

"We, my good boy. We shall be going northeast of here. To tour the mine camps and backwoods burgs of this most wild West. Call it a humbling journey, a revisitation of the places my family begat, the very mine camps where toil is as common as rock, where the agonies of daily living are unendurable, and yet . . . they are endured. Call this tour one of redemption. But most of all it shall culminate in one sweet, sweet reckoning."

"Jules!" The shout came from the man at the front desk who scowled toward the young man. "Stop bothering Mr. Valucci. He is a guest, not someone to be pestered. My sincerest apologies, Mr. Valucci. I assure you this waiter will not bother you again."

"You are correct about that, my good man. Because he is no longer a waiter."

"As you like it, sir. I shall turn him loose from our employ."

"Yes, yes you shall, because I have just hired him."

"What?"

"Close your mouth, you are collecting flies. Now, James," Giacomo reached into his suit coat and pulled out a long wallet. He unfolded it as one would a book and selected several bills. "Take this money and fetch one of each of the most recent periodicals you are able to find. I suspect the stand on Raskin Street will fill the order nicely. Do you know the one?"

He didn't wait for a response, but continued. "Buy them all and bring them to my rooms. I am here at the hotel for the next . . ." he plucked out his pocket watch and studied it. "Two hours, then I shall be dining with potential members of the troupe I am assembling." He looked up to see the desk clerk regarding him. "You're still here?"

The man reddened and backed away, bowing.

"Now where was I? Oh yes, bring the publications to my rooms as soon as you're able." He looked the still-stunned young man up and down. "On your return, we'll do something about your wardrobe and your worrisome ability to look confused." He held out the money, wagged it. "James."

The young man nodded and grasped the money, but Giacomo didn't let go of it. "Don't let me down." He narrowed his eyes, and their stares locked. "I do not tolerate shirkers."

Mr. Valucci said this in a low voice that did not sound like the one Jules was used to hearing from this wealthy individual. This voice sounded low, cold, coiled. He hurried out into the street, unsure of what had just happened, but convinced he was about to do what his mother had promised him he would do in life, be anything he wanted to be, if he only believed in himself.

She was right, once again. He had willed himself to be in the company of powerful, wealthy people, and that is how he had spent the past three months while working at the St. Charlebois Hotel.

What next? He wondered and did his best to ignore the chill he'd felt when Mr. Valucci had talked to him just now. He'd rather think of the possibilities of working for the wealthy man. Oh, what next . . .

"Our first stop shall be a little mining town north of here, tucked into the hills, called Dogville. I don't know why they named it that, nor am I certain I wish to learn, but I do know they need to experience a theatrical troupe of unsurpassed quality, don't you agree?"

If Jules had learned anything in the days since he began working for Giacomo Valucci, it was that nothing, nothing the man said or did, made any sense. And most of the time the things he said they were about to "embark upon," as he said it, hardly ever happened.

Oh, they visited all manner of shops and purchased a tremendous amount of gear, from trail wear to theatrical costumes, backdrops, and more. All this they had delivered to Mr. Valucci's home, a palatial residence not far from the St. Charlebois Hotel. But beyond that, they never actually embarked on the promised journey.

After the second full day of his employment, Jules had helped the delivery men unload the purchases and store them in a huge room with a crystal chandelier hanging in the center. "We will spend two more days outfitting for our expedition, then we will spend two more days readying it all. Then we will pack it, then we will have it brought to the Dew Street Freight Depot. The wagons should be ready by then. And in the meantime, I shall hire several seasoned trail guides, for we will be trekking the rough country." This last he said in a low voice, his eyes narrowed to match it.

Jules shuddered and thought about what "rough country" meant. He pushed the thought out of his mind and instead ventured to ask his employer something he'd been curious about for days. "Mr. Valucci?"

"Hmm? What is it, James?" The wealthy man was busy sorting through stacks of odd clothing.

"I've been wondering, why do you stay at the St. Charlebois Hotel when you live in this beautiful home not far from the city?"

Silence filled the huge room. Even the big clock in the hallway seemed to hold its breath. Valucci turned his handsome head slowly toward James and stared at him for long moments. Then he said, "James, I thought when I hired you, I made myself clear I will not tolerate impertinence."

Jules didn't know how to answer this, or even if he should. He shook his head, then changed his mind and nodded. Nothing he did seemed quite right. Finally, he cleared his throat. "Yes, sir, Mr. Valucci."

For the first time since beginning his new job, Jules wondered if he'd made the right choice. Too late to go back, he told himself. Besides, he could almost hear his dead grandfather saying, "What's life without a pinch of spice, huh?"

A week later, he would have cause to revisit this wisdom from beyond the grave. By then, it was far too late for Jules to do anything but look ahead and do his best to not say or do anything that might be considered "impertinent," even if he wasn't quite certain what that word meant.

Chapter Five

Rollie had no memory of how he got out to the street in front of the bar. Though it was darkening, likely a storm was coming, it was still daytime, so he couldn't have been sleeping. And why was it so quiet? It had been a long time since he'd seen the street so empty of people, horses, and wagons. Then he saw he was not alone. Across the way, behind the big low rock used by various men of a morning as a gathering spot, there stood a man shrouded in tree shadow.

Rollie couldn't see the man's face. Maybe the stranger had a kerchief tugged up. Though more than likely it had to do with the dark afternoon. A storm had boiled in, slowly for hours, lumbering its gray-black mass closer and closer to the little raw town until the sky, in all directions, had been consumed by it.

In the distance, jags of lightning ripped down, no sound from them. Then they advanced, and with them came the deep sizzle of the sky's rage.

A few weeks later, thought Rollie, and this would be a fast-moving blizzard. Nearer and nearer rolled the storm. Thicker and closer pushed the dark mass until the air felt like cotton wool. What sounds there were came to him as muffled, dull thumps. In all his years roving the West, he'd never seen, never felt, anything like this.

It seemed he'd been watching the storm for a lifetime before he remembered to look back to where the stranger stood. The man was gone.

"Great," Rollie mumbled, squinting about the darkening street. If it was going to be another vengeance-seeking desperado or a bounty-hungry killer, he had to make certain the street was empty of everyone else in town. What could he do? He'd have to wave them off and deal with this loner, and fast.

With no warning, cold, hard raindrops pummeled down. Rollie felt each one, like tiny pelting stones, until they smeared on his shoulders and turned his shirt into a clinging mass. He wore no hat and had to wipe rain from his eyes as he scanned up and down the long main street. Puddles formed, drops danced on their surfaces, and lightning snaked down as thunder rattled, rolled, and burst apart the dismal scene. It hadn't taken long to slick up the dusty through-fare.

Rollie wiped his face again.

Hoofbeats punched holes in the eerie muffled air about him, drawing closer. Rollie spun to his left, clawing free his six-gun as he turned. There was a mass of shadow, barely visible through the sheets of drenching rain.

A gun boomed, flame burst before him in the thundering gloom, and Rollie dove to his left, sliding in the rainsopped muck of the street. Too late, he was too late. He felt the sting of shotgun pellets. They'd peppered into him as he dove, and now he was half-useless, dragging himself forward in the mud with his left elbow.

His revolver was gone—he'd dropped it, but where? He never let go of his gun. He almost hated to look over at his right hand, the one that had held the gun. It was just a raw bloody stump, shiny and red and ragged. Before he could scream, hoofbeats hammered hard again, this time from the right, and a dark mass of shadow piled into view.

Rollie somehow knew it was the same man as before, who'd been hiding in the trees across the street. No, he could not see the man, but he knew, somehow he knew. And then the dark day bloomed bright once more and the last thing Rollie saw was a ball of fire coming straight for him. The last thing he heard was a phlegmy cackling laugh, as if from a dozen voices, all sharing the same sound but at different pitches.

"Hey! Hey Rollie!"

Something had a hold of him, jerking him hard back and forth. He reached once more for the Schofield and felt its comforting grips welcome his wrapping fingers. In a motion more memory than intent, he whipped it around, the hammer peeling back as if by magic, and jammed it hard into whoever was jerking his shoulder.

"Rollie, man, snap out of it! Wake up!"

Pops looked down at the face of his partner and for a moment saw a visage he did not recognize. It was gray, drawn as if pulled from below, gaunt like a week-old corpse, the normally waxed and twisted moustaches now drooped and soaked with dribbles of cold sweat, the same sweat that soaked the man's night shirt.

"Rollie! Come on now, wake up!"

With one hand Pops pushed the revolver away from his face, with the other he gently shook Rollie's shoulder. Rollie's breathing rasped, pumping hard like a smithy's bellows. His vision seemed to come back to him, he shook his head and said, "Wet, so much rain."

Pops maneuvered the pistol out of his relaxing grip and eased off the hammer.

Rollie looked up. "Pops? What's . . ." Then he gasped and held up his now-empty right hand. He stared in wonder at his fingers as they flexed. "Pops, I'm okay. Okay . . ."

"Yeah, you are now, Rollie. Just a dream. You had a bad dream."

Rollie's color crept into his cheeks. He shook his head once more and dragged a hand down his face.

"If you want to talk about it," said Pops, "I'll make coffee. It's more morning than night, anyway."

"No, no. I'm . . . I'm fine."

"You don't look fine, Rollie. You look like a man who's been rode hard and put up wet. Ought to change out of that shirt. You're drenched in night sweats, the leftovers of bad dreams."

Rollie grunted and said, "I don't dream."

Pops' response wasn't what he expected. The man laughed as he stoked the fire. "Okay, then. Believe what you need to."

Hours later, as Pops puffed his pipe and finished affixing the seat to a last bar stool, Nosey swept up the shavings, and Wolfbait quaffed his first beer of the day. Rollie had said nothing to any of them since he started his day. No one dared speak to him as a cloud of gloom seemed to hover over him wherever he went, hauling bottles in from the back room, stacking glasses, shuffling chairs.

Finally, Nosey said, "You know, it's nothing to be ashamed of, Rollie."

"What?" Rollie looked over at him, a glower on his face.

"Dreams. Everybody has them. It's a scientific fact."

Rollie gave Pops a hard stare. "Thanks for sharing that with everyone." And to Nosey, he said, "I do not dream." His moustaches twitched, and a nerve above his left eye jumped.

Nosey gulped. "Well . . . ah, yes, there are always exceptions to every rule."

Pops laughed. "And as we all know, Rollie is the exception to them all."

Chapter Six

The men in The Last Drop heard Chauncey Wheeler's shouts and rushed to the street to find out the cause of the ruckus. Rollie knew the mayor was a lot of things, but excitable for no reason was not one of them. There they were, watching his husky form hustle down the long main street. The man's gasping yips sounded gleeful, but with Chauncey, who knew?

The mayor waved his arms and shouted his way down the dusty track, looking more pained and winded with each jostling, wobbling step. Finally, he stopped in the middle of the street and bent over, hands on his knees, heaving for breath. Meanwhile, the various businesses and residents populating the street stood in front of their places, keen to hear the man's news but not so keen that they'd hustle over to him.

Rollie looked at Pops, then Nosey, then Wolfbait. None were inclined to move. He sighed, flipped a bar towel over his shoulder, and walked down to see what the mayor was yammering about. Even before he reached him the man was talking, or trying to.

"Ma . . . ma . . . ma . . ."

"Take it easy, Chauncey. And take a breath. What's all this about?"

The chubby mayor stood upright. "Maidens . . . maidens!" He was smiling.

"Huh?"

The mayor's smile confused Rollie and left him feeling not a little suspicious. Usually, any time the man grinned like that meant he was about to tell Rollie something he thought he could use to hold over the barkeep's head.

"Women, I'm telling you. Women are coming to Boar Gulch!" Chauncey had nearly gotten his breath under control, though his bright red face beaded anew with fresh sweat droplets.

"Yeah, that stands to reason. We have a growing number of families moving in, too."

"No, no." The mayor shook his head as if he were trying to explain something to a simpleton. "The soiled doves, for pity's sake!"

Rollie sighed. He'd heard Chauncey mumbling about his plan before, but never in full. "Come on up to the bar and you can tell me all about it over a cup of coffee."

To his surprise, Chauncey agreed. And he was still smiling.

Once they were inside, the mayor perched on a stool beside Wolfbait. Pops and Nosey and Rollie all waited to hear why the mayor was smiling.

Rollie said, "Why does this make you so happy, Chauncey? You miss having female companionship that much?"

"No, I mean yes, but . . . oh, for heaven's sake, Finnegan. Look, months ago I corresponded with a Mr. Gladwell in Billings about the prospect of him securing for me a selection of maidens, that's exactly how I put it. I implied, not without ample reason, that Boar Gulch was a boomtown on the cusp of becoming the biggest in all the West."

Pops sipped his coffee, then said, "You know, my dear Mama used to say, 'A little humility goes a long way.'"

"Smart woman," said the mayor, before proceeding. "I described it as the 'golden promise of Boar Gulch,' and it wasn't long before Gladwell agreed to send the women to this female-starved mine camp." He rubbed his hands together.

Rollie sipped his coffee. "That's your news?"

"Yes." The mayor nodded with enthusiasm, his smile sliding as he looked at the staring faces surrounding him. "What? You're not excited?"

"Be more excited if you told us when these here maidens were supposed to arrive," said Wolfbait.

"Oh, they're due any time now. Bone just arrived from his place to say he saw them on their way up the north road!" He hopped down off the stool and tugged out his pocketwatch. "Oh, I have to go get ready!" He ran to the door. "You all should, too." He looked around the room. "Do something to spruce up this place, will you?" Then he hustled out the door and down the steps.

"Was he humming as he left?" said Pops.

"I think so." Nosey shook his head. "The world is officially off kilter."

"You know," said Rollie. "Not that we needed him to say so, but this place could use a little tidying up."

"Good idea," said Wolfbait, sliding from his stool. "You do that, I'll go welcome the ladies. Ain't met one yet who could resist my charms." He winked and gimped on out the door.

"A selection of maidens," said Pops, laughing as he walked out the back door.

"Where are you going?" said Rollie.

"The only thing needs sprucing up around here is you and me. We been living like heathens for long enough. I'm going to find a clean shirt and give myself a fresh shave."

"Good idea," said Nosey. "I'll be at my place doing the same."

"But . . . but you work here," said Rollie.

"Technically not for another three hours. I just visit in the mornings because I find your lack of conversation so stimulating."

Rollie stood alone in the bar and ran a hand over his stubbled jaw. "Was going to shave today anyway," he mumbled, then closed the front door, locked it, and made for the back room and his shaving things, wondering if he had a clean shirt, too.

An hour later, they heard the sounds of a streetside ker fuffle that grew louder, as if a crowd were approaching. Pops beat him to the door. "Hoo boy, I hate to give him credit for anything, especially since I thought he was lying, but looks like Chauncey was right."

Rollie joined him on the front porch. "Looks like it."

From the north end of the street, a bare-ribbed Conestoga jostled its way forward. Beneath the wagging curved ribs stood eight women, most of them in dresses of rich colors, deep blues, light blues, purples, two in red with black lace trim. There was a redhead, three brunettes—

one of whom was a Chinese woman, another a black woman—and the others sported hair in varying shades of brown to corn-silk gold. Most of the heads were topped with fancy feathered hats that complemented their dresses.

They all waved and blew kisses to the gathering men about them. And sitting in the driver's seat, keeping a two-horse team walking forward slowly, sat a woman, older than those of her cargo, but by no means elderly. She wore a smart green velvet skirt topped with a white linen shirt, a matching green velvet jacket, and a green hat with black feathers atop her piled-high chestnut hair that sported streaks of silver.

Walking ahead of the horses, clapping his hands and gesturing wildly back toward the wagon, walked a beaming Mayor Chauncey Wheeler.

Miners three deep had flocked to town and surrounded the wagon.

"Don't know how he got the word out, but he did it," said Rollie.

"The man doesn't do much by half, that's for sure." Pops shook his head. "You going down there?"

"Me? Nah, that'd be too . . ."

"Desperate?" said Pops, laughing.

"Something like that."

The procession made it to halfway up the main street and the woman driving the team reined them to a stop, right in front of The Last Drop. The mayor kept walking but soon realized he was outdistancing the guests of honor. He waddled back to them, gesturing for the wagon to continue rolling forward.

"No, no, we're right in the middle, which is the very

place we want to be!" shouted the woman in the driver's seat. She smiled down at the throngs of cheering, hooting miners, then her gaze roved the buildings up and down the street and stopped as she laid eyes on Pops and Rollie still standing on the front porch of The Last Drop.

She nodded, and the two men, each thinking she was nodding at them, replied in kind, then looked at each other. Only Pops laughed.

She held up her hands and waited until the crowd quieted. "It has been a long journey, and I'm sure you all will agree that my ladies deserve a bit of refreshment."

Head nods and cheers greeted this statement. She set the brake on the wagon, looped the reins on the handle, and made to step down. Immediately a dozen hands offered to help her. She waved them off and with shooing motions, but with a smile on her face, she cleared a path through the men and made her way to the back of the wagon. She dropped the tailgate, two of the women passed down wooden crates, and she set them up as steps. Then she helped the women descend this royal staircase to the dusty street.

The hush that fell over the crowd as these mysterious strangers appeared among them made Pops smile and Rollie shake his head. One or two of the men reached out to touch a nearby lady, but the matronly woman in green smacked their hands, offering a knowing but barely tolerant smile at each of the offenders.

"She's something," said Rollie.

"Yep."

The procession of ladies made its way, much to the surprise of the two men, straight to their steps, then up their steps. They retreated to just inside the door. Rollie smoothed his moustaches, curling the tips quickly just before the ladies filed in, all of them smiling.

Up close, the men saw what a pretty selection of maidens had indeed arrived in Boar Gulch.

Pops looked at Rollie, who was, after all, the senior partner in this enterprise. Rollie was red-faced and couldn't seem to remember how to speak. Pops sighed. "Good day to you, ladies. Welcome to The Last Drop. We are honored to have you here. Won't you please come on in?"

He crooked his elbow and the handsome woman in the green dress laid a gloved hand on his arm as he led the way indoors. The eight pretty ladies followed her in like a rainbow of ducklings. Rollie regained his senses in time to gesture toward the bar and smile. "Ladies, please, come in. Welcome, welcome."

The crowd of leering miners pressed in through the door, clogging it a moment, then popping inward. Rollie turned around. "Keep your distance, boys. Don't give me a reason to shut the door on you."

He heard groans and growls of protest, but the men in front did their best to tamp down their enthusiasm . . . barely. Then the front-most men staggered to either side as if shoved from behind by a cannonball. It was Chauncey Wheeler.

"Now see here!" He elbowed his way into the room. "I'm the mayor of Boar Gulch, and its founder, too, so out of my way, make way for me, curse you. And you, Phillipe, you might try bathing."

The man he'd insulted sniffed his grimy shirt at the pits

and couldn't help but agree. He nodded, but showed no sign of giving up his prime spot at the front of the line.

"Mayor, come on up here," said Pops. "Make the introductions you're dying to make."

The mayor harrumphed and tugged his vest low. Rollie noticed the man had trimmed his beard and moustaches and slicked back his hair with something that smelled godawful, like cut roses gone sour in a vase.

"If I may . . . if I may! Ahem!" He held up a pudgy hand, and everyone in the saloon stopped talking. "Thank you. Now, as you all know, I am the founder of Boar Gulch, and the mayor, as well."

"Didn't you just say that?" said Wolfbait, who'd somehow managed to secure a stool at the far end of the bar. Rollie suspected the man had made his way through the back room. He'd be ticked off about that except he trusted the old man.

"That will be enough from you, Wolfbait. Now, Ma'am," said Chauncey as he walked toward the woman in the green dress. "Might I inquire as to when Mr. Gladwell will be along? Or did he send a letter in his stead? I was led to believe he would be escorting the ladies here. A letter, however will do nicely, as well. I do hope one or the other will be forthcoming."

A couple of the women giggled as Nosey wound among them with a tray, handing out drinks. He blushed, but Rollie didn't think the women were mocking him.

The woman in the green dress tilted her head toward Rollie, who'd made his way closer, so that he was standing next to her. "I wondered when this was going to come up." Then she winked.

Her words surprised Rollie, the only person to hear them. He was going to ask her what she meant, but she was already moving closer to the mayor. "Ah, yes, Mr. Wheeler." She held out her hand. "I'm pleased to meet you. I pictured you . . ." She eyed him up and down. "About the same as you are."

The mayor's smile slipped a bit but he held on. "Well, ah, thank you. May I ask who you might be?"

"I am Madge Gladwell." She let that sink in, then said, "M. Gladwell, to you."

"But . . . but . . ."

She held up her hands. "I never signed my letters as Mr. Only as M. I suspect it was a case of you wanting to believe you were corresponding with a man."

"No, I don't understand, madam. I am quite confident I corresponded with a man. You see, Gladwell always signed his letters to me as Mr."

"If you look closely, you'll see that's not the case. I always signed with an 'M.'"

With that, the mayor tugged out a sheaf of letters from an inner coat pocket. He fumbled with a couple of sheets and his red face turned even redder. He gulped.

"I hope you're not disappointed." She rested her hands on her full hips, canted to one side.

"I . . . uh, no, that is to say, no. You are a most fetching woman, if I may say so."

"You may." She continued to smile.

"I'm . . . confused," said Chauncey. The women giggled and rolled their eyes. Madge Gladwell said, "Ladies," and they shut up.

"Nothing to be confused about, Mr. Wheeler. It's all

actually very straightforward. You painted such a lovely picture, indeed such an alluring portrait of Boar Gulch and its immense promise, I sniffed an opportunity too large to resist. Why, it was all I could do not to ride on out here myself and begin digging for gold!"

"I'm so glad to hear that," said the mayor. His smile had still not quite returned.

"Fortunately," she said, "I have more experience with other matters. Those, as you may have guessed, include managing the talented women you see here before you."

"Hence the reason I wrote to you, yes."

"Indeed. So I took it on myself to assemble the 'selection of maidens,' as you so kindly put it, and decided to ferry them here myself in part to make certain my investment was not harmed in any way. This wagonload of worthy and willing women are the finest you'll find in the Americas."

Rollie was indeed impressed with the beautiful faces here before him, but he couldn't help smirking at Madge's claim. As if she read his mind, she turned and winked at him after she'd said it. He felt himself blush. There was something about this woman he liked, starting with how she wasn't afraid to talk to Chauncey as an equal.

"I'm afraid I don't quite understand, Mrs. Gladwell."

"What's there to understand? I brought the maidens to Boar Gulch and now that I see it and I see the opportunity, I will manage their care and handling myself, as I have for quite some time, Mr. Wheeler."

"But . . . my investment. I initiated this transaction. It's . . . it's mine!" He all but stamped his foot like a petulant child.

Rollie was enjoying this. He glanced at the woman, Madge Gladwell, who also was smiling, looking down at Chauncey as if he were about to break into tears. "Yes, yes, I understand. But to date you have made no investment, you have paid nothing, not even a retainer. You were, as your letter states, if I recall correctly, 'a bit strapped at present, but that will be overcome as soon as other investments free up, any day now, any day . . .' Something to that effect, anyway," she said.

"Now see here . . . madam! I will not stand for this chicanery!" Wheeler took a step toward Gladwell. His red face shook and he gritted his teeth as if he might lunge at her. She did not move.

Rollie stepped between them and pushed the chubby mayor back with both hands planted on the man's chest. "Not in my saloon, Wheeler. Get a hold of yourself. And get out of here while you can, you hear me?" He kept shoving the mayor backward toward the door. The miners parted and loved it, smiling at the exciting little confrontation unfolding before them.

"You can't ban me from The Last Drop! I sold you this place. I'm more welcome here than anybody else in town!"

"Nothing you just said makes any sense, Chauncey. Now go home and cool down. You're making a fool of yourself."

"You don't have any right to talk to me like that, you . . . you . . ."

Before he could finish his thought, Rollie balled his steely fists in the mayor's lapels and dragged him right up into his face. "You listen to me and you listen good, you little fool." Rollie's growl was like gravel ground between steel. "If you paid attention, you'd see I'm doing you a favor, giving you the chance to leave with a little grace. Don't piss me off . . . mayor."

Once freed, Chauncey whimpered and scurried out the door.

"I'm sorry about that, Mr. . . . ah . . ." She eyed Rollie up and down.

"Finnegan, ma'am. Rollie Finnegan, at your service." He offered a quick nod and a smile.

"Mr. Finnegan, very good. As I was saying, I apologize for this unpleasantness."

"No need. In fact, we should apologize to you since he's our representative of sorts. The man can be insufferable. I'd like to say he'll grow on you but . . ."

She laughed, and Rollie liked the sound. It had been a long time, he realized, since he'd heard a woman laugh, really laugh. Other than Mrs. Pulaski and Camp Sal, there were few other women in Boar Gulch, and none of them could be said to be happy to be there. Well, maybe Sal was happier since she'd partnered up with Pieder.

Talking with Madge Gladwell was refreshing, easy somehow. As the room filled with what looked to be ten men trying to converse all at once with each of the ladies, he realized that for the first time in a long time he was enjoying himself.

He saw Pops leaning on the bar from behind, talking with a plump redheaded woman who was ignoring all the other men who kept trying to talk with her. Pops had a reputation among the townsfolk as a man who was second only to Rollie in the no-nonsense department when it came to dispensing hard justice, so few folks dared tread on his toes, conversation-wise.

"I hope you don't think ill of me, Mr. Finnegan," said Madge Gladwell.

"Rollie, please," he said. "And no, I can't imagine I'd think ill of you . . . Madge, for much of anything."

"The deal with Chauncey Wheeler was just that, a handshake by mail. The hitch was that he promised to send money for the ladies' passage and to help set them up in acceptable accommodations, professional and personal, if you understand me."

"I do, and I take it he didn't?"

"No," she shook her head and sipped her whiskey. "He never sent money, so I paid for the trip myself, bought the wagon and horses, the provisions, the lot of it. A second wagon will be arriving in a day or two with more of our gear and belongings, professional attire, furniture, that sort of thing."

"I understand. And as far as I can tell, you were completely in the right in withholding management of the ladies from the mayor. He reneged on his end of the bargain."

"It is unfortunate, but I run a business, not a charity. And to be honest, I much prefer it this way. I didn't really want to send my girls out here without me. I'd secretly planned on accompanying them anyway. But now we can run our ship the way we want to. I leased out my building in Billings, and here we are."

Rollie pooched out his bottom lip and nodded. "Impressive. I'm not certain Chauncey had accommodations planned for you. As far as I know there aren't any places close to town where you can move in and set up shop."

"I figured that might happen. Are there any landowners

hereabouts, someone looking to sell a lot in town or perhaps just outside of it?"

"That's the trouble. You know that pudgy fellow you offended a little while ago? He's the biggest landowner hereabouts. Owns most of the vacant lots left here in town."

"Most . . . but not all?" she said.

"It's possible there are a few unspoken for that he doesn't have his hands on yet." Rollie rubbed his chin. "I'll have to think on it. Tell you what, let me talk with my partner, Pops. That's him behind the bar."

Madge looked over and nodded. "He's the gentleman who welcomed us into your establishment."

"That's him, all right. We own a claim with a tidy cabin on it, but it's not close to town. In fact, it's sort of out there. But it could serve you short-term until we can figure out a more convenient spot for you."

"I appreciate that, Rollie. And speaking of, this impromptu welcoming party is very kind of you, but it's been a long haul and we all really should get to where we need to be, set up somewhere and then get rest before daylight leaves us."

"I understand. You still have about three hours before dark. Let me talk with Pops and we'll see what we can get sorted out for you. I expect we can scare up all manner of volunteers to help." He turned toward the bar.

"Oh, Rollie?" She laid a hand on his arm.

"Yes, Madge."

"Thank you. I did not expect to be so . . . surprised by Boar Gulch."

"Pleasantly so, I hope."

"You bet," she said.

He touched her hand briefly. "Good. I'll be right back."

From a corner of the packed bar, a wiry man with a trim brown moustache nursed a mug of beer. He slowly made his way around the room, pausing as he sipped beer from his mug, not looking at anyone he stood near. He seemed to be taking in everything in the bar all at once, eyeing each person in the place before moving on to settle near others.

No one paid him any heed, not thinking that their conversations about the luck they were each having at their claims were being listened to. But they were.

Chapter Seven

"Ah, there was a time when people such as yourselves would not have been tolerated in public. You see . . . how do I say this without sounding indelicate? You are people who do not matter." Giacomo Valucci regarded the three men sharing the table with him. Not one among them understood what he was talking about.

Valucci shook his head and snorted. "So, Mother, it has come to this." He looked toward the strip-plank ceiling of the Rusty Bucket Saloon. "I am to be burdened by the weak and . . ." He snapped his fingers. "Spine-free! Yes, that's it, these men have no backbones. Still, in a big fight, I will be able to hide behind their stacked bodies. Ha ha!" He smacked his hands together.

The men to whom he spoke regarded this tall, broad-shouldered, clean-shaven man with oiled black hair, a square chin, and light blue eyes. Yep, he was handsome, even they could see that. But he was also offensive as all get-out.

"How come you talk to us like that, anyway? Ain't like you done so well for yourself, after all. Sure enough, you got money. But as you told us, it was your daddy who earned it. Way I see it you been suckling on his sugar teat. You come to us, remember that, mister big-time, fancy actor of the stage."

"Yes, yes, that is true." Valucci strode the room, his hands on his waist. "I will admit you have a point there. I was wronged by the man I seek while you three were riding here and there, looking for whatever it is you have been looking for. Maybe gold? Women? I don't know. Nor do I care. And now I require your services to track him, to right the wrongs he has committed against so many for so long."

His handsome face darkened and he gritted his perfect white teeth, his top lip rose in a sneer. "Oh, Mama," he looked skyward again.

The three seated men also looked toward the ceiling. The fattest of them, Rex, their leader, said, "There he goes again, talking to himself. Wonder why?"

Valucci spun back toward them, and planted his big hands on the table. The bottle and glasses jumped. "Because, you oaf, I am communing with my sainted Mother. There is no one else in all the world who understands me, do you hear?" He stood upright, fuming, his broad chest heaving as if he'd run uphill carrying a great load.

Rex rolled his eyes and began whistling and circling the air by his temple with a finger. The big actor grabbed Rex's doughy head from behind with both hands. His long fingers laced across the man's face, his broad palms mashed the man's cheekbones inward. The victim screamed, a strangling, pinched sound squeezing through his crushed lips. His chubby hands flailed and grabbed to no avail.

The other two men, flanking the struggling man, jumped to their feet, shouting oaths of surprise and stepping backward at the same time. They wanted to help their friend, sure, but they wanted to get away from this big crazy man even more.

The odd thing was that Valucci seemed unaware he was crushing the man's head between his massive hands, his arm muscles bulging beneath his crisp white shirt. His eyes had rolled backward in their sockets, the lids twitched, and his lips murmured inaudible words over the squawking, strangling sounds made by the man in his grasp.

One of Rex's compadres, Bean, clawed his Colt free of the holster and cocked it. "Hey, you . . . crazy man! You got to knock it off! We agreed to help you, but we didn't sign on to get ourselves killed by you! Now let him go!"

Valucci shook his head as if he'd just emerged from a river swim and his eyes flickered open. He saw the snout of the pistol pointed at him, and he smiled. His hands relaxed, and the man he'd been holding flopped forward, his forehead smacking the wooden table.

"Rex? You okay?" The third man, known as Shaver because he used to perform the tonsorial arts back in Teasdale, Oklahoma Territory, before the town dried up, touched Rex's shoulder and shook him.

Rex moaned and lifted his head. His face was a swelling, bleeding mask of itself. One cheekbone had been relocated, his nose looked to have scooted sideways from its previous spot of residence, twin streams of blood leaking down over lips that had both split and now bled.

But it was Rex's eyes that alarmed Shaver the most. They were bloodied where before they had been white. They also now looked to be permanently popped outward. He waved a hand before Rex's face, unsure if his pard could still see.

Then those eyes swiveled and Rex said, "Guhhh? Heppp . . ." A tooth dribbled out between the man's lips and bounced to the tabletop. They all watched it. Rex said, "Ohhh . . ."

"He appears addled now," said Bean, his nostrils flexed as if he were smelling a shank of flyblown meat. "Curse you, Valucci, you are to blame. What do you think of that?"

"Put down that pistol and I will tell you," said Valucci, smiling once more. Then he held up his big hands. "I apologize, gentlemen. This was rough treatment of your friend. I sometimes do not know myself, nor do I have control of my, how shall I say it? Whims? Yes, that sounds right."

Rex mumbled and moved his head back and forth slowly, his eyes seeming to roll loose in their sockets like clay marbles.

"Your friend here will be fine. He needs a little time and perhaps a drink or two. There is nothing that cannot be cured with drink. Bartender!" Valucci snapped his fingers and looked over toward the bar, but there was no one there. "Now where has that devil gone to?"

As if in answer, the batwings parted and a single-barrel shotgun inched its way into the room, a sweat-stained fawn hat visible over the slowly parting doors. "Okay in there, here's how it's going to happen. You all are going to set your guns on the table and sit back with your hands on your heads. Now do that."

Bean and Shaver looked at each other and shook their heads, and Valucci began to laugh, a big, loud sound that doubled him over, and he slapped his leg. "Oh, but I am having fun today. First it's all business, then it's all fun. Now perhaps we shall mix the two!"

The shotgun pushed into the room farther, the doors parted fully, and a man stood in the doorway, lit by the afternoon's gray sky. "You all better do as I say. I am Soldano's law."

"No, no, and no, sir. I am Giacomo Valucci, noted actor of the stage, and you will join us for a drink, okay? We are having a bit of fun in here before we vacate these premises."

The lawman walked in and eyed them over the raised barrel of the shotgun. "I don't know what that means, but you all need to pack up your gear and hit the trail. This town is small and peaceful, and it is my sworn duty to keep it that way, you savvy?"

Valucci looked at the lawman, brows drawn. "Yes, yes, I understand. However, we have already bought whiskey and we have rooms at the hotel, so no, we will not be moving on before tomorrow. But come tomorrow morning . . ." He held up a tall finger. "We will hit the trail, as you say. For now, though, I do wish you would join us for a drink. You see, we have much to celebrate." He walked back and forth, his tall form commanding the attention of everyone in the room. By then the bartender had joined them once more, having edged back into the bar behind the deputy through the batwing doors.

"I, for one, am so excited. You see, I am about to

embark on a great journey, a journey northward, to reunite with an old, old acquaintance of mine. Oh, but it has been far too long. Oh, the stories I could tell, but—"

"Mister," interrupted the deputy, lowering the shotgun a mite. "I don't know what you are going on about, and I don't much care. What I know about is this town, and what I care about is keeping it safe and free of folks intent on making a mess and a mockery hereabouts. I've about had enough of you big-city types from San Francisco, nosing on in here as if you own the place."

The big man offered up his booming laugh once more. "Of course, you have, and we do not blame you for feeling that way. But, in truth, that is of little concern to me. Now, we shall drink to our good fortunes."

The lawman shook his head. "Nope. I'll not be joining you. But I will keep an eye on you all while you're in my town." He backed out through the batwings and once they settled back into place, he peered up over them. Only the hat and a pair of eyes were visible.

Giacomo sat down at the table, poured a fresh round of drinks, and eyed each of his three companions. He spoke in a low voice and grew serious once more. The two men who were still coherent, Bean and Shaver, did their best to watch everything their new employer did. They felt better that he was on the opposite side of the table.

"Now that the fun is over with, I would like to tell you of our plans. For once a man takes money from me, he is committed to the full venture, from beginning to end. And since you three have taken my money, in the form of these drinks, as well as the soon-to-be-accrued livery charges for your horses and the reserved rooms at the hotel, you are fully committed."

"Committed to what, though? You perfume the air with a whole lot of words, mister, but I still don't rightly know what we're up against."

"Good question. As I told you a few moments ago, I will be reacquainting myself with the man who is responsible for the death of my beloved, and then imprisoning me."

"A killing? And prison?" said Bean. "You didn't say nothing about a killing, nor of prison." He smirked. "I didn't think I could say this, but I believe now me and you and Rex have something in common. Not Shaver, though. He's too good for prison." This struck Bean as humorous and he giggled. Shaver rolled his eyes and reddened but said nothing.

"No, you dolt. When I say I was in prison, I mean a prison of the soul. A most horrible place, far worse than anything you may have endured."

"Soul?" said Bean, shaking his head. "No, no, that's not a place I recognize." He leaned forward. "Hard on you, were they? I knowed a man who spent time in Yuma and he still walks with a cane. Busted him up something fierce. Cries like a child sometimes, too. For no reason." Bean nodded, as if in agreement with himself.

Valucci sighed. "The only thing that helped me to survive—"

"Let me guess," said Shaver, grinning and pouring himself another shot of rye. "It's talking with your sainted Mama. Am I right?"

Valucci kept his narrowed eyes on the man and did not

speak for long moments, long enough that Shaver paused with the fresh drink halfway to his mouth and gulped.

"I cannot tell if you are, as you say, having fun with me, or if you are sincere. For now, I will choose to believe you are sincere. But that will be the last time on this journey that you will mention my mother with your foul face. Is that understood?"

Nobody nodded.

He smacked a palm on the tabletop. The two men nodded. Rex said, "Ahh," and tried to lift his own drink to his mouth. He made it partway and dumped the shot down his chest. "Ahh."

"I fear Rex is not going to be right in the gourd," said Bean, whispering to his friend.

Valucci, who had been thumbing through his thick wallet, looked up. "He has until midday tomorrow to prove himself worthy of our company. If not," he shrugged. "Well . . ."

Bean and Shaver each gulped and nodded, worrying about their pard, but watching the wallet. They'd ridden together since they all deserted the army four years prior. They'd spent a goodly amount of that time edging south of the Mexico border, droving when they had to, borrowing horses and cattle from border-hugging operations when they could, splashing them back and forth across the Rio Grande.

Rex always swore he recognized most of the animals, and had begun naming them. Bean and Shaver were doubtful, but then again, Rex was the brains of the three, they all admitted that. He'd kept them in tobacco, whiskey, whores, and bullets.

Then this big, handsome man with the exotic name

swooped into Soldano, their town of choice, wearing a cape, of all things, and looking like he had just arrived from some sort of royal palace. He also toted along with him a wet-behind-the-ears kid Valucci called his "footman," whatever that was.

When they met the actor, he'd told them he had inherited a pile of money from his father and wanted to hire them as guides to take him north to meet up with an old friend. They'd been skeptical, until he started peeling out dollars for drinks. He'd bought the whole town drinks, and it seemed his cash wad never shrank.

That was earlier on the day before, and each hour since had been stranger than the one that led to it. Valucci was a crazy man, they all agreed. But it was Rex who whispered to Bean and Shaver when the newcomer had visited the privy, "Crazy or not, that big Italian fella has a wad of cash that will choke two horses. And did you notice how handsome he is?"

Bean sat up at that and eyed his pard. "What do you mean by that, Rex?"

"Now don't get to thinking strange thoughts, Bean. All I meant is that when there's a fellow as handsome as that one in the group, the ladies will try to climb him like a tree."

"Whoopie for him," said Shaver, adjusting his hat on his eyes and wishing the other two would shut up so he could get some needed sleep.

"And whoopie for us, you idiot. We can be there to catch the ones who fall off that tree!" Rex had rubbed his hands together lightly, looking around, lest they be overheard by the crazy, rich man. "Yes sir, I think that big rich actor man needs us to be his guides."

And now Rex was all-but-squeezed to death, sitting there between them with bloody drool leaking out of his saggy mouth and his eyes wobbling every which way. The three of them never had shot any people other than a few Apaches back in the army, so if it came down to it, Bean and Shaver didn't know how they'd go about shooting that big goober, as Rex had called the actor with the surname none of them could pronounce. But they had to figure it out fast, else it was going to be a long trip guiding him somewhere.

And that was the other thing, he said he would only tell them where he wanted them to take him once they were on the trail rolling northeastward. All around, it was an odd set-up, given that they were supposed to be the guides. But the sight of the man's bulging wallet had convinced them all to nod in agreement with everything Valucci said.

Still, it seemed to Shaver if a man knew where he was going, he shouldn't need any guides. Maybe he was afraid of the wild animals.

Chapter Eight

Colton Shepley woke with a sore throat and a sore head. He opened his dry lips, forced his dry-as-a-stick tongue off the roof of his equally dry mouth. "Gaah." He grunted out the word and wished he hadn't. It echoed in his skull, pinging like a ricocheted bullet, looking to force its way out. And in the midst of this, a tiny man with a sledge whomped without cease, up and down, fore and aft, alternating just behind each of his tender, red-veined eyeballs.

He'd been warned as he dove in the night before that the swill he'd be indulging in was called Ol' Splitskull by its maker, one Theobolus Ward, the owner of the next claim over.

He and Theo got together most every night. Up until the night before, they'd lived with little more than the dwindling remnants from Colton's last bottle of bourbon he'd brought with him. Then Theo's first batch of shine had come ready. Or as ready as the two thirsty men were willing to let it be.

It might have been a mistake, at least that's what

Colton was now thinking. He groaned again and wondered if Theo was feeling the same way. Not that he cared much. The man was a convenient enough neighbor, would lend a couple of hands when Colton needed them, and he offered the same in return, naturally, but still there was plenty about Theo that annoyed him.

Not like he could choose his neighbor. Hell, back home in Rheingold, New York, he had plenty of elbow room on the farm. He and his brother had grown tobacco and beans and corn and raised enough critters to keep the family in meat and eggs and cheese and milk, but it was the freedom their 600 acres afforded him that he missed most once he found himself in Oregon Territory.

The trip itself had taken four months and left him the weight of a child lighter—a welcome result—and nearly penniless—not so welcome—as the result of his team of horses taking on bad water somewhere in the Dakotas. They'd all but shat themselves green and foundered, and in the end he'd had to shoot them behind the eyes and call it a day.

Then he'd taken precious saved money he'd earmarked for purchase of a claim and equipment and bought two oxen because he'd heard they were, though slower and more dim-witted than horses, known for being long-lived and hardy and dependable. He imagined they'd be most useful, day after day, hauling out mountains full of gold-rich ore.

That, too, failed to happen. Oh, the oxen were all he'd been promised, but he hadn't reckoned on the wolves that killed one by the neck in the night and savaged the other badly. He'd also heard from another passing gold seeker that there might be Indians about, as to what tribe, the man had been uncertain, but he'd heard it on good account from a drummer that evil was afoot in those hills.

And so Colton had had to use his skinning knife to end the second ox's suffering instead of shooting it, as he was hesitant to draw the attentions, by way of gunshot, of the savages who may or may not be lurking nearby. Best not to take chances, he'd told himself.

He was left with his wagonload of goods, mostly pieces of furniture made by his grandfather, as well as a few farming implements, despite his vow to his brother some months before to never again take up the agrarian arts. Of course, without oxen, he had little choice but to leave behind these possessions, save for what he could carry on his back.

He was far from any place he might procure fresh stock, and if he did happen to find new horses or oxen or mules, he would have no money left for a claim. He wasn't even certain he had enough left to make that purchase. But he had to try, as confidence welled in his breast like a neverending spring of crystalline water.

Despite that, he waited by his wagon for nearly a week in hopes of meeting up with someone who might take him and his gear, sell him cheap stock, or at least purchase from him his furniture. In the end, no one came along.

This was in part because he, as was his nature, had chosen a northerly route well away from the trodden trails other fortune-seekers had made over the preceding decades. He was a loner, always had preferred his own company to that of others. He'd never even kept a dog, barely tolerated his brother, with whom he'd run the farm left to them by their parents. And he certainly never pursued taking on a wife, no thank you.

Now that buzzard had come home to roost and bit him square in the backside, to boot. That is how his luck had run these past months. One thing upon another was the phrase he had sighed to himself since arriving in the West.

And now, just when he was getting a leg up on life once more, a monster looked down at him, eyes blazing like hot coals, its face a ragged white thing that appeared to sway and flop. It made no sense. Then the monster spoke to him!

"You give up your poke and we'll let you live, you hear? But only because I'm feeling charitable today. Now, where's it at?"

By then Colton's vision had begun to clear and he saw it was no monster, but a man, a man wearing a mask.

The clicking of the man's gun had persuaded Colton to hand over his meager sack of savings, a combination of cash money and a paltry selection of teensy nuggets and two pinches of gold dust.

Then the man in the mask said, "Keep digging, mister. I'll be back." He laughed long and loud. "And because, as my long-dead Pop once told me, one good turn deserves another, I'm going to leave you with something." The masked monster man nodded to two others that Colton had not seen. Behind them stood even more, must have been six in all, maybe eight. "Boys?" said the leader. "Your turn."

Then two men stepped forward and dragged Colton

out of his shanty. He felt the first couple of fist blows, saw not the inside of his crappy little leaning cabin, but bursts of stars, even though his eyes were open. And then he saw nothing, for Colton Shepley was knocked cold.

Chapter Nine

"Boys!" said Wolfbait from the open doorway of the saloon. "I have just seen visions, mighty visions, I tell you."

"You been eating your own cooking again, huh?" Pops shook his head and smiled.

"No, Mister Know-It-All, I have been to the mountain. Or at least to the meadow west of town. You know, down the trail from Pieder's blacksmith shop."

"Ah, yes," said Pops. "That's where Miss Gladwell and her ladies have set up their little tent city."

"Yep," said a grinning Wolfbait as he settled himself onto his customary stool. "Where the bloomers are a-waggin' and the miners are a-draggin'. And that Madam Gladwell, hoo boy, she is a fine-looking woman, a seasoned dove with impressive assets. Hee hee!"

No one said anything, but a low grumbling sound came from Rollie's direction.

"Wonder how they settled up there?" said Pops, hoping to alter the course of the conversation.

Rollie said, "I helped Madge find a parcel of land to lease that Chauncey didn't have his claws into."

"I'm guessing the mayor wasn't too fond of that."

"You guessed right. Chauncey's fit to be tied. Thought he could gouge her for some of his land, after all. He figured if he couldn't get in on profits from the ladies' presence in the Gulch, he'd better make something on what he keeps calling his 'masterful idea' of bringing them here in the first place."

"Man's got a point," said Pops. "So I take it he doesn't have a horse in the race at all, huh?"

Rollie shook his head. "Pieder owns the land and is happy to let the ladies set up camp there, though he's still trying to decide if he wants to sell it."

"Well, somebody better decide quick," said Pops. "Because all the attention from miners still won't keep those ladies from freezing solid in a couple of months in those tents up there."

"I have it on good authority that Madam Gladwell intends to buy the land from Pieder. And what's more, she plans on building a large, sumptuous mansion on that very spot. She wants to call it 'the house on the hill,' or some such pseudo-poetic notion," said Nosey, wiping down the bartop.

"Oh, and how did you happen to come by this notion?"

Nosey stopped and looked at Wolfbait. "How do you think? It appears I am the only one in this establishment, perhaps in this town, who isn't afraid to share that he has partaken of the earthly delights of one Mabel Cummings, a randy little woman in the employ of one Madge Gladwell. Mabel also happens to have more than a passing familiarity with the Classics. Indeed, I believe she has a first-rate mind, and I look forward to spending more time in her company."

Pops leaned in the front door. "Hey, Rollie, somebody's causing a ruckus down at the assay office."

The ex-Pinkerton man was almost relieved to hear the news. He set down the handsaw and planks he'd just evened off out back and checked his gun as he walked to the door. He couldn't wait for the day when they would be finished with rebuilding the bar. If he ever had to go through this sort of thing again, he hoped to either be rich enough to hire it all done or to have sense enough to pack his saddlebags, climb aboard Cap, and ride off with a full coin purse and few regrets.

Instead, here he was in Boar Gulch, keeping the peace and, well, he had to admit it, despite his surly mood this morning, making good money. He sighed as he walked toward the south end of the street. Pops had already reached the cluster of six or eight men standing around a person in their midst.

Someone saw him and the crowd parted. "Rollie, over here."

As if I couldn't guess, he thought. Instead, he nodded. In the midst of the men stood a fellow he recognized, though he couldn't place him at the moment. That was probably because his eyes were nearly buttoned shut from swelling, his jaw was purpled and puffed, and he stood with one arm hanging askew, as if his shoulder were broken or out of joint.

"Rollie, you remember Colton Shepley," said Pops.

"I do now." He recalled the man and his friend, Theo Ward, two miners who lived some miles from the Gulch on adjoining claims smack between Boar Gulch and its closest neighbor, a newly sprung mine camp called Low Cat. Good men when they weren't drinking, but when they got lit, which was often, and usually together, they could be brutal toward each other. "Colton. You and Theo whomp on each other again?"

The man shook his head. "No, no, t'want nothing like that, Rollie." His voice sounded as if he were talking through a mouthful of sand. He looked at his worn boots. "You know I wouldn't bother you with that."

"What is it, then?"

One of the other men began to speak, but Rollie held up a hand and looked at Colton. Before he could answer, the same man interrupted again.

"Look here, Mr. Finnegan," said the chatty man who kept trying to butt in.

He was new to the town, but one of those sorts of men who wanted to be part of everything. Be a politician one day, thought Rollie with less-than-kind thoughts toward the newcomer.

"He's been robbed and we all have a right to know what's going on."

"That true, Colton?"

The bruised mess before Rollie nodded.

"Okay, tell you what, Colton. You come on back to The Last Drop with me and Pops and we'll all have a cup of coffee and talk about it." He turned to the nosey newcomer. "You can go on about your business. And if anything comes up that you should know about, you'll be told. Until then . . . stop being so annoying."

The man's eyes widened and he backed up. "I . . . I was just trying to help."

"Try harder. I dare you." For once the man had nothing to say. Rollie's quick glance at the other men confirmed they felt like he did.

The scowling man mumbled and stomped back inside the assay office. Rollie and Pops ushered Colton Shepley down the street. "Is that true, Colton, what that fellow said?"

"Landers, I think he said." Pops glanced at Rollie.

"Yeah, that's him," said Colton "But them that did this, I never saw their faces because they wore masks."

"Masks?" Rollie was already thinking about various cowards he'd tracked down in the past. "How many?"

Colton tried to shrug, then winced. "Six, maybe eight."

He knew Pops was thinking the same thing he was, because they'd talked about the possibility. Sooner or later in a gold-rich place like this, someone was bound to get robbed. He knew that a lot of the men along that stretch of the Little Falls Stream were still panning, and from all accounts, largely from the miners themselves when they turned up at the bar and got too drunk to keep their mouths shut about their recent good fortunes.

"Where's Theo now?" said Rollie.

"That's the thing, he's gone. Before I came to town, I looked quick in his cabin, then down by the stream, but I never saw him. I'm worried about him."

Rollie stood up. "Nosey, could you fetch Colton here a coffee? Me and Pops are going to be busy for a while. We should be back before the evening rush."

Once he and Pops were in their living quarters at the back end of the building, Pops said, "That fool is worried about Theo but I'm thinking Theo's long-gone with Colton's hard-won dust and nuggets. You?"

Rollie rummaged in his trunk and pulled out a second revolver and two boxes of cartridges. "Hate to judge a situation before I know what's what, but I'd bet money you're right. But it doesn't explain the six or eight masked men he says robbed him."

It took them an hour to ride out to where they recollected Colton Shepley's and Theobolus Ward's claims sat. They came on Shepley's first, with the shack almost visible from the road. "If what Shepley said is true, we should see lots of hoofprints."

Pops circled his horse, looking down. "And I do. Here and here, and there, a churned mess." They were easy to pick out in the gravel.

"See if you can pick them up, either coming or going. My guess is they came from the forest over that way. But they could easily have come from further up the lane."

"Okay," said Pops. "You thinking road agents?"

"I sure hope not. If you swing back by this way and I'm not here, I'll be at Theo's cabin further in that way." He nodded his head at the narrow trail that threaded past Colton's cabin and disappeared in the scraggly trees beyond.

"You got it."

"Pops." Rollie waited for his partner to halt and look back at him. "Be careful."

Pops hefted his Greener. "Lil' Miss Mess Maker's got me covered."

"I know, but it's been a while since we've had real trouble, and something feels like it's about to give."

"I feel it, too. Trick is to kill it before it kills us."

"Truer words, my friend." Rollie slid down from Cap and tied his reins to the spidery air-dried roots of a fallen pine, likely downed from too much digging by Colton or whoever owned the claim before him. Rollie knew little of the man, save for his drinking habit and his somewhat sober claims, always revealed to Rollie on the quiet, of his modest but hopeful success at finding placer gold about his place.

Oddly enough, Theo did much the same, though at different times. Rollie suspected if they weren't so hampered by drink, the two men could actually make a go of their diggings.

There were definitely a number of riders here, so that part was true. Which meant his initial suspicion of Theo was lessened, but not wiped out. Yet.

He drew his Schofield and thumbed back the hammer as he scanned the yard in front of the cabin. An assortment of broken-handled tools—two shovels, a pick, and a mattock—leaned against a boulder half-unearthed that looked to be a much-used spot by Colton, owing to a convenient rock shelf of the right height and depth for a man to sit and consider his situation. From the empty coffee cup and spent tobacco where a pipe had been knocked, it seemed Colton spent much time musing on his lot in that very spot.

The cabin, if you could call it that, was more a collection of leaning, wind-chewed boards and logs, gray with age, that looked to have been robbed from wherever the finder happened upon them and put to use here. None of them was of the length they should have been, as evidenced by the gappy wall facing him, with one boarded window and a plank door.

Rollie approached with slow, near-silent steps, pausing every few feet to listen. He could right now be watched by someone inside. The wall was breezy enough for a spy.

From the looks of it, Colton would never have enough spare clothes to wad up and stuff in the holes. Rollie made it to the wall, his back to the less-gappy left side of the sagging, leather-strap-hinged door, and rapped quickly on the door to his right. "Anybody in there?"

Nothing, no sounds but a high-up soughing breeze through the tall trees. He reached over and tugged the leather-loop handle and yanked the door open. It swung outward, giving up a long, slow squeak. Rollie peered around the door and, because the sun was to his back, took in most of the interior of the single room. There was little shadow where anything bristly on two legs might hide.

Dead ahead sat what Rollie assumed were the remains of a squat stool, one that had started life as a homemade affair by someone more suited to brute labor than furniture making. Crooked splits of stovewood, barely shaped by a dull axe, formed the legs, and a crude seat was woven of rope. No wonder Colton spent his sitting time outside on the rock in the sun. The crippled stool made Rollie feel a whole lot better about the tables, chairs, and stools he and Pops had built for the bar.

As Rollie entered through the doorway, he stepped around a smashed lantern and took in the scramble of bootprints, gouges, and drag marks on the dirt floor. The stink of lamp oil, man-sweat, vomit, woodsmoke, and burned food mingled, reminding the old lawdog of a wildcat's piss-soaked den he'd peered into once looking for stashed loot.

That experience hadn't ended well, and he still carried the scarred forearm—could have been his face—to prove it. He hoped that dredged memory wasn't a harbinger of what awaited him this day. He also hoped he'd gained a few more smarts since that long-ago day of his exuberant youth.

Eyeing left and right, he saw it wasn't only the stool that looked to have been smashed in a recent fracas. An equally oddly constructed trestle bed sagged against the right wall, its long pieces snapped as if stomped. Blankets and soiled clothing lay tussled on the floor.

A cracked dynamite crate tacked to the left wall served as a shelf for a jumble of items left after the majority of them had obviously been swept off the shelf to the floor. As if someone had been searching for something.

A small sheet-metal stove hugged the back wall—too close for comfort, thought Rollie—and still sat, surprisingly, upright, though its pipe had been knocked askew. Another wooden crate held a fry pan, a coffee pot, a cup, and a tin plate and utensils. Tucked in the close right-side corner, a stack of crates served as more storage for clothes and cans of beans, milk, and pears.

The shanty had only the front door and the one boarded-up window beside it, though given the gaps in the walls, Rollie didn't see further need for a window.

He knew Colton Shepley had spent at least one winter in this hovel, and he wondered how on earth the man had survived it. Right then and there he felt nothing but relief at his decision to stay in town and tend a bar.

His and Pops' digs there might be a far cry from his comfortable rooms back in Denver City, but they were downright sumptuous compared with what most of the miners in these parts endured.

Shaking his head, Rollie crept out of the shack, eyeing the vicinity. Nothing moved, no glints revealing sunlight on metal. As for sound he heard only the breeze and a chickadee flitting from mumbling to itself as it hopped branch to branch on a never-ending quest for bugs.

"Time to check on Theo." He turned to the trail, then decided to take Cap along. The man's cabin was farther up the trail, a narrow, windy affair that hadn't seen much more than foot traffic of late. No hoofprints. Rollie wondered if the man even owned a horse. From what he'd heard, Theo had likely traded it for a bottle of gargle.

The lack of hoofprints also meant Colton's alleged attackers hadn't ridden up here. Didn't mean they didn't walk.

They reached the cabin's clearing. Rollie tied Cap once more and held out the pistol. He advanced, sidestepping toward the shack. The dirt before it was a trampled mess of bootprints.

He wasn't expecting much and he wasn't disappointed. If Colton's cabin was a ramshackle affair, Theo's was its lesser. Size-wise it was smaller than Colton's, but the aged roof made it seem even smaller. The door had been pried or ripped off its hinges and a torn shirt hung from the bottom of the frame like the tongue of a dead man.

Rollie held up, scanning the scene. "Hello the house!"

No movement, none of those stray sounds folks in hiding often make and are unaware they make from fidgeting—heavy breathing, sniffing, the rustle of trousers or a shirt sleeve on a board or stone or branch. Nothing.

The cabin inside looked a whole lot like the first one, a jumble of broken, badly made furniture, clothing, empty bottles, and a knocked-over stove. This time the stink from the shanty made Rollie's eyes tear. The strong smell of urine and a sour gut's leavings—from which end he didn't want to know—hung in the small, dark space.

He held his breath and poked and prodded the inside of the cabin quickly, toeing piles of junk for the body of a bony drunk. Nothing.

Once outside, he gulped a couple of deep breaths and turned his attention to the bootprints once more. There were at least three men here, fewer than he'd seen at Colton's. They appeared in profusion in front of the shack, then he saw a barefoot print in the softer dirt off by the shack's front right corner. Boot prints followed. And so did Rollie.

It took three strides to walk the length of the cabin's north wall. The trail here likely led to an outhouse or pit where Theo did his business. Only Theo never made it up there a last time. He lay in the trail before Rollie, face down, arms reaching up-trail. His grimy hands clawed the dirt as if raking for one last hint of that elusive temptress, the promising sign of gold ore.

Then Rollie saw the twin bullet puckers in Theo's bare back, drilled close-up and angled into the upper ribs, left side, and gut level on the right. His befouled longhandles had been stripped from him down below his waist, exposing the upper half of his backside. His bare white skin reminded Rollie of pig carcasses hoisted up on a tree branch for cleaning after being scalded in a backyard rendering setup.

Rollie had only ever seen Theo a few times in The Last Drop, at night in the bar's smokey dimness. Out here, in the full sun of midday, the man looked much older than he'd thought him to be. His hair, greasy and stringy, was grayed and dull. The skin of his arms sagged, though the man was soft-fleshed and bone thin.

Rollie bent closer and saw more smears on the man's

head. He'd been shot there as well. He used the barrel of his revolver to part the hair draped on his neck to reveal a smaller pucker. Same as up higher on the side of Theo's head. These were smaller caliber shots, likely from a hideout gun. Odd.

Maybe Theo had been laid low by the big shots, then whimpered and was finished off by the smaller gun to the head and neck. Out of kindness? Not hardly.

He again used the barrel's tip to lift the dead man's fingers, but saw nothing but dirt balled beneath the hands. The knuckles atop were callused but not bloodied and cut.

Rollie stood and eyed the surrounding hillside, into the trees above, and back down to the cabin behind him. He saw nothing, heard nothing save for a squirrel chittering, and smelled nothing . . . yet. Theo would be ripe before long.

Rollie led Cap back down the trail toward Colton's shack, half-paying attention, half mired in thought. He'd been hoping that if this situation had a nefarious edge to it that it might have been instigated by Theo or Colton's drunkenness. It would have been far too simple to be able to lay the blame at Theo's feet. But he had not found the man hung over with a gun in his hand regretting stealing from and pummeling his neighbor.

Now that he'd found Theo dead, it would be likely and even expected to blame Colton for the crime. Trouble was Colton was the one who tipped them off. And his claim he'd been accosted by a number of men, and the wreckage and bootprints, of varying sizes, further confirmed his innocence. Rollie saw no sign on Theo's knuckles that he'd been the one to use Colton's face as a sparring sack.

He heard a whistling up ahead and his Schofield rose out of reflex even as he ducked low in a crouch.

"Easy, pard," said Pops, chuckling. "It's only me."

Rollie stood and holstered his gun. "I see that. Anything?"

Pops shook his head. "They lost me in the trees. Too dry and piney up in there. I'm no top tracker, but I'd say we're looking at six men, at least."

Rollie nodded, said nothing.

"Theo?" said Pops.

Rollie shook his head. "Dead behind his cabin. Looked to have been making a run for it. Didn't get far. Still in his longhandles, though it looks like someone grabbed them and tried to hold him back. They're bunched about his backside."

"How'd they get him? Gun him down?"

Rollie nodded and patted the back of his head. "One in the neck, one up higher, and two in the back."

Pops whistled. "That confirms what Colton said about hearing shots on his way to town. You think we ought to warn the other miners hereabouts?"

Rollie shook his head. "Not yet. Be more effective if we let the word out back at the bar. That and Theo's death. Besides, we'd spend the day riding these hills with no idea of where we're going."

"Yeah, and I'm sure Colton will have attracted a crowd by now. What do we do with Theo?"

"Leave him for now. I got all I can from him. He wasn't very talkative."

Pops arched an eyebrow at this rare moment of humor from Rollie.

"Besides, Colton can bury him. They were pards, after all, despite the squabbles."

"I feel bad for him," said Pops. "Now he doesn't have anybody to drink with."

"We could always send Wolfbait up here to keep him company."

Pops laughed. "Oh, now that I wouldn't wish on any-body."

Chapter Ten

Two days after he and Pops had surveyed the scene up at Colton's and Theo's cabins, Rollie stood out back of The Last Drop, splitting wood for the neverending maw of the stove. He stopped for a breather and scanned the hill behind town as he stretched his back and sipped water from a dented tin cup.

The scene reminded Rollie of how that day from hell had unfolded weeks before, when Cleve Danziger and his gang had trampled through Boar Gulch, stomping her citizens and making a mockery out of him. He'd nearly been undone by the affair, but the citizens had shown the pluck mountain folk are made of and had risen up to help him lay the bastard and his thuggish cohorts low.

Rollie's gaze took in the hillside behind the saloon, past the outhouse and up the rocky, stump-pocked slope, its long tufts of grasses gone gold and brittle and rattley in the coming season of cold and less daylight. They'd need to lay in more firewood, a whole lot more. And soon.

Was that black hump a rock or the top of a hat's crown? It looked out of place to him. He didn't have Pops around today to verify his suspicion, as Pops and Wolfbait had gone on their now-weekly supply run down to Bella Springs. Nosey wasn't due in for his shift behind the bar for a few hours yet. Then the black spot disappeared, sunk out of sight. Yep, he thought with grim satisfaction. You still have it, old boy.

But it only verified what his gut had been telling him. The rest of the world—or at least every inbred fool West of the Big Muddy seeking what they suspected was easy bounty money—knew by now he'd not died when Danziger came to town . . . and never left. And now Rollie "Stoneface" Finnegan was once more, in the eyes of every worthless bounty seeker, a chicken up for the plucking.

He'd give a dollar himself to know how much the bounty on his head was. A slice of vanity he'd not admit to many, but he hoped it was mighty, upward of $10,000. That would make shooting the vermin seeking him even sweeter.

Rollie thought back on the day Cleve had arrived in town. He should have shot the stranger right out of his saddle and been done with it when he'd spotted the first of them. But that wouldn't have changed anything, he knew, because there were all those other men, seemingly dozens at times.

What if that man had been one of the innocent folks drawn to Boar Gulch for the same reason Rollie had been? How could a body tell the good from the lousy? It was a question without answer, so far at least. And it plagued him each and every day he spent living in the Gulch.

He and Pops had spent far too much time talking about it, parsing the situation this way and that. Rollie had gone along with that line of thinking mostly to humor Pops. At times Rollie felt strongly he should have followed his gut instinct and packed up and gone away.

His musings clipped short with the reappearance of the hat's crown. Though he was always on his guard, he half-thought it might be a kid playing games. Then he remembered there weren't but two kids in these parts that he knew of.

One was the McGillicuddy boy, a fine young lad who did his pretty mama and hardworking papa proud. They worked a double claim northwest of town. The other kid had a name unknown to him, a waif hollow eyed and meager smiled, the opposite of the McGillicuddy kid.

This one was a nephew of Bone, who, along with his son, who everybody just called Bone Junior, wasn't much of a miner, but ol' Bone was one heck of a jack of all trades. You wanted a hole dug in the cemetery, Bone and his boy were your men. You wanted your privy dealt with, emptied, relocated, or filled in, he was your man.

And now he had a nephew. Rollie suspected everybody in whatever secret hollow Bone was from was much the same, all gaunt and spooked seeming. Rollie hadn't seen much of the kid since he arrived, couldn't be more than twelve or thirteen years old, but he was as tall as a man and weighed as much as a man's left leg.

Somehow, he doubted the hat was that of a game-playing kid. That left one possible answer. He backed to the steps and made his way inside to retrieve his rifle and extra bullets. While in there, he parted a wooden shutter and peered out. That's when he saw the black hat disappear once more from view atop the hill behind.

"Here we go again," he whispered.

Rollie pulled back inside, snapped his braces up onto

his shoulders once more, and pulled on his vest. He stuffed extra shells into his trouser and vest pockets, buttoned his vest, and lifted his rifle free of its sheath beside the door. He checked to ensure it was full, then ratcheted in a round and looked out again.

He hated to crank off a shot and rile the sleepy midday hour, about the only time the Gulch was somewhat quiet these days. But if he had to, he had to.

The black hat appeared again, rising up as if conjured by his mind. It was a tall-crown affair.

Could be there were others of them close by the bar, outside. But why tip him off with the obvious hat appearing and disappearing, over and over again? Only reason he could think of was to draw him out. And it was working.

He nudged open the door before the hat rose up enough for the eyes beneath it to get another look at the backside of the bar. Get out, shut the door, and get gone, that's what he needed to do.

He kept his boot scuffs to a minimum down the slight pegged ramp they used to help get goods in and out the back door. It looked to Rollie like an oversize chicken ramp. Pops had suggested they rename the bar The Hen House. Nosey said The Rooster Palace was more appropriate.

Rollie catfooted between two stacks of empty crates and a barrel of creosote, and made it to the cover of the leaning storage shed they used as a catch-all, mostly for horse feed and tack. He swore he was going to get it straightened up and tightened before snow flew. After he laid in the firewood. Lord, but there was a lot to do, and here he was about to deal with another bounty seeker.

He made it to the back corner of the shed, pulled off

his own hat, and peered around the edge. The rough, dried plank smelled good with the sunlight baking it, like the way pipe tobacco always smelled better than it tasted. At least it pleased his nose.

From this altered angle he couldn't see the divot in the land atop the slope where he knew the man sat, waiting for him to come out. He must have been on watch for a while and knew Rollie was alone today. Maybe he grew tired of watching him split wood? Why not shoot him then? Unsure of who he was?

Life was chance and chance was life, eh, Rollie, old boy?

He looked ahead, up along the line of tents and buildings lining his side of the street. If he could keep working his way southward, he could angle west, upslope, and circle behind the man, catch him before bullets flew. It was unlikely, but it was his only plan.

He counted on the fact that the stranger was unfamiliar with the town's layout, and hastened to scramble up closer and closer to the man. He was within fifty feet of him when he caught sight of the stranger. And as soon as Rollie saw the man's profile, he knew who it was.

Chin MacRae was a Chinese-Scotsman, and a peculiar-looking fellow, at least compared with Rollie's other acquaintances. The man wore a dragoon moustache, but it and the hair on his head was red and bristly. The man's face was ruddy, but his nose was long and narrow, and his eyes bore the almond shape peculiar to the Chinese. He was also loony, a trait Rollie attributed not to his having that odd cocktail of blood but rather because he'd likely been dropped on his homely head as a tot.

It had been six or so years back that they'd had their

run-in. The man was running a small gang that had pulled off two simple train robberies and had developed a taste for more of the same. MacRae had never tried to disguise his distinctive looks, so plenty of trainmen and passengers remembered him.

Trouble was, he up and disappeared. Not the three men in his gang, though. They turned up dead, along with an empty Pacifica Lines Railroad mail satchel he'd liberated on his last job. The man had gotten away with quite a haul. And then there hadn't been sign, sight, nor sound of the odd half-breed since.

Rollie had wanted to keep tracking him but Allan Pinkerton had quashed that notion, citing his needing Rollie as part of an elite hired guard team to protect brewery king Adolphus Schinnhelmer of St. Louis, whose portly life had been threatened. That had been a waste of time. Turns out the man's own spoiled-rotten son was the one doing the threatening. He ended up getting a scolding and an inheritance, which, the last Rollie heard, he'd lost in a bizarre scheme to harvest rubber somewhere in South America. Good riddance.

He wished the whiny beer heir had taken Chin MacRae with him, maybe he would have been bitten by one of those mammoth jungle snakes and died. But nope, here he was in Boar Gulch, likely fresh out of money and with an axe to grind. What better way for him to get his revenge on Rollie for helping jerk his train-robbing career to a halt, and make a wad of cash at the same time?

As Rollie recalled, the man had a tendency to chew licorice root and frequently spit the woody matter he'd pulped between his shiny horse teeth. And as Rollie watched, the slight man did just that, bent his head low and spit beneath his right arm. As he did so his eyes lifted and narrowed as he spied Rollie spying on him.

Chin MacRae uttered a word Rollie didn't pick up, then swung a rifle on him. Rollie barely had time to flatten against the gravelly earth before slugs panged into the stone and whistled over his head. He gave consideration to scooching backward on his belly, but that would only delay the inevitable. Instead, Rollie crawled forward up tight to the rock. It was tall enough to shield his head if he kept low and wide enough to keep from getting lead poisoning if he kept himself lined up right.

At the rate MacRae was discharging his weapon, he'd be out of bullets any second now. And yep, there was a pause. Rollie peeked around the right side of the rock quickly and saw the man had ducked down, stuffing in shells, no doubt.

No more wasting time, Rollie matched the man's rifle frenzy with his own. More difficult because he was prone, but he didn't dare risk prairie-dogging. He had to keep MacRae in sight. He recalled the man was unsavory, a backshooter and a thief, and Rollie had no doubt he'd not hesitate to lay him low, facing him or otherwise.

Rollie paused to reload. "Chin MacRae!" He shouted. "Give yourself up. This town's bristling with guns, and we saw you ride in. You're done."

The reply was instant, beginning with a howl of laughter, and followed with a fresh volley of shots. "Still crazy," muttered Rollie.

Dirt plumed to either side of his rock. Rollie knew he had to do something. He wished he had some sort of bomb he could lob at the man and call it a day. A half-stick of dynamite would do the trick nicely. The idea of lobbing something wasn't bad. He was surrounded with hand-size rocks.

Why not hurl a few? Maybe he'd get lucky. Unless his hand got shot in the effort. Maybe not such a good idea. Besides, they were a dozen yards apart. Rollie didn't have that much faith in his aim or his throwing arm.

By now he was certain the sleepy, mid-day residents of town were wide-eyed and fretting. He hoped they kept low and away from doorways. He also hoped MacRae was traveling solo. If his past was any indication, he was a lone wolf.

"You've saved me the trouble of tracking you, MacRae! You've been on my list of things I've been meaning to get to. How nice of you to show up here."

Another cackle of laughter.

"Who sent you? I'll mail them a thank-you note."

"Purely business, old man. Your homely old head is worth cash money."

Rollie knew they were trading insults, but being called old set his teeth to grinding. "Okay, junior. You asked for it." Rollie didn't let the words hang in the air but chased them with a fresh volley of bullets. He knew right where he was aiming and hoped to kick up enough dirt that he'd daze the oddball, bloodthirsty character.

Then something happened that Rollie did not expect. A white handkerchief tied to the end of a rifle barrel slowly rose up in the air, as if it were the head of a strange, timid beast. Up and up it rose until most of the rifle was visible. The man's hands were as yet unseen.

"What in the hell . . .?" muttered Rollie as he peered around the left edge of the rock. Had to be a trick, a gambit to lure Rollie into showing his face. He looked around but still saw no one behind or to his sides. Far across the way, to his left, the ringing of Pieder's daily work had long-ago ceased. A cold wind shuffled through stickleweed stalks, rattling them, then moved on.

The white flag waved slowly side to side. "Finnegan! I've had a change of heart. I walk away and you live, simple."

Now it was Rollie's turn to laugh. And he did offer a quick snort. He'd give MacRae this, the fool was ballsy. Could it really be that this ruthless grubbing killer and thief felt himself trapped with no way out? Doubtful as the day was long. So what was this game?

"What's the angle, Chin?"

"No angle. I go my way, you go yours."

"Why should I?"

There was a pause before the man responded. "Because if you don't, I'll kill you before the day's out. You know it, old man."

Rollie sneered, ground his teeth again. "You know . . . boy . . . a little humility goes a long way."

"Never found that to be true, old man."

"Get up and advance, hands high!"

"That's not the agreement."

Rollie rose to his knees, whipped the rifle butt tight against his shoulder. "We didn't come to an agreement." He fired. "And we never will."

The bullet hit Chin's raised rifle's forestock dead center, bursting the wood apart and slamming the gun backward. But Rollie was already on the move. If Chin MacRae tried to peer out or stand or do anything other than sit and whimper and wait for Rollie to descend on him, he'd be shot.

Even before he made it to the edge of the little divot in the land that the bounty seeker had holed up in, he knew he'd won. He heard a shrieking that was almost embarrassing to listen to.

"You ruined my gun! My lucky rifle! You!" MacRae looked up, both his hands clutching the shattered stock, one hand bleeding. The right side of the man's face looked like he'd been used as a target at a sliver-throwing contest. He screamed and carried on like a child denied a sweet at the mercantile. Rollie stood over him, rifle aimed down at him.

"Shut up! Now!"

How in the hell did this simpering fool ever manage to rob trains? He looked to be ill, thinner than Rollie recalled from his glimpses of the man years before. No longer was he a wiry, muscle-and-bone young man with weird hair, angry eyes, and a toothy sneer under that silly moustache. Now he was gaunt, and his hat looked too big for his bony head.

"What's the matter with you?" he said when the fool had simmered down to a snuffling whimper.

"Nothing . . . nothing. Thought I could make an easy pile shooting you. The head, the man said, just the head. That's all the man said they wanted. Said he'd know your ugly face anywheres." At that Chin smiled, and Rollie saw some of the breed's old fire and familiarity again.

"Toss that rifle away. Now!"

Chin sighed a disgusted sound and shoved it onto the crusty ground to his right.

"Now the sidearm. I can see it. Two fingers, easy. Lift it and toss it this way."

Chin regarded him with half-lidded eyes like a drowsy viper. What was wrong with this fool?

The half-breed tossed the revolver, but it looked to have cost him effort he could ill afford. Ill, that's what he must be, thought Rollie.

"Okay, now climb up out of there, slowly, with your arms up. If I don't see those hands, I'll shoot you in the head." Rollie backed up a step. "Let's go."

MacRae was already on his knees. He jerked one leg up underneath himself and wobbled. A slick sheen of sweat coated his face, and Rollie saw for the first time that the man had what looked like sores on the side of his face that hadn't been pocked with splinters from the gun stock.

"What's your sickness, Chin?"

The man looked back down at the dirt, hands shaking but still held up. "Don't know. Could be pox, could be I'm a syphilitic." He shrugged. "Don't much care. I have about an hour a day when I got strength to do anything." He looked up again, squinting at Rollie from beneath his nudged-back hat brim. "You know how long it took me to get to this forsaken place?"

Rollie didn't answer, just stared at the man. If it was pox, he could be contagious.

"What you gonna do, huh, Stoneface?" Chin smiled again, his teeth, once white and gappy and memorable in that odd face, were now grayed and browned. A couple had gone grimy and stumpy. It looked as if the man had been ill a long time. Pox, from Rollie's experience, didn't mosey. It ravaged in days, at best weeks. This poor fool looked to have been afflicted for some time.

Rollie let out a breath. "Same thing I do with hydrophoby dogs—shoot you in the head. On the other hand, if you are poxy, I'll have to torch you. That alone would do you, so I could save myself the wasted bullet and drop a match on you."

Chin's gaze faltered and he twitched as if he were trying to scare a fly off his cheek. "Now, Stoneface, I never took you as a man burner."

"You don't know me very well then, do you, Chin?"

Chin licked his lips. They were of a purple-red hue, like seeing veins through thin skin. He closed his eyes and smiled

Rollie thought he was about to speak, but he just knelt like that, as if waiting for Rollie to do something.

"Then again," said Rollie, trying to shake the eerie feeling the wraith of a man was giving off, like a rank odor. "You might not sit still for the flames to do their task, so I guess I'll shoot you."

Chin's eyes snapped open and he seemed to have gotten over whatever brief spell of sickness had passed over him in the past minute or two. "I want the law, Finnegan. I know what I have a right to and it's a legal public trial."

"Trial for what? You come in here blazing away and expect the law to protect you?"

The man's face grew brighter, redder as if heated from within. It began to rival the tufts of orange bristle sticking out from under his hat. "Why, yes, I do."

"Nah," said Rollie. "Besides, what sort of a lawman would I be if I went around freeing guilty folks?" He watched the man's face and relished what he saw—widening eyes and a drooping jaw.

"Did I forget to mention that? Must be my dotage creeping up on me. Yep, I'm the law in these parts. Well, technically not the law, since we're lawless. But I am the duly elected arbiter and dispenser of justice."

"I don't understand."

"That's okay," said Rollie. "I know how difficult it can be for a fellow who grew up simple in the head to follow regular conversation." Rollie wagged the rifle. "Drag your diseased carcass on out of that hole. You have a date with a rope."

Rollie didn't think Chin would make it that easy for him, and he was right, especially since he'd seen the transformation that came over the man's face once he'd gotten his wind back or whatever it was that had triggered the sudden recovery.

The scurvy-looking oddball grunted once and used as leverage the back edge of the slight graveled bowl he had fought from. He shoved himself up out of the hole as if he were crawling forward, but at a startling speed. His thin hands clawed toward Rollie, and the right hand snatched Rollie's left polished boot low, at the ankle. Rollie felt himself toppling backward even as he rammed the rifle butt down at the dusty crown of the black hat.

The snatching hand jerked hard, and Rollie's aim was off. The rifle butt shoved the wide brim, mashing it down against the man's head, before slamming into Chin's shoulder. Again, he grunted but was not to be put off his attack. He crawled farther from the hole, slithering, using his bony knees and elbows, resembling a lizard swarming up and over the backpedaling Rollie.

The barman had landed hard on his tailbone and hip, his old wounds from earlier in the year smarting and delivering instant, eye-watering grief. He slammed the gun sideways as he scrabbled backward, kicking with his free boot heel at the advancing, leering, ghoulish face of the half-breed.

A kick connected as the snarling man made to rise to his knees. The blow dazed him and as he shook his head, his hat, which Rollie's earlier blow had loosened, fell free of his head.

What Rollie saw seized him but a moment. Chin's once-red-haired dome was a scabbed, sore-covered mass of crusted pustules with tufts of bristly red hairs poking from them like grass in a baked desert landscape. The gun-butt blow Rollie had skinned off the side of the man's head had damaged his ear, ripping the top free so that it bobbed as he thrashed. It didn't seem to matter to the demon.

As Rollie pivoted on his right hip he brought the rifle barrel around on MacRae, who had freed a hidden Bowie knife in the melee and once more lunged, the blade pointed down, the grip held in the thin right hand so tight the skin whitened over the bones.

He didn't count on Chin's left hand to act as if thinking on its own. It clawed forward, found purchase on Rollie's knee and used its grip there to shove him, skewing his aim. The bullet sizzled between Chin's savaged ear and his shoulder. In the time it took Rollie to lever another round, the Bowie arced down and slammed into the scrambling calf of Rollie's left boot with enough force to drive it through the boot and lodge an inch into the dry earth beneath.

Rollie jerked his leg away, yanking the knife free of Chin's grasp. The blade whipped out of his boot and flew a few yards off. At the same time, he triggered the rifle, coring the spidery man's forehead with a bullet that traveled no farther than eight inches from the snout of the barrel to Chin's head.

Wide, almond-shaped eyes, yellowed and veined with red, topped those stained and rotting horsey teeth. Farther in, behind the teeth, the red-black clot of a mouth opened wide, emitting a raging shriek that trailed of in a wet, gagging sound. The unholy mouth puckered and a cloud of reeking gas leaked out.

Rollie shoved backward once more, wanting, needing, to get away from the thing that had just attacked him. It was no more a man than Rollie was a coon hound. He was about to put another round into the slumped, leering mess when he heard heavy bootsteps pounding, closing in behind him. He spun, levering the rifle, and landed prone. It took him a moment to realize the man approaching, shotgun held before him balanced on a stiff forearm, pointed toward Rollie, was his chum, Pieder Tomsen, the blacksmith.

"Okay?" shouted the man as he dropped to his knees beside Rollie.

Rollie relaxed, nodded. "Yeah. Thanks." He ran grimy fingers in his eyes to clear away the sweat. "But" —he held a hand up—"keep away from him. Some sort of sickness."

Pieder rocked to his backside and eased off the trigger of his trusty single-shot blaster. "I hear the guns, but not sure who is who. Then I get closer and see the fight."

Rollie sat upright beside him.

Pieder gestured with his chin toward the dead man. "You know . . . this?"

"Long time back, yeah. Like the others, out for the money on my head."

"Oh?" said Pieder, trying to suppress a grin but not looking at Rollie. "So . . . how much for that head of yours?"

Rollie smiled. "Sometimes I think it's overpriced."

"So this one, he is not well. Looks . . . ah . . . like a sick cat from the barns."

Rollie nodded. "That's about it. I think he had syphilis or some such. But I'll drag him to that far stump hole and burn him anyway. I don't want to risk the town getting sick just in case he had something that was catching."

"I can help."

Rollie began to protest but Pieder said, "No, no. I am strong. I am never ill. Bullets slow me, yes, but not sickness." He grinned, referring to the shot he'd taken to the shoulder in the scuffle with Danziger. As far as Rollie could tell, Pieder had healed completely and faster than any man he'd ever seen. Must be Sal's ministrations. "How's Sal?" he asked, standing and dusting himself off.

"She is, how you say . . ." he snapped his fingers and smiled. "Wonderful. A very fine cook." He smacked his belly, covered with his scorch-marked leather apron, but which didn't look to be concealing a paunch in the least.

"Glad to hear it. Give her my best."

"Yes." Pieder turned. "I'll bring a rope for this one. Hold there."

Rollie couldn't help smiling at the man's odd mastery of English, which, Rollie had to admit, was better than his poor grasp of Pieder's native tongue of Norwegian.

Or any other lingo. He knew enough Spanish to get him answers, a beer, and a knock on the head, which had happened more than once. He liked to believe if he had to make a go of it in a strange new land, he'd pick up the tongue soon enough, though.

He turned his attention back to the dead varmint at his feet. This was one of the odder attacks he'd ever experienced. The man was clearly sick, likely dying. But he couldn't have walked here in that condition. So he must have had a camp nearby, a horse, something.

He wanted to search the man for a dodger or note or something that might tell him who posted the bounty on his head, but he didn't dare. Every time he looked at the top of the man's head, what part wasn't blasted away by his rifle shot, he grew less interested in touching anything the man had touched.

And thinking that, he'd forgotten that Chin had stabbed him in the boot. He looked down but saw no staining, felt no pooling of blood. It must've gone through the gappy part of the shank. Luck, Rollie. Nothing but. One of these days . . .

Pieder loped back with a coil of rope on his shoulder, a ragged tarpaulin in hand, and instead of his shotgun he toted a glass jar stoppered with a wooden bung, filled with clear water and he held a small bundle of cloth. He unwrapped it and held it out to Rollie. There were two plump muffins as big as a man's fist, dotted with berries and shiny on top with butter and baked sugar. "From Sal. She says we eat before we work."

Rollie's eyebrows rose and his stomach rumbled at the tasty sight. The two men turned their backs on the dead mess. Rollie took a bite of a muffin, then patted his own belly. "I could get used to this." He closed his eyes and savored the tasty baked good. "Oh, that's good."

He chewed a moment, then said, "Sal ought to go into business for herself as a baker. As hungry as these miners are for homebaked fare, she'd earn more than me and you combined."

Pieder's brow wrinkled. "This is a good idea, and I will tell her. But I worry she will not want to bake for me."

"Are you kidding? You'd get first dibs." He finished his muffin, then swigged water and wiped his mouth on his sleeve. "Please tell Sal I said thank you and any time she needs somebody to make certain breads or cakes or pies are safe to eat, she knows where to find me."

With their boots and the rope, they managed to get MacRae dragged onto the canvas. He was surprisingly light, no heavier than a large child it seemed.

Pieder nodded at the dead man. "His guns and knife. You will burn them?"

"Only if you don't want them. Up to you, I don't think he's poxy, more like something that only he had."

Pieder shrugged. "I'll take them, yes. I have only the shotgun. They could be handy."

Rollie nodded and leaned down, impressed with his friend's mastery of the English lingo. It hadn't been that long ago he'd been unable to speak it. Likely Sal's influence. Rollie held his breath and, with a single finger, managed to unbuckle Chin's gunbelt. He grasped the buckle and slid it out from under him. "You give that a scrubbing with the rest, it'll serve you well. Fine quality." He tossed it on the small pile with the rifle, revolver, and knife.

"Thank you. I appreciate it."

"Don't thank me until you don't come down with something."

By then a handful of townies poked their heads into view. "Everything all right up there?" said what sounded like one of the Horkins brothers.

"All set, just taking care of a sickly cur. Nothing to see here." Rollie stood facing them with his hands on his hips. A few of them craned their necks and looked left and right in an effort to see more, but he was confident the dead man was well hidden from their curious gazes.

"Okay, then. We'll leave you to it."

It sounded to Rollie as if they were relieved to not have to deal with anything unsavory. That's why they elected me and Pops to this thankless job, he told himself. He also reminded himself MacRae was here in Boar Gulch because of him.

They propped the dead man forward, then lashed the rope around the tarp and up around Chin's shoulders, then cinched it tight. There was plenty of tarp left to drape up over the man from either side, which they then lashed with another run of rope cut from the longer piece.

Rollie dragged while Pieder walked beside him. Halfway to the distant stump hole where others had burned logging slash and trash, Pieder spelled Rollie.

The going was rough and a glance back now and again showed that Chin's crumpled black hat was still wedged firmly on his head where Rollie had jammed it.

They made it to the stump hole and looked in.

"First we need wood." Pieder strode to a nearby jumble of dried branches and kicked at it to dispel any resident snakes. Hearing none, he dragged branches to the hole. Rollie followed suit, and soon they had a tall, dense bed of dry wood, with layers of log-thick lengths criss-crossed atop, for a slower burn.

Without further ceremony, Pieder grasped the tarp at the man's feet, the boot soles the only things showing. Rollie lengthened the rope, circled the hole, and then dragged the dead man straight in. His hat flipped up in the process, half-wedged in the tarp, and Chin MacRae's ruptured face lay partly exposed, facing upward.

He was now nothing more than a jostled, rumpled skeleton of a man with a blasted-apart head. Rollie figured he should make one slight effort on the man's part. He was set to climb in and place the hat on Chin's face when Pieder grasped his arm.

The blacksmith nodded toward the pile. Rollie looked to see a big timber rattler, girthy and easily six feet long, worming its way upward through the densely packed wood. It paused, flicking its tongue at the canvas, then made its slow, cautious way up onto the body. A dry, dragging sound rose up as it traveled. It halted once more, this time at Chin's face, the quick tongue testing what it found there.

The snake's full length hadn't yet dragged atop the body before it worked its head beneath the canvas and slithered, soundless, into a shadowy gap beside the dead man's raw face. The rest of the snake followed it in. Soon the entire snake had disappeared beneath the tarpaulin. The only sign of it was a rise in the canvas as it passed over and around the body. It seemed to be exploring and caressing MacRae's corpse.

"I've never seen the like," said Rollie, swallowing back his shock in a sneer.

"Yah," said Pieder. "Never."

The two men turned away and walked to the pile of weapons and empty water jug. "I'll finish him off," said Rollie, shaking Pieder's hand. "Once again, thank you for your help. Pops and Wolfbait are gone on the supply run, or I expect I would have had an easier time of it dealing with him." He nodded toward the far-off stump hole.

"Any time."

"And thank Sal for me. Let me know the next time she's baking pie!"

Pieder smiled and nodded, lugging home his new gear.

Rollie walked back down the slope, checking his rifle and revolver, making certain they suffered little more than scratches. He'd have to stitch up the slits in his boot, but thankfully not in his leg.

He wanted to remember to replace Pieder's rope and tarp. He'd buy the man a new one of each at Horkins' Hardware and bring them by tomorrow morning. Maybe something for Sal, too. Good people.

He zig-zagged down past the storage shed and outhouse to the back door of the saloon. The front was still locked, but the back he had left closed but unlocked. He doubted anyone would be fool enough to sneak in and rob them, but most folks knew that's where they kept their bar stock and where Pops and Rollie slept, each having a new bit of privacy as the back was divided into two equal-size rooms with a half-wall on either side of the middle aisle.

He trusted that the folks he'd known the longest weren't up to filching from them. Well, most of them, anyway. But it had been trickier than ever lately to keep up with who'd been arriving in town since strikes in the hills all around had been drawing the hopeful from all over the nation like flies to a gut pile. Along with new gold strikes in the Gulch and surrounding hills, other mine camps had been springing up.

That led his thoughts to the killing of Theo Ward, and Colton's beating. He and Pops had continued to search for another day, but found no sign of further crimes by masked bandits. Still, Rollie guessed more of the same was going to happen. Always did in every mine camp he'd ever read about or ridden through or worked a case in or near. Gold brought out the worst in people.

He looked around the bar, and satisfied all was as it should be, he grabbed a box of matches and locked the back door. Then he retrieved the can of lamp oil from the shed, along with two rags, and made his way back up the hill to MacRae's funeral pyre.

As he walked, he ruminated on the day's events. Whatever Chin MacRae was and whatever stunted thing he'd become, he was not the thing in his dream, the thing that had stalked him. He'd not told Pops the details of the dream, let alone the others. They'd think him softening, and that was not the case. He'd not let it be the case.

What was happening, or was about to happen, Rollie did not know. But for the first time in his life, he was unsettled by an untouchable, unreachable, unseeable evil. And he didn't like it. Whatever that thing had been in his dream, it was still out there, and he felt certain it was coming to Boar Gulch for him.

Chapter Eleven

Wolfbait and Pops didn't roll on back into town until after dark. It wasn't unusual, given that daylight hours were beginning to pinch out this time of year, but that didn't mean they weren't dragging as they clomped up the steps. The bar was brimming and as folks recognized the two men, cheers and shouts of "Pops! Wolfie!" rippled through the smokey room.

Pops gave Rollie a weary smile and leaned his Greener beneath the bar. "Wagon's out front, packed up above the sideboards. Thought we were going to spill a few times—that north road's not getting any better with age, unlike myself." He smiled and reached for the beer Nosey drew him.

Nosey drew another for Wolfbait, who looked like he'd been dragged through a knothole and smacked against a table leg for good measure. The old man drank the beer down without pause, his Adam's apple working like a pump handle. Nosey took the proffered empty glass and refilled it. When it was set before him, Wolfbait elbowed a dozey miner in the stool next to where he stood. When the man saw who it was, he slid off the stool and Wolfbait took over.

He sipped again, then smacked his lips and said to Rollie, "How was your day, young fella?" Wolfbait looked as refreshed as an old, grizzled rock hound had a right to be.

"It began quiet and ended with a nice bonfire."

"Hmm," said Pops. "Something tells me there's a whole lot that happened between quiet and fire."

"Tell you later," said Rollie. He tossed a towel to his partner. "You help Nosey. I'll drive the team around and get started unloading."

"We're settled in here for now," said Nosey to Pops. "If you don't mind, I'll help Rollie." He walked out from behind the bar. "Besides, if you get busy, you can always get Wolfbait to help you."

"Ha!" said Pops. "The day we let him behind the bar is the last day we see a profit."

"I resent that cutting remark. I'll have you know I once went quite a long time without benefit of liquor-tinged libation. Was the worst day of my life."

By the time the stock was unloaded and a path made in the back room, path enough so that each man could thread himself to and from his bunk without scaling crates of booze, the bar had attracted even more of its nightly attention.

Rollie eyed the crowd and saw a number of faces he did not know. There were lots of them nowadays. One face he did know was that of Mayor Chauncey Wheeler. His scarlet cheeks and forehead looked as if it had been slapped a dozen times. He'd no doubt been drinking before he wandered in.

He'd made it known some time back that he preferred to do his drinking at the Lucky Strike at the south end of town. Fine with Rollie. He could only take so much blather from the little blowhard.

But tonight here he was, likely barred for the night from the other establishment. Not the first time. He could be a belligerent drunk.

At present he was holding court in the midst of a cluster of glassy-eyed men, all his new best friends, nodding knowingly at each slurred phrase he offered. "I should have laid claim to the entire valley when I had the chance. Should have . . ." He nodded his head in sorrow at the memory, then raised it again with a fresh thought. "Could have, too, if my old partner, Pete Winklestaff, hadn't held me back!"

The name was not unfamiliar to Rollie, as he'd heard it from Wolfbait some time before. Winklestaff had died under what Wolfbait would only refer to as "odd circumstances." This did not surprise Rollie.

"That's not how I heard it," said a high-pitch voice. "I heard tell he was all for it, but you tried to kill him for his share." All eyes turned on the stranger who'd spoken, who smiled and sipped the last of his drink. He was thin and dressed well enough, definitely not a miner. He wore a fine gray wool vest with a gold watch chain looped out of its pocket. The vest rode over a white shirt and black trousers. A worn but decent fawn hat, tugged low over his brow, topped his head. His moustaches were trimmed pencil-thin, and the rest of his face was clean shaven. He wore no gun.

"Do I know you, good sir?" Chauncey pushed his way through his gaggle of admirers.

The stranger shook his head. "No. No, I don't think so. And I don't know you."

"Then what are you telling lies for?" The words had barely come out of his mouth before Chauncey swung a sloppy right fist upward toward the taller stranger. The man seemed to be sober, because he dodged to his right and swung a curving right of his own that drove hard into Chauncey's left cheek and sent the chunky man flailing backward to land in a heap on his back on the floor.

Rollie was in their midst while the mayor still crabbed on the floor, dazed and grunting. Rollie smacked a length of stout oak, rapping it into a palm. He pointed it at the stranger. "You . . . out."

The man nodded, held his hands up. "That's fine, but I didn't start it."

"Actually, you did, by calling him a killer."

"Oh, I see how it is. You take his side because he's a big deal in town, huh?"

"Sure, whatever you think. Now go."

"I'm leaving, I'm leaving." He turned and walked to the door. Two men from the other side of the room, both strangers who'd been quietly playing cards, got up and followed him out.

"Okay, mayor." Rollie helped him to his feet and steered him to the bar. "Nosey, pour a cup of coffee into him, then I'll walk him home."

"No, I'm not done here. I got a lot of drinking left to do!"

"You're welcome to do that, mayor, but not tonight."

Chauncey leaned against the bar, belched, and shrugged.

Rollie asked a few locals if they knew who the three strangers were, but none did. By then, Nosey had done all he could to get coffee into Wheeler, which resulted in more on the bar than anywhere else. Rollie walked the man home and made certain he was good and passed out in his own bed, behind locked doors.

The next morning, as Rollie and Pops were sitting at a table drinking coffee and eating bacon, eggs, and fried bread, someone knocked on the bar door.

Pops got up, wiping his mouth. "A little early, even for Wolfbait." He opened the door and leaning in the doorway was Chauncey, or rather a sagged, rumpled, white-faced version of himself.

"Mayor, great to see you this fine morning." Pops clapped him on the shoulder, plenty hard, thought Rollie, trying not to smile.

"Come on in. We're in the middle of breakfast, but I could fry up more eggs. I like mine runny, you like yours that way? How about some gristly bacon? Again, I like mine so it's still squealing. Oh, and coffee. We have hot coffee."

"Coffee, that's all, thank you." The mayor walked as if he had lived a thousand years, scuffing his way toward their table.

"What brings you here this early, mayor?" said Rollie, sipping his hot coffee.

It took the chubby man a few moments to reply. He cracked an eye and looked at Rollie, who noticed up close the man carried the tang of vomit. "That stranger, last night. There was a stranger, right?"

"Lots of them these days, yeah."

"No, see, I mean the one who said something about me, something I took exception to. Do you remember that?"

"Better than you do, I bet. Yeah." Rollie nodded. "Something about how you killed your former partner."

"Oh." Chauncey held a trembling hand to his face. Then he looked at Rollie. "Do you men know who he was? Where I can find him?"

They both shook their heads. "No, why, Chauncey?"

"Oh," he stood wincing at the sound the chair made as it scraped backward. "No, no. I was wondering if he would be interested in buying a lot, as I still have a few left to sell."

"At this rate you won't have much land left over, will you, mayor?"

"I just need to make some quick cash right now. Say, that Gladwell woman, she isn't still in the market, is she?"

Rollie shook his head. "No, after you insulted her, I think she took her business elsewhere."

"Oh. Well, I have to go." And the mayor tottered toward the door.

"Maybe you should take a day off, Chauncey. Rest up."

"Can't," he said without turning. "Have to make money." He closed the door softly behind himself.

"Man surely is hurting some this morning."

"We've all been there," said Rollie, sopping up the last of his egg with a hunk of bread.

"That's a fact. Never again, though," said Pops.

Rollie looked up and they both laughed.

"He has been acting odd lately, correct?" said Rollie.

"You mean odder than his usual odd self? Yeah, I guess," said Pops.

"And he's more prone to flying off the handle, losing

his temper with everybody. It's always about money, too. He's overspent on that foolish hotel, and he's always looking for ways to make quick cash. Like with Madge Gladwell and the ladies."

"Yep, he's hard-up, no doubt about it."

"Then what do hard-up people do when they get their backs to the wall?"

"They break the law to get what they want."

"And who's broken the law around here lately?"

"You mean besides the man you lit on fire?"

Rollie rolled his eyes. "He was dead before I torched him."

"A technicality that I don't think would have slowed you down much."

"I'm talking about whoever has been robbing the miners."

"The masked men who killed Theo?"

"Yep."

"You don't think Chauncey's in on that, do you?"

Rollie shrugged. "He's desperate enough. And he has an axe to grind with all these folks getting rich off land he used to own."

Pops poured more coffee. "I'll need more convincing than that."

"It's all I have at the moment, but I'm not ruling him out. He's a greasy little man, and I want to head off whatever it is and whoever it is doing it before they hit Boar Gulch in a big way. I have a feeling it's not going to be long in coming."

"I hope you're wrong, but I bet you're not. How you want to start?"

"More of the same. We keep riding out and try to pick up signs. They're bound to slip up one of these days. Maybe we should talk with Colton again, too. He might have remembered something new by now."

"You think so?"

"Not really, no. But we have to start somewhere."

Chapter Twelve

"Welcome to the Gulch," said a man leaning against a long-handle spade. It was difficult to tell if he was holding up the shovel or if the shovel was doing the job for him. His face was begrimed. His hat, a time-gnawed affair with more hole than felt, sat tipped back atop his head, and wispy gray hair poked out from beneath, dancing in an unseen breeze.

The most striking feature on the thin man's face was the bulbous, purple-red nose in the midst of it, flanked by veined, ruddy cheeks. "What you all doing here, anyway?"

The leaning man took in the assemblage before him: A large, handsome, dark-haired man sitting atop the wagon seat, a rabbity-looking young man beside him, and three riders bringing up the rear.

"Yes sir, now I guess I seen it all. If you was alone, I'd say you were a tincture seller, what with that wagon and all. But now you other men, you all look like criminals, maybe on the run? Riding the owlhoot trail? What is it, huh?"

To a man, Valucci's compatriots were visibly riled by

the strange man's accusations, but only Giacomo smiled. "You are a refreshing sort of fellow, aren't you?"

The leaning man straightened, found that he needed the shovel, and resumed his slouched lean. "I will take your word for that, mister. Since I don't think it's right a man makes such a determination about himself. What I meant to say was we don't get many folks who happen on by here in Bear Gulch."

Valucci nodded, still smiling. The young man beside him said something in a low voice. "Excuse me, sir, but . . ."

"Yes, James, what is it?"

"That man," he nodded toward the staring inhabitant of the place, who seemed to be having trouble keeping his eyes open and standing upright. "I believe he just called this place 'Bear Gulch.'"

"Bear? No, no, you must be mistaken. We have at long last made it to Boar Gulch, am I not right, sir?"

The red-nosed man's eyes snapped open. "Huh?"

"I said, this is Boar Gulch, is it not?"

"Well now," the man ran a shaking, knobby-knuckled hand over his bristled face. "You do talk peculiar, but not so much that I can't tell the difference between the words 'boar' and 'bear.' Them being two different critters and all. Though if you were to mix them up together, sort of let them tangle beneath the sheets, if you see what I mean, why, I suspect you'd have yourself quite a beast after a few months. Something nobody had ever seen!"

The smile slid from Valucci's face. "I asked you a simple question, sir. Is this or is this not Boar Gulch, Idaho Territory?"

The man patted the air before him with his free hand.

"Now don't get your underthings knotted up, big fella. I'm working to it. As to this being Boar Gulch? Naw, naw, man. You've been led astray. I heard tell one time a few months back that this forsaken rat hole had a kin town some miles east of here in Idaho, but right now you are in Oregon."

He nodded and gnawed the inside of his bottom lip. "Close by, but not close enough. This here's Bear Gulch. On account of the fact that when I got here there wasn't nothing but bears. And then me. Pretty soon there was just me. I killed them off. A whole pack of them. Traveled in a pack they did, like wolves or moose or somethin'. Vicious things, too. I still have the hide off one of them, the last one. The rest I ate. Not the hide, though. I been desperate poor since I got here, but never so bad off I had to dine on bear hide. Nor hair, come to think on it."

He rubbed his face again. "You fellas wouldn't happen to have some libation of the gods with you, now would you? Being the only resident of a place is powerful thirsty work. I don't know how I stand it. Honestly, I don't." He shook his head at the terrible thought.

But his words fell on deaf ears, because Valucci had turned on his wagon seat and looked to his left. "Bean."

"Yeah, boss," said the man, who clearly knew he was about to receive wrath from their mercurial employer.

"Please verify for me that this pathetic wretch of a man is babbling incoherence and is indeed incorrect. I must be assured beyond doubt that we are in Boar Gulch and not a place called Bear Gulch."

"Uh, okay, boss." Bean rummaged in his saddlebag and tugged out a poorly folded wad of paper. He unfolded half of it, then traced a grubby finger along a flat section, then looked up at Valucci, then back to the map.

Valucci sighed and held out a hand. "Give the map to me, idiot."

The leaning man cleared his throat and said, "Thirsty work it is . . ."

"Shut up," barked Valucci without looking up from the map. "According to this crudely drawn mess—is this what you've been using to navigate by?" His gaze, two piercing chip-black eyes, made the navigator turn away.

"According to this childish rendering, we are somewhere north of where we began, thank God, but not northeastward enough to have made it to Idaho." He collapsed the paper into a ball in his hands and said, "Now tell me the truth, Bean. You were hired on as the principal navigator of this expedition, were you not?"

The man stared at his boss, eyes wide. He didn't say anything.

"Hmm?"

"Yes, yes sir. But—"

"And as principal navigator, was it not your duty to . . . oh hmm, navigate us to the place we are supposed to be going? Hmm?"

"Yes sir, but—"

"Stop interrupting me. Do you know what this means? It means . . ." He hopped down from the wagon seat and in a fluid motion snaked an arm around Bean's neck. The man had no time to flinch. He had barely raised his arms before he was encircled and enfolded by the big man's arms and torso.

Valucci's face tightened, and he growled a quick sound

as he squeezed Bean's neck in the crook of his left arm. "Now," said Valucci as he jerked and jerked, increasing the pressure with each tightening of his big arms. "If ever there was an error that was truly unforgiveable, it is this, you dull-witted oaf!"

He rotated on the spot, paying no heed to Bean's flailing arms, scuffing gravel beneath his big, dusty, black brogans, and swiveled to look at the other men in his employ. "I can forgive much, you see, including boastfulness. And while Bean boasted of his prowess in guiding people into these filthy hinterlands, never did he intimate he was not up to the task. Which means he lied to me." His arms squeezed tighter.

Bean's face bloomed from red to purple.

From behind, a scuffling sound turned Valucci around. The leaning drunk had hefted his shovel and stood surprisingly upright, weaving but the slightest. "See here, man. That ain't no way to do for a fella!" He raised the shovel up over his shoulder as if it were a spear.

Valucci's eyes widened and he released his hold on Bean. The man dropped to the dirt like a sack of wet corn meal.

His purple face stared outward from beneath a flopped arm, his eyes bugged and popped as if something were pushing them out from within. He didn't appear to his fellows to be breathing. None of them dared hop down off his horse to check on him. That might rile Valucci further.

In truth, though none of them liked him, they also couldn't be certain he wouldn't somehow be able to track them down and kill them, one by one. He was that menacing. Talk amongst themselves was that he wasn't quite all man. More like a demon man.

No person, Shaver had reasoned earlier in low whispers, could be that wealthy, that handsome, and that big and still be a real man. Had to have some assistance from something unholy and freakish. Wasn't natural.

Thankfully for them, the boss man's fired-up attentions were now turned to the wispy local with the shovel.

"You dare interrupt me when I am reprimanding my men?"

"Yeah, I guess I do. Now you just simmer down, you big nut. You're in my town now. I know it ain't much, but by golly, it's mine and mine alone. Got me a few other folks who pass through now and again on their ways elsewhere, but this here's Bear Gulch and that means I'm the boss of it. And as boss of Bear Gulch, I order you, no, no, I command you to get back up on your wagon and git gone! And take that plum-faced fella with you. I see he's breathing again, no thanks to you."

He waved the shovel like an awkward baton and jerked his head in time with his words, as if to punctuate the air with strident meaning.

To Valucci's men, it appeared to work, because Valucci's big ham fists eased out of their balled shape, and his shoulders relaxed. He canted his head to one side and said, "Yes, yes, I see you are a man of infinite wisdom, a man with patience where others have only hotness and anger. That is why you are the very heart and soul of this" —his arms raised and his fingers gestured outward— "your very own kingdom. Whereas I"—he hung his head—"I am but a lowly thespian, weary from a life on the boards and on the roads."

If they didn't know better, his men might guess he was a dejected specimen with little left to live for. Apparently, that's what the lone denizen of Bear Gulch thought, because he stepped forward and resting the shovel on his shoulder once more, he reached out to pat the big man's shoulder.

"There now, fella," he said.

His hand got as far as six inches from Valucci's upper right arm. Valucci's left hand whipped upward and his massive fingers clamped on the bony drunk's wrist. He squeezed. The old man's eyes widened and a thin rush of air wheezed from his mouth.

Valucci's smile broadened. The man's mouth sagged open. He dropped his shovel. He dropped to his knees. Valucci still didn't let go. In fact, he tightened his grip. Snapping, popping sounds greeted his ears and those of the old man, who also received the distinct sensations of having his bones cracked by a madman he'd never seen or heard of but ten minutes before.

Valucci raised him up to his feet. The old man was groaning and drooling now, breath coming in quick gasps. His gray face blanched, and finally he made a sound the rest of the assemblage could hear. "Gaaah . . ." he said.

"Yes, yes," said Valucci, his brow knitted, his head nodding in commiseration. "I quite agree. The only course of action, then, is to do . . . this." He gritted his big, perfect white teeth and jerked the old man's wrist behind his back.

With his other hand, Valucci grabbed what sagging, pale meat remained of the old man's small, pooched gut and twisted. Behind the old man's back, he worked the broken arm. He ground and ground, and the old man groaned and groaned, and soon he sagged forward over Valucci's hand like a soiled dish towel.

Blood drooled from his mouth dangerously close to Valucci's shoes. He stepped backward and let go of the man. The big man smacked his hands together and smoothed his lapels. "There now." He looked over at Bean, who by then had righted himself and sat upright, one hand rubbing his neck. His face was back to a sunburnt crimson, but his eyes were still rather bugged.

"Someone help our navigator back onto his horse. A navigator who owes his measly life to that old soak of a rat." He mounted the wheel and righted himself on the wagon seat once more. "As we turn ourselves and make for a route east, I hope you all will reflect on this most valuable lesson we have learned here today."

They waited for him to explain just what that lesson was, other than to not rile the boss. But no answer came. Instead, Valucci turned the team, and his smiling face, eastward and began humming a jaunty tune.

Chapter Thirteen

"If our destination is Boar Gulch up in Idaho Territory, why are we dragging all this junk up a mountainside in Oregon?" muttered Shaver some hours after the Bear Gulch incident. The bedraggled troupe was busy setting up camp for the night.

Valucci, who they called "the big boss man," sighed and closed his eyes. "Is it that I am paying you too little?"

"Well, no, but . . ."

"Is it that you are being asked to do too much?"

"Well, no . . ."

Valucci opened his eyes and stared at Shaver. "Then why are you concerning yourself with questions only I deserve to know the answers to?"

"Now, see, right there, that's what I'm talking about. If I had known we was going to be asked to act out farces and whatnot on stages in front of other men, why I guess I would have said no to your offer. But you said we was going on an expedition, and that you needed seasoned guides."

Shaver looked around at his fellows, one of whom was still bug-eyed and groaning softly, and the other was shaking his head in silent warning. But Shaver's back was up, and he was committed to bulling forth with his grievance. "Well, me and my pards, we are guides, trail scouts, we've worked on wagon trains, on ranches, for the army, gone down into Mexico and back up again. We been all over this big country and never once have we been told we had to act."

"Hmm," said Valucci, stroking his chin. "Fortunately for you, we have traveled past the point where you are allowed to leave my employ. Now, my good sir, you will complain no more and will instead shut your foul mouth and do as I tell you. Is that understood?"

"Or what, you puffed-up dandy?" Shaver stood tall, scratched a half-circle in the dirt at his feet, and held his hands at his waist, his fingertips dancing as if they were insect legs.

Once more, Valucci sighed. "I had no idea you were serious. Allow me to apologize to you. Sometimes"—he waved a hand near his head— "I get confused, you see?"

His accent, whichever one he was trying out that day, became more pronounced than it had been moments before. The other men noticed, but didn't say anything. They'd all witnessed Valucci's odd fits of anger enough that they knew to keep their mouths shut and their eyes looking anywhere but at the boss man's face.

It didn't much matter, because they realized there was no easy way they could get away from who they had begun to regard as a madman. They knew after his fits that he'd go sort of kind and soft on them, splash out with the whiskey, and apologize for being so odd.

It was one hell of a trip, that was for certain. Shaver would have a whole lot to tell the boys back at Clancy's

Bar when it was over with. And with the way the man paid, he'd be able to spend next winter doing little more than bedding Tillie upstairs at Clancy's, drinking and playing Faro downstairs, also at Clancy's, then moseying down the street to Miss Dot's restaurant for a good meal of an evening.

Thoughts of all that goodness waiting him back in Soldano were enough to force him to ease off from drawing his irons. "Apology accepted," he said, half-turning to wink at the other fellows.

He turned his head back, and the big fellow was about six feet closer, his head leaned to one side, a weird smile on his face, and lordy if it didn't look like the man wanted to hug him. Shaver tensed again.

"I hope my little outburst did not dissuade you from continuing in my employ. I realize I have been driving you men too hard. Yes, that is it." All the while he spoke, Valucci walked closer to him, arms outstretched. "Come, let us make up. I think this calls for a drink of whiskey, don't you all agree?"

Shaver nodded, a smile beginning on his face. "Now that sounds right neighborly of you, Valucci." That was the last word Shaver had time for, because his large, handsome employer had come within striking distance.

Valucci whipped a quick, tight-muscled backhand straight at Shaver's face. Everybody around the campfire heard the leather-gloved blow produce a sharp sound as Shaver's jaw bone not only dislocated from its accustomed hinge, but broke, separating in a place nature did not intend.

He staggered forward, facing the big man once more. The moment before the pain flowered up over his head and down through his entire body, Shaver saw the big man's face bend low, close to his, staring at him. The black eyebrows arched like the wings of a raven, the eyes themselves ebony, and glinting wet, like diamonds from hell.

"I will not tolerate impertinence."

Shaver managed a thin squeak of a moan that pushed out of his broken face as a bloody bubble. It burst as the big man's black-gloved fist arced up and Shaver's head whipped backward. Another sound, distinct as the snapping of a fresh carrot, reached all ears. The man's breath gushed out in a last rush, and he flopped forward, unmoving at Valucci's feet.

Once more silence reigned among the small gathering. Valucci straightened, faced the others, and smiled. "Now," he eyed the men. "If you will indulge me, I would like to toast to you all." His words were buoyant, shy of giddy, but his black eyes belied the man's real intent.

There was no mistaking the threat they carried. The men shifted from foot to foot, eyes flicking between the freshly dead comrade and the menace of the man they worked for, looming before them, suddenly seeming much larger than he did moments before.

Valucci sensed they felt they were on the cusp of revolt, of screaming, of drawing down on him, of collapsing into violent chaos. But he knew they would not raise a hand to him. He had them in his grip, yet only for the time being. He was no fool. He was rich, and he was likely crazy—this much he knew about himself. But he was no fool. Craziness dulled by money and whiskey will only be tolerated for so long.

How long would this sway he had over them last? *Long enough to get him to Boar Gulch,* he thought. *That's all I need*. But for now, he knew that to a man they were like all the others. They could be bought, shut up, paid for, first with threats, then whiskey, then money. That last would make all the difference.

"Gentlemen," he said, holding his arms wide. "Do not be alarmed. The man was impertinent. When we entered into this business agreement, between each of you and me, we agreed that for a fee, you would do as I say. But you had to agree that you would do so without question, without reservation."

He drew the corners of his mouth downward. "As you can see, this . . . buffoon" —Valucci nodded toward the man at his feet—"he chose to break with that agreement." He clasped his hands below his lean belly and cocked his head to the side, an indulgent parent looking at a wayward child.

"What do you say we have that drink and discuss the raise in pay you all will be receiving." He watched their faces slowly soften and their eyes glint with greed. They were thinking, "Perhaps we could tolerate one more week with this man." He knew he had them, even as they were also thinking, "Which one of us will be next? Which one of us will end up on the ground, head bashed in, neck snapped by those big, meaty fists?"

He wanted to laugh in their faces. These were not men, they were mice, wide-eyed and running here and there with no purpose. Waiting only for crumbs to be dropped, and they would scavenge for them, yes, even if the crumbs dropped right in front of the big black cat, tail twitching and mouth grinning.

After he'd placated them with a fresh bottle of the finest Kentucky bourbon, which they were passing around, including the boy, Giacomo, as had become his custom in the evenings, settled himself off to the side, at the edge of the firelight's glow. He sipped his drink and regarded them.

It never fails, he thought. I have been down this road before with others, maybe not trail guides, but men who were all the same. Women, too, though he had much more tolerance for them. Even if he had had no true and real dalliances with women since his lovely Ophelia died, a collapsed, wilted flower.

Oh, but he missed her trembling red lips, her nervous eyes, her lovely small ears, her stuttering breaths, even as they stuttered and stopped right in his very arms.

Come to think of it, he thought, she hadn't been so very different from the many other women he'd known. The ones who demanded he pay them for their time, the ones who ended up quivering and shrieking in his ear until he shushed their soft lips with a cupped hand, the only thing between them, their eyes locked on each other, their little noses struggling for breaths until his fingers pressed harder.

Oh, but they struggled beneath him. It was always the best time then, when they gave up the ghost, as he had heard that moment called. It was an old timer in a saloon who had shared that particular phrase with him.

So far, he had been able to avoid trouble with the saloon owners, the madams, the police, all such grubbers, when he went on his tours throughout the West, always under disguise, always alone. He called such trips his rehearsals. He would try out new characterizations, new costumes, new disguises in towns large and small. He was a one-man acting troupe, a tour-de-force like no other, playing to extremely exclusive audiences.

He always enjoyed those sojourns and then would drift back to his hometown of San Francisco, where he preferred to stay for extended stretches of time at the St. Charlebois instead of at his dead father's mansion. He still couldn't bring himself to sell the old pile.

But now he had a reason to bring others with him on this, what held the promise of being his most exquisite foray yet. On his own, he'd not ventured beyond the rail lines and stagecoach lines to get to the towns where he would try out new personas, disguises, and costumes.

Sometimes he would be a gambler, sometimes a professor from the East, sometimes a visiting scientist, sometimes a wayward farmer, sometimes a mute miner from Cornwall, and once he attempted to be a woman, but found the looks he received told him he was regarded as comical rather than convincing.

But this trip required he venture far from beaten roads and trails, far into the Bitterroot Mountains in the wilds of the far north, deep into Idaho Territory. Until now, he'd not had occasion to trek that far north.

Thanks to the newspapers, now he knew where to find the one man who had escaped his grasp and earned his lifelong wrath in the doing, Rollie "Stoneface" Finnegan, that vicious Pinkerton operative who had pursued him for far too long, who had caused him to lose the love of his life, dear Ophelia.

Finnegan had trailed him, dogged him, tried to run him aground for what he'd read the law was calling a "string of murders by a man in disguise." Imbeciles, what did they know? What could they know? Yet he had bested the man at each turn.

He had even sat across from him at a table in a hole-in-the-wall saloon in Nevada and still the fool didn't suspect that his quarry, the one and only Giacomo Valucci, that world-renown chameleon of stage and saloon, was but a fist's swing away. Ha!

Yes, for Ophelia's death in his arms, Giacomo Valucci blamed Stoneface Finnegan. For if Finnegan hadn't been closing in on him, he might well have dallied with that dear girl indefinitely. But the thought that Finnegan was closing the distance between them, might one day soon catch up with him, had driven Giacomo on that cold November night to cling too tight to his dear Ophelia for comfort. It had not worked. Instead, he had squeezed the life from her, as he had with so many before her.

Since that night he'd known only rage. And his rage led him to seek revenge. But he'd waited too long to seek it, wallowing in his anger and grief instead. And then one day he'd heard that the man had died! Stoneface Finnegan dead? The loss Giacomo felt could not be understated, no one would ever understand the depth of his seething hatred. It was a thorn in his very soul.

He had raged for days, and demanded to be left alone in the family mansion. Cook, the last of a long line of family servants, had dared to bring him food and he had fired her, only to rehire her soon after he tasted the toothsome lamb leg she had prepared. After all, it would not do to lose his strength at so vital a time.

He'd indulged in too much drink—a rarity for him. He'd howled his raw frustration, naked in the lashing rain in the overgrown rose gardens, clawing at his own flesh, and screaming at the injustice of being denied his sweet vengeance.

And then, the promise of redemption had been dangled before him. He'd heard tantalizing rumors that Stoneface Finnegan had not died, but had merely holed up, like the wounded vermin he was, healing and licking his wounds. But where? He'd hired men to find out, but they dallied in reporting back to him—Valucci suspected they had put little effort into the task, and he had paid them back dearly for their negligence.

Then he'd read an odd notice in the *San Francisco Courier-Dispatch* announcing that Finnegan had relocated himself to a far north mining camp, no doubt in an effort to evade Giacomo's wrath. It was a tempting, if less-than-credible scrap of information. Yet it was the only one he had had. So he hired the mercenary Cleve Danziger, who came highly recommended and led his own band of ruthless brigands and brutes. And yet even this infamous killer was unable to best Finnegan. And so now the task was up to Valucci, a task he recognized now was fated for him.

But how to get to the man's mountain stronghold, this Boar Gulch? And how to do so in a manner in keeping with his true thespian self? Above all else, and especially at this crucial time, he must honor the spirit of his mother, his guiding star and one true patron.

Giacomo had mulled over this pickle for nearly a week, and then the answer came to him, as if by divine inspiration. Surely Mother had sent the thought to him, like a gift from heaven itself.

He would do what he does best, he would play a role,

as yet to be contrived, and he would bring a modest yet moving stage play to that most-murderous fiend, Finnegan. And what's more, he would force him to participate, and then . . . Oh, but it would not do to dwell on the delicious details too soon.

That had been weeks before. And now he had guides enough—two gruff men plus the annoying youth from the hotel. The boy had proven a fair hand at cooking, but useful for little else save for carrying baggage and driving the wagon. As long as the lot of them got him to the silly little town of Boar Gulch, that was all he needed them for. After that, he didn't much care.

At the edge of the campfire's light, two dozen feet from where his trail companions guffawed and hooted like the fools they were, Giacomo Valucci raised his glass and toasted to the most brilliant man he knew—himself. He would finally have his revenge, his retribution, his reckoning. It would be his finest performance. Oh, lucky, lucky Boar Gulch.

Chapter Fourteen

The saloon owners, Pops and Rollie, took to the trail, riding hard patrolling the draws and ridges surrounding Boar Gulch. They rarely traveled together, wanting instead to cover as much terrain as they were able in their limited time away from the saloon.

Pops knew Rollie wanted little more than to stay out all day, every day, until he solved the murder of Theo and the molestation of Colton. The assault had taken place nearly a week before, but they'd turned up little to go on.

Hoofprints, bootprints, and a couple of broken branches, sure, but there'd been nothing tell-tale or distinctive about any of it. It frustrated Pops, but it downright gnawed at Rollie's innards, if the scowl on his face and the grunts he offered by way of conversation were any indication.

On this particular day Pops was doing his best to keep one eye on this back trail and the other on the well-trammeled track he'd not yet been down that week. It was a snaking route more than halfway between Boar Gulch and Low Cat. The ride was smooth, the wind soughed high up in the pines, accompanied by the occasional piercing stab of a screech from an eagle riding a current in the far blue above, pinned there like a mote in Pops' vision.

He chuckled and tried to stifle a yawn. If he wasn't careful, he was going to doze off and tumble out of the saddle, land on his dumb head, and die then and there. He shook his head and almost spoke to his horse—a sign he was getting saddle-weary—when he heard quick, whooping cries far to his left, down a slope that swept up at the bottom, topped with a thick cluster of trees and huge rocks like spires.

He reined up and listened but didn't hear it again. Once was enough. More than likely it was a miner scratching for his fortune. Or hers. He'd been mildly surprised in the past few months to meet not one but two women who had taken to the solitary mining life.

After meeting the first, he told himself he shouldn't be surprised since women were, in his way of thinking, every bit as formidable as men when it came to work and adventure and . . . well, just about everything. Frequently they could be so vociferous in their pursuits that they were downright frightening. Which brought to mind a woman from his past, a woman who was vociferous in pursuits of a different sort. But that was a thought for another time.

"Come on," muttered Pops, nudging the horse into motion once more, tacking left then right down a switchback slope more suited to growing stunty pines and rocks than to putting up with a man and horse.

Once more he heard a howl of joy followed with a quick yip, down below him from that protected-looking knob. Then he thought maybe he heard more voices, and Pops regretted taking the horse along this route. He hadn't made it but quarter way down, so he dismounted and tugging, coaxed the horse back up the scree-slidey slope.

"Has to be a smarter way to live," he whispered as he lashed the reins to a low jut of branch and slid his Greener out of the sheath. The fingertips of his right hand checked the nickel-plate derringer riding on his hips. Pops also wore a sheath knife hanging off the opposite side of his gunbelt as well as a hideout gun tucked in an armpit holster riding half-concealed beneath his overalls.

He clapped his worn brown bowler on his head, patted his chest pocket and pulled out his corncob pipe and clamped it between his teeth. "Don't you go anywhere," he said to the horse, then retraced their route back down the slope.

He did his best to switchback and avoid causing a landslide, while also concentrating on staying upright. He did not want to kick off a cascade of stones that would tip off whoever was in the woods below to his presence.

He wasn't as bothered with having his boots fill with gravel. He wore lace-up boots more common with loggers and farmers than the slip-on boots preferred by some of the folks of his recent acquaintance, among them Rollie.

What would he find when he got down there? The best he could hope for was a handful of men he knew from town, sitting around a lazy little campfire, brewing up an afternoon pot of coffee. The thought of a steaming hot cup of trail mud brought a smile to his face. And that momentary lack of focus is what got him into trouble.

From behind him he heard a rough voice, as if barbed from shouting too much for too long. "Well, look what we got ourselves here. It's a darkie sneaking around the hills."

Pops ground his teeth together hard. He didn't bother turning around, but he did shift Lil' Miss Mess Maker in his arms so that he could swing around fast, thumb the triggers, and fire all at once. That wouldn't help him if the man already had his gun drawn.

Click-click—the smooth steel sounds told him what he suspected. He'd already been drawn down on from behind.

"Take 'er easy, boy. I got you dead to rights. Don't move a thing."

Pops heard the man pull in a quick breath, then shout, "Hey! Got us an intruder—get on up here!"

Hell, thought Pops. I must have slid and scrambled right by this fool. Except he's not the fool here, I am. Now what?

In answer, he heard voices from below, right where he'd heard them before. Only now they were drawing closer. Then he saw a brown hat pop up through the trees, then a shoulder, then a man's torso. But it was the man's face that pulled Pops' eyebrows upward as if they were tugged by strings.

The three, four, five men who emerged from the trees and rocks were faceless. Or rather they all wore masks, not kerchiefs but gunny sacks with eyeholes cut in them. Two wore ragged mouth holes, none of them looked to be made with care. The hats sat askew, the bags bunched at the throats, sagging like too much skin, so the men's faces looked bizarre, the stuff of bad dreams.

"We gone have to kill him, huh, boss?" said one of the sacks without a mouth.

"Shut yourself," said a high-pitched voice. "And yes, I reckon. But first, we'll have ourselves a little fun."

Chapter Fifteen

Just when Rollie thought he'd seen the whole of the region, he cut a trail downslope, threading through stands of aspen and knobby glades of tall, brittle grasses. Before and below him lay a long, narrow chasm stippled with the near-blackness indicative of dense stands of ponderosa pines that straggle sparser the higher they grow up the steep, graveled slopes.

"Now where in the hell did this valley come from?"

Cap, as usual, did little more to respond than to flick an ear.

"Still not talking to me, huh?" said Rollie, as if trading comments about the weather with someone. He mused on the scene a moment longer. He was certain he'd been this way before, and yet . . . yet eyes told him otherwise. He shrugged and eyed the scape for a logical path downward.

He chose downward because he thought he detected a thread of smoke rising up from the dark crotch of the valley below, muting with the wispy gray of rising mist, though it was past noon.

That could mean miners, and since he was northwest

of the Gulch, whatever waterway was down there likely fed the impressive rushing Boiling River that carved below town. Before he'd arrived in town, a handful of enterprising miners, at Chauncey's insistence, had diverted more of the flowage into town through a rushing feeder stream that now supplied clean water to all. He had to give Wheeler credit where it was due. The man had had a vision when he'd come to this part of the Rockies, even if that vision was some, or all, supplied by his former, and now conveniently dead, partner.

"As well," he said to Cap. "Nobody's perfect, eh?"

The route he chose looked to have been traveled a time or two before, but not heavily. There was no sign of recent use, which told him little until he figured out what lay at the bottom of the valley. He kept to a long traverse, switchbacking until they met with a well-trod trail wide enough for a narrow two-wheel cart at best.

If this was a primary route down to the valley floor, it was not for heavy wagon traffic, so whoever was down there was working light. Sluicing, he suspected. The trees grew close enough at times to rake him and the horse as they wound downward. None of them were too sharp and Cap plowed on through.

The water made itself known to him before Rollie saw it. The trail wound its way around boulders before opening up at the river.

Rollie reined up at the edge of a small cleared area eight or so yards from the edge of the water. It was a fervent, bubbling flow, especially so given the rains they'd had of late. Alongside stood a wet sluice. A shovel leaned against the trough and it, too, was wet. Whoever was working this spot was nearby. He assumed they had heard or, given the noise of the brook, had at least seen him approach.

He slid his Schofield from the holster, thumbed back to half-cock, and rested it atop the saddle horn. From left to right he took in the entire site. Light rising smoke showed him where the fire sat. He glimpsed the edge of a campfire ring before looking on to his right, toward denser growth, man-height, behind a boulder. Movement behind the brush stopped his gaze and he angled the pistol at it. He bet it was a man tending to his business back there over a latrine. The river sounds would have masked Rollie's approach. He would wait.

Throaty metal clicks spoke first, telling him the man had a weapon hidden low, likely a rifle. And here Rollie thought he'd caught the man with his trousers down, hunched over a cat hole.

"What you want, mister?" The voice was not hurried, but not kind, either.

Rollie sighed but did not raise his hands. "I'm from Boar Gulch. Looking for sign of road agents hereabouts."

The man snorted. "You are a long ways off your beaten path if you come out here looking to molest me, fella."

The man's voice scratched at an ancient itch in Rollie's mind. Familiar, something about it reminded him of one of his captures . . . And it was the man himself who, when he stepped out from behind the scrub brush, said, "I know you?"

Rollie kept his head angled downward, but his gaze steady on the man. He was an eyeblink from shooting should the man decide to open the ball.

The man did not do that, but stepped farther out, fully exposed now. He held his rifle chest height. Rollie saw the work-reddened hands wrapping the rifle firmly, the trigger thumbed back to the deadliest position of all.

He eyed the man's features, easy to do as he wore no hat. His dark, short-shorn hair was peppered with gray. He wore a week's worth of beard but full moustaches. The face was wide, as was the nose, which looked to have been mashed a time or three in fights. As to height, the man was average but with a broad, bull chest.

He kept himself neat in appearance, with green twill trousers, mended here and there with squares of blue cloth. They were tucked into the tops of tall, lace-up logger's boots, half-calf in height, oiled, and well cared for. The man's shirt was a button-up, blue chambray, over which rode faded red suspenders.

"You didn't really answer my question."

"I'm the law, such as it is, in Boar Gulch. Miners a ways from here were hit some days ago by masked riders. One killed, the other worked over."

"By hit you mean robbed?" The man sounded more serious, kept the gun raised.

Rollie nodded.

"What's that got to do with me?"

Rollie shifted in his saddle. The man tensed. Rollie held still. "I should think that would be obvious. I'm trying to find the ones who did it. Checking on all the miners hereabouts. And judging from how far off the beaten trail you've squirreled yourself away, you can see my task is cut out for me."

"Pardon me if I don't commence to tearing up."

Rollie couldn't help but grin.

A breeze shifted, and the enticing scent of fresh-bubbled coffee reached Rollie's nostrils. He glanced toward the campfire. "Coffee smells good."

The man sized up Rollie once more, then lowered his rifle to waist height. He nodded. "If you want to, step on down. Water your horse and have some coffee. I only have the one cup."

Rollie nodded. "That's all right. I brought my own. I always travel with a tin cup."

The man nodded as if Rollie had offered sage wisdom.

Something told Rollie the man was not a threat, despite the prickling on his neck and scalp telling him there was something about him, a familiarity from the past.

He slid down off Cap, keeping the horse between them, and his revolver in his hand. With the other he rummaged in his saddlebag for the cup. He found it and peered over the horse. The man was still watching him, but had bent down at the fire, prodding the coals, and glancing up at Rollie every few seconds. He'd lowered the rifle, then when he saw Rollie walk out from behind Cap with his Schofield in the holster, he sat down on a log and laid the rifle across his knees.

As Rollie walked closer, he saw a jagged scar across the top of the man's scalp, shining through the dark hair like a lightning bolt. The past popped back into Rollie's mind with fingersnap speed.

"H.A. Clements."

The man did not seem surprised that Rollie knew him. He nodded. "Yep. And I know you, Agent Finnegan."

"It's just Rollie these days." He sat on a log across the fire from Clements.

"And I go by Harold these days."

"Fair enough, Harold."

Clements poured the coffee. Rollie noticed the man's hands were hard, thick, and tracked with thin white scars, as if he'd been through a few knife fights. Death by a thousand cuts, he'd heard that somewhere. He found he was relieved to see that Clements had made it through his own hardships alive. Maybe not unaffected, but alive.

As if he were listening to Rollie's thoughts, the man said, "I hold you no ill will, just so you know. Some might, but not me."

Rollie sipped. "Good coffee," he said and nodded his thanks for the cup. "I'm glad to hear it. I did my job, that was all. I reckon you've paid your bill in full, so as someone wise once said, 'The past is a dead thing. Leave it be.'"

"You give up the Pinkerton line, then?" said Clements.

"I did. Or rather it gave up on me."

Clements nodded as if that was all the explanation he required, which was good, thought Rollie, because he wasn't about to offer more.

After a few quiet moments, Harold Clements said, "Masked riders, you say?"

Rollie nodded, stuck out his lower lip. "Truth is, I don't have much to go on. If I hadn't seen all the prints at the one man's camp, I'd be disinclined to believe him. But he's not the sort to spin yarns. Not much else to go on as yet. So I'm making the rounds."

"I thought you said you were out of the detecting game."

"I am. Or I was. Bought me a bar in the Gulch. At first

I thought I'd strike it rich doing what you're doing." Rollie waved a hand at the man's set-up. "But I'm too stoved up to dig for gold. It's a younger man's game. Me, I'll mine the miners." He sipped his coffee. "No offense."

"None taken. I don't think I'm all that much younger than you and I'm about done in at the end of each day." He shrugged. "What else am I going to do? Got out of Joliet with a clean shirt and a kick in the backside. I read about the strikes hereabouts and figured it can't be any worse than what I been up to."

Rollie looked the site over. "Living rough? Winters are hard hereabouts."

The man nodded. "My sister staked me. Soon as I can I'm going to pay her back, then lay claim to this little valley. Truth is, now that I'm here, I don't picture myself going anywhere else."

Rollie looked around and nodded. "It's a good spot. Quiet, pretty. Got water, timber, critters. I'll wager the deer like to mosey down for a drink. Yes sir, you could do a whole lot worse."

They sat like that, finishing their coffee, listening to the river rushing to get somewhere, but never quite leaving.

"You have any neighbors I should pay a visit to?"

"Don't think so. But as I say, I keep to myself. Been here about two months now, seen one other fellow. A digger like myself, was looking for much the same thing I have here. He didn't want any neighbors and I didn't encourage him to stay. He kept on plodding upstream. That was a month or more back."

Rollie nodded, rose, heard the inevitable popping of his knees and quelled a groan. "Well" —he shook out his already empty cup, then straightened his back—"I know you said you don't intend to leave here, but Boar Gulch isn't too far. Got a mercantile, a couple of bars, decent eatery, hardware, assay office. Oh, and we have sporting women now, too."

At that, Harold's eyes widened a pinch.

"Yep. Wagonload of the prettiest ladies you're likely to find here or anywhere, I reckon. I'd say we lucked out."

Clements remained seated, his forearms resting on his knees. "I'll think about it."

"Good. Hope to see you. You do make it in, stop by The Last Drop, that's my place. I'll stand you a beer to repay your kindness for the coffee."

Harold Clements set down his cup on a rock and stood. Rollie held out his hand for a shake. Harold looked at it a moment, then at Rollie, and shook hands with him. For the first time since Rollie arrived, he noticed that the man almost smiled.

As he rode on up out of the sweet little river valley, Rollie thought that maybe H.A. Clements, or rather Harold, might be the wisest of them all. He had a spot to himself that most men would kill for, some had, in fact. He almost hoped the man didn't strike a big lode of gold. It would ruin the simple beauty of the place, the soothing balm the spot obviously was for Clements.

Chapter Sixteen

Pops shifted his weight from his uphill leg to his right foot, angled downslope so he could spring forward, maybe dive to the side. But there were men downslope of him, one behind, and maybe more in the bushes and rocks. Don't be hasty, Pops, he told himself, even if every muscle and nerve in his body told him to run somewhere, anywhere. Play it out, maybe it'll end better than you think.

But thinking is exactly what he did as he remembered Theo's shot-up body and Colton Shepley's face, pummeled. They were not good memories of what these men were capable of. And he was as certain as a shovel to the head that these were the road agents Colton had told them of. How many other masked men could there be out here?

At least we know now he told the truth. And at least I found them, he thought. Fat lot of good it's going to do me or anyone else if I end up dead. I'm not too proud to wish to see Rollie ride up and open fire.

The man who'd shut up the other, whiny, tall man in the back, stepped forward. He was of medium height, lean in the middle. His hat was squashed down on his sacked head, forcing the burlap to puff. At his waist he wore a plain black leather double-gun rig, no tassels, no conchos, not even shined and polished leather. The gun butts were darkish wood, maybe walnut.

His clothes were plain, too, though lean and crisp. His boots were black stovepipes, again, not polished and shiny, but oiled and clean. Pops took it all in, knowing details could be useful at any time for anything. He didn't hear any horses fidgeting and whickering off somewhere out of sight, but the men had to have mounts nearby. If they were lazy enough to steal from people, they were lazy enough to not want to walk far to get to their horses.

The leader said nothing as he snatched the shotgun from Pops' fist.

"A Greener? Who'd you steal that off of, darkie?"

Next, he plucked Pops' six gun from his holster and the sheath knife from the other side of the belt. He tossed the shotgun to the rocky earth a couple of feet away. Pops winced as he heard his beloved Lil' Miss Mess Maker clunk and clatter. The revolver and knife he held out and the man nearest him, a burly fellow in a gray slouch hat with a flop brim, grabbed it and jammed it in his belt.

"Arms, higher."

Pops complied.

"Ah, a hideout gun. Good. I would expect no less from the law."

"Law?" said Pops. "You got me wrong. I'm not law."

"Aw, bull, son. I saw you at the saloon, standing there like you own the joint."

"Matter of fact, I do. Some of it, anyway."

"That a fact? How did a darkie come to own such property?"

"Lucky," said Pops.

"I should say." He expelled a tired breath. "Now, you and the other one, that old lawdog or whatever he is, you go everywhere together?" The man looked around, up toward where Pops had come from, searching for sight of Rollie. His voice was high-pitched, not womanly, but not quite mannish. And something about it was familiar, he thought.

Pops shrugged, tried to read the man's eyes, sunk as they were in the folds of that burlap sack. Must be smelly in there.

Burlap on a good day smells like dirt, and on a hot one such as this afternoon had turned out to be, his breath must be backing up in his face something awful, even with that silly little mouth hole. It looks like I'm being set upon by scarecrows, thought Pops.

"Why you boys wearing bags on your heads? You escapees from Mother Pritchard's School for the Homely?"

He didn't see the man come up behind him, but he heard one, two quick, heavy bootsteps. Pops tried to side-step but the man was fast and drove what felt like the butt of a long gun into his kidney on the right side. He grunted and sagged sideways, slamming the gravel hard on a knee.

He tried to rise but the man before him shook his head. Pops didn't want another club to the back, so he held his ground. The man had hit him hard and he found it difficult to pull in a breath.

"I'll not suffer cracks nor speculation," said the boss man. "You got that . . . darkie?"

Pops grunted, rubbing his back and sucking wind. He tried to even out his breathing, but failed.

"I said you got that? A nod will suffice."

Pops nodded, his lips stretched tight over his teeth. "Why not give me a hood, then?" Pops was thinking if he had a hood, he wouldn't know who these men were or where they were taking him. And if that were the case, he'd be less likely to recognize them or find them later. He got his answer right away.

"Nah," said the man. "Where you're going you won't need it. Or this," the man snatched the corncob pipe from Pops' lips and tossed it on the ground, then jammed it hard with his boot heel, crunching and smearing the pipe into unusable bits. "Far too uppity for one such as yourself."

From the back of the little gawking group came a grating voice, "We just going to end up killing him anyways, boss. Why we got to keep these sacks on our faces?"

The man who'd scolded Pops, obviously the boss, turned and sized up the whiner. He walked to him as one might stroll over to greet a neighbor, and quick as a blink, kneed the man in the grapes.

Pops saw burlap puff outward as breath whooshed from the stricken man's mouth.

"Now," said the boss, turning back to face Pops. "You might as well stay down there. Don't worry, we'll not kill you . . . yet. This particular stretch of the roadway is a-bloom with hardworking miners as dumb as the rocks they spend their days gnawing away at. So I don't want any of them scratching a curiosity itch and coming around to nose into my business. We'll see them all soon enough."

He looked past Pops. "Tie his arms behind him and hobble his feet. He'll ride on Myrtle."

Pops thought he heard a smile on the man's voice. Not much of a guess since the mention of "Myrtle" brought a round of guffaws from the men.

"What's Myrtle?" said Pops as the man from behind him jerked him upright by the back of his coveralls with ease.

"Not so much a what as a who. Meanest mule you ever . . . well, you'll see." With that the boss turned and walked right through the other men, who parted to let him pass back into the bushes.

One of the men remained behind, with a big revolver drawn and aimed at Pops. It wasn't cocked and Pops wondered if he had enough time to bolt forward, snatch the gun from the man, and spin on the brute behind him. But the brute never let go of him, and he nearly dangled as the man jerked him left, then right again to lash his hands behind his back.

When he'd been tied, the man behind him said, "Watch him, and pick up that shotgun of his. I'm gonna go get his horse up yonder."

Pops had hoped they'd overlook his horse somehow. In time, Bucky might have gotten loose and made his way back to Boar Gulch. How long did he have before Rollie would suspect him missing?

They had in the past each spent time away from the saloon, but that had been planned and for purposes of rest. That was something in Pops' favor—maybe Rollie would be alarmed and strike out to look for him. But how long that gave him, he had no idea.

He heard the man from behind clucking and coaxing

Bucky down the scree slope. They were almost to him when the man said, "Get moving, darkie."

Pops followed the first man, cut left as the man did, and glanced over his left shoulder. The man leading his horse wasn't far behind, as he could tell from the sound of his horse's hooves stepping and sliding. But he did get a look at the man. He was big, as he'd guessed from the sound of the man's voice. Sloppy-gutted and narrow-shouldered, but north of six feet tall. He wore a flapping, much-mended brown wool coat, flapping because the buttons were nowhere in sight. He also carried a rifle in the crook of his right arm. With the left he tugged the reins of Bucky.

The man's boots were worn leather, tall, and he looked to be stepping with a limp on the right side. Good to know. Tied as he was, Pops couldn't do much about it yet. He only hoped he'd have a chance to put the meager scraps of information he'd gleaned from rubbernecking into play once they got to wherever they were walking.

"Ain't too far now," said the big, slop-gutted man behind him. It sounded to Pops as if he were talking to himself, buoying his own spirits at the thought of having to walk on his gimpy pin.

"You fellas have a claim up in these parts?"

Instead of telling him to shut up, the big man said, "You could say that. Ain't that right, Joe?" This was directed at the man ahead of Pops. Who was quickly outdistancing them.

"Huh?"

"If you slowed down and did your job you'd hear what I was saying."

"Oh, yeah." The man ahead of Pops, Joe, eased his gait and looked back. "What now?"

The big man sighed. "Man asked we got a claim here-abouts, and I said yeah, you could say that." He chuckled again at his own wit.

Joe didn't see the humor. "Well, if you call rousting these rock hounds, separating them from their—"

"Shut it, idiot!" growled the big man.

"Okay, then." Joe glanced over his shoulder past Pops. "Man, you the one who brought it up."

"What's all that noise?" said the boss's voice up ahead behind a lean of boulders. Pops saw no face, but the scant trail they were following cut between great juts of stone tall as two men atop one another and wide enough for a horse, if the horse wasn't rambunctious. Up at the top the gap narrowed to no wider than a man's head.

As they marched into the declivity, daylight lessened. Pops smelled the mustiness of damp soil and felt the wel-come chill pulsing off the rock faces. Above, the line of sky looked like a blue river, as if he were viewing the heavens from beneath the water's surface.

The march wound on for a couple hundred feet. Sound closed in tight. Footsteps echoed and his horse rumbled and nickered. "S'okay, boy. Okay," said Pops to Bucky.

"Shut it."

Pops was tempted to say something about catching more flies with honey than with vinegar, but he suspected the man would think he was calling him a fly or some such. He kept his mouth shut and his ears open.

The well-tramped trail curved around a big belly of gray rock to the right and opened up and widened to reveal a bowl about forty feet across. It bore smooth sides and hollows where gear and lanterns were nested, and in the center smoked a modest camp fire, puffing out the last of near-dead embers. Beside it a large, dented, gray-enamel coffee pot leaned on a slope-topped rock.

Most of the men he'd seen before were visible, leaning against the rock walls that stretched up at least twelve feet. Others, including the boss man, were seated on rounded black and gray lumps of rock arrayed by nature in no design around the floor of the big stone bowl. Despite his situation, Pops couldn't help but feel awed by the natural stony spot and nature's ancient and immense power.

"Coffee?" said the boss man once he'd been shoved forward toward the center by Slop Gut.

"So, the tools you use for freeing up mined goods, nuggets and dust and such, are guns?"

The boss man nodded. "Yeah, and knives."

"Oh," said the idiot from before. "Don't forget axes! We give that fellow a few days back a good workin' over with his own axe. That was somethin'." His gunny-sacked head bobbed at the memory. Pops pictured a smile of fond remembrance on his dumb face.

"Cletus?"

"Yeah?" said the idiot.

"How'd you like an axe to your own neck?"

"Oh . . . uh, no. No."

"Good. "The man turned back to Pops. "Now have a seat and I'll fetch the coffee."

Pops sat on the rock about five feet from the man, facing him. "Obliged," said Pops. "But I can't drink coffee with my hands behind me like this."

"Yep, that does present a problem. Joe? Untie our guest."

"But . . . boss. He seen where we're at, so there's no going back for him." He turned back to Pops. "Am I right, mister . . . ?"

Pops nodded. "I reckon."

"That's right, Joe." The boss man lifted off his hat, then shucked the burlap sack covering his head. Beneath, his somewhat-thin face was red, sweaty, and familiar to Pops. He placed him right away as the man who'd challenged Chauncey that night not long ago in the bar, the night the mayor had been drunker than usual.

"I see by your face that you recognize me," said the man. He was smiling now and smoothing his pencil-thin moustaches.

"Yep, I do," said Pops. "And I expect that means you know me."

"Yep, I do," said the man, mimicking his captive. He looked up at Joe. "Untie the man's hands so he can enjoy his coffee."

"You sure?"

The boss sighed. "How many times have you heard me repeat myself?"

The man shrugged.

"And how many of those times ended poorly for the oaf who questioned me?"

Joe stared at him a moment, then nodded and untied Pops' wrists.

Pops eased his sore arms out in a stretch before himself and rubbed his chafed wrists. "How come you nabbed me?"

"You were somewhere you ought not to have been." The man poured two cups of coffee.

Pops saw the steam rising from the black brew and thought that if the last thing he took in was a cup of coffee, he could do worse.

"Thank you," he said, receiving the cup. He blew across the top and sipped. "Mmm, nothing better than camp coffee." He looked around the rocky bowl. There were eight men that he saw, including the boss and the man who'd led his horse out through another narrow cleft on the far side of where they'd entered.

From the looks of the place, it had been their camp for a while.

"I see you find our spot of interest."

"Good camp you got yourselves here." Pops sipped and looked at the man. "What do you want with me?"

"Ah, cut right to it, eh? Okay then, you work at that bar? The Last Drop?"

Pops nodded, sipped.

"But you're more than that, as you mentioned earlier?"

Pops shrugged. "Every man has more sides to him than you can see in one go, so yeah, I am more than that."

Instead of annoying the thin-skinned boss, Pops saw the man was enjoying himself. "I think you are one of the lawmen in Boar Gulch. Deputy to the man with the fancy curled moustaches, and I'm pretty certain he owns the bar. I doubt your claim of being part owner of the place is true, though." He let that speculation hang in the air. No sound came from the camp, save for a far-off whicker from a horse and the dry creak of a leather holster as one man shifted his stance.

"There a question in there somewhere?"

That nipped at the boss man's ire. His right eye twitched. "Will you be missed in Boar Gulch?"

Pops took his time sipping. He knew he was risking something here, and how he answered might determine a whole lot of things. On the other hand, what harm could the truth bring? He was beginning to guess the man's angle. Truth it was, then. But only enough to inch forward in the conversation. "Got me a stake in the bar."

"A stake? You really do mean you, a darkie, is part owner of the bar? Come on now, you expect me to believe that?" He slapped his knee and looked round. Three or four soft guffaws rose up from the men.

Pops shrugged again. "You asked, I answered."

The man's smile slipped. "Hmm. I think you are telling the truth. Are you also a lawman?"

"Nope," said Pops. "No law in the Gulch."

"No law, eh?"

"Nope. Only justice."

"Aw, same thing."

Again, Pops shrugged. He knew he was going to have to come up with a better response and soon. He just didn't know what it might be. But if his hunch was correct, this man was going to try to lure Rollie out to rescue him, then they'd kill them both and make their thieving easier.

The boss stood and tossed the rest of his grounds hard at the ground at Pops' feet. Here we go, thought Pops. He tensed, tried not to draw attention to the fact he was still untied, but he'd be ready, even if all he could do was snap the man's ankle if he tried to kick him.

Before it came to that, a skinny kid without a mask hustled in from the far side of the bowl, from the direction Pops guessed they hid their horses. Straw-color hair poked out from beneath a flat-crown fawn-color hat with sweat stains and a ragged edge to the brim that looked as if it had been gnawed by rats.

"Boss!" he said, glancing at Pops but not paying him anymore heed than that. "Boss!" he repeated. All eyes were turned on him as he loped across the rocky spot.

"What?"

"Oh, it ain't good, ain't good."

"Let me be the judge of that." The man flashed a narrow-eye look at Pops, then said to the kid. "Tell me in my ear."

The kid did as he was told. Pops looked at his cup and tried to make out what the kid was saying. He'd like to have filled it up again. One thing he was guilty of—or one of many, he thought—was his fondness for coffee. Even poorly made coffee was better in life than having no coffee in hand.

Words from the kid's urgent whisperings made their way to Pops. Turns out the kid was not all that quiet. Pops heard the word "shipment" and "dust" and "armed guards" and then the clincher, the name "Stag Horn," and he put it all together.

Stag Horn was a new mine camp tucked back in the mountains even farther in than the Gulch. The thinking by a handful of newcomers had been that there were already plenty of people milking the grounds around Boar Gulch for gold, and while they were finding it, what harm would it do to venture farther out. So they had, and from the sound of it, some of those souls had found luck. But if this gang had its way, that luck would not hold for long.

The boss man stood. "Gentlemen, tomorrow's job has

been unexpectedly moved up to today. I want everybody saddled and ready to ride in two minutes."

Men pushed away from the walls, stood from rocks, stretched, and checked their guns, their gear, but none seemed in a hurry.

"I said move!"

That did the trick.

"Except for Joe, and you, Ben."

"Me?" said the big man who'd been behind Pops when he'd been found. "Why?"

"Because somebody needs to tend to our prisoner here. I have more I need to know from him before I figure out what to do with him. Now bind him and keep a sharp eye. Right?"

The two men nodded, neither clearly pleased with having to be left behind.

"I said . . . right?"

"Right, boss," said the two men in unison.

"Good. Now tie him up. Wrists and feet. And set him over there." The boss man jerked his chin toward a spot free of gear off against the side wall.

He was the last of the departing men to leave. Before he disappeared down the cleft, he turned and pointed at Pops. "You and me, we're not through yet."

"Looking forward to it." Pops forced a smile.

The boss man almost smiled as he left the stone bowl.

The big man stepped closer. "Hands behind your back again."

"Okay now, I'll make you a deal. I have an old shoulder wound from the war and it just about kills me to have my arms bent back like that."

The man smiled. "Good."

"No, now I mean it. Just tie my hands in the front of me. Won't make no never mind anyhow, I can't go anywhere with my hands and my feet tied."

"Aw, let him, Ben. Ain't no harm and like he says, he can't get nowhere."

The big man sighed. "Okay, but one twitch I don't like and I'm going to tie them back behind again. After I beat the snot from your head." He smiled.

"I'll be sure to not let that happen. Doesn't sound pleasant in the least."

"You darn right, darkie. Keep that in mind lest you get notions of crossing me."

Pops shook his head. "Nope. No notions from me." *Crossing you, no, but getting away from you, yes,* Pops thought. *I have to, because it will likely be my only chance. No better time to try than with only two guards instead of another half-dozen or so, and one of them that touchy boss man.*

Ben tied Pops' hands in front of him. Pops tried to flex somehow, to make his wrists thicker. It didn't do much good. He jerked the ropes hard until Pops felt the pulsing of blood in his fingertips. He said nothing.

Ben grunted as he bent to tie a rope round Pops' ankles. Pops cursed himself for wearing lace-up boots and not wide-shank tug-on boots like Rollie.

He looked up. The other man had gone, maybe to tend the remaining horses? To relieve himself? He didn't see him in the stony encampment, nor did a quick glance up to the ring of stone above show he was guarding the scene from on high.

Good a time as any, thought Pops as he gritted his teeth. Before Ben looped the rope around his second foot,

Pops kicked upward with every effort he could make from his cramped position on the ground. His left boot toe connected hard with the big, soft man's bottom jaw.

Unfortunately for Ben, he had a lifelong habit of sticking the tip of his tongue between his teeth whenever he set to a challenging task, like saddling his horse or playing poker or lashing a prisoner's feet.

Blood spurted and something meaty and pink popped up in the air between them. The big man made a shrieking sound that pinched off as Pops rammed his right boot hard and fast into his left temple. It didn't knock him out cold, but he was addled enough that he flopped to his side and lolled like a sloppy barnyard hog in a wallow.

Pops knew he had mere seconds before the man regained his senses. He also had mere seconds before the other man would come upon this happy little scene and open fire.

He rolled up onto his left side and got a knee under himself, then thrust himself upright. His hands were throbbing something fierce, but he used the pain to keep himself focused.

He kicked hard, ramming his boots into the writhing man again and again, in the throat and head, until the gagging, quivering, bleeding wreck stopped thrashing, then trembling, then the trembles subsided into tremors, and finally he lapsed into either unconsciousness or death. Pops didn't care which.

All told, he figured it took about twenty seconds. Twenty seconds of precious time he did not have an excess of. He had to get his hands untied, but how? Then he spied the fat man's belt knife.

With his fingertips he slicked it free of its sheath and

dropped to his backside once more. He held the knife's handle tight between his boots, blade aimed skyward, and he worked his wrist ropes up and down against it.

The blade was sharp enough but the position was awkward, and the knife kept pushing forward. He scooted ahead and planted his boot soles against a big sitting rock, and clamped the knife once more between his boots. This time the blade stayed put, and he sawed away.

Sweat ran in his eyes, drizzled down his long nose, and droplets dangled, then dripped off its tip. He blew them away with a quick breath, and only then noticed his own rasping breath, keeping time with his sawing efforts against the blade.

"Any second now, Pops, and that man will be back," he whispered to himself. "And then you'll be a dead man."

He felt the strands popping free as he sliced. He heard boots on gravel, looked left toward where they'd all come from, then right toward where they all left. That was where Joe had to be coming back from the latrine or some such. Pops sawed faster. The steps ground louder, closer.

"Come on!" he growled, and it did the trick. He pulled his hands apart, snatched up the knife with his left, and rolled up onto his knees, then to his feet. Already he was moving forward, tucked low, catfooting across the camp toward the rough chasm.

He made it, slamming upright against the rock wall, just as Joe stepped into view. "Hey Ben, you suppose the boss will—"

That was all he had time for because his pard's knife, now clenched in Pops' hand, swung as if driven by a locomotive's piston, straight into his chest. It pierced the left lapel of his brown leather vest, drove through his wool shirt, the undershirt beneath, then straight through flesh, blood, and bone. It cored his lungs and the top right edge of his heart, before being yanked out, hard and fast, for a repeat drive.

His eyes popped wide and a long, thin, mewling sound leaked from between his lips, followed by a trickle of blood that flowed up and out. As he tottered, then took in a second plunge of the knife, the trickle of blood became a torrent, then a quick gout as his innards convulsed at this sudden and final of all shocks.

Then Joe's legs gave out and he dropped forward to one knee, then flopped face-first to the graveled ground.

It took Pops a few heartbeats before he breathed for the first time in long moments. "My word," he said, gasping. He considered using the knife on the big, sloppy man, unsure if his kicking him had killed him or just slowed him down some. A sudden flush of weariness came over him. "To hell with it," he said and tossed the knife on the dead man's back.

He shook his face, walked to the fire and filled his tin cup once more. The coffee was tepid but he didn't care. It was wet. He glugged it down then dumped the rest in the cup and strained that, grounds and all, through tight teeth. While he did this, he regained control of his breathing and kept a sharp ear on any sounds that might indicate someone advancing on him. He had to find his weapons and get on out of there.

Turns out they were right behind the rock the boss man had sat on. He must have laid them there when he came into the camp. Other than a few scratches and dirt, his revolver, his hideout gun, and knife looked fine. He holstered and sheathed up, then snatched Lil' Miss Mess

Maker from her resting spot, checked her, and found she still had her two shells ready to roar.

"Now for Bucky, and then ride hard and fast to the Gulch," he said out loud, more to comfort himself than for any other reason.

Pops slid back to the wall where he'd hidden to lunge at the unfortunate Joe, and peered around the cornice of rock. More rock. He heard nothing, not even horse sounds. He had to get moving, as his back was exposed to the entry path behind him.

With no more dithering or encouragement, Pops slid into the passage hewn so long ago from this mass of rock and hugged the right wall, the Greener cradled in his left arm's crook, his revolver drawn and held up in his right. The passage was darker than the stone bowl they'd been in and narrowed at times a dozen feet above him to little wider than a knife slit letting in a piercing ribbon of blue sky. He heard nothing save for his own stepping feet, pausing every few yards to listen. Nothing.

Pops sniffed as he advanced, but smelled no cigarette smoke, no pipes, no musky sweat of unwashed road agents, but there was a smell, faint but becoming stronger. From ahead. Yes, and he knew that smell—horses.

The passage widened and lightened and Pops once more was willing to believe it was still daylight. One more turn and the rock wall he'd been hugging ended. So did the rest of the mass of rock. The passage stopped, and revealed a plateau of ponderosa pines clustered close, but gappy enough that they were used as an open-air barn. Smaller trees had been hacked down and lashed horizontally to the bigger trees as rails, both for hitching and as a makeshift corral.

And right before him were two horses and one mule, two of the beasts were unsaddled and unfamiliar. He figured the mule to be the infamous Myrtle. From the boss man's earlier crack about him going to ride her, he guessed it was likely for a lynching.

The third beast was familiar, and still saddled, jerking his head up and down like someone working a pump handle. That was his Bucky.

"Easy, boy. Easy, Buck. Pops is here."

He eyeballed the scene, saw a paltry mound of musty-looking hay, no doubt pilfered from someone, and leaned against the rock mass that stretched out to both sides. Not seeing anything he didn't want to see, namely two-legged vermin, he ran for the horse, loosened the reins from the rail, and thanked his luck that Ben, the big softy, had been too lazy to unsaddle his mount. "How thoughtful," mumbled Pops as he mounted up.

He slid the Greener into her sheath and looked about. He didn't want to make his way back through the stony garrison to find his old path home, but neither did there seem to be much of a trail from this corral. But the outlaws had to have left from here on their mounts.

He nudged Bucky forward, leaning out to either side, and finally caught sight of hoofprints angling through the trees toward the southwest. Had to be their trail out of there.

He had little choice, so he clucked Bucky toward the brush-shrouded trail. Then he heard a weak, wheezy shout from behind him. He raised the revolver as he spun the horse, and saw Ben, the big slop-gutted man he'd all-but-kicked to death standing at the end of the stone passage.

The man no longer wore a sack on his head. He was

nearly bald but had a fringe of dark hair and a sparse beard. He held one hand to his neck and held a long-barrel revolver in the other.

Pops noticed the gun shook slightly, but that didn't matter. One lucky shot, even from a palsied hand, and he'd be done. Taking in the distance between them, about twenty yards, Pops peeled back the hammer and sent a quick shot at the man. It was too far to the right and spanged off the rock.

The close bullet didn't flinch the man, and he let loose with a shot of his own. Pops hunched low, but even then, the shot caught him. Or at least he thought it did. Something, not blood nor bone—then what?—shattered and bloomed upward, stinging his left arm and face.

He felt it hard and so did the horse. They both jerked to the right, the horse prancing. Pops considered sliding off the beast, but he didn't want to risk losing the horse now that he was on his way out of here.

He'd worry about his or his horse's wound later. Right now, he had to kill this devil. Should have done it before, he thought. He gritted his teeth and held the reins tight in his right hand, then cranked off two more shots at the man, trying to compensate for the thrashing horse.

One of the shots did the trick, slamming the fat man against the rock. He wobbled back and forth against the gray, cold mass as if he were being jerked to and fro by unseen hands.

The man's right hand jerked upward, and the long-barrel pistol whipped from his grasp and spun in the air before landing some feet away. Then the big man stared at Pops with wide eyes, gasping from his beached-fish mouth, still grasping his collapsed throat.

He slid down the wall, the weight of his large body collapsing his knees. He sat propped against the rock, looking like he was dead, but still staring at Pops, still wearing that surprised look. Not fearful or angry, just surprised.

"Serve you right, you devil," muttered Pops as he sawed the reins and worked to get his horse under control. He managed to stave off a fresh fit of crow-hopping and got the beast directed toward the trail he'd been heading out on before he looked down to his left, afraid of what he'd see there. A bullet wound in the horse's shoulder? A gaping hole in his own leg? He'd felt no pain.

No, none of that. Instead, he saw the freshly blasted stock of Lil' Miss Mess Maker, chewed and hacked. Somehow the man's bullet must have hit a line of the wood's grain and forced the entire rear stock to blast apart.

He gave full vent to a groan. He wanted to shout but was afraid the already-flummoxed horse would slide back into its stomping state. Pops tucked low and jammed Bucky hard in the belly with his heels. The last thing he needed was those road agents to hear shots and come pounding back to their camp. He had no idea how far they'd ridden to waylay the transport wagon from the good miners of Stag Horn.

He departed from the well-hammered trail when it veered westward, toward Stag Horn. The Gulch was east-southeast from where he was, and he guessed about two-hours of hard riding would get him there—right where he wanted to be. He guided the horse switchback style upslope, picking a path between clots of gray boulders and jumbles of fallen trees.

Pops' head was on a constant swivel, keeping an eye

behind for sign of masked men thundering hard on his trail. "Let's go, Buck! Check you over at home for any grievous wounds. I hope you don't have any to match those poor Lil' Miss Mess Maker earned for herself on this fine day."

Pops mashed his hat down tight on his head, set his teeth, and rode toward home. It would be long miles, however, before he stopped snagging glances at his back-trail.

Chapter Seventeen

Rollie rode in near dark, trail dusted and hot and tired of the day. And he still had to serve booze to hot, dusty, tired miners all night long. He slid from the saddle and stood by Cap a moment, his arms draped across the saddle.

He'd spent hours, the best meat of the day, riding up one tree-riddled slope and glen after another, half of which he'd had no idea existed. And all for naught. Oh, he'd seen plenty of pretty scenery, but that didn't get him any closer to figuring out who was robbing the hard-working miners and where the thieves were holed up.

He didn't see Pops' gray in the corral and figured he was still out sniffing up clues, too. "Hope he's had more luck than we have," said Rollie to Cap, stripping off the saddle.

He finished tending the horse and stripped to the waist, then scrubbed down before the dented white wash basin out back. He dried off inside and pulled on a fresh shirt. After he slicked back his salt-and-pepper hair and smoothed in fresh wax on his moustaches, he made his way into the bar through the living quarters at the back.

The Last Drop was half-filled with men and one woman from Mrs. Gladwell's enterprise. Rollie offered her a smile and a nod. She was a pretty young thing, red hair and a modest dress. It looked as if she was in a non-professional conversation with Nosey Parker, who was, surprisingly enough, pouring a drink and holding a conversation with her.

Rollie never figured the young man had the ability to juggle more than one task at a time. He chastised himself for thinking hard thoughts about Nosey, but admitted the man had earned it. Nosey was plenty smart but annoyingly odd at times, lost in books and in his own head or scribbling yarns in his notebooks when Rollie expected him to be paying attention to what he'd been saying.

He assumed a spot behind the bar and with barely a nod, Nosey leaned on the bar and continued his conversation with the comely young redheaded woman.

It was more than an hour later, after she'd left and Nosey returned from the back stockroom with a couple of bottles of rye that he said, "Pops is back there, sitting on his bunk, staring at the ceiling."

Rollie looked at him as if he'd just said he was a cannibal looking for a snack.

"I'm not kidding you," said Nosey, looking mildly annoyed.

Just then Wolfbait walked in and stood by his usual stool, which happened to be occupied by a newcomer to the Gulch. The old rock hound stood unnervingly close to the man on the stool but never looked at him.

Finally, the newcomer slid off the far side of the stool and carried his beer to a front corner of the room where hopefully strange, bearded old men wouldn't stand so close. Wolfbait assumed his seat and waited for Nosey to slide a beer to him.

Rollie walked around the bar and into the back room.

"You all right?" said Rollie, leaning close to Pops, looking him up and down.

"I've had quieter days." Pops smiled and rubbed his face. That's when Rollie saw the raw marks on his wrist. He grabbed Pops' hand and turned it this way and that. "What happened here?"

Pops looked at him squarely for the first time. "Nosey out there tending things?"

"Yeah," said Rollie, wondering what his pard had gotten up to.

"Good. Maybe you could get us both a beer and a bump, bring it out to the back steps. I don't feel like talking to a bunch of drunks just yet."

Rollie stared at Pops, brows drawn.

Pops grinned. "Then I'll tell you all about my day, okay?"

"Okay." Rollie sighed and went to fetch the drinks. By the time he returned, Pops was seated out on the back steps. In the light, Rollie could see how weary his friend looked. And both his wrists were indeed chafed.

Pops looked up, accepted the beer and the shot with a nod. He held up the shot. "To our continued good fortune."

Rollie drank with him and was about to speak when Pops shook his head and knocked back half the beer. He let out a long, loud sigh of satisfaction, and said, "Okay, pull up a step and let me tell you what I've been up to while you were riding around the countryside, enjoying yourself."

Pops winked and commenced his story, beginning at the point where they'd taken separate forks in the trail.

The entire time, Rollie sat beside his friend and held his beer, sipping occasionally but not interrupting.

Pops finished, sipped his own beer, then said, "I now regret not chasing after the men. I keep wondering if I could have prevented their planned heist of Stag Horn's transport wagon."

"Could be the men who rode shotgun on the wagon were able to drive them off."

Pops nodded, said nothing. But he knew Rollie only said it to make him feel less guilty.

They were silent for a bit. Rollie rubbed his chin.

Pops began to speak once more, but Rollie held up a hand. "Hang on, this is a two-beer situation." He grabbed their empty glasses and returned in short order with freshened beers and shots.

When they'd resettled themselves on their accustomed perches, Rollie said, "Sounds to me as if your guess is right. They wanted to draw me out to look for you. Then they'd kill me and since your usefulness as the cheese in the trap would be over with at that point, they'd kill you, too. Then they'd ride roughshod over the entire region."

"That's about what I was thinking, yeah." Pops sipped his beer. "You know what me escaping means, though."

Rollie nodded. "Yep. It means they'll be after us." He grinned.

"You find something humorous in all this?"

"Yep."

"Oh, please explain."

"Why wait for them to come to us?" said Rollie. "Let's give them what they want."

Pops stretched his legs and rubbed his knees. "When were you thinking of lighting out?"

"Oh," said Rollie. "Not for a few hours yet. I know old fellows such as yourself aren't as limber as you used to be."

Pops chuckled, then let out a full-belly laugh, shaking his head. "Funny. I heard the same thing and thought of you."

Rollie joined him and they watched the sun set far to the west, each thinking the same thing: They'd be up before it rose again, and in hot pursuit of the bandits.

Chapter Eighteen

The big Italian was a curious sort, that much was certain. He kept rattling on about how wonderful he was. Didn't seem to Bean the man was all that secure in the head. If you asked him a question, he'd wander around and around in circles with his words. Then, when you were ready to give up and change the topic, the big man would surprise you and settle on the point.

"I tell you something, Rex," Bean had said the night before. "If that big Eye-talian fella didn't have so much money, I'm not so sure I'd stick with him." He said it in a whisper, but tried to make himself seem as if he'd decided something mighty important for all of them. "In fact, I'm not so sure he is an Italian."

"What do you mean?" said Rex. "He has the name and the look. He even said he was."

"Yeah, but he's also one of them stage actors. You can't trust one of them. Liable to whip back on you like a gob of spit in a heavy wind."

This was interesting to Rex, who had been concentrating more during the day on staying in the saddle than on listening to Bean yammer on. But now that he was beginning to feel something close to his old self again, after that rough treatment the big fellow had given him, he fell to wondering if maybe, for once, Bean wasn't right.

What if the boss man, Giacomo Valucci, wasn't Italian? Sometimes he spoke all odd and exotic, sometimes he sounded like the rest of them. They'd all marked it down to the fact he was an actor, and though none of them had ever been acquainted with one of that breed, it stood to reason they'd be an odd lot.

But what if he was just a man like the rest of them? Granted, he was a big fellow, handsome, and all that. And other than squeezing a man's gourd too harsh, and flying off the handle about nothing much at all, and killing folks in one of his rages, Rex had to admit that Valucci had impressive manners. You couldn't just pick those up any old where. All this made Rex more curious than ever about their traveling companion. And he'd been curious about him from the start.

After supper around the campfire, at the urging of Rex, Bean cleared his throat and said "Well now, Mr. Val, um, Valucci . . . we have been wondering about something, yes sir, we have. It's this: If you seem to know where you are headed, why do you need me and Rex here?"

There, he'd asked it. It was the one thing he and Rex had whispered about for nights around the campfire. Though in truth, half the time Rex was still off his nut, mumbling and drooling since that mighty head squeezing Valucci had given him. Bean had to admit it had been nice not having to listen to Rex yammer all day about how he was the brains of the outfit. It occurred to Bean that for the brainy one, he sure was stupid to get himself puckered up by Valucci.

The big, handsome boss tapped his lips with a long finger and squinted into the fire. Finally, he nodded and his manly voice rose into the silent night air: "What you really want to know is, how did a cultured thespian such as myself end up in the vile clutches of such a pig as the infamous Stoneface Finnegan?"

No, that's not what Bean had been asking at all. But he felt like he could not risk correcting the man. One squished head in the bunch was enough, so he nodded. "Yeah, that's about it, Mister, ah, Boss. I am curious. I don't know as I have ever heard of this Stone-whatever you called him. But I'd like to, if you don't mind telling us, that is."

Rex tensed, sipped his coffee, eyeing the big man over his cup's rim. He had to be ready if the big goober was going to throw another beating on them. As to the kid, as usual he kept to himself, looking about how the rest of them felt, as if he regretted ever signing on with Valucci. He pitied the kid, but he couldn't much worry about him as he had himself and his pard to consider first.

Valucci stretched out with his boots to the fire, combed both hands through his black hair, then folded his arms across his big chest. "It is mostly in the autumn of the year when the fever afflicts me. Oh, it had been with me my whole life, but it sleeps for a time, then emerges as if from a nap. And it hungers for satisfaction. I am helpless under its spell. I merely obey. There are consequences, always consequences, that I learn of later." He waved his long fingers as if shooing a fly.

"The newspapers call them victims. Bah! Prostitutes with a distinct lack of breath, gamblers missing eyes and tongues, sometimes their heads, that sort of sordid thing."

Again, he waved, but this time passed his eyes over the two men and the boy staring at him. Giacomo smiled.

"All this activity has waxed and waned for weeks, months, years, and now and then I read in the papers that a fresh assortment of lifeless individuals has emerged, leaving a trail of sorts. Their appearance naturally attracted the attention of certain badge-wearing individuals. None of them could make heads or tails of these so-called crimes. Ha! Of course, they couldn't. How dare they think they might cast a rope about a master of disguise!"

He clenched his hands into fists and gazed at the fire. "And yet it bothered me. For one among them truly was intent on discovering the perpetrator of these so-called crimes. It was one of that reprehensible breed known as a Pinkerton Man. And this one, a savage known as Rollie 'Stoneface' Finnegan," Valucci spat the name as if it were a mouthful of spoiled food. "He was the worst, and relentless. I was still not worried, and yet . . . his presence in the newspapers plagued me, irked me, and I soon succumbed to the bleak, black fever.

"Yet shortly before that I met Ophelia of the Racine-and-Tokyo Traveling Circus. Oh, but she was a vixen, at least that's what she called herself. She was also my savior, and I craved her like I have never craved anything in my life, you see. Her buxom body, her raven-black hair, her stroppy wit, her comely ankles and neck—and everything between. Oh yes, she was all a man such as I could ask for, could yearn for. And yearn I did. For days, weeks, nearly a month. You see, I headlined the touring retinue of players. The unimaginative name of our band of thespians was hardly worthy of our talents, I alone among them being an award-winning actor of the world stage.

We performed all manner of works from the Bard, of course, and those of lesser writers, too, which my presence alone elevated to near-legendary status."

Bean and Rex glanced at each other, reading the confusion in the other's eyes, but not daring to comment or even raise a brow in puzzlement.

"It all began while I was treading the boards at Chicago's Cragmore Playhouse, suffering through an abominably directed production of Delahanty's *Spring Rites of the Fallen*. I caught sight of that voluptuous maiden in the first row. It was all I could do to keep my eyes from her divine face. But professional that I am, I did. It turned out she was a performer also and was in town with a circus, of all things. Well, I reminded myself that even the most flawless performers, such as myself, emerged from humble beginnings.

"We spent much time together over the following days. And on our last foray we were shadowed by a menacing-looking fellow in a sad little dented bowler and ruddy cheeks. I wanted to thrash him and show her, I suppose, of what mettle I was made.

"Much to my surprise, she explained that he was her guardian. The very next night, after a particularly grueling performance, I don't mind saying, he braced me with a brandished pistol and informed me she was no longer free to see me. It seems the maiden had been less than forthcoming about her relationship with another of her troupe, the fire-breathing, sword-swallowing Swami the Great. I had taken in his act, as it happens. The man was anything but great. He was a rube with a long gullet and a freakish lineage that, I have little doubt, he could trace all the way back to something lurching out of a cave deep in the Appalachian Mountains.

"I found her after her final turn on the trapeze under the mighty tent set up outside town limits and quizzed her without mercy. She sobbed, hung her head low, and would not meet my righteous gaze. Nothing I could say would dissuade the little minx from what I had assumed was a lie on her guardian's part to keep me from her. Alas, I learned it was true. She was married, had been for some time, to he who ingests cutlery and sparks. I succumbed to something then to which I alluded moments ago. The black fever has plagued me since birth, a fever that settles over me as if a scrim of opaque madness. I lashed out. I barely recall this."

He stared skyward, tears sliding down his temples from his eye corners. Bean and Rex exchanged looks once more. Rex sipped, and Bean cleared his throat. "What happened then, Boss?"

"When I came to, I looked about me and saw that someone had lain the little goddess low. In three pieces: head, torso, and one leg. Why that combination, I will never know." He sat up and eyed the guides. "Bah! As if a man would do such a thing to the woman he loves!"

"But . . ." Rex said it before he could stop himself.

Valucci glared at him. All three men were silent a moment, then the big man's face softened. In the firelight, only his eyes remained hard-looking. "You want to know something, eh? Something more?"

Rex shook his head, but Bean said, "He wants to know what all this means. You said yourself you have an affliction of sorts that has plagued you since you were a baby. Madness, I think you said it was."

"Yes." Valucci nodded, a thin smile on his mouth. "That is true."

"So." Bean licked his lips. "Did you . . . kill the girl?"

The big man settled back against his mound of blankets and laced his fingers behind his big, perfect head and shrugged. "That is what Stoneface Finnegan believed. Oh, he didn't know who I was, still doesn't, I'll wager. You see, I traveled incognito as part of the acting troupe. Even my fellow thespians knew not of my true identity. I left town at that very moment and seethed at the little attention the newspapers gave the foul act that befell my dear Ophelia."

Valucci stared at the fire's dimming coals with bright eyes and distended nostrils. "But it was he, you see, Stoneface Finnegan himself, who did the deed. He and he alone rendered her a lifeless thing, no one else."

Giacomo Valucci turned his icy gaze on his companions. "But now, at long last, I shall taste the sweet nectar of vengeance."

Chapter Nineteen

Both Pops and Rollie found the early-morning ride to the bandits' rocky hideout a tense couple of hours. It took them longer than they expected, but they picked their way, guns drawn and reining up, eyeing every boulder, pine, and bend in the trail for a sign that something, anything might be off. But the early birds kept warbling and the breeze kept soughing and the horses never once acted balky.

Halfway into the trip, at Pops' suggestion, nothing more than a gesturing nod, they departed from the beaten trail that most folks used to travel west from Boar Gulch. Pops reined up, and Rollie rode close.

"Down that way." He nodded ahead. "Another hour at this speed."

Rollie nodded, and they moved out. They took to the same wooded, sloped terrain Pops had traveled what felt to him like mere minutes before.

They rode, a dozen yards apart, slow going, cautious and keeping a check on where Cap and Bucky would put their feet. They paused, stopping and starting, looking with caution at everything. Pops rode point since he'd been there before, and Rollie was seeing this particular slice of scenery for the first time.

He was amazed, as Pops had been, that he'd not seen any of this side valley. As his own foray showed him yesterday, the country hereabouts was immense. Rollie wondered if you flattened out all the peaks, how vast a region would it cover?

Ahead, Pops rode as he always did, straight-backed and alert, his Greener resting across his saddle before him. He was wishing the head bandit hadn't stomped his old corncob pipe. He'd had it many a-year, and now he had to shell out for a new one.

A low, birdlike whistle sounded. He stopped and held still. Rollie also stopped, not breathing, straining and listening for another whistle. It didn't come.

Pops cut his glance toward Rollie quick. The ex-Pinkerton man had far more experience than he in such potentially grim situations. Branches rustled ahead and a blur of brown hurtled out, gliding through low branches.

Pops let out a breath. It was a grouse, good eating, bad at staying silent and worse at not scaring me, thought Pops. Didn't mean the bandits weren't even now arranged throughout the woods, sighting on them. This was foolhardy, but unless they had scouts out, there was little chance they would know they were coming. If they were at the camp.

If I ran that outfit, thought Pops, *I would have cleared out as soon as I came back from my robbing run and found those two fools dead.* He knew the boss man would think like he did on this matter, that Pops would no doubt bring hell down on them. But not this soon, right? He hoped so. The logic was flimsy, but he had to at least try to think like the boss man of the bandits.

They crested a berm, recognizable to Pops, and he halted once more. Rollie did, as well, then after a pause, cut to his left and rode close to Pops.

"Down there," Pops whispered. "See those rocks?"

Rollie nodded. There wasn't much to see.

"Don't let them fool you, they're massive." Pops nodded. "Land slopes."

Rollie nodded again. "Leave the horses here?"

"Yeah," said Pops, sliding from his saddle.

They tied the horses to branches and in the still-brightening morning light, they checked their guns and proceeded downslope. At about the spot where Pops had been taken, they split by mutual nods, and continued, making as few branch-crackling steps as they could.

Gray boulders loomed larger and larger before them. The two men finally reached the rock mass and flanked the cut where the thin path wound inward. It was dark in the declivity, and a cold, bitter morning breeze carried through the cleft as if escaping from a cave. Escaping that place of death, thought Pops. They walked, one in front of the other, Rollie in the lead.

They advanced slow, one step, stop, one step, and listen. No sound reached them. Pops touched Rollie's shoulder and nodded ahead, then held up a hand and curved it in the air, as if mimicking a swimming fish, then closed his fist.

Rollie nodded. Around the corner, then there it would be. Would they catch anyone there? If so, would they be sleeping? It all seemed doubtful. Any road agents worth their salt would have posted guards at their hidey hole.

Rollie walked on, Pops right behind, the patched stock of the Greener resting on a raised forearm, thumb on her triggers. Rollie's Schofield was poised and at full cock. There would be no hiding themselves once they rounded that last curve in the rock.

Rollie's mouth felt as dry as a sun-puckered plank. He ran his tongue over his lips and peered around the wall.

The morning light shone down brighter before him, where the mass of rock opened up into the great, time-carved bowl. And he saw no one. No one alive, that is. He stepped aside and Pops emerged beside him.

Rollie gestured with his chin toward a figure stretched out face-down on the ground. Pops took that as a question and he nodded.

With another jerk of his head, both men stepped back into the shadows of the passage. Pops said, "That's the one I knifed. I shot a second man, he should be just outside, on the far side."

"Okay," said Rollie. "I need to inspect this mess. There have to be clues we can use. I'll wait here while you go back, then up on top. That way you'll be able to cover me."

Pops nodded. They both knew Rollie was the man to do the snooping. He'd spent his entire career as a Pinkerton man doing just that.

"Keep an eye," murmured Rollie, which Pops knew meant look up, look down, and cover him.

"Count on it," whispered Pops, then he said, "I'll whistle twice when I'm up. If it's safe, I'll check on the second body." He turned back down the stony corridor.

Rollie waited for him to find a way out and up top. In the meantime, he edged closer to the bowl again and eyed the scene. Though it was indeed brighter than in the passage, there were enough mansize rocks and other unknown features causing holes filled with shadows or worse that Rollie wasn't comfortable risking exposing himself until Pops gave him the double whistle.

All was silent as he gazed and let his eyes and the morning sun reveal more of what he faced. One dead man, given that's what Pops had said he'd laid low inside the bowl. He would bet good money that the road agents were long gone from here. But what if they weren't? He'd learned over the long years to never underestimate killers and thieves.

Two low-pitched, hollow whistles, like the husky sounds of a mourning dove, reached him. He offered one in return and, bending low, crept into the bowl. He catfooted straight for the body, twenty or so feet away. It was a tall, lanky man, stiffened, and facedown.

No way was this one going to rise up and attack. If he does, thought Rollie. I am going to scream like a schoolgirl. A great pool of blood had leached beneath the man, though now it was little more than a stain on the gritted earth.

Up top, Pops skirted the great stone bowl until he reached the far side. Down below, leaning against the rocky wall, sat the big goober he'd shot before riding out. Same spot where he collapsed. Good. He retraced his steps to watch over Rollie.

Satisfied that the man was beyond fighting, and that Pops was protecting his back as well as his own, too, up there somewhere, Rollie backtracked. He made it to the campfire and held a palm over the long-dead coals. He rummaged, poking and nudging the rocks, wishing he had a lantern. Though it was morning, full sunlight hadn't pierced the trees to brighten the gloom of the cold, unwelcoming bowl.

From what Pops said, the spot had been filled with men and gear. And from the prints and the drag marks, they left in a hurry and didn't leave much in the way of clues.

"Psst!" The sound came from above. Rollie looked up and saw Pops gesturing. "To your left—paper?"

Rollie spun and narrowed his eyes. Yep, good eye, Pops, he thought. There looked to be something protruding from one of the rock wall's niches. He walked to it, coming up on it from the side, ever cautious. It was indeed paper, held down by a rock.

Before Rollie tugged it free, he eyed the thing all over. He'd seen some sort of triggering device set up on a train car once, rigged to kill lawmen. And it had. Ever since then, he'd been cautious about sticking his hands near or in or on anything that might have hidden intentions.

He tweezered the paper free with two fingers and opened it, two folds. It still wasn't light enough to read by full sunlight. He expected in here it might not be until the sun crawled its way up beyond the tree tops above. He thumbed a match alight and saw words printed in large block letters:

WELL, HELLO LAWDOGS!
YOU MEN SHOULD HAVE LEFT WELL
ENOUGH ALONE. WE KNOW WHO YOU ARE
AND WE KNOW WHERE YOU LIVE AND WE
ARE WATCHING YOU . . . RIGHT NOW. YOU
BEST KEEP YOUR WITS ABOUT YOU.

—THE HARD RIDERS

Rollie shook out the match and suppressed a chuckle. It was possible they knew who they were and where they lived, most folks in the region did. But watching them right now? Doubtful. They would have laid them low already if they were smarter than they proved themselves to be.

Rollie refolded the paper and stuffed it in his vest pocket and made for the far side of the bowl, stepping over the dead man blocking the corridor in the rock.

Behind and above him, Pops' boots ground gravel as he, too, made for the far side. Rollie would give a couple minutes more to inspecting where Pops said the horses were kept, but as thorough as the gang had proven to be, he didn't think they had left behind much in the way of evidence or clues.

He made it to the obvious spot where horses had stood—mounds of drying road apples rolled with prompting from his boot. It had been a few hours since horses were kept here. He heard light footsteps and glanced over his right shoulder. Pops, as he expected. The man was swiveling his head left and right.

"Any more of that and you'll look like an owl," said Rollie.

"Owl, rat, don't care what you call me, as long as I'm a live one."

Rollie handed Pops the note and, as he thought, Pops chuckled, too. "Saw the second one. He's as dead as he was when I left him. Maybe deader."

"Good. And just to be safe," said Rollie. "Keep looking around and stick to the walls as we walk back. You never know."

"I hear that," said Pops as they retraced their route

back through the passage. They stopped once more in the bowl-shaped cavity where the dead man lay.

"If you want to do something for the two of them, we best get at it," said Rollie.

"Naw," said Pops. "But it is a shame this one inside has to sully the place, though. It's a rare spot. Makes you wonder how long the tribes used it in the past. Almost as if it was built for a campfire in the middle."

"And long nights of storytelling after a hunt," mused Rollie. "You're right. Let's at least drag this one on out of here, put him with the other, where you said the horses were."

Each man grabbed a handful of coat at the dead man's shoulders and rid the spot of him, then Rollie snooped for more clues, but found little of use. The endeavor cost them another ten minutes.

Rollie brisked his hands together then rested them on his hips. "Well, we have two choices. We can try to track them or head back to the Gulch."

All of a sudden Pops felt as if somebody had loaded six or eight fifty-pound sacks of cornmeal on his shoulders. He shrugged, hoping his hesitation hadn't been apparent to Rollie.

Rollie turned and stretched, worked his shoulders and said, "I must be getting old because I am plumb tuckered out. All this getting up early. I don't know how you do it, Pops. What say we head back home?"

Pops chuckled. "All right, old man. Last one there makes the coffee."

By the time they made it back to their horses, the sun had topped the trees. Cap and Bucky were still there, and not impressed with a second day dawning of trail work.

The ride back to Boar Gulch was a quiet one, each man considering a next move that wasn't presenting itself. They were also busy eyeing their back trail and the road ahead.

Town came into view as they rounded a bend, and Pops said, "Well, I wouldn't say it was a waste of time but we didn't gain a whole hell of a lot of wisdom out of that adventure." He yawned. "Plus, I am beat. I feel like somebody hit me with a length of stove wood without letup for an hour. You?"

Rollie grinned. "I can't say I feel that bad, no. But I could use a few hours of sleep before we open for the night's rush of drinkers and liars."

Chapter Twenty

Late the next day found Rollie and Pops at the bar trying to hash out a next step for their investigations.

"I know what you said about Chauncey, but I tell you there's something there." Rollie ground his teeth together, then poked a finger on the bartop as if he were driving in a nail. "He's mixed up with these Hard Rider thieves somehow, I just know it."

Pops shrugged. "Unless you have proof, that's a whole lot to dump on a man."

Rollie sighed. "Yeah, well, I'll prove it." He walked out and the door slammed behind him, harder than he intended. But so be it, he was tired of pussyfooting around. They'd attacked Pops, they'd threatened him and Pops, and they were robbing and killing throughout the hills. It was past time to do something.

An hour later found him all stomped out and up atop the western rise above town. It was hours to dark and he didn't feel like heading back to The Last Drop yet. Up ahead, a light thread of smoke rose up out of Pieder Tomsen's chimney, and not the one from his shop. That was odd, especially since it was still daylight. The man never seemed to take time off. Indeed, the steely ringing of his hammer blows could often be heard well after dark.

But now that Rollie thought about it, since Camp Sal had nursed Pieder back to health after the fracas with Danziger, the sounds of activity from the shop, while still daylong affairs, had not leaked into nighttime hours. Sundays, too, had grown to be unusually quiet from his direction. Several residents of the Gulch had commented to Rollie that the taciturn blacksmith had been smiling more of late, and they all knew Sal was to blame.

Rollie was about to turn around and make his way home when he heard a woman's voice say, "Well good evening, Mr. Finnegan."

He turned to see Sal walking along a path to his left, lugging two water pails.

"Hello, Sal. Here, let me help you." Rollie rushed over to her side, hands out.

"No, no, that's all right," she said. "If you do, I'll be unbalanced. It's easier to carry two than one." She set down the pails and pushed stray hair from her forehead with the back of her hand.

Rollie noticed she looked happier and more fit than he'd ever seen her.

"What brings you out and about this early evening?"

"Oh, I'm just strolling. Thinking, if truth be told."

"About those terrible road agents?"

"You know about them?"

She smiled. "Everybody does, Rollie. The bar isn't the only place gossip takes place in a little town like this. You want to hear the latest and from sober people, spend time at Pieder's shop in the mornings. I've taken to serving coffee and biscuits!"

Rollie smiled. "Pieder doesn't mind?"

"No. In fact he encouraged me to. He seems to think it's good for business."

"I'm sure he's right."

"Say, I'll make a deal with you. You help me lug these pails home and I'll feed you supper. I always make more than enough and we've been wanting to have you up anyway. And next time, bring Pops along."

"Oh, I don't want to intrude, Sal. I was just out for a walk."

"So you said. But maybe talking with Pieder will help. He might have heard something that could be useful to you. I know he'd not forgive me if I didn't invite you."

"Maybe just a cup of coffee, then."

"Okay," she said. "But in our house that means elk steak and greens and potatoes and apple fritters for dessert."

Rollie stared at her a moment, then said, "Give me those buckets and look out!"

She giggled and they walked up the trail to the cabin.

The meal was better than Rollie could have wanted. No wonder Pieder seemed to be thickening slightly about the face and chest. He'd always had a gaunt, bachelor look about him, but now he appeared well-fed and happy. After they ate, Pieder and Rollie, on Sal's insistence, retired to the cabin's setting porch and, over pipes and hot coffee, they discussed what each knew of the villainous gang.

"Dustin Schenker, from south," Pieder gestured with his pipe stem in that direction. "He brought a work wagon to be mended." He puffed and mused, then continued in his own time, looking Rollie in the eye. "He said Mayor

Wheeler has been to see him and others." He puffed again, then said. "Some of them get robbed later." Pieder shrugged. "I only tell you this because he told me this. I know nothing more than that."

Rollie nodded and drew on his own pipe, deep in thought. The coincidences were there and could be little more than that. But coupled with the common knowledge of Chauncey's financial woes and you had a growing reason to question the mayor.

"Well," said Sal, drying her hands on her apron. "I leave you two to chat, and I come back to hear crickets and see a cloud of blue smoke. Anybody need more coffee?"

Pieder stood. "I can get it. You should sit. You've made the meal, cleaned up." He held her by the elbow and tried to steer her to a third chair. "Here now."

She kissed him on the nose, shook her head, and went back in for the coffee pot. Pieder sighed and sat down again, smiling.

"I am happy for you and Sal," said Rollie.

Pieder nodded, then said, "Thank you. Yes, it is good."

Rollie stood and straightened his back, listening to the pops and creaks. Sal returned with the coffee pot, looking at him. "Is my coffee that bad?"

Rollie smiled and patted his full belly. "On the contrary. I am too full for anything else. Thank you both very much. This was unexpected and just what I needed."

Pieder rose and walked with Rollie a ways down the path. "If you need help with those men, come get me." He nodded, not taking his piercing eyes from Rollie's. "They are bad men and many of them. You and Pops are only two."

Rollie nodded. "I appreciate it, Pieder." He clapped a hand on his shoulder. "We'll see what comes up. But I'll keep the offer in mind. Maybe we can avoid a big dust-up yet."

"And . . . how do you say . . . pigs might fly."

Chapter Twenty-one

"But Rollie, you have to believe me!" Chauncey squealed and stamped his feet and Rollie noticed then that the man seemed fatter. When he'd first arrived in Boar Gulch, Rollie's assessment of the mayor had been of a portly fellow, soft in his habits and soft around the middle. Why do it when you could hire it done.

That had rankled Rollie, but to each his own. Though he had to admit that Chauncey's constant bustling drive, something he couldn't seem to quell, was a trait Rollie admired. He himself had always been more inclined to move through his day at a measured pace.

But the mayor had definitely put on weight, and it wasn't even winter. That sat at odds with his constant cries of poverty.

"You feeling well, Chauncey?"

"What do you mean?"

"I mean you look like you've, well you're . . ."

"Aw," Wolfbait smacked a hand on the edge of the bartop. "What Rollie's getting at is you look fat, Chauncey! Now don't you deny it. You've porked up these last few months."

The mayor's face had rarely been redder. Then he did something that surprised the rest of them. He nodded. "You're right. You're right. It's the money I've been spending on the hotel. I get worried like this and I eat. Can't help it. Doesn't help that I own a store now, does it?" He stood looking at his belly and shaking his head. "But that's not why I came here, dang it!"

"Why, Chauncey," said Pops, eyebrows raised. "You swore! I never thought I'd see the day."

"Have your laughs at my expense, I know about all of you and what you get up to when my back is turned. But I'm here on official lawful business, and I demand you hear me!" He'd worked his rage up again into a red-faced fury.

"Okay, Chauncey, let's hear it," said Rollie, eyeing the others to keep their comments to a minimum.

The mayor took a deep breath and said, "I'm being . . . tormented."

That made everybody perk up.

"I know the feeling." Rollie muttered, then said, "I'm kidding. Who's doing the tormenting, Chauncey?" said Rollie, pouring the man a cup of coffee.

The mayor looked at him, eyes wide, and said, "By a ghost."

The barkeep sighed. "Chauncey, in all my years as a Pinkerton man, I've come across all manner of oddness in the world, people claiming they were driven to do various bad things by ghosts, ghouls, specters, spirits, angels, demons, dead folks come back to life, and more.

"One lady told me she had poisoned her village's well because her cat threatened her with eternity in the hellfires of damnation, if I recall correctly. So take heed when

I tell you that not one of them did I believe. And what's more, I found out the real causes of their various misdeeds and none of them had to do with anything from the spirit world. So when you tell me you're being blackmailed by a ghost . . . I'm skeptical."

By that time, most in attendance were shocked that Rollie had spoken that much at once, more than any of them heard him say in a week's worth of conversing. They were also beginning to laugh, but none more so than Pops, whose shoulders were jerking up and down and eyes were tearing.

Chauncey Wheeler narrowed his eyes. "I don't appreciate being mocked, laughed at, and certainly don't like it when I'm not believed." He turned to go, but Rollie said, "Okay, okay, I'm willing to hear the rest. But only because you aren't usually what I'd . . . insensible."

The left-handed compliment seemed to mollify the mayor. He paused and shot the softly chuckling Pops a hard glance, then turned once more to face Rollie.

"I don't care what you believe or not. I know what I saw and I saw Pete Winklestaff."

A loud moan rose up from the end of the bar. All faces turned to see Wolfbait sliding off his stool, backing toward the door, doing a poor job of crossing himself and preparing to spit on the floor.

Pops walked up to him and pointed a big finger in his face. "I thought we talked about this. I catch you doing anything like spitting on my floor again, superstition or no, and I'm going to tan your hide! I don't care if you're old enough to be my pappy!" He snatched the old buzzard by the collar of his coat and held him still. "Now what's got into you?"

Wolfbait looked over at Chauncey. "You tell 'em! I said I'd never utter a word . . . and I ain't about to now!"

Rollie looked at them both and said, "Somebody better say something and quick, or I'm liable to lose my temper."

Nosey, who up until now had been silently regarding this scene, scribbling in his notebook, said, "Wasn't Winkle-staff the name of the man who co-founded this town with you, mayor? Also known as . . . your dead partner? A man whose grave was the first to grace Boot Hill at the northwest corner of town?"

"Out with it, Chauncey." Rollie glared at the man. "And you" —he looked at Wolfbait— "sit down on your stool and keep quiet."

"I could use a beer to calm my tremors," said Wolfbait.

"Maybe after we hear something useful from you."

"Okay."

"We're all waiting, mayor."

The chubby man cleared his throat, said, "I need a drink. Whiskey, Rollie, then I'll tell you everything."

Rollie complied, then resumed his stance, arms crossed and his cheek muscles bunching as he watched the mayor drink.

He finished, set down the glass, and said, "It began, as so many such stories do, back in St. Louis. I was thin then, a younger man."

Wolfbait snickered, and the mayor looked at him but narrowed his eyes and continued.

"Peter Winklestaff rescued me from a sure beating when I found I was penniless and it came time to pay my bar bill. I was waiting out my days to tag along with a family trekking westward. Turns out they'd left in the night, so I was left at loose ends. I had gold fever, like anyone else. Along came Pete Winklestaff. We were about the same age, but he seemed older, wiser. He was a pudgy man, no comments, please. He dressed nicely, had money. He said he was looking for someone to help him on his new venture, do the heavy lifting, as it were. I signed on, as his venture sounded more promising than going back to Pennsylvania and putting up with my sister and her annoying husband and their brood of five children.

"We made for this very place, a region it turns out he'd discovered several years before as a promising spot on his way back from the gold fields of California. He'd gone back East with the intention of marrying his sweetheart, who was supposed to have waited for him. Well, she didn't. He showed up with a small fortune, enough to set them up nicely. Her loss was my gain, as it happens. He was eager to get back out here to the West and really strike it rich. He staked us on gear, a wagon, stock, provisions, the works. I had little to offer save my eagerness and my brute force."

Wolfbait snorted.

"Knock it off," said Rollie. "Can you get to the meat of the story, Chauncey? We open for the night in a couple of hours."

"Well, as you all know by now, we made it to this place, and set to work staking claims and digging. I worked my fingers to the bone, yes, every test hole dug, every sluice-box filled, every pan swirled in those early days, I was the one to do it. I wasn't complaining, though, as that was my job. Pete, he was busy staking out the claims. He was dead certain we were going to strike it rich and he wanted to grab as much land as he could."

"I know it!" said Wolfbait. "I was here before you rascals! That's why you gobbled up all the land around me but you didn't get mine!" He slapped his knee as if he'd just pulled off a great caper.

"Yes, well," continued the mayor. "There were a few impediments in those early days, but by and large it all worked out according to Pete's plan. Then he began running out of money, even though we were bringing in some with the diggings. It wasn't enough for him. Turns out there was a side to Winklestaff that I hadn't known about. He began to get greedy. Even though from the start he insisted I have my own share, not an even split, mind you, which was fine since he had fronted the entire operation, but I got a decent share. I wasn't complaining. But he began to."

"How so?" said Rollie.

"He'd get drunk and berate me. Tell me I was a moocher. Then he'd disappear for days at a time. Pretty soon, I had saved up my money in a tin can and a whole lot of gold dust in a sack. I was hedging my bets, wondering if I would have to leave in the night. Well, I came back to the cabin from a long day of work and found him tearing the place apart, yelling that I'd held out on him. He had my can and was counting out my money! It was all my share, I tell you. But he would hear none of it. He barreled out the door past me and stalked down the mountainside. Well, I finally caught up to him out by Wolfbait's camp. And wouldn't you know, that old reprobate was out sunning himself in his front yard."

Nosey had to hold Wolfbait back from launching himself at the mayor. "Reprobate! I'll show you a reprobate! Don't think I don't know what that means! I was a schoolteacher in Connecticut before I came out here on my own back when you were still in short pants, you bloated little weasel!"

Chauncey backed up a step and held a hand to his throat.

"Back to the story, mayor," said Rollie. "Pops, give him a beer, will you?"

Pops nodded, suppressing a smile. He was loving this.

"Yes, well," said Chauncey. "I grabbed Winklestaff's shoulder and spun him around. I told him to give my money back. What would anybody do?" Chauncey looked around at the four men as if daring them to disagree with him. Nobody did. "He swung at me, unbidden! I wanted to talk, he wanted to fight.

"I could smell the whiskey on him. He'd become a drunken sot by then. He hit me good, right in the face. Why, I thought he'd broken my nose! I saw stars, doubled over, then dropped to my knees. But he wasn't through with me. He kept beating on me. I fell to my side, my hearing buzzed, and I heard voices."

"That was me trying to stop Winklestaff from beating you to death, you damn fool!" said Wolfbait between sips of beer. "Would have, too, if I hadn't stepped in, you ingrate! How's that for a two-dollar word?"

"Yes, well, you've been thanked, and plenty over the years! Anyway, the beating slackened and I could barely see, so puffed up had my eyes become. Then I felt him beating on me again! I crawled forward, and my right hand touched a shovel leaning against something. Turns out it was a cabin."

"Yeah, mine!" said Wolfbait.

Chauncey ignored him. "I used it to pull myself upright. As I turned, I saw Winklestaff's leering face come at me and, without thinking, I grabbed that shovel and swung it around as hard as I could, to keep him away from me. I couldn't take anymore beating. I was sure he was going to kill me."

He paused, his voice shaking. "My blow connected with his head."

"Yeah, ol' Winky dropped like a sack of corn meal!" said Wolfbait.

"I was mortified. Even though he'd been trying to kill me, even though he'd stolen from me, he was my friend, my business partner. Heck, he was responsible for bringing me out here in the first place, wet as I was. I owed him so much. And now I'd killed him!"

He rested his elbows on the bar and rubbed his face in his hands. "I could see better by then, after I'd wiped the blood out of my eyes. I felt for a heartbeat, nothing. No breaths from his mouth. I tell you it was self-defense!"

"What happened next?" said Rollie.

"My mind began to race. I wondered how I would protect myself. All I had worked for all those long months while he was out carousing and spending our money. Yes, I know how that sounds, but why, I recall thinking, why should I lose it all because he'd become a drunken thief? We were so close to a breakthrough. I knew we were. Why couldn't he just wait for the strike?"

"What did you do?" said Pops.

"I decided to cover it up. It would have been a simple matter, too, except for one thing."

"Yeah, me," said Wolfbait.

"Yes, you," sighed the mayor. "I paid him off, produced deed and claims aplenty, and generously gave him the deed to the claim he was squatting on."

"It was mine anyway. I lived on it, didn't I?"

"Not legally, no, but I bought you off, paid you to shut up."

"What did it matter to me? You killed him in self-defense, fair and square," said Wolfbait. "I would have told the law that, too, but you had to go and insult me by threatening me and then buying me off." He shrugged. "What did I care? I never asked you for a thing. Why not? I figured. You were fool enough to give me that when there was no need, so be it. My conscience is clean on the matter. All I saw out my front door was two fools fighting. Heck, I see it all the time—sometimes I'm one of them!"

"What about Winklestaff's body?" said Rollie. "What did you do when it turned up missing?"

"How did you know it turned up missing?" said Chauncey, wide eyed.

"Yeah, you accusing me of grave robbing?" said Wolfbait.

"Let the man speak," said Pops.

The mayor gulped and nodded. "It's true. I got my mule and fetched him back to our camp. About where my store sits. I laid him out on the rise up there where Boot Hill is now. I went back to the cabin to get his good togs. I felt awful about it, wanted to send him off right. I took a drink to steady my nerves."

He sighed. "Well, that one led to another, and before you know it, I was drunk and crying and then I passed out. The next morning, I woke up stiff as a plank and swollen from the beating he'd given me, and hungover, to boot. When I finally remembered what I should have done the night before, I stumbled up to the spot and he was gone."

"What?" said Wolfbait. "But he's buried up there. You told me so!"

Chauncey shook his head. "No, no he's not."

"I won't ask again," said Rollie, his jaw muscles bunching and his moustaches twitching. "What about Winklestaff's body?"

"I . . . I thought perhaps wolves or bears dragged him off," said the mayor. "You know how these wild animals can be!"

"So you faked the burial? The grave's empty?"

Chauncey nodded.

"That part I did not know. I thought the man was dead all this time!" said Wolfbait. "Now I don't know what to think."

"I do," said Rollie. "Sounds to me like you're trying to play us for fools, cover up a murder you committed all those years ago."

"Why would he do that?" said Nosey.

"Yeah, why would I do that?" said Chauncey.

Rollie shook his head and made a sound as if he'd just seen a dog drop a cigar in a church. "You are a piece of work, Mayor Chauncey Wheeler. Wasting our time like this." He slammed a glass on the counter and poured himself a shot, then pointed a stiff finger in the mayor's face. "The next time you're tempted to share something else with us, maybe about how leprechauns visit you in the wee hours, I suggest you go back to your store and count your money instead. Maybe have a snack."

"I don't understand," sputtered Chauncey. "I'm telling the truth here!"

"Maybe yes, maybe no, mayor."

"But . . . but don't you believe me?" said Chauncey.

"Believe you or not, it doesn't really matter now, does it, mayor? You got all the land, it's all in your name, by hook or by crook."

"Or shovel," said Pops, meeting Chauncey's hard stare. The mayor looked away.

"But don't you see? I didn't kill him. Now I know that! I saw him, I tell you! I know he's back. He's alive and he's back. And he wants revenge!"

Chapter Twenty-two

After they closed up that night. Rollie and Pops each turned in, mindful of the other's tender mood. Pops noted that Rollie grew especially prickly whenever he was in the midst of a potential fight, which the gang's presence was showing signs of becoming.

Finally, Rollie said, "Hey, Pops. You awake?"

"Yep."

"I have to head out tomorrow, try to find out more about this gang."

"Sounds like you don't want company."

There was a pause, then Rollie said, "I don't want to offend you, but I need to do some of this on my own. I can travel faster, like I used to before I came to Boar Gulch."

Like when you got yourself stabbed in that alley, thought Pops. Instead, he said, "Uh huh. Well, I'll mind the bar and the town. How long you expect to be gone?"

"No idea. Hopefully not long."

"If you get in a sticky situation, send word if you can. I'll be along."

"I know. And I appreciate it."

* * *

Rollie felt awful about leaving Pops behind, even though it made the most sense. Somebody had to watch over their business and the town. And Rollie was the most experienced in tracking men, not that his lack of success recently was any indication.

He also hated that he felt guilty. There was a time when he was a whole lot more footloose and devil-may-care about his own comings and goings.

He'd ridden for two hours since sun-up and was contemplating stopping and building a small fire to brew up coffee. He hadn't wanted to kindle a fire, all but an invitation to raid his camp, should there be nefarious sorts about.

Rollie flexed the fingers on his right hand that held his Winchester repeater. He rode with it resting atop a makeshift cradle he'd fashioned out of knotting a small cotton sack about the top of the saddle horn. It provided the forestock enough support without allowing it to slip off the smooth leather knob.

He slowed his pace and looked for a cluster of boulders, plentiful hereabouts, where he might brew up. That's when a scruffy character stepped out on the trail about five yards ahead.

Cap shied but Rollie held him in check.

"What you want here?"

The man was old, maybe not as old as Wolfbait, but old enough. Still, he looked fit enough to pull the trigger on his single-barrel shotgun. The thing looked to have been repaired a good many times. From beneath the man's arm Rollie saw wraps of twine around the stock with what looked like varnish slathered all over it.

If the gun looked oft-repaired and rickety, the old man was anything but. His voice was solid, if raspy. The two dark eyes glaring out from under the flop-brim hat and above the thick shrub of a beard told Rollie enough. Here was a character with plenty of sass but maybe not enough to back it up should it come to it. He trusted his gut.

"Passing through," said Rollie.

"Well, you can't!"

"You own the trail?"

"No."

"Then I can."

"Mister, you do and it'll be the last thing you do!"

"Like hell," said Rollie and he nudged Cap forward to within five feet of the man. On closer inspection, Rollie saw he'd been right. The man kept licking his lips and blinking sweat out of his eyes.

"What are you afraid of, old timer?"

"Who says I'm afeared?"

"I do." Rollie leaned forward, pivoting his rifle with him so that it aimed at the man. "You haven't seen a gang of men hereabouts, have you? Men who steal honest miners' pokes?"

That got to the old buck. His bottom lip quivered and his eyes flinted up again. "You know them fellas, huh?"

"Nope," said Rollie. "But I am tracking them."

"Well, you're too blamed late, that's what! Robbed me blind and my neighbors, too!"

Rollie sighed and considered the situation. "Am I near Stag Horn?"

"Yeah, you are. Why?"

Rollie ignored the question. "You get a look at them?"

"Yeah, but they was all dolled up in bags. Cowards is what I call them. Used to be a man wanted to rob another man he'd show his face, be proud of breaking his mama's heart. Nah, these men are useless."

"How many?"

"Eight that I saw. I was one of the shotgun riders, but it didn't matter none. We still got took. Shot Elmer and Lily, too."

"Shot a woman?"

"What? Naw, Lily's a mule. Right in the traces. Elmer, he was the driver. He's dead, too. I buried him, read over him. Couldn't bury Lily, too big and I'm too old. But I read over her, too." The old man sniffed and looked away a moment.

"How long ago was the attack?"

"Yesterday, about four hours after noon o'clock."

"Where did the robbery take place?"

"Why, no more than a half-mile up the road, you'll ride on through it getting to Stag Horn. We'd heard there were rogues afoot, so we armed up and rode along with the wagon, but it didn't do no good."

"Where were you headed with the ore?"

The man shook his head. "Wasn't no ore. Was all our savings, all the dust and nuggets we've collected. Decided to band together, transport it to a town for safe keeping."

"What town were you going to bring it to?" Rollie thought this sounded insane. As far as he knew there weren't any banks or strongholds in these parts of the Sawtooths.

The old man shrugged his shoulders. "We got rabbity. Figured we'd make for Boar Gulch. Never did, though."

Rollie said nothing, then the man said in a loud voice, "Well, we didn't want to get what Stumptown got!"

"What's Stumptown and what did it get?"

"Stumptown's a poor ol' mine camp southwest of here about half a day's ride, barely alive anymore. And even poorer now that she got robbed. Diggin's started to give out so some of us moved on, some stayed, figuring they were goin' to hit it any day. You know how it is."

Rollie nodded, guessing he was talking of the gold fever that grips everyone at some point in their lives, be it for cards or dice or poker or love. He added Stumptown to his mental list of places robbed by the gang.

"Others of us come up here, founded Stag Horn. Our luck stuck here, too." For a moment the man cracked a smile, then it faded as his present condition came back to him. "Now I got nothing. None of us do."

"You're alive. That's more than Elmer and Lily can say."

"Oh, I know that. Don't you think I don't know that?" The man rubbed his head and lowered his shotgun.

"I was about to stop and brew up some coffee. Care to join me?"

The old man really smiled then, and Rollie saw he had half the teeth he used to have. "Well now, that's mighty fine of you. Don't mind if I do. Step on down. Name's Sam. But most folks call me Sam." He paused, smiling at Rollie, then cackled and slapped his leg.

"Good one," said Rollie as he slid from the saddle and stretched his back.

An hour and two cups of coffee each later, Rollie learned a bit more from the old man about his quarry. One of the men, likely the leader, had a highish-sounding voice and part of his mouth was visible through his gunny sack, unlike most of the other men. Sam said the man wore thin moustaches.

Pencil-thin moustaches, eh? Same as the one who'd captured Pops. Rollie remembered the man in the bar who'd challenged Chauncey. He'd been a stranger, no one knew who he was, and he'd left with a couple other men, also unknown to regulars. High-pitched voice and thin moustaches.

As Rollie dumped out the last of the coffee from his battered, gray-enamel trail pot, the man stood and rubbed his rump, then eyed Rollie. "You're him, ain't ya?"

Rollie tensed, let his hand drift down to his holster.

The man saw him. "Don't worry yourself none. But if you're Stoneface Finnegan, then the head of the bandits said you was around these parts. Said you wasn't to be trusted, but not to worry as he'd be laying you low soon enough."

"Hmm," said Rollie.

"Yep. Well, far as I'm concerned, any man who shares his coffee pot with a stranger is a friend to me." He stroked his leather braces up and down and rocked back on his heels. "Yes sir, what's more, you let me know what I can do to help you, and I'll do it."

"Thanks," said Rollie, cinching the flap on his saddle-bag. "Keep an eye and ear open and don't challenge them if they ride back this way. And I'd appreciate it if you don't tell them you saw me."

"Easy enough. I'd ride with you but I ain't got a mount." His eyes grew wet and he looked away.

"Lily?" said Rollie.

"Yeah, yeah." He dragged a finger under his nose and snorted. "Okay then. I best get back to my diggins. Otherwise, I'll die old and broke. I'm already both of those and I can only fix one before I meet my maker." He thrust out a knobby old hand. "Good huntin', boy."

Rollie nodded, they shook hands, and he mounted up and rode on, offering Sam a quick two-finger wave over his shoulder.

Chapter Twenty-three

"There's something nice about a day when rain keeps you from tending to your tasks that ain't nothing but hard work outside. Wouldn't you say, Finchy?"

The burly, dark-bearded Reginald Finch, who his younger companion insisted on calling "Finchy," looked up from sniffing the stewpot. "I would have preferred to do my cooking out of doors, but as you say, it is raining."

"Aw now, Finchy, don't you fret. That little sheet-metal stove ain't let us down yet. Why, I even laid in enough wood to keep it glowing cherry red for hours to come. Yes, sir." The younger man, a skinny drink by the name of Wally Porter, rubbed his callused palms together brisk enough to kindle flame.

"I only wish we had some applejack to rasp the edge off the day. My arms sure are tired from swinging that pick and toting them satchels. But you say you think we're close, right? Huh, Finchy?"

The bearded man didn't bother looking at his chatty partner. He'd heard it all and then some over the past seven months they'd been working the claim. They'd met on the trail West, Finch from Pittsburgh and Wally from somewhere in Tennessee. Finch could never recall the name. It had the word hollow or gore in it. But he didn't care. The younger man had talked non-stop from the time they met and decided to throw in together to make a go of a claim somewhere, anywhere of promise, until today.

Even at night, when Finch lay awake thinking of more efficient ways of using their time or puzzling about different spots they might dig, even then he could hear Wally, plain as day, yammering nonsense in his sleep.

Finch had always been a patient man, one of the things his wife had harangued him about. She'd said he wasn't one for excitement or stimulation. He had to agree there. All he ever really wanted was to make a lot of money and open a small book shop in a small city somewhere far from Pittsburgh. Without Irene. And as soon as he and Wally made that fortune, enough to satisfy both of them, he would find that city and open that shop. Without Wally.

". . . expect we'll have to go for supplies one of these days, maybe we could afford a small bottle of applejack, you know, for medicinal—"

A sharp rapping rattled the door to their drafty little dugout. That shut up Wally. Both men stopped what they were doing—talking and stirring—and looked wide-eyed at the door. Neither could recall ever having a visitor. Maybe it was the wind.

Then the wind rapped again, three hard sounds, followed with, "Hello there—anybody home?"

Finch looked at Wally, held a thick finger to his lips, and dried his hands on his flour-sack apron. He crossed to the door and lifted down their sole weapon, a squirrel rifle they used to hunt small game and once, a slow-witted young buck. They had butchered it poorly and the meat tasted of strong musk that made their teeth grit and their nostrils flare. But they ate the whole thing, just the same.

Finch didn't know if the weapon was loaded, but he felt more confident in having it in hand when he opened the door. He flashed Wally one more quick glance. The young man's eyes were wide and his mouth, for once, was closed.

"Who is it?" said Finch, trying to make his voice lower than it was. It ended up sounding as if he had a cold.

"Why, what would that matter? I'm likely a stranger to you. I am getting soaked to the bone, friend. Can I come in and warm myself?"

It did sound miserable out there, maybe one of the worst storms they'd had since he and Wally had arrived in this remote mountain place. Finch was surprised their roof hadn't yet begun to leak on them.

Finch unwrapped the twine they used as a locking device by wrapping it from the handle over to a nail in the post doorframe. Twelve wraps it took. He knew because he had to go through the procedure at least once a night to urinate outside.

When he swung open the door, he was greeted with a man who looked to be horribly disfigured. The dim light from within the cabin, their sole lantern turned low to save on oil, moved as Wally shifted it. It showed Finch that the hideous man, no taller than he, was actually covered up on the face with sack cloth of some sort. Maybe to keep the rain off, thought Finch.

Then the man stepped forward and held before him a revolver, slick and shiny with raindrops. Finch didn't know much about guns, but he knew that revolver was fully cocked.

"Okay now," said the man. "Lean that rifle against the wall beside the door and back it up."

In that very moment of seeing the revolver aimed at him, Reginald Finch felt all the years of his life he'd spent as a quiet, bookish man flare with a sudden sharpness. And in that sharpness, he saw as clear as day that he'd accomplished nothing of worth.

Yet somehow, in that moment, the one thing he could do, should do, was fight back. And so Mr. Finch raised the rifle and rammed it forward, intending to knock the rain-slick pistol from the stranger's hand. It didn't work.

"Why?" shouted the stranger as he pulled the trigger on his revolver. In the small dugout, the muzzle erupted in a blast of flame once, twice.

Wally screamed and dropped the lantern as his pard, Finch, collapsed backward. His head knocked the stewpot off the stove where it clunked against the corner of a rough-split log bed frame.

"You got yourself killed and you wasted a perfectly good meal!" The masked man shook his head and stepped over the still-twitching man. He opened the door on the stove, and the low orange light was enough to see who was where in the little dingy room.

"You . . ." He wagged the pistol at Wally. "Light that lantern. Now!"

Wally gulped and found the lantern. He looked up when he heard voices and footsteps drawing closer. Three strange faces appeared in the doorway behind the masked man. They, too, wore bags and stared at him with freakish, owly eyes.

"Oh Lord!" said Wally, shaking so hard the cracked glass in the lantern rattled.

"Boss, you okay?" said one of the men.

"Yeah, yeah." The first man brushed at the soup glop dripping off his left sleeve. "You grab that drooling dough head over there, though. And don't hurt him. We'll need him."

Two of the men stepped by the boss and snagged hold of the now-whimpering Wally. He not so much fought them as sagged against them. "Stand up!" said one of the men, jerking him hard by the arms.

The third newcomer lit the lantern while the boss stuffed more wood into the stove.

"What'd you do to Finchy?" Wally couldn't stop staring at his dead partner.

"Well now, what does it look like?" said the man they called boss.

"You . . . you shot him! Why?"

"That's just what I asked him. He begged for it, though. Wasted all that soup. I could have used a bowl or three of that inside me. You boys?"

The three newcomers all declared their agreement.

"So now," said the boss, standing and jamming the barrel of his revolver under the clean-shaven chin of Wally. "You're going to do us a favor and if you do, then we'll do one for you, okay?"

Wally couldn't take his eyes from his unmoving friend on the floor.

"Hey!" The boss jerked the barrel hard up under the young man's chin, forcing his head upward.

"You understand?"

Wally nodded or tried to.

"Good. Now, it's simple. You tell us where your stash is, your gold, your dust and nuggets, and anything else of value you might have dug up, and then you'll get it for us. And then . . . we won't kill you. Okay?"

Wally nodded again.

"Good. And hurry it up because after that you're going to make us more soup. I have a hankering for some, and your stupid friend there ruined it for me."

"We . . . we don't have anymore potatoes."

"Huh?" said the boss.

"Potatoes," said Wally, as the two men holding him loosened their grips. "In here. I . . . I have to get the potatoes."

"Well, where are they, smart man?" The boss looked at his chums and winked. They laughed.

"In the root cellar. Out back."

"Worry about that in a minute. Where's your claim papers, your deed, your money, and your dust? Now. We're going to take this place apart anyway, so if we find you held out on us. you'll go the way of your friend, here, what did you call him, Finchy?"

Wally nodded.

"Well, you and Finchy can be pards after death, too. But it'll take a while. I know how the Apaches torture their victims, okay? I learned their techniques. It will take you a long, long time to die. Likely days." He leaned forward and looked into Wally's eyes.

Wally barely saw light glinting off the two dark eyes sunk deep in the holes in the wrinkled brown burlap sack, the mouth a collapsed thing beneath them. "You ever see a buzzard eat a man's innards while the man was still alive? No?"

Wally shook his head, his eyes wide.

"Well, let me tell you a thing, kid, it's not something you want to see. Especially if you're the man it's happening to." He nodded. "Yeah, it's that bad, kid. That bad."

"You," the boss pointed to the man who'd lit the lantern. "Take him and the light out to the root cellar for potatoes. He can get us some water while he's at it, then get him back in here so he can fix up the soup. Once that's bubbling, we'll see to that stash, okay?"

Wally knew there was little he could do to get out of the situation. It's not that he was a simple-minded fellow, as he liked to remind Finchy, it's just that he was like a dog when he was with someone who was smarter and better at taking care of things when they went awry, like he was with Finchy.

Finchy had never said much to that. He'd always just grunted and pushed past Wally without speaking. Now, with a killer in a mask nudging him outdoors and into a lashing rainstorm, Wally thought maybe that logic wasn't kind to Finchy. Maybe it looked to Finchy as if Wally was keen to shirk his duties.

"Not like it matters now," whispered Wally. By then they were out of doors, and the lantern was already sputtering and sizzling as heavy raindrops pelted it. Wally envisioned the entire mountainside taking flame, the only noises from rain hitting the roof, so he had to do something fast to avoid a fate such as Finchy had experienced.

Wally and the armed oaf rounded the back of the cabin and Wally's nerves quivered his legs as if they were bowls of water. They actually did have somewhat of a root cellar, but he would be damned if he was going to let these bums have any of their hard-earned money. The pouch was a ways off the southeast corner of the house, buried beneath a pile of rocks that looked like they'd been stacked that way forever and a day. That was Finchy's idea.

Man, Wally thought, *am I going to miss my pal Finchy.* And thinking that made him all the madder because just then the man with the lantern in one hand also had a revolver in the other, and he prodded Wally in the back again.

Usually, Wally would get in trouble with Finchy for not thinking a thing through. But as Finchy wasn't with him anymore, Wally decided to let it rip.

Emboldened by the intensity and roar of the pounding rain, the darkness of the night, and the sputtering of the lantern, Wally came up with a plan. One of his own special little-thought-needed plans. He gestured slowly with a pointing finger toward the slope behind the dugout and said, "There!"

The man prodding him nodded and jerked his gun toward the slope. "Well, get to it!"

Wally walked forward, the scree of the slope becoming slickened and oozy with the rain. He jammed in the toes of his boots, but his left foot slipped. He hadn't planned that, but since it was unexpected, it caused the man behind him to collide with him. Wally wrapped his hands around a flat rock twice as long as his head.

He was used to hard physical labor all day long and so hefting and swinging the rock was not a taxing task. He swung it from left to right, colliding with the gun in the man's right hand.

The gun did not go off, for which he would soon be thankful. Instead, it knocked clean out of the man's now-crumpled hand. The man screamed and let fall the lantern.

The glass broke, and the light pinched out for good. The bandit dropped to one knee and, cradling his battered limb, howled his rage, trying to rise once more on the rain-sodden slope. It did no good.

Wally lifted the rock again and swung it, this time from right to left, connecting with the howling man's grimy sack-covered head. He felt a peculiar sensation as if telegraphed up through the rock to his fingers and on up through the arm to his brain. It felt exactly like smashing old squashes left in the field too long in the autumn back home in Feeley Gore.

It was a satisfying feeling, he had to admit, as if he'd collapsed an entire range of mountains. Wally was invincible.

Wally stared down at what he thought might be the man he'd just laid low, but couldn't be certain because it was so dark. Any time now the men from the dugout would come after him. He had to figure out what to do. Now see, Finchy would have said, that's what you get for not thinking a thing through. You've got yourself trapped in a corner with no way out.

Then Wally smiled. Because for once, Finchy wasn't right. And would never be again, he reckoned. Wally spent about five seconds scrabbling for the lost revolver before he realized he'd never find it in all this darkness. He looked upslope, into the night, and ran a hand down his face once to clear away the rain, rain that soon covered his face as fast as it drove down.

He howled low once, a wild dog free, but for how long he did not know. Then Wally clawed his way upslope and prayed that the rain held out all night long. That would be long enough to make it to the Delphi Trading Post, especially if he cut crosswise over the jut of rocky range separating him from the sack-headed killers.

He didn't think the men were folks he knew, they acted like strangers, somehow. And they didn't sound like locals at all, which was good for Wally. That meant they wouldn't know the countryside like he did. A small bloom of hope, cupped in smugness, blossomed in his pounding chest.

He gained the top of the ridge in minutes and still heard no shouts or gunshots from below. Good. Even if the rain was masking the sounds, he felt sure he could outdistance them now. He knew where he was going, had to, or he'd end up dead. His biggest hope was that the rain would hold out and that night would go on for extra hours, for in it he was the masked one and they were blind.

It didn't work out that way for Wally. Within an hour, the rain had slowed to a drizzle, then by the time his legs felt as though they could not lurch another step, the rain ceased falling. It was still plenty dark, but now he could see stars here and there up past the sparse treetops. Then after another little while, he saw more stars. The clouds had passed by, leaving a cold clear night with plenty of starshine and a glow from the moon from somewhere. He didn't dare stop to take it in.

Wally kept limping forward, doing his level best to ignore the creeping shivers that had been with him all night but now felt as though they were settling in for a good, long while. His teeth rattled like rocks in a can, and his fingertips, under the nails, were near blue.

By the time the sun had risen enough for him to see, he recognized where he was, and it was close to where he wanted to be. He topped a slope that overlooked a river valley and down below saw thin trails of smoke rising up from the chimneys in each of a cluster of shacks ranged along the glinting snake of water far below, which bristled with sluices and mounds of dug gravel.

"Beetle River," he said, pleased with himself for choosing this direction. It was a mine camp he'd seen only once, four months before, but it was home to the Delphi Trading Post and to what looked to be a dozen or more miners. Surely, they were enough to stand up to marauding killers and thieves.

He felt renewed by the sight of the shacks, and he looked behind himself once more, but still saw no one. Switchbacking his way downward through trees and rocks and low, stunty bushes was not as simple as his new-found happiness wanted it to be. His legs began cramping once more. He'd stopped several times in the night to rub them but did not want to do so again.

Now that it was light out and his path ahead was taking him through open terrain, he would be an easy shot from above. "What were you thinking, Finchy? If ever there was a move that one of us didn't think through, it was raising the rifle on that man."

He'd been talking to Finchy all night, off and on, and the more tired he'd become, the more talking to his dead partner made sense. After all, Finchy wasn't much for keeping up his end of a conversation, so Wally had had to fill in both sides for as long as they'd known each other. So it wasn't unusual for him to not receive a response for hours.

Fifteen minutes later found him hobbling down the last of the slope, his breathing raspy, but a smile spread wide on his sweaty face. Somewhere along the trail he'd gashed open his right trouser leg below the knee, but though he felt the wound, he didn't care. Soon he'd be able to drink from the river and then shout to whichever cabin was closest.

That was the last thought he had, just before a bullet chewed a rock to his right. It came from behind him, up above on the slope. He half turned as he crouched low and stumbled to the left.

Another bullet whined close, too close. He flinched as he felt the spray of gravel as it burrowed into the slope above and another, on its heels, found soft purchase in his muscled left shoulder. He pitched forward to his knees, gripping the arm with his right hand. He felt the warm trickle of blood, his blood, and rose once more, beelining for the river and cursing himself for taking one too many breaks in the dark.

How had they followed him? He'd tried not to leave a trail, tried not to make too much noise . . . except for the talking. Yes, he'd talked and talked most all night long. Finchy always would smile and say that Wally's mouth would get him into trouble one day.

He lunged for the river, felt the soft squish and squelch of the bank as it sank and gave beneath his wet boots. He saw a man across the river, then another emerged from the closest shack. They visored their eyes against the morning sun, unsure of the commotion so early in the day, and right out their front door, too.

Wally waved to the men with his right hand and shouted, "Help! There are masked—"

That was all Wally would get to say because another bullet delivered from on high drove into his back and pitched him forward, both arms up as if he were finding salvation in the water he slammed down into.

He was still alive but somehow unable to do the one thing that had never before failed him. Wally could no longer speak. And soon, even the rich colors of the graveled riverbottom, through the ice-clear water, were lost to his sight.

Chapter Twenty-four

Twenty minutes after he finished nosing through the remnants of the wagon robbery, which included eyeing the carcass of poor Lily and taking stock of the boot- and hoofprints pocking the scene, a savage wind nearly peeled off Rollie's hat. Only a quick smack of his hand squashed it down, clamping it to his head. He lifted it off, freed up the stampede strap, and snugged the hat down nearly to his ears once more, cinching the strap tight beneath his jaw.

A glance over his shoulder revealed a menacing swirl of purple-black clouds barreling at him low from the east. Fingers of wind daggered into him, and he knew it was but a sampling of a gullywasher of a storm. Thunder pounded the thought into place and twenty seconds later, lightning razored the bleak sky.

He'd sensed something earlier, pulsing aches in his joints and old wounds, divots in his hide from a score of knife fights, creases from bullets. He felt throbs from the deep wounds in his leg and back and lungs from his near-death attack from the alley in Denver City, barely half a year ago since the attack.

"Cap," he said, knowing the horse likely didn't hear

him and wouldn't care if he had. "We need to find shelter, and quick."

No sooner had he uttered the words than he felt the first tiny fists of rain pelt into his vest's back, felt the cold of the rain through his thin shirt sleeves. They were traveling upslope, and he heeled Cap into faster action, to gain the top and then get off trail. Thunder and lightning were pounding and stitching closer together, booming across valleys now hidden by gloom and low, eerie fog, lighting for the briefest of moments the land about him, revealing the raw stalks of trees and bald faces of rock.

He didn't want to be in anything resembling a worn sluiceway, just like the trail looked from months of the digging hooves of animals hauling people and goods. He felt Cap's powerful muscles working to carry them both upward. He guided him off trail to the left, threading between sparse pines and low, stunty brush. The slope leveled off and a thicker stand of trees looked as though it might offer some relief from the coming rain.

Rollie slid from the saddle and, in his stiff-legged lope, led the much smoother-walking horse to the trees. He parted smaller trees crowding the base of the larger, and a man-size flash of brown and white startled him, staggered him backward into Cap, who jerked, nearly taking the reins from Rollie's hand.

He regained his stance, already tugging free his revolver, but he stayed his hand as he watched an equally befuddled mule deer bolting away and out of sight.

"Sorry, chum," said Rollie. "Didn't see you there." He poked deeper into the copse and found it wasn't too bad, plenty of still-dry needles on the ground. He palmed the spot and found fleeting warmth there from the deer. All in all, the spot could have been worse. They could have used more branches up high to deflect the rain, but beggars can't be choosers.

He scraped together a mound of needles and toed them under a close-by jut of ledge. It looked tall and deep enough that he might be able to squeak under there seated, maybe make a warming fire should the storm prove to have any lasting power.

He tied Cap to a low branch, hobbled him, and wasted no time in uncinching his waxed duster from behind the cantle, where it rode wrapped around his soogans. He looked to the sky and didn't need to, as the darkness felt like a mighty shadowing presence looming over him. Certainly, felt like it was going to be a long, drawn-out corker of a storm.

As soon as he was dressed in his raingear, Rollie stripped his saddle and blanket from Cap and shoved them beneath the ledge. It ran long for a few yards, deeper at the close end, deep enough that he was able to nudge the saddle in and have plenty of room left over to protect a small fire and still sit with his legs nearly extended.

Cap wouldn't fare, as well. Already the horse stood hip-shot and with a hangdog droop to his head. He seemed resigned to the soaking he was about to receive.

Rollie felt bad about it but not bad enough to slow his gathering of a goodly supply of sticks and duff for a fire. It had been a few hours since he'd had coffee with Sam, the old crotchety miner, and he was about ready for a round of food and a hot drink. It was unlikely any bandits were doing anything but what he was doing—holing up and huddling around a fire.

The late afternoon storm turned into a long-term soaker

that the region needed. It had been a dry spell of late, so Rollie didn't much mind. "Not that I have any say in the matter," he said, sipping his coffee.

He dribbled a little whiskey in the cup, aware he shouldn't overdo it, then he mused on the rain off the lip of the ledge above him, dripping just beyond his boots. He'd always enjoyed rainy days and felt happier and more relaxed in the rain.

Never could understand folks who whined about rainy days and called them "bad weather." Seemed to him rain did nothing but good things for crops and water supplies. Of course, too much rain could lead to flooding, but that was unlikely for him today.

Rollie sighed and flexed his tocs in his boots. He hoped the scalawags would stay hidden until tomorrow. Cap appeared to be dozing, half covered in the marginal shelter of the branches and he himself was downright comfortable in his little rocky niche.

He'd laid in enough wood to keep his tiny fire fed for a few hours yet. After that, since it was close to dark and still raining without sign of let-up, Rollie figured he'd spend the night in the spot. Could do worse, he told himself and pondered what he was going to fix for supper.

"Let's see," he said, rummaging in his saddlebag. "Either a handful of Geoff the Scot's hardtack tooth wreckers and a can of pears, or jerky, hardtack, and pears. So many choices." In truth, Rollie knew it wouldn't take much to make him happier. Combine his meager but filling supplies with hot coffee and a few splashes of whiskey, and he was set for the evening.

And that's just how Rollie's evening went, with nary a sign of an outlaw emerging out of the gloom between the steady, driving drizzle. The next day, he felt sure somehow, would bring success of some sort.

Shots, he thought he heard shots in the middle of the night. Far off, but gunshots, nonetheless. He'd bet money on it. Unless they were branches snapping close by.

Rollie listened but heard no more. He nudged his hat back off his face and waited. He heard nothing but the steady, driving rain. His fire had gone out, and he was cold and stiff. What hour it was he did not know. He could flick a match and check his pocketwatch, but why? Dark was dark and he couldn't do anything in it but wait for light. There was a time when he could have guessed, within a few minutes, the time of day or night, without problem. Those days, much like his ability to run without wobbling, were long gone.

He sighed. "You good, Cap?"

He didn't expect the horse to reply, and he wasn't disappointed when he didn't. So what if he'd heard shots? Not like he could do anything about them in the rain and at this hour. He crossed his legs again and tugged his hat down to rest on his nose once more. But he was still awake, and he stayed that way for a long while.

It was still raining, but slightly less dark, when he grumbled and growled and scooted on his backside to the lip of rock. A half-dozen drops of drip water found that spot between his collar and his neck when his head was bent forward as he struggled to his feet.

The cold water sluicing down his back shivered him and forced his eyes open wide. He stamped his feet to rid himself of the pins-and-needles feeling pestering them and made his way over to Cap. The big horse still stood with his head bent. He swung it around and nickered soft and low.

"Hey, fella." He patted the horse's neck. "You look as miserable as I feel."

He gazed into the drizzling gloom, but still saw little. Not much else to do but make water, then make coffee. He retrieved his pot, which he'd set beneath one runnel of drip water drizzling off the rock. It had filled in minutes. He drank a couple of cups of water, then dusted in more of the beans he'd ground back home for the trail. If he wasn't careful, he'd run low. "Should have brought more coffee. I always say that."

An hour later found him cleaning out his coffee pot, chewing on a particularly unappealing strip of jerked elk meat, and repacking his gear. He could see much of what he was doing because of the morning's increasing light and because the rain was thinning by the minute. He used the outer canvas wrap of his soogans to wipe down Cap, who seemed perky, given the night's long, wet conditions he'd endured with stoic resignation.

"Almost there, boy. Be on the trail in no time, you just wait."

He doubted, if the horse understood his lingo, that Cap would find much in the way of excitement at being saddled and hauling Rollie's carcass over the rocky terrain.

Rollie rode upslope, crossing brown gushes of stream emboldened by the storm. At one point he thought he heard gunshots far ahead. At least three. He waited but heard no more.

He made it to the top of the ridge several hours after breaking camp, and paused there, gazing downward.

The hillside led toward a river. Across it squatted several low shanties cobbled together with logs and a few rough-plank doors. Smoke drifted up from most of the chimneys. The river, really more a glorified brook, thundered with last night's rain. Sluices dotting the flow stood empty, and several men were in sight, ambling to the river or off to outhouses tucked by the trees.

"Well, Cap, let's see what this place calls itself, and if the miners here have seen any sign of malcontents."

Halfway down the long, rocky slope, Rollie saw the remnants of tracks in a long trail that joined his, but wound down from north of where he'd emerged from the trees at the top. There were many of them, and as he switchbacked he kept them in sight. They were not much bothered by rain so that means the riders who made them, at least a half-dozen of them, had come through within the past couple of hours. Could well be his quarry.

He glanced upslope, saw no one, and pulled out his pistol, kept it in his left hand as he guided Cap down the trail. The men across the river had caught sight of him and stopped what they were doing. One of them said something to another, then rushed over to a cabin. Before long there were a dozen men standing outside their cabins, some with cups of coffee in their hands.

He'd almost reached the river when he reined up. There were boot tracks here, then scuffs, as if someone had run, shoving off the gravel? This, too, had happened after the rain had stopped. Not unusual, but the thing he saw next was.

He'd seen enough blood in his years, had caused it to

leak out of others, witnessed the blood of his quarries' victims, and on occasion watched his own leak out. So the black-red stains on the rocks and the dark patch of gravel near them all told him one thing: Someone had been shot or stabbed.

He climbed down out of the saddle and toed the bloodied rocks, eyed the surrounding gravel. There, finger marks, as if someone were down on their knees or flat on their belly, digging with their fingers, trying to . . . what? Crawl forward? Likely.

"Hey!" he shouted across the river. "What happened here?"

The men did as he expected—nothing. They stared at him. He mounted up and walked Cap across the river. The closer he rode, the more he took in of the place. It wasn't so much a mine town as a rough camp. The men looked like half the fringe residents of Boar Gulch. Lots of beards, unwashed faces, and grimy hands. They were greasy and dirty, their trousers and shirts, and faces and hair stiff with it. Some of the men looked half-wet, as if they'd spent the night in worse conditions than he had. Maybe their roofs leaked, thought Rollic.

Cap walked up out of the river, and Rollie saw the mass of hoofprints again. Whoever the riders were, they rode right through here. Rollie angled Cap alongside the river, his left side toward the men, his right toward the river and the mountainside he'd just ridden down. He held the cocked Schofield balanced on the saddlehorn and aimed at the men.

"What happened over there?" Rollie jerked his head to the right, indicating where he'd yelled from the opposite bank, at the bloodied spot.

No one said anything. He looked them each up and down. Up close they didn't seem menacing so much as uncertain, maybe even frightened. One of the men shrugged, looked away. One of them wore a revolver, an ancient looking thing in a holster that sagged off his thin frame. None of them looked particularly healthy.

"The riders who came through here, were they masked?" Again, the men said nothing.

"Did they go anywhere or are they still here?"

They were frightened, now he could see that. He felt a prickling up his neck, but knew he was close to something. Some sort of moment. He sought out the weakest-looking one, a younger man. Under his thin, sparse beard he saw dark eyes and an unlined face, a narrow frame, shoulders not yet thickened with the weight that hard labor drapes on a man.

Rollie looked straight at him and in a lower voice said, "They still here?"

The young man said nothing, but looked back at him, and in his eyes, Rollie saw the slightest of widenings, as if the kid were trying to nod without using his head, just his eyes.

Okay, then. That was something. Time to play along so I can get more answers. Rollie sighed. "Well, if you don't mind, I'd like to step down."

"No!" said one of the men, a middle-aged fellow with a paunch belly and a thick beard the color of honey.

"No?" said Rollie, hoisting his leg up and over the saddle. He finished dismounting, then faced the men. "Now what's that mean? Not very neighborly of you."

"He means we . . ." said a skinny old man.

"Yeah?" said Rollie.

"We have a sickness hereabouts. You'd do well to ride on out of here."

Nods circulated among them like they were contagious.

"Well, nobody wants to be sick any less than me. Boy, I tell you, nothing worse than an autumn chill that won't leave you alone." As he talked, Rollie kept his revolver drawn and keeping the men to his left and the river to his right, he led Cap past them.

The kid looked at him again, and Rollie offered a quick wink. "Yep, I was telling my friend, Pops, any of you ever met him? No? Well, you'd like him, he's got a sense of humor that won't quit. Anyway, I was telling him just the other day that there are few things in life a man would like less than coming down with something like a head ailment or chesty croup or worse. Yes sir . . ."

He lashed Cap's reins to a stout-looking log and slid the rifle from its scabbard. The group of men had turned and watched him as he walked and talked. None of them unfolded their arms or changed their expressions. Rollie didn't much care. He'd seen all he needed to in that young man's eyes. Somebody who shouldn't be there was in camp, and unless it was one of the rag-tag bunch of miners staring him down, which he doubted to high heaven, he'd find them.

There were ten or more cabins arrayed before him, along the river's edge. They'd be lucky to live through one of these flooded mountain rivers when the big melt came as it did every year. They had his sympathy, but little else. Even a dolt could see the chewed slope where the river had gnawed its way up out of its regular course sometime last spring.

Rollie walked upslope, angling toward the closest of

the cabins, his revolver holstered, the rifle levered and cocked and laid across his arm. He didn't walk full-on toward the shack but stepped sideways to it, presenting a thinner target, he hoped, to whoever was hiding in one of these shanties. He tried to take in everything about the structure, and those beyond. Any movement and he'd drop and fire. He hated to be in this exposed position, but he had little choice.

A chill morning breeze belied the bright sunlight and promising clear, blue sky. It should still be summer, he thought. I'm not ready for autumn, and I'm damn sure not ready for winter. A flap of dried bark wagged on one of the upright logs that formed the uphill corner of the first shack. There was no window on this side, but that didn't mean whoever might be inside couldn't see through a poorly chinked gap.

The wind soughed down the river valley, lifting a swirl of dust. Despite the heavy rain, the high desert setting would not be denied.

Rollie glanced to the cluster of men by the river, downslope to his left. Only hat brims and bushy beards waggled in the breeze. The eyes stayed rooted on him. A raven sawtoothed above the clearing, winging north-westward.

Rollie was within ten feet of the cabin when a raspy cough sounded from beyond. It wasn't from this cabin. He covered the last feet quickly and jammed himself right to the corner. The chinking on this end of the cabin was intact and the logs were tight enough that he didn't think a gun barrel could be poked between and make him a bleeder.

Scabs of pine bark felt rough against his cheek as he peered around the corner toward the next cabin. He could see half of it. The smell of dried pitch tickled his nostrils. It was a good smell, though, and reminded him of warm summer days, insects buzzing, and cold beer. Then the cough rasped once more, was stifled by something, almost sounded like something that said, "Shhh!"

"Okay then," whispered Rollie. "Next cabin it is." He leaned out, saw most of the next cabin. If anyone were in this one, he'd have his back exposed to them if he tried to creep closer to the other. As it turned out, he didn't need to worry about it.

A shout burst from the cabin as the crude door whipped outward and slammed into a rock that held up the front wall. A man lurched out of the black mouth of the doorway, a pistol aimed roughly in Rollie's direction. He was shouting and staggering, and even from this distance Rollie could see the man was not well. His face was bright red and streaming with sweat. Rollie could practically feel the heat leaching off the man.

The lurcher didn't look like the other men. He was dressed more like a gun hand than a miner. His clothes were not overly mended, he wore a short-waisted coat, a stiff-brim hat, and a dagger beard, though his cheeks bore scruff and his eyes were red-rimmed and wild. The clothes might have been nice once, but they were now sodden and soiled, as if he'd spent the night in the rain.

"Hold there!"

The stranger, still facing him, raised the revolver.

"I said hold!" shouted Rollie again, peering around the far corner of the shack, his rifle aimed at the man.

In response, the man cranked off two shots.

Rollie jerked back behind the corner in time to see part of the log inches from his nose bust apart. Fevered or no, that man was a decent shot. Rollie peeked again and saw the man in the open, weaving in place, as if unsure of which way to turn.

Rollie bent low, pivoted out on his left leg and shouted, "Hey!"

The man spun his head and fired from the waist, but not before Rollie sent a bullet of his own at the man. It caught him in the upper left arm and spun him. His revolver flew from his grasp, and he spasmed as if he'd slammed his hand in a hot stove door. He continued his weird dance, spinning completely around until he dropped on his back, writhing and screaming.

Rollie ran to the man and stomped on his wounded wing, feeling the bones grate beneath his boot. The man howled, long and loud.

"Shut up!" growled Rollie. He bent low and stuffed the rifle's snout in the man's face, an inch from his nose. "Who are you and what are you doing here?"

He glanced over at the miners, and was surprised to see they had moved closer. Their faces had lost some of that nervous wariness he'd seen when he first rode up.

"Is he the only one?" Rollie shouted at them. They mumbled, still not meeting his gaze. He stomped again on the arm of the man sprawled at his feet, then he jerked the rifle up to aim at the mass of the weak-kneed men. "I asked you a question—kindly answer me."

As a group they staggered backward, and one man held up his hands. The burly one with the honey-color beard. "Look, mister. We had nothing to do with this!"

"With what?" said Rollie, easing up the rifle barrel. He didn't like to play the hard-nose with them, but they gave him no option.

"He was one of about eight," said the man, walking forward. He looked back to his friends for support and received ardent head nods.

"When?"

"Not but an hour, maybe two before you arrived. Rode on through, but this one—"

"Shut up!" shouted the man on the ground. "Shut your mouth—you'll pay for the misdeeds . . ."

Rollie waited for the man to finish his odd statement but he fogged over again and made mewling, whining sounds as he writhed beneath Rollie's boot. Any man in his right mind would have tried to flip Rollie off him by now, maybe twist a boot or drive a knife into his leg. But this fool was addled, that was plain to see. Addled and fevered. The second likely led to the first.

"Don't pay him any mind," said Rollie as he ground his boot once more into the wounded man's arm. He howled a blue streak, but his fevered ravings soon took over. Rollie hoped it wasn't something catching.

The blond man swallowed and licked his lips. "The men, they shot a fella here."

"Across the river, where I shouted from?" said Rollie.

"Yeah." The burly miner nodded. "Fella they shot wasn't from here, this is Stag Horn, by the way. But we knew of him and his partner. This one's name was Wally something. His partner went by the name of Finch. Good men, have a claim a ways from here, back up east, toward where you come from."

Rollie considered this a moment. That would mean

the road agents likely attacked those men at their camp, then this Wally fellow escaped and they tracked him here.

"This Wally, is he dead?"

The miners nodded. The kid spoke up. His voice suited him, all squeaks and nervousness. "They shot him twice, never gave him a chance!"

"Why did they leave this one?" Rollie kicked the man in the ribs. He moaned and fluttered his eyelids. He was in a delirium, that was certain.

The big miner shrugged. "Sickly, near as we could figure. But they said they might be trailed, like they was expecting you to come along. They also said that if we told anybody they'd been here they'd come back and kill us. They already took our pokes, all our money. Wasn't much. I don't know why they bothered. The gold's scant hereabouts. Been that way for months."

Rollie worked to suppress a smile. If he had a nickel for every time one of his customers told him that about their own claims, he'd be a wealthy barkeep.

"Anybody have any rope?"

The men looked at him as if he'd just asked for a pillow and a hot meal. Finally, the young man said, "I do. Me and Pap, we brought too much of some things with us, not enough of others."

Nobody of an age to be the kid's father stood near him, so he figured Pap must have met with an untimely end. Hard life for a slim chance at a motherlode.

"You the law?"

Rollie was tempted to say no, because he wasn't really a lawman.

He pulled in a deep breath and nodded. "Yeah, yeah,

more or less. And the gang that rode through here and shot your friend, Wally, has been robbing the miners all through the hills, from south of here at Black Rock, over to Stumptown, Low Cat, and then up by my town of Boar Gulch."

At that the big man with the light beard raised his eyebrows. "You're him, ain't you?"

Here we go, thought Rollie. "Depends who you think him is."

"Stoneface! Stoneface Finnegan! I heard all about you. They said you were in these parts. I never figured I'd meet up with you."

"A couple of the other men mumbled, one or two looked impressed, but still guarded, with their arms folded before them. But the blond-haired man smiled broadly and walked forward, a hand out. Rollie lowered the rifle to him again. "Not yet, son. Stay back, if you don't mind. Things need doing here, and they need doing in the proper order."

"Oh, okay, sir."

"Try to remember exactly how many men there were. And you, boy, go fetch that rope, if you please."

The kid nodded and gangled off toward a small log hut at the far end of the camp. Rollie looked down at the man at his feet. He had passed out. Then he looked back to the miners, who had become more relaxed, but still didn't quite know what to do with themselves.

"Which way did they ride?" Rollie eyed them all, hoping for a flinching look. He got several. "Well?"

The blond-bearded man said, "Straight west," he

pointed with a thick, callused hand. "You can just make out the trail from here."

Rollie could, a well-chewed path that cut left, right, left through the nearby trees, then across a small meadow, up and back into the trees again.

"How many men were there?" said Rollie, trying to smooth his voice to something less than a bark.

"Eight," said the burly man. Then he looked over his shoulder. "Eight?"

His townsmen nodded, shrugged.

"Including this one?"

"Yeah . . . I think so."

"Why didn't you overpower him if you knew he was the only one left here?"

Again, the man shrugged. "He was armed. They took all our guns. Only one they left us was Clem's service pistol there." He nodded toward the man with the drooping gunbelt.

Clem looked at his boots. "It don't work no more. Seized up in a rain once, never got around to fixing it."

"We were discussing what to do when you rode out of the trees on the eastern trail above the river."

"Come to any conclusions?"

They looked at each other. "Not much, no."

"Well, I have. I'm going after them. But first I'm going to get this one to talk. Then I'm going to hang him."

"Oh," said Clem and stepped backward.

"That necessary?" said the burly blond man.

"Yep. He's a thief who rides with killers, might be a killer himself. Me and my partner have tracked them for some time now, and they keep eluding us. I need to stop them before they rob more folks such as yourselves and kill others such as Wally."

"What do you think happened to Finch?" said a gaunt man with dark, piercing eyes and ears that stuck out like handles off the sides of his head.

The young man returned with a big coil of decent rope, long enough and new enough to do the job, reasoned Rollie. "Thank you." He nodded to the youngster.

To the others, he said, "I'm guessing Finch is dead. Likely why Wally bolted from them. The rain covered his escape, but they ran him aground here." Rollie shook out the rope and smoothed one end. "I'm surprised they didn't kill you all."

"We begged," said the kid, not looking up.

"No shame in saving your life however you can, son." That raised the kid's gaze. Rollie nodded to him as he finished tying the noose. He doubted, from what he knew of the gang, that begging would have dissuaded them from killing them all. It was as likely that the leader suspected he was being dogged and wanted to make tracks. To where, Rollie wished he knew.

"What's west of here, the direction they rode?"

"Whitneyville," said the blond man. "About fifteen miles."

Rollie was surprised. He didn't think he'd ridden that far west. He knew of Whitneyville, of course, it being a sizable town, bigger than the Gulch, at any rate. But he had thought it too far to venture to for his supplies.

"There's something else, Mr. Finnegan," said the boy.

"Oh?"

The kid turned red and looked at his boots, then up at

Rollie again. "They were all wearing masks. Like you said."

Rollie nodded. "Thanks."

"Even him," said the kid, nodding at the man on the ground, who was coming around.

"Where's his mask now, son?"

"Probably in that cabin. He holed up in there when he saw you coming. Told us we had better not say anything or he'd make sure he'd kill us all when the boss came back."

"Did the boss or any of the other men say anything else to you? Anything at all that might be useful to me?"

"Naw, just a lot of threats. Took all our money, all our nuggets and dust. Drove off our horses and mules."

"Where's Wally's body?"

"In that same cabin where that fella there was holed up."

"Could you go get that hood he wore?"

The kid nodded and went off to retrieve it. Rollie motioned to the miners. "I could use help in fitting him with his necktie."

The eager young blond man hurried over and hoisted the rogue to his feet. "Put this noose around his neck before he comes to fully. Then take whatever of his you find of value and divide it up if you can."

The blond man hesitated after he slipped the noose over the man's head. Another fellow someone had called Clem strode over and began taking the man's gear off him, from the vest and shirt all the way to the boots. They soon had the man stripped down to his woolen long johns.

The kid returned with a burlap sack with crude eyeholes cut in it. He handed it to Rollie. "Thanks." He gestured with his gun. "Those boots look decent. Serve you better in the coming cold than what you have, I bet."

"Here," Rollie handed the blond-bearded man the rope. "Hold this. I have to look in your cabins, I don't mean any offense. But where there's one rat, others are sure to linger."

Nobody argued. They were all busy rummaging through the meager pile of goods and clothes with vigor. The kid took the boots and sat down on the ground with a sigh and held the boots next to his own. Rollie noticed his own were worn clean through the sole leather in a big spot on each, with what looked like paper or cloth poking through the holes.

He knew that without money or means to trade for goods at Whitneyville, and with no mounts to get them there, these men would not last long into the late autumn, let alone winter. He had to find the bandits and make this right.

At least he knew where they were headed. He only wished Pops was here with him.

By then the man had come around again, he'd been coughing and snotting himself. Rollie didn't think whatever the man had was contagious, likely a chesty cold worsened by last night's damp-bringing storm. But to be safe, he did his best to keep from firing range of the man's raspy coughs.

"What . . . what's this rope?" The man's grimy fingers crabbed the knotted hemp affair about his neck. "I don't understand . . ." His voice was higher than before, a sign he was getting worked up. He spun on his backside, trying to get up, and noticed he had been stripped clean down to his longhandles. Given the man's sickness, nobody had tried to remove those from him. "Where are my clothes at? Where are my—"

"Shut up," said Rollie. "Until I tell you to talk." He jerked the rope, and the man gagged and looked at him.

For some reason the man seemed to understand him and complied. Good, thought Rollie. Save me having to jerk him by the neck again. "Stand up," said Rollie. "Now we're going to take a walk over to the trees. Get out of this blazing sun, okay?"

The man nodded, his head lolling a little, then he looked up at Rollie. "What?"

"Oh, Lord." Rollie had officially lost his temper and began dragging the man by the noose. They reached the nearest thicket of stout pines.

He selected a branch not more than a dozen feet high at the edge of the trees.

"What are you going to do?" screamed the man, trying to edge himself away from the trees.

Rollie was having none of it and jerked the rope again. "Where did the men go?"

"What men?" A coughing jag doubled the man over as he held his gut.

"Poor try," said Rollie. "One more chance."

"Okay, okay." He dragged his forearm across his mouth, then touched his thin lips tight as he tried to swallow. "Hurts," he said, "to swallow."

Rollie jammed him in the gut with his rifle barrel. "You don't hurry up, that sore throat's going to get a whole lot worse."

"Now, now, hold on there a minute, fella. The others will be dancing, I think, some time soon," said the sickly man.

Rollie sighed. It seemed to him that during the rain, this weak-kneed outlaw had gone too far around the bend in his sickness. He felt raw animal heat from the man's fever wafting off the sick devil. He wasn't going to get a single useful word out of this fool and might just end up with a chesty croup himself if he kept near the spittle-spewing bastard.

Rollie looked over at the miners. Most of them didn't move, and none met his gaze. "I'll need a chair or a stump for a few minutes." He looked at the miners. One old man raised a finger as if to say, "Hold on a moment, I'll fetch one." And he did, from the nearest cabin, about two-hundred feet down the easy slope.

"Thank you," said Rollie as the old buck returned with a stout, hand-built chair. He nodded and resumed his spot at the rear of the small group.

Rollie jerked the man, who'd begun to babble and drool again, over to a spot beneath the stout limb he'd selected. He was going to tell the man to stand there but instead the bugger collapsed to his knees. Blood pumped once more out the bullet hole Rollie'd given him in the arm earlier.

He whipped the rope upward, and it sailed right over the branch, first try, about six feet out from the trunk. He snagged the swinging end and held it in one hand. "Somebody help me get this fool up on the chair."

The blond-bearded man strode up. Rollie noticed the glint of eagerness in his eyes had lessened. The man licked his lips and helped Rollie hoist the delirious man up to a standing position on the chair. The outlaw's knees refused to stay locked.

"Hey!" shouted Rollie. "Wake up and stand up."

It helped. The man revived, came to himself enough to stand. The burly young man steadied the outlaw and the chair while Rollie walked the rest of the rope to the trunk. He took up the slack until the rope ran in a rigid course from the man's neck to the branch above. There was enough to loop it around the tree's trunk twice, then tie it off.

"Don't know!" the man screamed, the rope biting into his throat and making him gag. "Boss is always around, I tell you. Why—" The man spun on his heels, looking into the trees, then downslope toward the little cabins and the river beyond.

"Boss said he'd always be around, would know when we were betraying him and would be there to shoot us dead before we could turn on him! He's out there right now. Oh Lord, I can feel it!"

From there the man slipped into his whimpering, sobbing routine, sagging against the rope, mashing his left ear hard against his head. It looked to Rollie as if the thing might peel right off.

He was getting nowhere with this jackass. He also didn't have time to wait for the man to get well. And he didn't trust these men to keep guard over him while he went on after the rest of the gang.

"Okay, son. It's your lucky day," said Rollie. "I'm about to heal that arm of yours and your chesty croup and your deliriums. All of your ailments, all at once."

"Huh? You a magic man like I heard about one time?"

"Something like that," said Rollie as he steadied the man's legs. "You have anything you need to say to anyone, like God?"

"What? Heal me! Wait, what are you fixing to do? Man, you go to hell . . ."

"You first," said Rollie, and he kicked the chair sideways.

The man shrieked and dropped. As he gagged, he jerked hard, his untied arms clawed at his neck where the flesh bulged and bunched above the rope. His face purpled and his eyes bugged, wide and veining. Ropes of sickly spittle and blood burst from his mouth, laced his heaving chest and whipping legs and arms.

Rollie glanced at the miners. Most of them regarded the scene as if a two-headed mountain goat had just strolled into camp. The rest, the boy included, looked away. Rollie felt bad about the boy. Maybe he should have warned the kid. Too late now.

It took the man several minutes more to settle down and stop his thrashing.

Rollie walked down the slope, the chair in one hand. He handed it to the old man who'd given it to him. "Obliged."

He joined the cluster of miners and looked up at the hanging man, slowly spinning at the end of the rope. "I'd give him a few hours before untying the rope."

"Where you going?"

"After his gang. If I can recover your goods, I will. You said they drove off your stock."

"Oh, they can't have got far, we was fixing to send someone after them before you rode up."

Rollie nodded. "One last thing—any of you know where Wally and Finch's cabin is?"

Clem raised a hand. "I do. Been there a few times."

"Okay, you might want to go up there, couple of you.

I expect you'll find Finch dead, maybe not. But you might want to bury him, too. Maybe lug Wally back if you can find a mount to do the hauling. Be a kindness, them being pards and all."

"Yeah, we should do that, should do that," said the old man with the chair. "Finch and Wally, they was good boys. Didn't deserve this."

Rollie walked down the slope, still holding his rifle in his right hand and slid it back into its scabbard. He untied Cap, who'd been tied loose enough to crop at the still-green grass along the river's edge. He led the horse to the river for a drink.

Rollie mounted up and rode Cap slowly back through the narrow trail that bisected the scatter of crude cabins. He gazed once at the men who were watching him. The old man said, "Good luck to you, mister."

"Get 'em!" said another.

"Get 'em for Finch and Wally!"

Rollie nodded once more at the grim, but now vaguely hopeful faces. "I'll do my best." He touched his hat brim and heeled Cap into a lope, following the barely visible trail that threaded uphill into the dark forest beyond.

Chapter Twenty-five

The trail of the outlaws wasn't difficult to find and then follow. Too easy, in fact. And that told Rollie plenty. It was as if he was expected. Again, he wouldn't mind having Pops along. Funny, he mused, on how dependent he'd become on having a partner in these shenanigans. And it hadn't taken long, just a few short months of intense trouble in and around Boar Gulch, for him to rely on Pops.

"But he's not here," said Rollie. "And I am." He forced himself to focus on the trail, on the grim possibilities awaiting him, especially if he didn't tighten up and think like he used to when tracking criminals—think like a beast on the hunt.

Early on the ride he stopped several times and checked tracks, horse dung, and obvious spots where his quarry had also stopped for a rest, usually where their route took them to a stream. Here and there Rollie found the deadened ends of cigarettes.

Three hours after leaving the miners, he came across a small fire ring, sloppily built for the purpose of a cup of coffee. He knew this because a mound of spent ground beans sat in the midst of the fire, sodden with what smelled like urine.

"At least they took pains to put out the fire," he mumbled. A hand held low verified what he suspected. Cold.

They weren't but a few hours ahead, three, four at the most. But that only meant he had to advance slowly, for they could have split up. It was difficult on some of the terrain he was passing through, to keep track of the number of horses that had come this way.

Not long, perhaps twenty minutes after leaving the fire ring, their trail departed from the worn path obviously taken by many travelers over previous months, perhaps years. He suspected it had been in use for some time by tribes as it cut through a series of notches layered like great, raking, rocky teeth rising to either side of him. If he continued on this trail, he suspected it would lead west deeper into Oregon Territory, in due time.

But the men he was tracking, he counted seven of them now, which agreed with the miners' assessment of their numbers, had departed from that worn trail and now chose a rougher, unproven route alongside the east flank of this series of ridges. Such features, he pondered, had to be why the Sawtooths got their name.

The land was still forested, and they were now headed in a northerly fashion. What was the man's game? Luring him far from wherever they thought Rollie was most comfortable? He sneered and adjusted his grip on the Winchester, flexing his thumb. He was comfortable wherever a handful of blood-loving killers happened to be.

They could lead him straight into the fiery gates of the netherworld and as long as he had life in his limbs and a gun on his hip—and perhaps his long knife—Rollie

Finnegan was right at home. It was a good feeling he'd come to learn over the past year. He didn't need a badge to justify his actions, not in a place where evil slithered like spring rattlers snaking out over the land.

Dark would come soon and he was no closer to them than he had been all day. But their leader was a bright one. He might well guess Rollie would plan a surprise attack in the night. But he'd be wrong. Not on this night. He'd gotten poor rest the night before and he was trailing seven men who knew he was behind them. Or guessed he was, at any rate.

No, he'd seek out a rocky grotto among the massive tumbledowns to his left and before night would give him away with reflected firelight, he'd kindle a small cookfire, have a hot meal and coffee, and then douse the flames. It would be another cold night, but at least it didn't feel like rain was in the offing.

With any luck he'd be up and on the trail before full light. It was his favorite time to travel, before the night critters had exhausted themselves and gone back to their trees, nests, dens, for the long day. Before full sun baked a man's skull like a stewpot on a hot stove, but after night's full blackness had given way to the subtlest of purplings.

It was a coloration not even noticeable by a man until he had been in it for some time. And then, almost before it was too late, it would change to become something lighter, barely a graying in the high-up places.

All this would happen even before the birds somehow agreed all at once to begin twittering their excitement at waking for another day. That was Rollie's favorite time and it would find him, come the early, early morning, leading Cap along the route he knew they were headed. By the time enough light showed itself, he might have gained an hour on them. As long as they hadn't molested another miner and his camp before then, he was confident he could make up the time in the coming day.

But not yet. Now he'd make camp and coffee, give Cap a well-earned rest, and catch some shut-eye, just enough to keep him alert tomorrow.

The late afternoon light faded long after Rollie reluctantly doused his meager fire. Something about killing a fire always tugged at him a bit. Like killing something innocent and life-giving. And a fire at night in the wild was always a welcome thing. He could sit all night with his back to the dark, cold world, but with a fire at his front, warming his feet and hands and cherrying his cheeks, he was fine.

"Ah well, Cap," he said, "we've had cold camps before, we will again. Rest while you can, mister. We're lighting out early."

With that, he leaned back against raw rock, one of a mass of jutting boulders that from the looks of the worn earth within, others had used as a camp spot who knows how long ago? He had seen odd renderings of animals on a rock coming into this place off the trail.

Something that looked to once have been red in color, and shaped like a running deer . . . Nearby was depicted something that could have been a man with a spear or bow, hard to tell. Other bits of the artwork were scattered on various rocks hereabouts, but it had been getting too late and too dark to investigate them all. One day, perhaps.

Still, the idea of them having been painted on these

very rocks who knows how long before, for they did not look fresh and new, set Rollie's mind to thinking of other people who had roved these high places, long before greedy men, himself included. And as he thought, that skunk called sleep sneaked up on him and pulled its dark sack over his head.

He dreamt deep and hard about other men with sacks on their heads, men with holes cut for eyes and mouths. But when he drew close to them, there was nothing in those holes cut in the sack cloth. Nothing but blackness that reeked of despair, woe, and evil.

He woke twice in the night, each time cursing himself for sleeping more soundly than he'd intended. Each time his first thought had been something akin to . . . what if the devils had backtracked and found him? But even if they did, he'd kept a cold camp, was well off the trail, and it was black as ink. No, he'd hear them should they decide to roust him. And he'd be ready. And each time he slipped into sleep again, he was thinking those same thoughts.

When he jerked awake for the third time, he knew, though it was still full dark, that it was time to rise. Cap seemed to know, too, and whickered low. "G'mornin' pal," said Rollie as he stumbled by him to make water in the bushes off to the side of their stony camp.

He'd kept a full tin cup of coffee set off to the side, covered with the charred, fist-size scrap of hide he used for grasping the hot bail of the coffee pot and hot pan handles. The rest he'd packed the night before. All that was left to do was drink his cold coffee, pack the cup, saddle the horse, and visit the bushes once more, so the ride wouldn't be too painful.

He started out trusting his night vision. Shapes were visible in the dark, you just had to be open to their presence. He couldn't think of it anymore plainly than that, nor did he intend to.

He led Cap on foot for the first hour, barking a shin and stubbing a toe on rocks that failed to announce themselves to him before he got too close. *So much for my wonderful vision in the dark,* he thought with a wry grin.

Finally, that glow came when he realized he was seeing more than he had but minutes before. Dawn was coming. He reasoned he still had another hour before the men he was trailing would rouse themselves. He was partially right in that assumption. One hour after he'd mounted up on Cap, he found their camp.

The gray light had allowed him to make better time. He hunched low, a small effort at keeping from riding too tall and being seen. The camp was closer than he thought it might be. And he smelled it before he saw it. They'd had a campfire, proper size, from the smell of the ash and greasy meat stink hanging low over the upcoming clearing.

Rollie reined up and slid down out of the saddle, lifting free the rifle as he ground-tied Cap. He bent low and catfooted the last fifty feet. It looked like five men lay rolled in their blankets, unmoving in sleep. He smelled cooked meat and ashes and something else he couldn't quite place. It was a wild, feral, natural stink, and it hung over everything.

Could it be this easy? No, his pricked neck hairs, and his tightened gut told him otherwise. In Rollie's experience, nothing in life that was easy had ever been worth the outcome. He didn't hear horses fidgeting, no snores, nothing. All that and his neck hairs felt like needles, warning him in a silent scream that this situation was not right, not right at all.

Rollie lowered to one knee behind a boulder and waited, not daring to draw anymore breath than was necessary to remain silent. If anyone were here, standing guard, they would have heard him approach long minutes before. So why weren't they firing? Creeping around to get in a position to shoot him? Jump him?

No, the set-up was all wrong. Maybe the bodies he'd seen were not even that. Maybe they were bunched branches or rocks tucked under blankets. For what purpose? It would explain the lack of snores, but little else.

No, he had to find out what all this meant. Patience, Rollie, he told himself. You'll find out as soon as it's a little lighter. He couldn't maintain the pose, resting on one knee, leaning against the rock, tensed for action, for much longer. He'd have to shift.

What was it Pops always said? In for a penny . . . Rollie repeated the phrase in his mind and, scrabbling with his fingertips, he plucked up three thumb-size rocks. He tossed one at the nearest body, a good twenty-five feet away. A dead hit. It made a soft thunking sound and rolled off. Nothing moved. He tossed a second stone. It landed short of its mark, a second body, but it, too, roused no response. The third did the same.

Gray light worked its way in and still Rollie held his position. His rifle poised, unlevered so as to not draw attention. But wasn't that what he wanted? He waited a few moments more, made out three, no, four bodies laid out sloppily, as if thrown from on high, about the campfire. One lay close by the fire, as if curled around it for warmth.

And then he became aware that the stink was more than a mere smell. It was something else, a curdled, burnt rankness, more than a poorly cooked supper, more than off-meat. But what it was, he couldn't say. It hung in the air like filth smell hovers by a latrine.

Cap nickered and Rollie watched, wondering if the sound might prompt action. The horse was the only one with guts enough to open the ball, he thought. He levered the rifle. Nothing. So he shoved off of the rocks, stood slowly, still hunched, and rubbed his numb left knee, not taking his eyes from the sleeping men.

Far off he heard a bird, maybe a jay. Not the prettiest sound you'll hear, but an interesting bird. Why would a jay be startled into sound? How far off? Now he was playing foolish mind games. Concentrate, Rollie. Do the job. He forced himself fully upright, the rifle held before him ready to bark its orders, and he walked closer.

A quick kick to the first shape, mid-body, told him it was a person, and that the person was a deep sleeper, or a dead one. He kicked again and again, nudging harder each time. No response. He bent low and tugged the edge of the blanket back. A man lay on his side, looking for all the world as if he were sleeping.

With a boot, Rollie nudged him to flop on his back. The man's head waggled, and then he stared upward at him with two wide eyes and a third, smaller eye drilled up high between them on his forehead.

So much for worrying about waking him. Rollie bent low, palmed the ashes on the fire, and felt the faintest trace of warmth on his outstretched fingers. A couple of hours.

He moved to the next body, still glancing about him with as much caution as he was able to dredge. It was the body closest to the fire stones, as if to warm itself. He pinched the blanket with two fingers and flipped it backward. It was another man, curled as Rollie suspected, around the fire stones, but one part of him had gotten too close, apparently.

The man's head was a crisped knob of burnt hair and blackened, charred flesh. And it was fresh, for though it stunk as only human meat and singed hair can, it had not stewed and aged. Soon it would, and the flies hereabouts would fill the air with their bloated death song.

On the man's right temple, Rollie saw a pucker with something black welled in the center. Blood. Hopefully he'd been shot before the agonizing pain of the burns had plagued him. In all this, he heard no other sounds save the occasional movement by Cap.

Three more to go. Rollie walked to the next, expectations that he'd find a living man huddled beneath his blankets were low. The third man was also dead, shot in the head, as were the fourth and fifth. By then the light had bloomed to a dull gray-purple that gave the scene a freakish glow. It was almost as if he were in the midst of a horrible dream and the ghouls of the newly dead were about to rise and savage him.

What to do now? He circled the camp wider, wider, and found where they'd kept the horses. In fact, he found the horses. Well, six of them. One for each of the dead men, plus one. Puzzling. The extra could be a spare, used as a pack animal. Each one had been, as the men, shot in the head. That bothered Rollie far more than seeing the dead men. He'd done his share of killing of men, but an innocent beast laid low in such a self-serving way soured his gut. He made his pass back to the camp and searched each dead man for clues.

He flopped them this way and that. Nothing. He toed at their possessions, saddlebags, and saddles, nothing looked to be of use. His boot kicked an empty whiskey bottle that rolled and clunked against a small rock, and sat still. It wasn't likely they were robbed, for two of them were gone. The one thing he'd expected to find if they were the men he'd been chasing was some sort of loot, sacks of gold dust, excessive amounts of money for saddle bums such as these.

In the end he found a burlap sack mask beneath each man, same spot under the back on each. As if they had either rehearsed where they would place it when they went to sleep, or it had been stuffed there by someone knowing he might come along.

The stink rising off the burnt-headed man filled the air of the place. Rollie gave up trying to sip his breaths and instead made his way back to Cap, who had drifted from where he'd left him back uptrail. He gathered the reins and mounted up. "Come on," he said. "We have a few things to think about and two men to catch up to."

He skirted the bloody encampment and slowed when he reached the far side. The dead horses lay beyond a low bramble of bushes to his right. Cap perked his ears and balked at the smell. "No worries, pal. I won't let him shoot you. Okay?" He patted the horse's neck, knowing he'd not be able to live up to his promise should they get jumped, and urged him on.

The men he tracked took no pains, as before, in hiding their trail. They had a couple of hours on him, and as the dawn grew, he saw he was tracking three animals, two rode lighter than the third, which followed along behind. A riderless horse packing stolen goods? How many men had they robbed from to accumulate enough weight in gold to weight down a horse like that?

Where did they intend to go with it? And why did the boss of the outfit kill his own men? Were they planning a mutiny and he got wind of it? Or was he just greedy?

"Maybe I'm thinking of it all wrong," said Rollie. "Maybe they did mutiny and he was one of the dead men left behind."

But no, none of the dead resembled the man with the pencil-thin moustaches. And from what Pops had said and what he'd seen so far, the man was a demon who cared little for anything save money. Woe to the man riding with him.

The morning dawned full and bright and clear. It was another of those dry, hot days in the mountains that seemed to come without end, such that when a dark day appeared, you were startled by it.

He sorely wanted to stop and make a fire, boil up some coffee, and think. But he settled for a quick stop at a creek to refill his canteen and let Cap sip long, then crop bankside grasses. "Enjoy it while you can, Cap. Winter's coming, and you'll have to make do with oats and what hay I could buy from Bone and the boys."

He worked another strip of that godawful elk jerky as he mounted up and rode slowly across the creek. The tracks on the far bank were obvious and still those of three horses. They'd not stopped at this creek. Another pile of dung prompted him to dismount and check it The road apples were not warm but not yet dried out.

He didn't think he was gaining on them, but neither was he slipping behind.

How had that man's head become burned and why? Was he trying to protest the shooting? And how could one man shoot four, each in the head, without the others rising up and trying to stop him? He couldn't, not without help. Two men alive made more sense. Perhaps they'd divvied up the killing. How far would this loyalty to each other last? Were they brothers who would stick together to the end, whatever end that might be?

More than likely, given what he remembered of killers in the past, they would tolerate each other out of convenience, then at the first opportunity, one would kill the other. Part of the reason he never rode with a partner. Until Pops.

At thought of him, Rollie sighed. He'd left under a bad cloud. He'd given in to his old itchy-footed ways and used Pops as a scapegoat to shoulder the burdens of the bar and as a punching bag for whatever Rollie had been ticked off about.

He rode for hours and began to feel the close-fitting garment of the coming chill, much earlier in the day than months before in the deep, hot days of summer. He knew this was partially because they were in the forest. Still no sign of the men having slowed, so he kept urging Cap on.

The horse slowed and Rollie knew enough to pay attention to the beast's senses. Any animal's senses were keener than any man's, any day of the week. And once again it paid off. The vista before him began to open, trees thinned, and more blue sky was visible.

The trail cut an abrupt right, eastward, and widened. He could tell they were coming to the edge of some cliff-side with a sizable drop. He slowed Cap and they walked closer.

The sky beyond was bluer than any sky Rollie could recall seeing, and there was a whole lot of it. Enough that a man, if he had enough steam built up, could ride his horse hard and fast right off the edge and, without a cloud to push off of, they might launch out a good twenty, thirty feet before dropping. But what a ride. Not fair to the horse, but what a ride anyway.

"Maybe when the time comes, we'll talk about just such a departure, eh, boy?" He patted Cap's neck and looked to his right, following something that had perked the big gray gelding's ears forward. Far down the cliff-edge trail, along the bottom a few hundred feet below, there was smoke, but more than you'd need for a cook fire or even a chimney from a cabin. And he didn't doubt there were miners along that river below. Likely good gold waters.

As he looked down at the spot from on high, he saw tiny glints of amber, flashing through trees, and guessed them for what they were—dancing flames.

Forest fire? That would not be good, but no, on second glance it looked to be set in a clearing of sorts. He cursed himself for not bringing his spy glass. Another reason to not pack and depart in haste and anger. Fool that I am, he thought.

"Come on, Cap, we best get down there. If someone's in need of help, okay. If not, we'll get that fire behind us."

No sooner had he nudged the horse forward than he

heard one, two, three cracking sounds, like branches snapping over a knee. Gunshots.

The sounds rose up to him like a taunt from below, near that mysterious fire. Yes, somebody was in trouble, and Rollie guessed that whatever or whoever he found down there would be beyond his assistance.

Chapter Twenty-six

The canyon-rim, hard-rock trail seemed to go on for days without beginning a descent. At times the trees were thick enough ahead that he couldn't tell if they were close to the far side of the rocky gorge. He needed to get to the bottom, but nature was not complying. But he was getting closer because he smelled smoke about the same time Cap whickered and jerked his head.

"I know, I know. But that's too bad, because we're going down there."

He didn't dare force the horse to move any faster than he was walking because the edge of the precipice lay a few yards to their left, and the land to their right, mostly unforgiving rock with a scatter of clinging pines and rabbit brush, inclined up and away from them.

He hoped this was the right trail to take and not a raw disappointment that would taper to a spot they wouldn't be able to navigate in. Sign of his prey had been scant since taking to this rim trail. But the gunshots and the fire urged him on.

At the point when he really began to doubt the trail he'd taken, he felt Cap's front legs dip down and bear to the right, leading them downslope and away from that eerie edge. This was the correct trail, because it turned to more dirt than rock and he clearly saw a recent hoofprint. Had to be the same men he was trailing.

Down, down, they rode, the trees more abundant now and giving him a sense of safety. Ahead he heard a dull roar he guessed was the water source that created the cleft he was making for. It would cascade down to the bottom, however far that was now, and form itself as a river once more. And that's where the cabin, or whatever lay along those banks below, was burning,.

Spray too fine to see tickled his nostrils and perfumed the air with the promise of the freshness of cold, clear mountain water. That, combined with an increasing steady, churning roar, told Rollie they were coming to a river, but one that had already decided to begin its tumble downward. The trail still cut southeastward, but he figured once he crossed the river he'd cut north once more. For the first time the notion occurred to him that this stretch of the river actually flowed north. He did not find this as unusual as he once might have.

A number of times in his days roving the West he'd paralleled or crossed over or camped alongside northerly flowing waters. It had more to do with the shape of the land than anything mystical, as one old freighter had sworn it did over a campfire one night a dozen or more years ago.

The old toothless man had been convinced that sorcery of some vague sort was responsible for such oddnesses in the world. He had also been half lit on his own jug of homebrew that he brought with him on every run. He called it "Satan's Own Spittle." Rollie declined to share of the proffered jug, feigning a riled gut. He figured he would soon have one if he sampled from that jug.

The river presented itself within minutes, a tumbling mass of clashing water spattering off a jagged jumble of rocks that had been there longer than anyone alive could remember. The rumbling torrent upstream dropped down at him from twenty feet above before settling in a deep, clear pool. If he hadn't been in such a hurry, he would have liked to spend time there, cut a whip for fishing, and maybe even soak in it. Nothing like a dip in a mountain river to wake up a man.

"Another time," he said, his voice lost in the thundering rush of water.

The crossing lay below the pool, a wide ledge of rock covered with a steady flow of clear water up to Cap's knees. The horse didn't much like the traverse, but he plunged in at Rollie's urging. They were halfway across when Rollie glanced once more upstream at the falls. It was an impressive spot, and one he'd surely visit again someday. He wanted to share it with someone. And Pops was not the one he had in mind. Maybe Mrs. Gladwell.

As he hoped it would, once across the river, the narrow trail, so recently used, cut to his left, following the river downward. It wound, snaking around massive boulders and through chasms of rock, none so impressive or violent as the falls above.

At one point, the river narrowed to no more than a man's stride across, overhung with thick vegetation. But it soon reappeared in full force and loudness. He knew they must be getting close to the cataract he'd suspected from way back on the ledge trail. He hadn't been able to see it, but knew it must lie upstream of wherever the shots had been fired.

They trailed away from the river, but stayed close enough he could see it through the trees. The path was more forgiving than close by the flowage, and he and Cap finally made good time cutting downward.

When they were forced to switchback repeatedly, he knew they were closing in on the bottom. He hoped he could get there in time to help whoever was being shot, burned, or otherwise tormented by whoever he was chasing.

It was frustrating to have so few answers, though it was not an unfamiliar position for him to be in. One more switchback in the trail and he'd be alongside the river. How far downstream the trouble spot lay, he did not know, but already he heard the waterfall he had suspected would be there, tucked in the rock cliff face to his left.

They emerged from out of the closely treed trail and there was the roiling river, clouds of spume rising up, the sheen of a faint rainbow wavering in the air in a dagger of late-day sun fifty feet above the water.

Instead of tumbling the full hundred or more feet from on high, the river had over many thousands of years carved itself a cradled path, a rocky route that when it finally emptied its burden did so a mere fifty feet above the river's lower course. Another tempting, pretty pool lay at the bottom, surely aswim with trout.

Despite the potential dicey situation he was riding into, Rollie couldn't help thinking of a thick bull trout broiled slowly on a stick over a solid campfire that licked and crackled the skin. It made him detest all the more the satchel of funky elk jerky he'd toted along.

They pushed on down the thin riverside trail that wound according to the snaky course of the flow. Rollie unsheathed the rifle once more and cocked and cradled it as they rode. From that position, he would be able to swing and squeeze.

Now and again, he smelled whiffs of smoke, but as yet saw no raging forest fire ahead. He estimated they were within a half-mile of the trouble spot. He urged Cap onward, jabbing the horse in the barrel with his heels.

Rollie knew the horse was by nature a cautious sort, but now since he felt he'd wasted so much time getting across the river, then down the steep mountainside, a sense of urgency gripped Rollie from within. What if the bastards had laid low another miner and he'd been but minutes too late to help?

And then, as they picked their way through a thick stand of aspen, late golden leaves still fluttering, there lay a cabin. Oddly, it did not seem to be on fire. But ample clouds of gray smoke boiled up from something sizable to the east, hidden by trees.

Rollie rode forward, unsure of what he was about to see, but suspecting the worst. Given that he was trailing killers, it was not going to be good.

He didn't have long to wait. Ten paces more and he saw a smoldering wreck of what had once been a stable. One side was gutted, the roof leaned, and great clouds of black smoke boiled from beneath it. Through the smoke, he made out a meadow. That would explain the smoke. Hay, thought Rollie. Put up wet.

That's when he saw a figure stumbling out of the smoke, bent at the waist and coughing, then standing up again and charging back into the sagged structure.

"That fool," muttered Rollie and climbed down from the now-fidgety Cap. He tied his reins to a nearby pine and advanced on the fire, keeping the rifle raised and checking his revolver. As he drew closer, the man once more stumbled out of the smoke, coughing and bent over.

"Hey there!" Rollie barked his words and stood with his rifle pointed at the man.

The soot-faced man looked up, genuinely surprised by the sight of the gunned stranger. Then he shook his head as if to wake himself, and shouted, "Help! Help me! My . . . daughter! In there!"

Rollie ran closer and peered at the wreck of a barn with now more smoke than flame issuing from it. "Which direction?"

"Please! My daughter! In there!" the man pointed at the middle of the mess. Rollie nodded. "Okay!" He laid his rifle down and tugged his hat low, and his kerchief up onto his face. He would have liked to have wetted it with his canteen water first, but there was no time. He doubted anybody was still alive in this blackness, but he had to try.

The fire was contained to a stall in the back left corner. Beyond the few flames, he saw little more than clouds of black, thick smoke. A raw stink of smoldering grass and charred wood filled his nose and throat and he began coughing. "Hello? Hello?"

He turned, but saw no one behind him, not that he expected to see much through the smoke. He groped forward, grasping nothing but air, then his right hand felt an upright timber, a stall, perhaps. He followed along it.

After another few shuffling steps and shouts of "Hello!" his boots toed something soft on the floor. He bent, gagging on smoke. He would have to get out of there soon.

He patted whatever it was, expecting it to be a dead horse, but it was a person, had to be the daughter. She was unmoving. He patted along a leg, trousers, then felt a boot. He reached for the other, found it, and dragged backward toward where he'd come from.

A cough boiled up in his throat, snagged like a bad dream, and he tried to keep it down. His lungs rebelled and he turned his head to the side and retched. All the while he kept dragging the body backward. Through his teary eyes he saw light from the outside, and kept stumbling backward toward it.

He kept going past the point where he thought the barn door might have been, then his boot caught on a rock and he fell to his backside. He rolled to his side, coughing and gagging. Then he felt the weight of something on his right leg and remembered the girl. He turned over and through burning eyes he saw a man lying on the ground. Was it the girl's father? None of this made any sense.

He crawled alongside the body and saw it was not a girl he'd dragged out, but a man. A man with a bullet hole in his forehead. Before he could pull his Schofield free, he heard the unmistakable sounds of a rifle being levered. Right behind him.

"That's right, lawdog. Raise those hands of yours—and keep them high, you hear?"

Rollie was on his knees, facing the smoking wreck of a barn, his arms raised, and coughs rising up from his gorge unbidden. "What . . ." He coughed and gagged, tried to speak again. "What is this?" His words came out as a hissing whisper. He turned his head, somewhere along the way he'd lost his hat. Must be in the barn.

Behind him stood the man he'd found before, the one who said he'd lost a daughter. Except there was no daughter. And that meant this was the leader of the outlaws, the man Chauncey had killed all those years before, the man with the pencil-thin moustaches. Pete Winklestaff.

"That was mighty gallant of you, Finnegan. Or should I say Stoneface? Oh, I know who you are, you foolish man. And I know you would like to kill me about now, wouldn't you?"

The man smiled, and his teeth were the only things white on his whole body. The rest of him was sooted. He nodded, "Yeah, now you know who I am. I'm him. The one you've been chasing. I'll give you this, you are a relentless sort. Remind me of a dog I had once as a child. Never gave up on a thing. Until he tangled with a hydrophoby raccoon. Then he gave up, all right, with a shot between the eyes!" This struck the man as most humorous, and he doubled over, his laughs turning into coughs.

Rollie jerked around, got one foot under himself, but the man jerked back and shook his head, his toothy smile gone.

"Yessir, betwixt the eyes, just like Corby there. You didn't really need to drag his sorry carcass out of there, you know. He's the one who started the blaze, after all. Tried to double-cross me. Me! Can you believe the nerve of that man? It was my idea to set all these fool miners straight."

"Why all the killing, Winklestaff?"

He shrugged. "I woke up this morning, and it wasn't fun anymore."

The two men stared each other down for long moments, then Rollie said, "If you're going to kill me, shut up and get to work."

All the while the man held steady, Rollie's own rifle leveled on his own back. He turned again. If the idiot was going to drill him, he might as well face it like a man.

"Nah, it's not going to be that easy, Stoneface. What's about to happen is you're going to unbuckle that gun belt, then toss it over here."

Rollie complied, taking his time, trying to figure how he might fire without getting shot first. But no, the risk was too great.

"Good. Now get up off your knees! We're going to march to the river, beyond that cabin yonder, and you're going to fill two buckets over there and bring them back and walk back in there and douse that smoldering fire. You understand? And you're going to do it like you have an investment in the outcome. Because you do. You fail me and you'll die where you stand with a bullet in you, delivered from your very own rifle. You know I will do it, too. Understand?"

Rollie didn't nod, but he did get to his feet, his right knee offering up an audible popping sound. That made his captor laugh. "You surely are an old dog, you know that? Now get going." He jerked the muzzle of the gun toward the cabin and river beyond.

All the way there, Rollie puzzled out the oddness of this request. Must be there's something of value in that barn. He'd guess it held the loot the man and his cronies had been stealing from the miners in the surrounding countryside.

Just as the man said, there were two wooden buckets on the far side of the small log cabin. The cabin itself was a tidy affair, maybe two rooms, and with a nice setting porch overlooking the river. Under different circumstances it was a spot Rollie could see himself spending time visiting whoever owned the place. That thought made him wince. Likely whoever owned it was now dead by the hand of this vicious bastard.

"Pick them up, Stoneface, and fill them, before I fill you with lead!" Again, the idiot cackled at his own wit, ending his glee with a coughing jag.

Rollie coughed himself, as if just hearing it induced his own wracked body to comply. He reached the river's edge, down three stone steps, and knelt, splashing the cooling water on his face, over and over, then slaking his nagging thirst with scooped handfuls of water.

"Enough!" shouted the man behind him. Rollie ignored him and continued to drink his fill. He reckoned there was no way the fool would shoot him yet because he needed him to do his work, a task he himself wasn't willing to tuck into.

The man ranted and prodded him once in the back with the gun. Rollie stiffened and spun, snatching at the rifle, but the man had backed away. "Uh uh uh! No, no, bad Stoneface. You behave like that once more and you'll be down this river without a paddle or a heartbeat."

Rollie considered repeating himself in telling the man to prove his threats, but he was wearied. He filled the buckets and walked back to the smoking barn. As he passed him, Rollie took stock of the killer. He was so sooted that his eyes and teeth were the only things of brightness about him.

But he could tell the man, thin and of medium size, wore decent clothes, not miner's rags, and sported that trim moustache, a sculpted thing on the top lip that looked to require effort to maintain, so precise was the shaving job.

That told him the fellow was a bit of a dandy, but not so much he was hesitant to get dirty. When Rollie had come upon him, he'd been scrabbling about the blazing barn, probably had just killed his partner, Corby, the one he'd said had kindled the blaze.

That meant the barn fire was not planned and Rollie's appearance was a lucky coincidence. Did the man have something hidden in the barn? Buried beneath its dirt floor? If so, how long had they been using this hidden little riverside oasis as a hideout?

"Get in there and douse those flames! Dallying will only get you killed sooner, Stoneface!"

The man's barked orders became harsher, more frenzied. He was losing his patience and getting worried about whatever was in there getting burned. Good.

Rollie set down the buckets, tugged off his kerchief over his head, and dunked it in a bucket.

"What are you doing? Get in there!"

Again, Rollie didn't answer, but arranged the kerchief on the bridge of his nose and, giving the man a last glance, lifted the buckets' rope handles and walked back into the still-boiling mass of black clouds issuing from the mouth of the sagged barn.

"You come right back out and get more water! I want

that blaze fully out, and then we'll talk about what I'm going to do with you. Might be I'll let you live a while!" He laughed and coughed as Rollie disappeared inside.

It was as black inside as before. Rollie ducked low and walked to where he'd seen the blaze in the back corner. The paltry flames were having a time licking at the mound of wet hay put up there, which produced a whole lot of smoke and very little flame, good for him.

Instead of wasting the water, he crouched before the back wall, the logs warm to the touch, and kicked at them, but they were stout. It would take too long to try to dig under the wall, then prairie-dog up outside. But he did have this water.

And he knew the man wanted something inside here, something bad enough to risk giving Rollie some amount of power, no matter how slight. That decided it. Rollie dunked his face in the cooling liquid and held there, breathing through his parted lips just above the surface of the water. Waiting.

Soon he heard the man shouting from outside. He couldn't make out the words because the flames were close enough to the outer walls that they'd begun to lick and chew at the logs. Soon they would gain purchase and really blaze.

With any luck he wouldn't have to wait all that long.

He pulled his head up from the surface of the water and covered his face again with the kerchief. The water helped clear his tearing eyes, if but for a moment. To his left he saw something on the floor, an arm's length away and reached for it. It felt familiar as soon as his throbbing fingers touched it—his hat.

He dragged it close, sloshed water inside it, and jammed it on his head, then waited, his left hand slipping into his trouser pocket and pulling out his trusty Barlow folder. He picked out the big blade, clicking it into place, a leaner version of what it had been when new, some years before, thinned from meticulous honing, but no less sharp than when new.

Seconds later a shape appeared in the shifting, smoky gloom. "Where the hell are you? Where are you at?" A pause, then: "What are you doing?"

From his crouching position, Rollie lunged at the man, drove straight into his legs and knocked him to the ground. A loud "Oof!" burst from the man's mouth as he hit.

And as he hit, Rollie's blade drove once, glanced off something, likely the man's boot top. He pulled his arm back and drove it forward again. Rollie could tell by the man's screaming that it found purchase in flesh.

A grim smile spread on the old Pinkerton man's mouth beneath the kerchief. He clawed wide with his other hand for the rifle as he pulled the blade back for another stab. But the little killer was a fighter and his legs lashed out, kicking like he was dancing a fiery jig on his back.

One kick landed square in Rollie's crotch, and he groaned but kept up his crawling attack. He punched, landing a blow that glanced off the man's shoulder before smacking with a solid feeling to the jaw. With his left hand, Rollie clawed for the rifle, while trying to get a knee up onto the squirming man's gut.

He almost succeeded, was half-raised up when he felt something hard slam into his head. The near-darkness of the barn pinched to a burst of stars against a pure black vista. Sound muffled as if he were hearing from underwater.

He felt his own grip on the man weakening, and tried to force his fingers to resume their clawing task, but they would not mind him, nothing would.

He felt weak, so weak, not since the attack in the alley, when he'd almost died, had he felt this way. All he'd ever fought for, to be taken by a lucky blow in the dark by a killer, a killer and a thief who would keep on killing and thieving until someone or something could stop him.

But it won't be me, thought Rollie. And then he thought no more.

Chapter Twenty-seven

"Hey."

Something was pecking on him. No, that wasn't right. Pounding on him. Felt like a hammer to the face. He tried to shout. He heard it. It came out like a wheeze.

"Hey."

Something punched him again. Once more, he tried to shout.

Then the thing gripped him. Felt like his head was being squeezed between two planks, tightened in a vise, like the one at Pieder's shop. Wait now, if he was feeling something, that meant he wasn't dead. Didn't it? And if that were true, then . . . yes, that meant all those bad things—the fire, the body, the buckets, the fight—had actually happened. He'd stabbed the bastard! But did it do any good? Maybe only in the leg.

"Hey, Rollie!" Smack! Hard on the face again. This time, though, it felt like a slap and not a pummeling with hardwood blocks.

That voice, it was familiar. But who?

"Come on now, man! Wake up! I know you're in there! Rollie, tighten up now!"

"Mmfff . . ."

"Well, sounds like you're chewing oat porridge like some old toothless man, but it beats that snoring sound you were making."

"Ksss . . ."

"Huh?"

Rollie felt breath near his face, as if someone leaned in close. He forced the words to come out of his mouth, quiet but clear, as clear as he was able to make them. "Kiss . . . my . . ."

That was all he got out because he heard a deep chuckle from way down in the belly and he knew right then who it was tending him. Pops. His pard.

It took more coaxing and what felt like a cool rag laid on his eyes before he felt like he could try to force his eyes open again. His right eye popped open and light lanced in like a needle. He shut it again and groaned.

"Take it easy. Now that I know you're alive and in there, you take it slow. Got a cool rag here for your face. You're a little crisped up, but you're going to be okay. Pops is here. Take it slow."

That was the last he remembered for a while. When he came to again, it was to hear a bird singing and what felt like warmth on his face, then brightness on his eyes. Sunlight? He concentrated on opening his eyes and then remembered Pops. Yes, something about Pops, a cool rag. Was Pops here?

"Hey Rollie, you with me?"

Rollie heard and said, "Uh . . . huh."

"Good. Good!"

He heard what sounded like a handclap, then: "Take it slow. You've been out for a few hours since I found you. But you're safe now. Going to be okay, you hear me?"

"Yeah." He tried so hard to open his eyes, felt them fluttering, then his right eyelid popped open, a slit, brightness seeped in. Then his left eye opened, a crack, but it was enough. He saw blurry images, something moved, he heard a sighing sound, then someone took a deep breath and he felt a coolness on his forehead, a cloth maybe. "Okay, I see you opened your eyes. They're clear now, got the funk off them. Can you see me? Rollie, can you see me?"

He tried to nod, but it hurt his throat, his neck. He slid a tongue out on his lips; they were cracked and scabbed over. "Yeah."

"Good. Take it slow. I'm going to get you a drink of water. I'll raise your head and hold the cup to your mouth."

He did, and cold, sweet water touched his sore mouth, ran between his crusted lips, spilled out, ran down his cheeks and neck and it felt so good, so cool and welcome. Only a dip in a crystal-clear pool beneath a waterfall . . . like the ones he saw on his way . . . way where? To the cabin in the woods. By the river. The fire, that's it. The barn was on fire, and the man he'd been tracking, the killer, Winklestaff, he drew down on him, got the better of him. But he'd stabbed him, right?

"The man . . ."

"Take it slow," said Pops.

After a few minutes and a couple more sips of water, Rollie croaked out, "What are you doing here?"

"I had me a hinky feeling, you know, because whenever you are off by yourself, you're always ending up in hot water."

Rollie looked up at him with wide eyes, and Pops laughed. That was a joke because it was Pops who'd had the most-recent headache while alone.

"So I rode out to see if I was right. And I was. Saw the smoke, black smoke, in the distance. It didn't look normal, so I thought I'd ride over to investigate. I got here, saw the cabin first, then rode on through the trees and saw the barn, or what was a barn, smoke boiling out. 'That's not good,' I said to myself and when I got closer, I saw a body in the middle of the barn yard and another one half in-half out of the barn doorway. Turns out that last one was you."

"I appreciate it." Rollie sipped more water and rested his eyes. "Any sign of Winklestaff?"

"That's who was here?" Pops stiffened in his chair and peered out a window.

"Yep. Tracked him. Long story."

Pops nodded. "Had to air out this cabin. Turns out the man who lived here, an old gent, had been shot some days ago right in his bedroom. That's why I have you out here. I buried the old man and the other dead man from out front."

"Corby."

"Huh? Who?"

Rollie swallowed and licked his lips. "Winklestaff said the dead man was Corby. Not the old man, the other one. I dragged him out of the barn, too late."

"He one of Winklestaff's men?"

"Yep."

"Well, I buried them both anyway. Seemed the thing to do. You were sleeping."

"How long was I out?"

"Oh, not long, six eight hours."

"Got to find Winklestaff."

"He can't have gone far," said Pops.

"My money's on the Gulch. He's going to do what he needs to do there and then come back here for his money."

"What money?'

"That's buried in the barn. Money, nuggets, dust, what have you. Everything he and his men stole. I expect he thinks it's safe. He thinks I'm dead and he doesn't know you're here. In fact, I bet you're part of the reason he's headed back to the Gulch. "

"More of a side reason," said Pops. "You can bet he's going straight for Chauncey."

"And the others . . ." Rollie pushed himself up on an elbow. "We have to get back there."

"Rollie, you're in no shape to go anywhere. I'll go. You stay here and rest."

"Like hell." The ex-Pinkerton man gritted his teeth. He felt like he'd been dropped in a stewpot of boiling water. But no way was he going to give in to the pain.

"Rollie, don't be crazy!"

He wanted to reply but he had to get himself upright. Rollie knew from experience that if he didn't force himself to shove through the thudding pain in his head and the bubbled, pulsing mess that was his hide, he'd always regret it and would never accomplish anything of worth ever again in his life. At least that's the threat he held over himself. It had always worked and would this time, too.

As he stood, he glanced up and grunted through his clenched teeth and saw Pops staring wide-eyed at him. "You know," he said, trying to sound normal when he felt like anything but normal. "Other than a headache, I feel pretty good."

"Uh huh," said Pops, shaking his head. "Well, it doesn't matter because we only have the one horse, mine."

"Cap? Where's Cap?" said Rollie, forcing his eyes wide, despite the pounding headache.

"No idea. I haven't seen him. I'll look, though."

"You do that," said Rollie. "And don't ride off to the Gulch without me."

"Wouldn't dream of it. While I'm doing all the heavy work, why don't you figure out how you're going to stay in the saddle without falling on your bean, okay? I'll be back."

The quiet of the cabin was eerie once Pops left to scout up another horse. Where had Winklestaff gone with his own, plus the horse of the man he'd killed and the pack horse? Oh that's right, he recalled seeing at least one in the barn, expired from the smoke, no doubt. Maybe more than the one had died in there. None of them deserved that.

Rollie slowly paced the narrow dining room and ventured glances into the little cabin's other rooms. This was a quiet spot of respite for a contemplative man who wished little more for himself than to be left alone. And for his quietude and pains, he'd gotten himself killed.

He didn't know how long it took Pops to return, but the man was smiling. "Good and bad news. I found a mount and I found out where Winklestaff's headed. And it ain't anywhere near here, I can tell you."

Rollie's frustration at . . . everything in his life at that moment made him stare at Pops, who shrugged. "It's a mule, but he'll get us there."

"A mule? Out here?" said Rollie.

"From the look of it, I'd say it belonged to the old man who lived here."

"Bone rack?"

Pops shrugged. "Could be worse. He's been fending for himself since they killed the old man, but he was right tame. I have him outside. I'll ride him with a hackamore, you ride Buck."

"Nope," said Rollie. "I'll ride him. Not fair to you."

"Ain't no fair about it. I can move faster than you. I'm riding the damn mule, and if you give me anymore lip, I'll leave you right where you stand." Pops smiled. "Now if that's settled, come on out. I'll tidy up in here, fill the canteen, and we can get gone."

Once they were mounted, Pops unstrapped his gunbelt and handed it to Rollie. "You'll need that. I have Lil' Miss Mess Maker here." He stroked the hastily repaired stock of the Greener. "I'll do a better job of fixing her up once we get through this foolishness with Winklestaff."

As they rode out of the barnyard, Rollie looked back. "I like this place. Despite what's happened here."

"Yeah, I figure you would. Just your style. Maybe you should lay claim to it."

"I might just do that, Pops. I might just do that."

For the first few minutes of smooth riding, Rollie filled Pops in on Winklestaff, the killings, the men at Stag Horn, and Winklestaff's killing of his own men.

"He is one nasty piece of work," said Pops.

"Yep, and he's crazy. I mean it. Told me everybody in the Gulch owed him. And that they stole what was rightfully his."

Pops nudged the mule forward. "Hope this old mule has some hidden strengths because we need to get back home, and fast. You up for the ride, old timer?"

Rollie looked over at Pops to see him looking back. "You better have been talking to that mule, Pops. . . ." Rollie smiled for the first time since coming around.

"Maybe . . . maybe not!" Pops drummed his boot heels against the mule's ribs and took off up the trail. Rollie grinned and despite the pounding in his head and blistered back and face and hands, he kept pace with his partner.

Chapter Twenty-eight

"I'll tell you what," said the man entering the bar.

Nosey looked up from the book he'd been reading. He liked to get a few hours of reading and writing in before the late afternoon crowd began to dribble in, especially on a day like this, a quiet treat since Pops and Rollie were both gone. But now here was someone standing in the open doorway, daylight framing him as a silhouette.

Nosey sighed. "What?"

"That's what I said . . . ha!" The man slapped his thigh and chuckled. He walked with a slight limp into the bar, and Nosey finally was able to see his face. He didn't look familiar, not a surprise since it seemed half the folks in town were newcomers. Made him feel pretty good, an old hand, as it were, having arrived many months before, and well ahead of the latest round of gold strikes. Maybe this one had a story to tell.

Another benefit of working at The Last Drop was talking with interesting people. Now, if he had been back at his paltry claim, digging in futility for gold that never seemed to be there, he'd miss out on all these rich veins of information and stories, stories he could turn into grist for writing dime novels . . .

"What can I get you, stranger?" he said, closing his book, a copy of *Moby-Dick*.

"Well, let's see. What I am looking for is a glass, a whiskey bottle, and the answers to a couple of questions."

"I can help you out on all counts." Nosey set a glass and bottle on the table before the man. He was a slim fellow, none too tall, with a pencil-thin moustache, but he looked trail tired, dusty, and smudged, and he reeked of smoke. Stronger than the usual campfire stink most men exuded.

"Is the man who owns the bar anywhere about the place?"

"Rollie?" said Nosey. He wasn't about to answer the question anyway.

"No, no actually, the fellow I'm looking for is a black man."

"Oh, Pops. He's um . . ."

"Don't tell me he's not here." The stranger seemed genuinely annoyed. "Rode all this way and . . . wait a minute, he didn't go after Stoneface, did he?"

"You know Rollie?"

The stranger's eyes narrowed again and he forced a slight smile. "No, not really."

"What do you mean 'went after . . .'? Do you know something about Rollie?" Nosey backed toward the bar but the stranger was faster and stood, knocking over his chair and drawing a six-gun at the same time.

"That's right, Bookworm. Just back up nice and slow. Now, what we're going to do is tie you up and if you open your mouth, I'll make certain it's nearly the last sound you make. The actual last sound will be moaning as you watch your own blood leak out onto the floor. Got me?"

Nosey nodded and wondered if he'd be able to palm the two-shot derringer Pops gave him a while back. It was in his trouser pocket. Ever since the dust-up with Cleve Danziger, he'd been reticent to leave his shanty without the little firearm. It offered scant protection, but he found the confidence and comfort it gave him over-shadowed the gun's obvious shortcomings. Until now.

"What is it you want with Pops and Rollie?"

"You are a dumb one, aren't you?" said the man as he swung the revolver up hard, clipping Nosey on the right temple and collapsing him in a senseless heap behind the bar.

Winklestaff glanced around but saw little save for stacks of bottles, cleaning rags, a bucket of murky water, drinking glasses drying on a towel beside it and a wooden box of utensils. Then he saw the spare apron hanging on the wall.

He snatched it down and, using his hip knife, started a tear. He split the apron in two, then used half to bind the unconscious barman's ankles. The other half he used to bind the man's hands behind him. He stuffed a bar rag in the man's mouth and dragged him to the far end, back by the wall.

He was tempted to snatch up the cash box, but figured he'd do that later. So that Pops fellow was gone, huh? Off looking for Finnegan, no doubt. That means he might find him, but the odds were against it. The old man's riverside cabin was well off the beaten trails. And even if he did find it, he'd be too late to save his friend. Stoneface Finnegan was dead, burnt to a cinder.

Winklestaff grinned and made for the door. "Don't go anywhere, Bookworm. I'll be right back. We're going to have ourselves a party!" He giggled as he descended the stairs outside. He knew right where he was headed. To pay his old partner a visit. Maybe invite him to the bar for a drink or two. Yeah, that was a fine idea.

Pete Winklestaff felt certain when he walked in the door of the mercantile and saw his former partner, Chauncey Wheeler, that it was his lucky day. Smooth riding from here on out. He'd get all he wanted in Boar Gulch and without the headache of the law snapping at his backside. Then he'd swing back by the old man's cabin, dig his buried loot out from under the charred wreck of the barn, and make for California.

If Pete Winklestaff expected his old partner, Chauncey Wheeler, to run screaming at the sight of him, he would soon be amply rewarded.

The mayor of Boar Gulch heard the door's bell clunk and clank. "Be with you in a minute."

A few moments later he looked up from the ledger book he was penciling notes in, and his eyes widened. His jaw dropped down, and his breath stopped. But only for a second. Then he shrieked and bolted for the back door.

But despite his limp from the Barlow wound Rollie gave him, Winklestaff was faster and slid between Chauncey and the door, one hand resting atop the butt of his revolver. "Well now, Chauncey Wheeler. I will not insult you by saying how good you look. You look like hell, truth be told. You've gone fat and, well, distressed, yes that's the word for it. Positively distressed. I thought that when I saw you at the saloon some time ago. I believe you were disparaging my name in a rather undignified, drunken manner."

"I . . ." Chauncey swallowed and tried again. "I thought that was you. But I thought it was, that is to say I thought you were a ghost."

"Yes, well, I heard that a lot. But no, it's me. A little leaner than you remember, I'll wager. And a whole lot poorer. Well, that is until lately. You see, I've come into some money."

He let that thought hang in the air. Chauncey bit. "You have?"

"Yes, I have." Winklestaff leaned forward until his nose was inches from Wheeler's. "But it's not enough."

"It's . . . not?"

"Nope." He waited a few moments, then said, "Here's where you ask what is enough."

"What is enough?"

"All of it, Chauncey. I want it all. This store, that odd hotel you're building, the town, the claims, the title of mayor. Hell, son, I want your life. Then I might start to feel full."

Chauncey's face bloomed crimson, and he began to shake. Winklestaff grinned but didn't move. "I know that look, Chauncey. And if you do what I think you want to do, it will not end well." He tapped the revolver with his fingertips. "I am quick with this thing. Ask the men who gave all for these here notches."

Chauncey looked down briefly and gulped. There were at least a dozen tiny but defined notches sliced into the walnut grips of the gleaming revolver.

"Now," said Winklestaff, drawing the gun slowly and motioning for Chauncey to back up. "What we're going to do is close up shop for the day. Then we're going to take a walk."

"To where?"

"Up to The Last Drop Saloon, of course. I have unfinished business there with a man named Pops. I expect he'll be along sometime today. If not, well . . . I'll find him. But in the meantime, let's us go up there and talk turkey. There's a fellow waiting for us, a nosey character who wants me to hurry on back."

He herded Chauncey toward the door. "Oh, and Chauncey? Don't yell or run or anything you are ill-equipped to do. I can draw this thing and drop you faster than a tinhorn drops a full house. You hear me . . . partner?"

The Mayor of Boar Gulch ground his teeth and nodded as he locked the front door of the mercantile. He made to slip the key into his vest pocket, but Winklestaff held out a hand.

"Uh uh, see now, that there key belongs to me. Always has. You know it, and I know it."

Chauncey dropped the key into the killer's hand and bit back a salty mix of tears and rage as they walked down the main street of Boar Gulch, the chubby man slightly ahead of the stranger with the sooty grin on his face.

Chapter Twenty-nine

Wolfbait gimped on up the street from the trail north of town. He'd had a long day of soaking in the sun and thinking about a next move at his diggings. He really should make a decision or two before snow caught him with cracks in the walls that needed filling and no firewood laid in. Not to mention a distinct lack of gold, no promise of any to be scared up on his place. But it had been such a fine morning and noon, then even finer afternoon, he'd decided to table that motion until tomorrow.

He spied Rollie's mount, Cap, gray gelding, saddled and tied out front of The Last Drop. That was odd, usually Cap could be found out back in the corral the men kept for the two horses or pastured in the meadow above. The closer he walked, the odder the scene looked. Cap was smudged and looked ganted-up and drooping like an old flower.

"What's the matter, boy?" said Wolfbait, running a gnarled hand along the horse's neck. He was lathered, too. That was definitely not the condition Rollie would leave his horse in, unless he was in trouble of sorts. Something fishy was in the air.

Wolfbait mounted the steps and tried the handle of the closed door. The thumb latch didn't give, the door didn't swing inward. He rapped on the plank door. "Hey there! Open up! Got me a powerful thirst and a few questions for you gents! Hey there!" He rapped again, then put an ear to the door. Nothing.

"Yes sir, something's off when a man can't get a drink of an afternoon. I'm that close to passing out from want of liquids, I am. Why . . . ?" Wolfbait looked around him but though there were a few folks visible at the south end of the street, no one was in hearing distance. He rasped a hand under his stubbled jaw once more and looked down at that south end again.

There sat The Lucky Strike saloon. But they would want money and he had some, but he was loathe to spend it too early in the evening when he could usually cadge a round or three from Nosey and the boys in exchange for useful information or a smidgin of elbow grease, easily the least of options, but a fellow did what he had to.

That's when he heard a clunk from inside the bar. Someone was in The Last Drop! "I knew it! I knew it, I tell ya!" He rapped his old knuckles on the door once more. The planks rattled but did not budge. "Hide from me, will you? Me?" he growled. "What'd ol' Wolfbait ever do but help you in your times of need?" He cocked an ear. Nothing. "The gall of some folks."

He stumped back down the steps and stood by Cap once more. The horse needed a drink, but he didn't feel right unhitching him and taking him to the trough. "Guess I had best bring the water to you, old fella," he said, and ambled down toward the stable, with the public trough out front filled by the diverted stream.

He was on his way back to Cap, doing his best to not spill the filled bucket, when he heard horses from behind, making their way up the main street from the north road. He set down the bucket and visored his eyes. There was Pops on a mule and someone beside him riding what looked like Pops' gelding, Bucky. But that other fellow, something about him seemed familiar, but he looked rough. About as rough as ol' Cap looked.

"Wolfbait," said Pops, riding up fast and sliding down off the mule while he was still a few feet from the old man. "You seen a stranger hereabouts? Well, he wouldn't be to you."

"What are you doing on a mule, Pops? And what are you talking about, anyway? And who's that . . ." Then Wolfbait saw the other man was Rollie, but a singed, crisped-up version of Rollie. "Rollie, you look like hell-and-a-half!"

"Never mind about that, Wolfbait," said Pops. "Have you seen Pete Winklestaff?"

"What?" he said, swinging his attention back to Pops. "Why would I have seen him? He's dead, and I don't care what ol' Chauncey told us. He's off his bean. Trying to ease a guilty conscience or weasel out of some responsibility, that's all he's doing. Why, I told him . . ."

"Not now, Wolfbait," said Rollie still climbing down from the horse. "Cap all right?"

Wolfbait looked from Rollie to Cap, then back to the singed barkeep. "Yeah, he's been rode hard and put up dry, but he'll live. About like you, I expect. Say, what's going on here, anyways? I thought you was in there, holed up and having fun without me! Which isn't possible, I know, but . . ."

"What do you mean? Somebody's in the bar?"

"Yeah, I expect it's Nosey. But now that you mention it, the whole town's gone quiet on me. I stopped by Chauncey's for some tobacco, and his shop was closed up tighter than a bull's backside, then The Last Drop, same story. What's going on?"

"Nosey in there?"

Wolfbait shrugged. "How do I know? Heard something inside, but no telling who or what it was. Now what's all this about Winklestaff being alive? I thought Chauncey was making it up."

"Nope," said Rollie, checking Pops' revolver. To Pops he said, "I'll take the back, you take the far side."

"Now hold on," said Wolfbait. "Tell me what's happening. Maybe I can help."

"You have a gun?"

"Not on me, no."

"Then go get Pieder. Tell him there's trouble, bring guns, he'll loan you one. I think Winklestaff's in there, maybe holding Nosey and Chauncey hostage. He's crazy and bent on revenge."

"That's all you had to say!" Wolfbait legged it sidelong up the slope to the top meadow, which in turn led to the blacksmith's place.

"What are you going to do with me . . . us?" Chauncey Wheeler glanced briefly at the trussed-up Nosey.

He couldn't help himself, so he said, "Why tie him but not me?"

Winklestaff glanced at him from the window. "Are you serious right now, Chauncey? You are being held hostage and you are complaining because I bound him but not you?" He chuckled and shook his head. "Aren't you a prize turkey. I suppose you are miffed because being tied up somehow makes that bookwormy fellow better than you. If someone else has something, then you want it, too. Ain't that about right?"

Chauncey blushed and shrugged.

"Truth be told, Chauncey, I am not worried about you doing much of anything. The only burst of energy I ever saw from you was when you laid into me with that shovel. I still carry the scars beneath my hat. But I will gladly give you credit for shaking me out of my dark mood of those days. I was dazed for a time, but awake enough to get on out of there before you came at me again and finished the job. It's not my fault you thought I was dead. But it did work to my benefit. Made me feel like a newborn bairn."

"You know how bad I felt for all these years, Wink?" said Chauncey.

"Oh, well, wait a moment, let me pull out my hanky!" Winklestaff's glare didn't match his carefree attitude of moments before. "You want to know how poor I felt? And I don't mean just the brain fits that take hold of me now and again from that shoveling you gave me. I mean poor, without money, you understand me, you fat beast?"

Chauncey leaned back in his chair. He didn't know whether to be afraid or offended. He decided a mix of both was in order. "You don't look so bad off, Wink. You got nice clothes, a good gun." He regretted saying that right away. No need to call attention to something that might lay him low.

"No thanks to you . . . partner. You want to know how I got this finery? I healed up and vowed to myself if I didn't wake up dead, I'd return one day to Boar Gulch and get my revenge on you and the whole lot around here. Then I'd get everything I deserve, which just happens to be everything here." He waved his arms wide, then let his left drop. His right still held the revolver.

"Funny thing happened, though. I needed money in order to make my way back here and take this place by force. So I did what most men in my position would do." He paused as if waiting for an answer.

Just then Nosey groaned and tried to shift to a leaning position behind the bar. Winklestaff glanced back at him. "Shut up back there or I'll drive a knife in your ear, you got me?"

Nosey stopped moving.

"Where was I? Oh yeah, so I set myself up in business once more. This time as a road agent. I like that name so much better than an owlhoot or thief or any of those common names thought up by people who have little imagination. I was doing all right, too, out Oregon and Washington way, when I got wind of an interesting development I read about in a newspaper. You know what that was?"

He sipped a mug of beer. "No? Well, I'll tell you. I read that the little mine camp deep in the Bitterroot Mountains, name of Boar Gulch, which rang a bell or two, I can tell you, why it was the place to be, a hot spot. And what's more it wasn't just Boar Gulch that was something special, but the entire region.

"Folks were flocking there in droves, pulling out nuggets the size of a child's head from rivers, panning up sacks full of dust, and the ore, barely concealed beneath the thin soil of the local slopes. Why, to hear the reporter tell it, miners were practically tossing away the lesser rocks in favor of the shiniest."

"I hope you didn't believe that, Wink. It's not been that way at all."

"Shut up, Chauncey. It's my story. One more word . . ." He wagged the revolver at his old partner's pudgy face.

"I decided then and there it was time to relocate my gang—did I tell you I have a gang? Oh, well, I don't anymore. You see, they all recently left my employ." He laughed and shook his head.

"That's one way to put it. And then we moved on into this region. Been plying the trade hereabouts for a couple of months now. Got a base camp and everything. It's a spot your pal, Rollie Finnegan, knows well. Seeing as how that's where he died not long ago."

"What?" said Chauncey, standing up and knocking the chair to the floor.

"Oh yes, didn't I tell you? He burned to death in a tragic barn fire."

From behind the bar, Nosey Parker managed to finally expel the wadded bar rag from his mouth with a loud "Gaaah!"

Winklestaff stepped into full view at the open end of the bar and leveled his revolver on the tied-up journalist.

"I told you one more peep and you were going to pay for it." Then he smiled and said, "Nah, too loud. I don't want to draw flies until Pops arrives."

"You're lying, Winklestaff. You aren't man enough to do Rollie Finnegan in!"

"Oh, is that so? Well" —he shrugged—"believe me or not. I don't care." He slid the revolver into his holster and drew his hip knife, a wide-bladed staghorn-handled weapon of heft and menace. He tested the blade on his thumb. "But he is dead. Which, coincidentally, is the very thing you will soon be."

He never heard the wooden chair whooshing through the air behind him. It slammed into the back of his head and drove him forward, his knees buckling as Chauncey grunted and swung the lone chair leg left in his hand. His second blow missed and clunked against a cupboard door.

Winklestaff's knife arched through the air and stabbed quivering into the wall beside Nosey's head, which he shifted to his right with a quick jerk, watching in terror as if time had slowed, as the great gleaming blade spun toward him.

Struggling to rise off his knees, Winklestaff lurched forward toward Nosey.

"Nosey!" shouted Chauncey as he stepped around Winklestaff.

The clubbed man growled and, though weaving in his addled state, he snatched out with his right hand and caught a fistful of the mayor's black wool trousers. Then he pulled. Chauncey flopped to his belly with a tight scream, two feet in front of Nosey, struggling to stand.

Chauncey spun around, his jowled face vermilion in

effort and rage. He snatched back at Winklestaff, spewing spittle and words without meaning as he forced his girth up off the floor and at the man he'd long ago assumed he'd killed with a shovel.

"Not this time!" shouted Winklestaff and dragged himself to his feet, with Chauncey's trousers gripped in one hand and the fat man himself hanging off him on his left side.

As he spun, he clawed for his revolver, but Chauncey heard Nosey shout, "Chauncey— his gun!" and flailed his free arm even faster.

"No!" His thrashing limb scored a lucky hit, and the revolver dropped from Winklestaff's scrabbling fingers. At the same time, the mayor jammed forward with his feet and rammed his prodigious weight into Pete Winklestaff's already unbalanced body.

His former partner growled a mélange of bitter oaths and animalistic sounds as the two men over-ended across the barroom, caroming into tables and chairs, upending them in the process, and slammed into the front door, which cracked apart at the frame and snapped open, sending jagged shards of fresh lumber exploding down the steps and into the street.

The two men followed, howling anger and pain in equal measures as they tumbled and bumped down the wide plank steps. Shouts from up and down the street rose as residents turned to see what the ruckus was all about.

A two-mule team parked across the street balked and dragged their ore wagon, though the brake was set, a good fifty feet before the shouting owner launched himself aboard and worked the lines on their heaving backs.

Rounding the corner of the bar, just having sent Wolf-bait scampering up the hill for Pieder's help, Rollie and Pops stopped short and stared as wide-eyed as the rest of the town at the tumbling mass of grunting, ragged men.

"My word, it's Winklestaff and the mayor!" shouted Pops, nudging back his bowler and rubbing his forehead. He raised Lil' Miss Mess Maker, but couldn't decide just what to do with her.

Beside him, Rollie held up the borrowed revolver. "They're like two dogs fighting! I can't get a sight on either one without shooting the other."

"Would it matter?" said Pops, watching the spectacle in unabashed awe.

Rollie nodded in agreement, but couldn't bring himself to risk it. Chauncey was a thorn in his side. But not bad enough to shoot him, even accidentally. Besides, though he had a gripe with Winklestaff big enough to fill a bank vault, this particular part of the fight was all Chauncey's. Rollie was pleased to note that Winklestaff had a wet, dark smear on his lower left leg. That'd be the work of his trusty Barlow from earlier.

"Would it be so bad if I said I was sort of enjoying seeing this?" Pops laughed.

"Let's not forget that Winklestaff is a butcher, tried to kill both of us and has left a trail of bodies hip deep all over these hills. Time to stop this."

Just then they heard shouts from inside the bar.

"Nosey!" said Pops, making for the stairs. He took them two at a time and barreled through the open front door. Unless Pops shouted for help, Rollie was intent on peeling apart the two snarling ex-partners before one of them damaged the other mortally. The way they were going at it, the possibility was all but a guarantee.

Chauncey screamed from beneath Winklestaff, and received a volley of hard, quick blows to his face and neck in return. With a clawing hand clapped to his now-bleeding scalp, Chauncey tried to roll away from his adversary.

Rollie walked forward, the snout of the revolver extended, but before he could reach them, Winklestaff raised high a fistful of Chauncey's hair and shouted, "Hee-yaah, ha, ha!"

Rollie barked orders as he loped toward them. They had the advantage of distance on him, and he wasn't feeling too spry given his recent dance with fire and brimstone.

But his shouts seized Winklestaff's quick gaze. And what the sneering, shrieking killer saw froze him long enough that Chauncey was able to land a solid hard right fist to Winklestaff's left temple. At the same time, the chunky mayor sunk his teeth into the slackened hand of his foe that had but moments before been tightening about his fleshy neck.

It was all the opening Rollie needed. As Winklestaff leaned back, howling and holding his face with one hand and shaking his bleeding, bitten hand, Rollie closed in on the remaining dozen feet that separated them. "You!" he shouted at Rollie. "Can't be!"

"You bet it is," growled Rollie.

From his back on the ground, Chauncey wiped at his bleeding face and said, "Why, Winky?"

"Why? Because you all owe me. Big time. You and all these filthy miners. You took and took and took from me."

Rollie bit back the urge to laugh. "How do you figure that?"

"Because this land was all mine. I was the first to ever see this entire region. This entire valley. Hell, all these valleys!" He waved his arms wide to take in everything visible. Rollie was certain that in Winklestaff's mind his statement included a whole lot beyond what everybody could see, too.

"I had great plans!"

"Yeah, and you blew it. Stewed yourself in booze. So what makes you think you deserve a thing from anybody? They all worked for their pokes, and on land they claimed. You have no claim to it at all."

Winklestaff snorted and pointed at the mayor. "That ungrateful animal tried to kill me! He attacked me with a shovel, then left me for dead. And to think I took him in, gave him all the advantages, paid for his journey west, set him up in business as my partner! A man I chose as a business partner turns out to be a killer!"

"Why murder, Winklestaff? You could have taken Chauncey to court, gone about your claim legally."

Winklestaff convulsed in laughter, not quite forgetting that Rollie was close by, waiting for the opportunity to pounce. "You have to be kidding me, you buffoon! And miss all this fun?"

"What's the fun in killing?"

"I'll show you how fun it can be!" Quick as a bullet, Winklestaff snatched at something beneath his half-buttoned vest.

Rollie was quicker and shouted, "No sir!" as he sighted

and pulled the trigger. The pistol barked and bucked and recoiled for another bite, a serpent on a short leash. But a second shot wasn't needed. The first had done the job, drilling a smoking hole in the center of Pete Winklestaff's sweat-stippled forehead.

He stiffened, arching as if he'd been stung in the back by an angry hornet.

A drop of blood leaked from the hole down along the bridge of his nose. Bloody froth bubbled from his mouth where the severed tip of his tongue dribbled out between his lips and landed on Chauncey's trembling face. Then a long, high-pitched wheeze peeled from Pete Winklestaff's mouth, and he flopped on his right side.

For a long moment, there was no sound, then Chauncey squealed like a spooked child and bucked and squirmed until he was out from under his former partner. He crawled on his hands and knees a few feet, then grunted upright, his hands wide as if he'd just performed a feat of magic. "What have you done? Pete! Pete!"

He ran to Winklestaff's side and nudged him with a toe, then looked at Rollie, who stood with his gun drawn on the flopped man.

"You killed Pete!"

Rollie stared wide eyed at the yammering man, then shook his head and walked toward The Last Drop. Behind him, the bleeding, bedraggled mayor of Boar Gulch swayed in the dusty street over the body of his murdering old partner, screaming his righteous rage about something Rollie would never understand.

Chapter Thirty

"Now, now, Mrs. Gladwell! No call for that! I was just about to pay her—I swear it!" The skinny miner held his balled-up longhandles before his crotch and tried to stomp into his boots. He managed to get his left foot into his right boot, but the other boot had flopped onto its side and wasn't accommodating the situation.

Madge Gladwell stood tall at the foot of the bed, her gaze pinned hard on the scrambling man. "My girls don't lie, mister. There are a number of things I will not tolerate in this life. Near the top of the list is bilking my girls, which means the bilker is bilking me. You understand, whoever you are?"

The man stared back, his mouth working like that of a beached fish.

"Nod if you understand."

He nodded.

"Good, at least you're not as simple as you look. Now apologize to Mabel here and we will endeavor to not repeat this foolishness in the future. You hear me?"

Again, the man nodded, still staring at the double-snout

of the sawed-off shredder the fetching but frightening madam held tucked under her ample bosom.

From the brass bedstead, half-buried in a mound of quilts and sheets, a giggle bubbled up out of a fetching doxy's mouth. She raised her head and said, "Madge, maybe just this once don't kill him. He wasn't like most of them." She winked and wiggled her eyebrows at her boss.

"Oh?" said the woman with the shotgun. She wagged the barrels up and down. "Okay, mister. Let's see what you got. Might be a deciding factor."

"What? No, I . . ."

She thumbed the second barrel alive. "Drop the clothes or I drop the hammers."

He swallowed and nodded. "Okay." He let go his wad of clothes and looked up at the tent's close ceiling while the woman whistled. "You're right, Mabel. He's a plow-horse."

The man let his gaze trail down to the woman, and she was smiling at him and lowering the hammers. "Okay, pay up and get out. And don't forget to tell your friends that this is not a charity ward. We are selling a service and you agreed to the terms before you came in. My girls don't lie."

The man stumbled out, half-clothed, into the night, and the two women shared a laugh. Mrs. Gladwell sat on the bed and sighed. "I hope I haven't made a mistake, Mabel. This" —she waved at the tent—"will keep the rain off, but it's getting cold at night. I've never spent much time in the mountains, and I'm not sure I want to after this. We need a house and not a scatter of a half-dozen tents on leased land. No matter how much we make up here, we won't get warm by working in these conditions."

Mabel giggled. "We can try."

"You really like the work, don't you?"

The girl looked down at her hands as she tied the top of her shift closed. "I do." She looked at Madge. "Is that so bad?"

The older woman shook her head and smiled. "No, girl. Not at all. But you're young yet. Think about what you'd like to do after all this. Maybe save up your money and set yourself up in a business of your own."

"Or marry rich," said the girl.

Mrs. Gladwell nodded. "I did that once. Best month of my life. Then I found out he'd lied."

"What do you mean?"

"Turns out he wasn't rich, just had good taste in clothes." She stood and smoothed her skirts. "And women." She winked and left the tent.

Chapter Thirty-one

Sol Tiggs blinked his eyes and the thing he didn't think he could have seen was still there. He jammed his knuckles into his eyes and rubbed hard before opening them once more. Yep, the wagon was still there, and in the driver's seat sat a large, handsome man with dark, oiled hair staring down at him. Next to him was a slender young man, not long out of boyhood.

"Good morning, sir," said the big, handsome fellow.

It took Sol a moment to realize the man was addressing him. It took him another moment to see the men on horseback emerge from behind the wagon.

"Morning. What do you want?" Sol's voice came out hoarse, croaky, as if he'd been spoonfed powdered rock. Not far off the mark, he thought. He'd spent the night with a pint bottle of raw white liquor and it was disinclined to let him forget it.

The big man in the wagon smiled. "Want? Why, we came here to entertain you." He waved his arms wide.

Sol saw then that the man was wearing what looked like a woman's cape, all shiny and purple and black. I can't be awake, he thought. Curse that Pooler and his rotgut gargle. I will never drink again.

"Well, I don't need entertaining," said Sol. "What I need is a decent strike and a neighbor who knows how to make tanglefoot that is easy on both ends."

"This is Boar Gulch, is it not?" A look of genuine concern darkened the big man's broad face.

"In a manner of speaking, yes." Sol stomped a boot and regretted it. "But this here's my claim. I'm Sol, by the way. Sol Tiggs. Gulch proper, I guess you'll be meaning the town, is yonder." He nodded at the narrow trail that wound through the ponderosas in a southwesterly fashion.

"I see. And how far would yonder be?" The big man smiled at him.

If I wasn't so laid up with my gut-ache illness, Sol thought, I could do worse than to wipe that happy look off his big face. "Follow the roadway. You miss it, you'll be the first to do so." He shook his head. "Never thought I'd see a grown man togged up in womanly finery."

"Come, gentlemen," said the big, handsome man. "Let us find Boar Gulch so we may begin our thespianic ministrations."

Sol watched the wagon, which had the look of a tincture-seller's rig, slowly rumble past, the two hard-looking horsemen behind each giving him a cold stare. He might be more bothered had he not felt like something a stray hound had dug up, gnawed on, and covered over again. He also had to make it to the privy before his tender situation got a whole lot worse.

Chapter Thirty-two

Rollie watched the treeline beyond the south end of town and hoped Pops and Pieder were successful in their task. He'd sent them off three days ago to the burned barn and the cabin on the river to dig up the stashed loot of Winklestaff's masked gang.

On their return, they were going to circle wide, distribute what he hoped was a fair amount back to the men of Stag Horn so they wouldn't starve in the coming winter, then bring the rest to Boar Gulch.

Once word of the gang's demise leached out, Rollie figured the surviving wronged miners, such as Colton Shepley, would turn up looking for their rightful earnings. How much each deserved, he had no idea—he hoped honesty would win out, but he wasn't naïve enough to believe it—nor how to get shares from the dead men to their families, wherever they might be. But they would try, and Nosey promised to help wrangle the complex situation.

"Rollie, is anything wrong?" said Nosey. "You keep

looking toward the timbers as if you just saw a ghost hovering."

"Thought I saw someone up there, maybe someone I recognize. Can't place him, though."

"Who? Where? I don't see anybody." Wolfbait craned his old, reedy neck, looking toward the door.

Rollie glanced at his pocketwatch, then out the front door. "North end of the street. Twelve, thirteen minutes ago."

Wolfbait began hastily crossing himself, then forked two grimy fingers and spat through them.

"What are you doing?" said Rollie. "Nosey just swept that floor. Take your mangy old backside out of here if you're going to spit."

"Ain't right, is all. Mention of that number."

"What number?" said Nosey.

"You know," he nodded toward Rollie. "The one he just said."

"Thirteen?" said Nosey, smiling. "You're not superstitious, are you, Wolfbait?"

"Call it what you will, I seen and heard too many strange things about that number. Why, on that day, in each month I been alive, something odd has happened somewhere in the world."

"How come this never came up before?"

"Because it never did, is all. I try to keep such things to myself, because I know how certain people like to walk through their lives unen—what's that word, Nosey?"

"Unenlightened?"

Wolfbait snapped a finger and nodded. "That's the one I was groping for. Unenlightened. And since I see I am surrounded by such folks, I can't take much more of this just now. I will bid you good day and I will take my charms with me."

He stuffed a mangy old rabbit's foot and crumbling sprigs of sage back into his coat pocket and made for the door.

Still looking out the window, this time with his spyglass, Rollie said, "Huh."

"Huh, what?" said Nosey, glancing up.

"There's a wagon parked by the mercantile. Looks like an acting troupe. The side says he's touring the West and the world—not certain how that will work—delivering speeches and monologues and one-man performances."

"Sounds like a hard way to make a living."

As if beckoned, Chauncey strolled in through the front door. "The place is shaping up, gents," he said, thumbing his lapels and looking around at the rough-hewn pine poles that formed the outer walls.

He inspected the room, not quite looking at Rollie. "By the way, Finnegan, I have decided to forgive you."

"Forgive me? For what, exactly?"

"Why, for killing my old partner, Pete Winklestaff, of course."

"You're forgiving me for saving your life and laying low a man who murdered who knows how many men, and who tried to kill me, Pops, and Nosey?"

Chauncey's face reddened. He swallowed and said, "Well, yes. Yes, that's about the size of it."

"I am so relieved to have your forgiveness, Mr. Mayor. A weight has been lifted from my mind."

Chauncey cleared his throat and changed the topic. "This structure looks rather larger than the original." He turned to face Rollie. "Be certain you have not exceeded the parameters of your lot, Finnegan. I don't want to make an example out of you to the rest of the downtown merchants of Boar Gulch, but . . ."

"But what, mayor?" said Rollie, walking over, hefting a hand sledge. "We own this lot, and in our contract there are no words telling how we can and can't use it."

"Yes, well . . ." The mayor stepped backward. "There are provisions in this town that prevent folks such as yourselves from building too close to the outer edges of your parcels."

"No, there aren't." Rollie leaned close, hefting the blunt hammer enough that the mayor gulped.

"Well," the mayor said, breaking the spell and stepping backward, dusting his coat sleeves as if he'd come in from a sandstorm. "Thank goodness there are some people in this town who aren't heathens."

"What do you mean, mayor?" Nosey laughed and lifted full bottles from a wooden crate. "We're all heathens up here."

"All, that is, save for the internationally renown stage actor who not but an hour since arrived in our humble town."

"Actor? Here in Boar Gulch?" said Nosey. "Why?"

The mayor looked as if he'd been slapped. "And why not? With the Hotel Wheeler nearing completion, it would not surprise me to learn that acting troupes from all over the country, nay, from all over the globe will descend on our fair burg. Especially once they hear about the hotel and the performance space I intend to incorporate into the second floor."

"I thought that was going to be for town meetings and such?" said Rollie.

"Yes, well, those, too. But the primary use will be for stage plays, musical recitals, concerts. Oh, think of the culture we'll finally experience in this parched place!" He clapped his hands together and smiled so brightly Rollie didn't have the heart to poke fun at him.

Rollie turned back to his work.

"That is why I came to see you gentlemen. In honor of his arrival in our town, I would like to host a soiree, if you will, at my mercantile. I would hold it in the downstairs of the hotel but the place is a mess. They are not the tidiest builders I have encountered. I am inviting a number of folks, primarily business owners, and I wondered if you might like to attend?"

"That sounds . . . interesting," said Rollie. "What time is this soiree?"

The mayor said, "Ah, six o'clock would be a good time."

"Great. Pops and Pieder should be back by then. I know Pops never passes up an opportunity to attend a soiree."

"Yes, well . . ." The mayor scowled, then said, "I wondered, too, if you folks might supply the liquor."

"Ah, so this isn't so much an invitation as it is you needing somebody to pour booze down your newfound friend's gullet," said Rollie.

"If you want to be crass about it, then, yes, in a manner of speaking. Of course, Mr. Valucci will drink for free. I will see to that. But his attendants, an admittedly rough-looking crew of two men and a boy, will have to fend for themselves."

"Why does a man need two men and a boy to attend him?"

"I should think that would be obvious."

"Not to me," said Rollie.

The mayor sighed. "He is an actor of world renown!"

"And how do you know this?" said Rollie, trying to hide a grin.

"Why, because he told me so!"

"Uh huh."

Hours later, while a wind storm rattled and snapped at The Last Drop, and dust rolled in a boiling cloud down the hoof-pocked main street of Boar Gulch, a big, boisterous voice boomed above the dozen or so others in Wheeler's Mercantile.

Giacomo Valucci held court with a glass of bourbon in one hand and a silk handkerchief in the other. Most of the women in attendance, among them Sal and even pinch-faced Mrs. Pulaski, as well as all of Madge Gladwell's ladies, were visibly moved by the handsome stranger's Italian-tinged accent, his bespoke attire, and his lilac-perfumed hair oil. A number of the miners in attendance appeared impressed with the size of the man, if not in his taste in clothing or perfumery.

The entire time, Rollie eyed the big man who, noticeably, returned stares with smiles and gentle bows of the head. But the man's eyes never smiled. And that's what Rollie would recall hours later, lying awake in his cot in the back room of the slow-to-emerge new version of The Last Drop. The eyes were the clue to him remembering who this man was. He was certain he'd seen him before, certain he'd sought him in the past, but when was it? Months? Years? How long ago? And for what?

He sighed and tossed and rolled in his blankets for

what felt like hours, cursing himself for becoming too soft, for losing his skills of deduction, such as they were. And for asking too many questions without finding answers. He was beginning to sound like Nosey Parker, for pity's sake.

Finally, from across the dark room, Pops' deep voice cracked the silence. "You keep that up, you're going to wear out your blankets—be threadbare by morning."

Rollie growled.

"That won't help, but talking might. And if we're going to talk, might as well have coffee. I think better with a hot cup of it in my hand. Sometimes I think even better when I put something in my coffee."

"Me, too," said Rollie, swinging his legs over the side of his cot and stretching in the dark.

Pops padded across the floor and grabbed the coffee pot. "You poke the coals. I'll fill the pot from the barrel."

In twenty minutes, they were pouring hot coffee and lacing it with whiskey. "Now," said Pops, after his first sip. "What is it about that actor fellow you don't like?"

"That obvious?"

"Oh, just to me and everybody else in town. You glared at the man all during the mayor's silly little soiree, then you kept your trap shut tight all night after that."

"Well, you'll think it's odd, but I swear I've seen his eyes before. I know it, in fact."

Pops shrugged. "Not odd at all. In fact, I was going to tell you that I believe that man recognized you or knew you somehow. You think he's here looking for that bounty on you?"

"Wouldn't surprise me. I don't much buy this theatrical deal, either."

"Yeah," said Pops. "I'd say it's all an act." He smirked behind his cup.

Rollie grumbled but got Pops' point—he was prone to getting worked up about something.

"I'd feel better if we treat him as if he's come to the Gulch looking for you. That is to say, with suspicion."

Rollie nodded and sipped, still musing on the big actor's eyes. He knew the man, knew him from some dark, ink-black well in his past. But from when? Where?

It would come to him, it always did. He just hoped it would before the actor and his attendants came knocking with guns firing.

Chapter Thirty-three

For a large man, I am impressively nimble. Giacomo Valucci glanced about himself in the dark of the night and breathed deep. It felt good to let his lungs fill, expand with the cool night air.

He stepped ever closer to his intended destination, placing each foot with care lest he make a tell-tale noise tipping him off to the busy occupants of the tents. It would not do to ruin the surprise he had planned for Stoneface at this late moment in the game.

He paused behind each of the tents, listening to the low murmur of voices or the cooing of a woman pretending to feel something for the grubby man who rode her like an old workhorse.

The fourth tent was lit from within by the soft honey-glow of a turned-down lamp. He heard what he hoped to hear—a man grunting into his clothes, mumbling about how he liked her, and would it be all right if he were to come see her again.

The oaf, thought Giacomo. Of course, she'll say yes, yes, do come again. It was her business. As if a baker would say no, I'm afraid I'll only sell you the one loaf of bread forever.

Then the sound of coins dropping onto a plate, perhaps. Yes, a tip. Isn't that thoughtful. Then the goodbyes, a longing in the man's voice, a murmur of faked parting from the woman, and the soft rustle of the canvas flap, boots on the wooden planking out front, then crunching gravel beyond, and gone. Now was the moment.

Giacomo wasted no time in rounding the tent. He stepped softly with his quiet brogans on the planking and parted the canvas flaps with a long finger. There was the woman, standing before her washbasin, a robe parted as she bathed herself before a mirrored vanity table.

In the low light he saw she was red haired, one of the women he'd seen at the pathetic little soiree they'd thrown four nights before, on his first night in town. Any of them would serve the purpose. He waited a few moments longer while she finished her ablutions and tied her robe.

Now she will make her way to the madam's parlor tent, as he had heard it called, to await her next customer. Not tonight.

Valucci opened wide the flaps and stepped inside the tent. She turned with a slight inhale of breath. "I'm not ready yet—oh, it's you." She slowly smiled.

"Yes, it's me," he said, closing the flaps behind him. "I hope you don't mind," he said, "but I am eager." She likes what she sees of me, he thought. This is not a surprise. All women like to see Giacomo Valucci.

She crossed to the bed and sat down, patting the spot beside her. "Please, come sit with me."

So that was how it was going to be, the kindly young girl who wishes to play innocent games. Fine with me, he thought as he sat down beside her. Two can play this game. He looked about at the inside of the tent, a crib as he had heard it called in many other towns, in many other places far from here. But they were all the same. A messy place that could never quite rid itself of the stink of base-level humanity, grunting away their lives.

"You're the actor," she said, resting a hand atop his right knee.

"Yes, that is I."

"I've been looking forward to seeing your perform-ance."

"You haven't seen any of the short shows I've put on yet?"

She shook her head. "No, not yet. I've been . . . busy here."

"I see." He nodded in understanding. Then he turned to face her. "You are a pretty young woman." He took her face in his big hands and held it tenderly. "You remind me in some ways of a woman I once knew."

She cooed, a soft sound meant he knew to convey she found what he said to be sweet and sad. Perhaps he had lost someone dear to him. He stared at her long moments.

In truth, her eyes did remind him of Ophelia's. Large for her face, but the rest of her, a straight nose, too long, her chin pronounced, her hair, a reddish brown, all wrong, all wrong. Still, he held her face in his hands and was tempted to end it all there, that quick. But no. He must have patience. But not too much, for the madam, that large, coarse woman, would lumber in on them and raise the roof of this pathetic tent with her mannish voice.

No, best to cut to the chase, as they say.

"Would you like to . . ." she said, pulling her face back

from between his hands. She gazed toward the rest of the rumpled bed behind them.

"Yes, yes," he said, smiling. "You lie back and I will make ready."

She did so, untying her robe and parting it as he dallied with a button at the top of his shirt. He sat once more beside her and with his left hand reached up to stroke the hair from her face. She smiled.

His right hand found her throat. He softly stroked the fair skin there, then ran his fingers harder and harder, deeper and deeper until he saw that quick flick of change in her eyes, from softness to slowly widening alarm. This, he knew she was thinking, this is not right.

No, my dear, this is entirely wrong. For you, anyway. He smiled as his massive right hand closed over her throat and squeezed, a quick push to collapse her windpipe before she could screech in that annoying way women always did when he was showing them how very fond he was of them.

The entire time he squeezed he watched her eyes, and loved that moment that always happened when they widened as if they were seeing something for the first time. Perhaps they were, a man who had just then gone beyond the point anyone had ever gone in her life. And then the very next moment, when they widened more and bulged outward, her mouth working fast but allowing no sound to pass other than tiny, gagging noises.

Her hands slapped and clawed at him now, but she knew, deep down, in her last moments, she knew there was no hope for her. Because she knew he was a large man and healthy, not like these coughing, worn-out miners looking for far more than she could ever give. No, he was a fine example of what a real man should be, one of the few she had ever seen, and the last she would ever see.

This had not occurred to him before. As he snatched her flailing wrists and held them tight in his free left hand, still smiling down at her, he thought that yes, indeed, he was bestowing on her a great kindness in allowing her to see him and not some bumbling oaf as the last face she would ever see on this earth.

She fought and fought, kicking and bucking, just as in her occupation, and he squeezed, and even in the dim light he saw the color of her face change from the pale hue of when he'd first arrived to the deep, dark purple, now nearly the color of a day-old bruise. A once-pretty face, though not a beauty by any stretch of the imagination, had now gone puffy and bulbous and oh, look, her tongue did that thing they all do, just before the eyes cease to look at him, on him, the very man who offered her release.

He held her there a few moments longer, for he had been surprised once, down by the wharves in the Barbary Coast, back home, when a fallen woman had surprised him by gasping back to life, even after her eyes had glazed and her breath had stopped. No, that would not do any longer, and certainly not here. For this evening was to be a special one, a leaving behind of a calling card for a long-lost acquaintance, one he sorely wanted to meet again.

He gingerly lifted his big fingers one at a time, free of her throat. There it was, the imprint of his hand, his calling card, as he thought of it. Yes, it was risky in such a small place as this, for there were few men here the match of his stature and thus, hand size. But no, he did not care.

For it would bring him what he came to find. It would bring Rollie "Stoneface" Finnegan crawling to him, sniffing for clues in that devoted doggish way of his.

"Now, my dear," said Giacomo. "One last thing." He arranged her hands by her sides and lifted free his razor-sharp needle-like knife from a pocket inside his frock coat. "There is one last thing we must attend to, or Stoneface may well miss out on the clues, ample and obvious though they are. He is a dullard, you know. A simpleton, a life-long, plodding fool."

Giacomo smiled, but the girl did not return this. He sighed, flipped open the long, slender blade, and patted up high on her belly. "Now, my dear, after play-acting at it all the long years of your sad little life, you shall finally give your heart to someone." He leaned close and whispered, "Me!"

Chapter Thirty-four

The woman's screams ripped through the quiet night air, jerking awake the men and women in tents lining what the locals had come to call Heaven Hill.

It was Clarice who found her. She'd walked over between customers to borrow a hair ribbon. She'd knocked on the pole at the front of the tent, but heard no response. "Mabel?" she'd said. Still no response. There was no lamp light in the tent.

Since she lived and worked in the tent to the left of Mabel's, Clarice went back to her tent and retrieved her lamp. The girls were forever borrowing one another's things, so if Mabel was not in just now, Clarice felt sure she would not mind her entering and borrowing a ribbon. She'd lost hers, not the first time a miner or ranch hand would have walked off with it.

What they did with them, she did not know, sniff them, maybe. Reminding them of their girls back home, wherever that was. The men, especially the young ones with funny, back-East accents, were forever telling her about the girls waiting for them back home.

She knew if she were one of those girls she would not

want her young man sharing a bed with a whore. But she had no such boy on her arm. There were plenty of men who wanted to be her boy, or so they thought.

Dally with a man a few times and they would always try to get her to give up her ways and live with them. Why? So she could raise ten children and cook and clean and listen to him complain about how they didn't have any money and live in a soddy out on the prairie and worry about rattlesnakes and wild hogs?

No sir, she thought as she returned to Mabel's tent with her lamp turned low. I grew up in just that sort of family. Why did they think she was flat-backin' for a living? She was answerable only to Madge, she had pretty dresses, all the food she could eat, fancy perfumes, and hosiery and hats. She even had a parasol and two pairs of boots. And good friends, too. And Madge promised them all a bigger cut of the earnings once they built their own place here in Boar Gulch, which sure did have the makings of a boomtown.

"Mabel? You in here? I hope you're not sleeping. I just came to borrow a hair—"

That's when Clarice nearly dropped her lamp. No way could she be seeing what she knew she was seeing. She did the only thing she could think of doing.

Clarice screamed and screamed and screamed some more. She didn't stop screaming until the tent was filled with half-naked men and women all wide-eyed and wondering what the ruckus was about.

It took but two minutes for someone to fetch Rollie and Pops, who came barreling up the slope with half the town in tow—news spread quickly.

By the time the two men made it to the hilltop location

of the ladies' camp, armed men had spread out into the surrounding darkness, lanterns held aloft.

"Somebody's going to get shot by accident before sunup," muttered Rollie to Pops as they closed in on the crowd before them. The women of the place were wrapped in quilts and stood in a group by themselves, huddled and hugging each other and crying.

Someone, Rollie didn't see who, recognized him and Pops. "Here's the law, let them through, let them through!"

The closer they got to the inside of the tent, the quieter folks became. Two oil lamps were turned up, filling the small space with light and stuffy heat. Madge was there, her eyes were red, and she held a hanky to her mouth as she stared at the shape of a body on the bed. It was covered with a blanket, but they could see red hair pecking out.

Madge turned to Rollie. It was strange to see this woman, one of the strongest he'd ever met, turn a grief-ridden face on him, her bottom lip quivering, doing her best to hold in the sadness caused by what lay under the blanket.

"Madge," he said softly. She took a step toward him, and he met her, gathered her in his arms, and she leaned her head on his shoulder. He held her for a long few moments while she cried. Pops backed up and closed the tent flaps blocking the view from those outside.

She straightened, dabbed her eyes, and looked at them both. "Clarice found her. Mabel has been . . . killed by someone. A beast."

"Has she been touched at all by anyone? I mean, since you found her?"

At first Madge looked as if she were angry, but her face softened. And she said, "I closed her eyes, that's all."

"Okay."

She said, "I've only ever read about such things happening. In cities. Never did I dream . . . one of my girls . . ."

"If you'd like, you could wait outside, Madge." Rollie looked at her.

She returned his gaze, then nodded. "Yes, I think I will. I can't look again. Not yet."

Rollie didn't tell her that he'd seen plenty in his time and whatever lay under that blanket would be shocking but likely not something he hadn't seen before. That didn't mean he wanted to see it.

After she left and the flaps had been secured from within once more, Rollie turned to his partner. "You ready?"

Pops shifted the Greener to his other arm and nodded. "Yeah."

Rollie carefully pinched the blanket on each side of her head, then lifted it and pulled it downward to reveal her face and neck.

Other than her closed eyes, the rest of her face told him what had happened. Around her eyes, purple lines showed where tiny veins had burst beneath the skin. Her lips were purple and her mouth was parted, her tongue a swollen blue-black mass that looked unfit to be in there.

But it was the girl's neck that held Rollie's gaze. Specifically, it was the massive handprint, as if painted on her fair skin, a print that wrapped around the slender neck, a print left by a big hand that had crushed the poor young woman's neck.

And it reminded him of something, something from his past. From years before. The handprint mesmerized him, his vision blurred and then he heard something . . .

"Oh, Mabel," whispered Pops.

At first Rollie didn't seem to hear him, and then he did. "What?" Rollie looked at his friend. "You okay?"

"The girl. Nosey was fond of her. I think she liked him, too."

"I didn't know he came up here."

"He didn't, not so far as I know."

"Oh."

Rollie breathed deeply again and pulled the blanket down farther. It would never not embarrass him to his very roots to see a dead woman's naked body, but it was part of the job. A job he did not want, and he never felt that more strongly than at that moment. He didn't stop at her chest, but kept tugging the blanket back until it reached her navel.

And as soon as he saw what had been done to her, just below the fan of the ribcage, he realized he was looking at something that simply could not be. Something that had happened years before, crimes against women, mostly, but some men, too. And they were replicated here, first with the crushed throat by a big hand, strong enough to leave a deep dark imprint.

Second, the sliced-open upper belly, a vertical cut long enough to accommodate a hand, a large hand. A hand that reached inside the girl and pulled out the heart, her very own heart, that now rested, glistening with drying blood, on her sunken belly.

Chapter Thirty-five

Dawn found Rollie alone in the back room of The Last Drop, his right eye-corner jouncing from too much coffee. He'd just sent Nosey and Wolfbait out on the west road in search of clues. It was the least likely trail out of town, but they were riled and determined to do their part. Nosey was especially worked up, understandable given how he felt about the murdered girl.

Pops rode off to track Valucci's attendants, who were, as with their boss, nowhere to be found. In truth, Rollie didn't much care if they found the man's helpers. It was the big actor himself Rollie wanted.

Ever since that actor and his 'assistants,' as he called them, had arrived in town four, almost five days before, nothing had been the same in Boar Gulch. Somehow the actor hadn't wanted to talk with Rollie up close and personal for very long since they arrived. Now Rollie knew why. And he knew who the man was, or rather what he'd done, for years.

All those brutal, bloody murders from southern California to Arizona and beyond, all of which Rollie knew about, some of which he worked on, none of which he cracked. They had been the source of his greatest personal failings as a Pinkerton agent. And now here was the killer, come looking for him, in little Boar Gulch. Here was his opportunity to end it, too late for Mabel . . .

He'd already spent two minutes too long rummaging for more ammunition. Every second he spent grabbing more was a second Valucci was still alive and not paying for gutting the innocent girl.

Images of the sliced-up girl's belly and chest stabbed unbidden into his mind. He shook his head and gritted his teeth as he thumbed shells into his rifle.

"Hello! Hello?"

Rollie sighed and dumped the rest of the box of cartridges on his rumpled bedding. He snatched up a handful and shoved them in his vest pocket. The last thing he needed was to talk with Chauncey Wheeler. But it was too late.

"Ah! There you are, Finnegan."

"Yeah, here I am."

The fat man thumbed his lapels and puffed up his chest. "As mayor of Boar Gulch—"

"Chauncey, I'm busy!"

The barked interruption stopped the chubby man for a brief moment. Then he resumed his pose and began again. "As mayor of Boar Gulch, I demand to know what you are going to do about this most heinous crime. It cannot stand, Finnegan, do you hear me?"

"Doing it, Chauncey."

"What, specifically?"

Rollie sighed. "Pops is tracking Valucci's men, and I'm tracking Valucci."

"For heaven's sake, why?"

"Because he's the killer."

"What? You must be out of your mind, Finnegan! I have had enough of your loose-cannon ways. I absolutely forbid you to pursue this line of inquiry."

Rollie bent down over the fat man's face and in a low voice said, "Walk carefully, mayor. You're on thin ice."

"But, but . . . he's a man of culture! An esteemed actor of the world stage! We should be thanking him for visiting Boar Gulch, not vilifying him!"

"I'm not going to vilify him, Chauncey, I'm going to kill him."

"But . . . but . . ."

"You want to be useful, Chauncey, sell that damned hotel to Madge Gladwell. She has money to finish it, and she has the need for it. You don't. Hell, partner with her. Rent it to her, I don't care. But those girls don't deserve more hardship, especially not after last night, you hear me?" By the time he'd finished talking, Rollie's face was an inch from Chauncey's and the rifle's snout was poked into the porky man's gut.

The mayor nodded. Even in that instant Rollie could see the fleeting glint of a deal working in the mayor's eyes. It would work out. And with any luck, Chauncey would meet his match in Madge Gladwell.

"Now go away, Chauncey." Rollie levered the rifle. "I'm not kidding."

The mayor whimpered and bolted for the door. Rollie walked through the empty, dim bar and was about to open the front door when it swung wide. He palmed his Schofield and stuffed it in the sniffer of the man who'd opened the door. Bone, town odd-job man with the gaunt hawk face and now, wide eyes.

"Don't shoot me, Rollie!"

"What do you want?"

With a trembling hand the man held up a folded paper with a blue wax seal. Rollie growled and snatched it from him. "Who gave it to you?" he said as he thumbed it open.

"That kid, the one with the actor."

"Where?"

"Out front of the mayor's hotel."

Rollie grunted and walked to the bar. Bone followed.

Rollie laid the paper on the bar, still gazing at the note written inside, in fancy hand. He drew a glass of beer and slid it to Bone. "Take it with you."

"Huh?"

Rollie stuffed the note into his vest pocket and ushered Bone out the door. They both emerged into the morning light. "And bring the glass back for a refill."

"Sure thing, Rollie," said Bone, smiling and quaffing this unexpected morning treat.

On the steps, Rollie pushed past him and stalked up the street toward the north end and the unfinished hotel, Chauncey's Folly, with the note's words echoing in his head:

Dear Rollie "Stoneface" Finnegan,
You are cordially invited to a private
performance in your honor by the one and only
world famous star of the stage, Giacomo Valucci.
The time? Now.
And don't be late . . . unless of course you wish
for a repeat of last night's masterful performance.

Your humble servant,
Sir Giacomo Valucci.

Chapter Thirty-six

One hundred feet from the entrance of the hotel, Rollie veered to his left, cut upslope behind the building, noting, not for the first time, its impressive size. And one mighty waste of money and time.

The ground was dry, despite the recent, pounding rains. Without deep topsoil, the wet weather drilled in, and the thirsty earth sucked it up, leaving the surface loose and dusty.

Despite the situation, Rollie noticed the sunlight. Later in the day it would take on that particular golden sheen so prized by artists. He learned of this years before when he'd ridden through the east slope of the Teton Range as fellow guide and guard with a native Lakota man named Takes Wing. They acted as hired protectors of a young married couple, each of whom was an accomplished painter.

On top of finding the work easy and enjoyable, and learning more than he'd ever care to know about painting, Rollie learned about the golden light, as the painters called it, and how that time of day was the most valued time in which to work their talents.

She had been the daughter of a wealthy brewer in Milwaukee, and the young man her new husband. Afterward, Rollie had followed their careers when he could, and had been unsurprised to learn the marriage did not survive. The young man took to the bottle and squandered his pretty wife's money until her daddy put an end to it, bought the young fool out, and kicked him to the curb.

But the woman's artistic renderings of the grandeur of America's unexplored West had become the talk of social circles in Europe to such an extent that she drew the attention of a young Earl or Duke or Lord or something and had married him, had become the Lady of a castle, and a mother to future royals.

Rollie often thought of her and hoped her aspirations and passion for her art hadn't been lost, or worse, buried alive under the false glow of money and high society and responsibility. Most of all he hoped she was happy. Of what he remembered, he knew nothing made her happier than her art. Not even, Rollie had remembered, her young husband.

His boots slid and raised puffs of dust as he angled toward the top of the low ridge behind the town. He cut north and came back down between the few close-by trees lucky enough to have survived the axes of residents eager to cobble together cabins and get to digging for gold.

The top of the slope was roughly level with the building's second floor, but too far to reach without a catwalk, which did not exist, bridging the span.

The rear of the building thus far offered no windows, just a dizzying wall of horizontal clapboards, or clabbers, as he'd heard a few old-time New Englanders call them.

And down below, three steps led to a small platform and a large, plank door.

With Schofield drawn, he cut left, then right, the left again down the steep slope that ended within a dozen feet of the rear of the building. He saw that the knob on the door above and ahead was on the right side, meaning it would swing to the left. He made for the right. If someone were to open it while he was out here, he wanted to see them first. And them to see him soon after, with dread in their eyes.

Inside, he guessed there was an odd clot of seasoned rattlers waiting to strike. He'd find out soon.

That's when the door cracked open a smidgin, as if whoever was inside was expecting to see someone. They must have seen Rollie because the door squawked open hard and fast, slamming outward against the back wall. Before it settled, spasming and clacking, the man from inside opened up, squeezing off a bullet. It whistled a couple of yards past Rollie's left shoulder and splintered into a stack of rough-sawn planking.

As it chewed into the wood, Rollie squeezed one, two shots from his revolver into the dark slice of doorway. He was rewarded with a yelp and a gag that tailed off into a groan. He wasted no time in bolting up the steps and stomping his way to the twitching man who'd flopped half out of the frame.

"Help . . . me . . ."

"Nope," said Rollie, recognizing the man as one of the "assistants" of Valucci. He peered around the doorframe into the darkened room. He saw little but long shadows from the early sun's glow.

Rollie thought back on what he remembered of the

interior of the slow-to-emerge building. He knew the open-roofed top floor of the place had still not been divided into rooms. There was a second floor and this floor, but beyond that he knew little.

Chauncey had told Nosey he hoped to keep the upstairs open for stage plays and various productions for what he considered inevitable visits from touring theatrical companies.

Valucci's presence in town had only emboldened the mayor, who considered Valucci "a fellow man of culture and refinement." From what Rollie knew of Chauncey Wheeler, Rollie wasn't so certain the mayor knew what culture and refinement might be.

"Come, come, come," said a large voice from somewhere deep in the building, deep in the dark space. "Welcome to the show. Welcome to your very own private performance."

And so Rollie walked on in.

Pops heard gunshots from The Last Drop, where he'd stopped to check in with Rollie, see if he'd had any luck.

"Wonder if that's the direction Rollie went," said Nosey.

"Me, too," said Pops, setting down his glass of water and reaching down for Lil' Miss Mess Maker, then ran toward the door, his fingertips brushing his holstered hide-out gun, worn up high on the left side of his chest, checking to see it was still there.

He pounded up the street, leading several other Gulchers doing the same. He knew in his gut at least that one of the shots he heard came from Rollie's gun. But he did not know the outcome. He did know that no one, not even Stoneface Finnegan, was that lucky, or that good, forever.

Nearly to the hotel, Pops spied one of the men he'd been looking for, one of the characters who worked for Valucci. He was hotfooting it to the stable where the company had been keeping its wagon and mounts.

"Got to keep him from leaving town," he muttered to himself, and angled toward the back door of the barn. He reached the cool, darker interior a few paces ahead of the man, who burst in, breathing hard, taking in the dim space for a moment. Pops watched him from behind a half-open stall door. Motes of hay dust hung in narrow shafts of light.

"Can't let that lawdog get wind of me," the man muttered. "If he survives Valucci—though ain't nobody has yet that I know of—I might well be next." He looked around himself. "Now, where them horses at?"

"Over here," said Pops, standing and leveling the hefty Greener at the wild-eyed man. "Raise them high, boy, or die thinking about it." He cocked both barrels.

The man did as Pops bade, but not quite high enough.

"Higher or we're done."

"Okay, okay!" He complied, then said, "Who are you?"

"I am justice, such as it is, in these parts. And you are a known associate of that killing devil, so you are guilty, too."

The stranger groaned and protested and cajoled and whimpered and whined as Pops tied him up. It was a crude job, but served to keep the man immobile, at least until he could get someone to watch over him. The man, a seasoned trail hound, from the looks of his worn garb, cursed him and called him foul names he'd already heard a thousand times throughout his life.

Pops worked fast, and as he cinched the last of the knots tight, he said, "I'd like to stay and chat some more, but I have another engagement. Rest assured, I'll keep all those kind words in mind as me and my pal, Rollie, pass judgment on your neck."

With that, he lugged the man's weapons outside and beckoned Bone, who was strolling by with another clot of curious townsfolk toward the hotel. "Do me a favor, Bone? There's a beer in it for you."

"Like what?"

"Like go tell Nosey to lock up The Last Drop, then have him and Wolfbait come down here to the stable to tend to a headache I have tied up inside. And make sure Nosey gets this." He handed Bone the gunbelt off Valucci's man.

The gaunt man draped the belt on his shoulder. "Sounds like a two-beer job to me."

"You're right. But only if it works out as I want. Might be there's a shot of whiskey in it, too."

Bone didn't need to be told twice. He bolted for The Last Drop as fast as his sticklike legs could carry him.

The sky, already a darkening thing, clouded even tighter, and a cold wind came calling. Pops stifled a shiver that zinged up his back, and made for the hotel. Just in time for the show.

Chapter Thirty-seven

With cautious steps, Rollie winced at the slightest wood creaks and scuffs his boots made on the rough planking as he ascended the half-built staircase. He paused as he reached the second floor. Two open window holes in the front of the building cast gray light and let in a sudden, frigid breeze. To his right, shadowed by a tangle of cast-off plank ends, a shape shuddered and sniffed. Rollie walked straight to it and jammed his gun into it.

"Oh!" said the shape as Rollie snagged at it with his free hand and dragged.

"Who are you?" growled Rollie in a low voice.

Then he saw who it was—the kid who'd accompanied the actor. Add him to the one he'd shot downstairs and that left one man unaccounted for.

"I had no idea what he was like!" The young man whimpered and stuffed knuckles into his mouth.

Little more than a boy, the youth sported two puffed eyes, a bloodied nose that did not look as if it would heal well, and a bleeding gash trailing from his mouth. "I wish I never came. I . . . I didn't know!"

"Where is he?" whispered Rollie.

The kid looked upward toward the rough ceiling of the second floor.

"He alone?"

The kid nodded.

"Yeah?"

"I swear it!"

"Get out of here. Go find Pops, black man, bowler hat. Tell him I sent you."

The kid's eyes widened.

"You'll be safe with him. For the time being. And tell him I said, 'No rope.' Got that? 'No rope.'"

The kid nodded and scurried for the stairwell.

Rollie waited until the youth was out of hearing range, hoping the rope comment would keep Pops from stringing up the kid should Rollie not make it back down.

He worked his way up the last flight of steps toward the open-trussed top floor, the day's cold air chasing him as if urging him upward toward some higher, odd encounter.

He peered above the floor, the faint, sweet tang of fresh sawdust tickling his nostrils, and didn't have to scan the gray space to locate his quarry.

There stood Giacomo Valucci, looming large at the front of the building, facing Rollie, his back to the open air and the street below, the steepling raw rafters open to the blustered, graying sky above.

As if whisked by the push of the sudden, frigid breeze, Rollie was taken back to the dream, the cold-sweat terror-soaked dream. The man before him was the vicious death dealer in the dream, glimpsed in profile, in shadow, never in full. A brute specter wrought massive and all-too-real. The cold pricking of Death's beckoning bone finger sliced an icy trail up his spine.

The big ghoul raised his arms high as if he were about to take flight. Rollie stepped up out of the stairwell and faced him.

Valucci whipped his arms even higher, a flapping, gaudy, high-collared cape gripped in his large hands. Big, murderous hands, thought Rollie, the massive mitts that had crushed the life from, who but Valucci really knew, how many innocent lives?

Twin lamps flanking the big brute cast an eerie light, making his shimmering cape a living thing. "Welcome! Welcome to the show of all shows, Stoneface Finnegan!" His voice boomed outward from a mouth stretched wide in a full smile of confidence and satisfaction, his words reaching not only Rollie but the assemblage of townsfolk far below.

"By now you must have it all figured out! You see, I am here because one Cleve Danziger failed me. Yes, that was my doing, but I am pleased with this outcome, aren't you? I needed to be here to tell you all this. To reveal the truth to you."

The news that Valucci was behind the Danziger attack did not surprise Rollie. In fact, it made all the sense in the world. "I'll bite, Valucci. What's this truth?"

"Why, it's about all those murders years ago, yes? Your failures, hmm? You see, there's a reason you could never solve those murders, Mr. Finnegan, and it is simple—you were too close! Too close to the cases. So close you could not see it, or perhaps did not want to see it. It's starting to dawn on you now, isn't it, Stoneface? It's because you, yes you, were the killer! Yes, now I see that you understand." His rant tapered off into a deep, manly laugh.

"You're a fool," said Rollie, striding forward, ignoring

the gasps rising up from below by his fellow Gulchers. He laid the rifle at the top of the stairs, but kept the Schofield peeled back and held steady on the big man.

"The only reason I didn't catch you back then was because of your silly costumes. I will give you credit where it's due, though. You were a good actor. I said 'were' because you've lost your edge. Just like your looks, they're beginning to fray. You're rough in the daylight, Valucci."

Rollie walked forward, hoping his digging comments would draw out the man, force him to do something quick and foolish. He held his gun drawn and steady on the large, posed form standing before him. Valucci whipped his arms downward with a mighty flourish. Yards of shimmering blue-black satin whispered and fluttered.

Rollie held still, eyeing the crazed man. Now that Valucci's arms were down, hands at his waist, Rollie could see the front of the man's suit, a black velvet affair with a vivid, blood-red ascot tied wide about his neck and puffed beneath his chin, vivid against the crisp white of a dress shirt rising from a blue velvet vest.

The man's long, black shoes shone, outmatched in sheen only by his gleaming black hair, oiled and coiffed in a fanciful dollop atop his wide head. Two onyx eyes glinted beneath arching black brows. Beneath his long, perfect nose, that cruel mouth framed wet-white teeth, and smiled impossibly wide.

But it was the glint of metal at the man's waist that most interested Rollie. Something that looked like a small wire cage rode at the man's left-hand hip. It didn't look much like any weapon Rollie was familiar with.

As if reading his thoughts, Valucci grasped at the silver fist-size cage and pulled. With a slick, metallic sliding sound, a slender silver sword emerged. The man held it aloft and then lowered it vertically until the handle's basket hovered before his mouth.

His eyes peered at Rollie around the slender blade, an ornately carved thing more ceremonial than practical, but Rollie did not wish to find out just how useful it might be. He guessed that even dull it could skewer a man.

"And so the play opens," said Valucci in a grave, solid voice. "Imagine if you will a cool autumn evening. A man and a woman are alone, locked in a deep embrace, gazing into each other's eyes, happiness such as mortals may never know abounds between them."

"Stop talking, Valucci, and lay down the sword."

Valucci smiled and nodded and continued as if Rollie were not there. "Ah, yes, that glorious blush of new love. And then darkness falls. Enter the villain! Stoneface! Here he comes, the rumble of thunder, the rattle of bones, the screams of his victims—oh, it is too much!"

The big man draped his free hand across his forehead and sighed deeply.

"I should shoot you now and be done with you," said Rollie. "The world would thank me. The families whose lives you gashed apart for years would thank me. Mabel would thank me."

Rollie advanced to within ten feet of the big man, who roused himself from his reverie, snapping open his eyes. They were darker somehow, and any trace of a lurking smile had skittered off into the shadows. In a low voice, barbed and thick with emotion, Valucci said, "You made me do it. You and no other. If you had only left me alone, not insisted on tracing my routes, tracking me, annoying me with your petty, snooping ways. If only this and more, my dearest Ophelia would be alive still."

"Another innocent woman whose life you gutted and ruined, eh?"

With no warning, the big actor screamed, "No!" and lunged, slashing the sword downward as if it were a buggy whip. The action caught Rollie off guard and he faltered as he dodged to his right and squeezed off a shot. His bullet buzzed through the big cape and continued skyward.

A second shot lodged somewhere unseen. If in the man, Valucci showed no sign of it. He wheeled and advanced, growling. "How dare you interrupt my performance!"

Rollie's back was now to the open gable end facing the street. And Valucci was one stride from him. In that fingersnap of time, a sudden notion stayed Rollie's hand from delivering a third shot. He would sidestep, simple as that, and Giacomo Valucci would bull and roar past him and out into the unforgiving bleak air, and that would be that. Justice done . . . and a bullet saved.

But it did not happen quite as smoothly as Rollie had hoped. Valucci was quick and closing in, and his sword closed the gap between them even quicker. The big man's long arm shoved forward with the sword as he lunged. Rollie spun to his right, but not fast enough.

The ceremonial blade shimmered and darted forward like a metal snake. It slid beneath Rollie's flapping vest, shoving into his shirt, and, with a popping sound, pierced his left side, below the ribs, inches away from the intended target of his heart, before it popped again as it drove out through his back.

"Aaaah!" he roared, dropping his revolver and slamming hard into his right knee.

The actor lost his grip on the sword as he jerked as if in a spasm, and scrambled to stop himself from falling out the open-ended wall.

Giacomo's right ankle turned, buckling under the big body it had held up for years. A shriek of pain and anger and surprise burst from the big man's mouth. He collapsed on the now-useless ankle, and his momentum carried him, as if planned, straight between two thick upright timbers in the very center of the open wall facing the street.

It was the very spot where Rollie had once heard Chauncey say he'd like to one day mount a clock face for all the town to see, to use, to rely on, to stare at throughout the days of a golden future for Boar Gulch only the fat mayor could foresee.

As the wide shoulders clunked the timbers, then disappeared over the edge, Rollie heard desperate sounds that were not words, but animalistic, tearful grunts. He saw the big hands scrabbling, dragging over the edge, clawing for purchase on the half-finished trim boards as the weight of the man fought them and, slowly, inch by desperate inch, lost. The fingers all but slipped from sight, the tips still visible, white and trembling on the very edge.

Shouts and screams rose up from the crowd below.

Rollie staggered to the edge, and holding one of the timbers, peered over. In Rollie's fogged, pain-steeped mind, what he saw seemed impossible, and yet, there he was.

Valucci kicked and bucked, snotting on himself and blowing fierce breaths through clenched teeth. Tight, whining sounds rose from his gorge. His big, gleaming shoes bumped against the planked face of the hotel and could not find purchase, and then one did, the barest of crevices. It was enough to allow one big hand to snatch higher, to slap the floor at Rollie's feet. Then the other.

Rollie leaned out, extended a hand . . . then straightened and saw the crowd staring up from below. The clouds had thickened, and stinging pellets of ice shot down on them, but still they stared upward.

Rollie looked back down at his feet, at the big hands clawing their way closer. They were the hands of the man who had moments before tried to kill him, the man who ran him through with a ceremonial sword. It hurt like hell.

He was losing blood. He bent low, looked Valucci in the face, and smiled, then stood full height.

"Help me, you oaf!" The big man's words came out in a desperate, gasping whisper.

The words were like a tonic, and Rollie's pain-fogged mind cleared. "But of course." He raised a boot and stomped the man's right hand. Valucci screamed. Rollie lifted his boot, and the hand let go.

The man swung precariously from the white-knuckled fingers of his left hand. Rollie stomped once more. The man screamed once more and fell. Four feet.

Valucci's red silk ascot snagged on a protruding spike, looking to Rollie's addled mind like a shining rope of blood that held the flailing, gagging man aloft.

Valucci's scream sounded as if it were being dragged like a thread through a thin hole, then for one long moment, it pinched out, and there was silence, save for the whistling wind and pelting ice.

The ascot seemed to stretch as if made of India rubber, the red silk ripplings reflecting the scant rays of cold sunlight. Then the man's large body grew even longer, as if his neck were stretching.

People would later comment on this, wonder how it could have been possible, until in the next instance they saw how.

Giacomo Valucci's eyes bulged wide and popping, his face purpled, his neck bulging as if he were a fat man. And in that instant, he was hideous, and more like his father than he ever had been.

The body separated from the head at the ascot, and bobbed as if by magic a moment longer, as if in disbelief of what had just happened.

The big man's body dropped, dropped, as if time had slowed, then hit hard, a ragged heap on the wide, deep steps, then slopped to a stop.

The great, gleaming leonine head followed, bouncing down the steps before rolling to a stop at the mayor's feet.

For a brief moment, the crowd stood stunned in silence.

Then Pops began to clap. Nosey joined in. Behind them women screamed and Mayor Chauncey Wheeler flopped backward in a faint.

"This is, without doubt, the best play I have ever seen," said Nosey.

High above, beneath the gable of unfinished rafters with the gray sky over all, beside a sloppy stack of planking and a poorly swept mound of sawdust, Rollie "Stoneface" Finnegan dropped hard to his knees, peering over the edge of the building.

His mind was tricking him, he knew, having crawled

down this particular mental path a number of times in his long career. It was mortal pain, the spawn of grievous wounds. This was the dream, but worse, it was real. And he knew it could only end one way.

He was closing in on a bad place, a place where his body and his mind would go despite his wishes, and he could do nothing about it. His mind and body fogged, pulsed with waves of dull, ceaseless pain.

What happened here? A man, yes, that man who had tried to have him killed, who had hired Danziger, that one. Yes, the actor, the big man, handsome, young, all the things Rollie was not, and some he'd never been, that brute beast had tried to kill him.

Rollie shifted his gaze to his flat belly and the odd sight of the blood-slick thing he was holding before himself. Wait, it was in him, a part of him . . . a sword. Yes, that's what it was, the big actor had stabbed him with it.

A sword! He chuckled, and tasted something sticky filling his mouth. He smelled the warm stink of blood clog his nose.

A sword, though, now that was funny. Who used swords anymore? Except those dunderheads in the military, the ones who parade around clanking and clinking while real men do all the work.

And where was this light coming from? He saw sun breaking through a rift in the dark clouds. Like the reflection off a horse's eye in lamp light.

He heard a soft, fluttery sound somewhere out before him, in the air, what was that? Below him that's where it was. He leaned, dizziness pulling at him.

Something red fluttered out into his vision, retreated. He leaned out farther. There, a few feet below, too far down to reach, even if he wasn't holding a sword in his gut, there was a something . . . what? A cloth? A scarlet flag?

No, smaller than a flag, but familiar somehow, just below him, attached to the building. One of the workers had maybe nailed it there. But that made no sense. Then a sliver of sunlight reflected off it, and he saw it and knew it.

The actor's tie, another of the bright neck scarves he'd worn so proudly, parading up and down the street of Boar Gulch each day of his visit. The silk thing had puffed beneath his big square chin, attached to that big square head, topped with a pile of oiled black hair.

Pops and Nosey bolted for the building, shouting Rollie's name. The crowd closed in around the wreckage of the actor. As if by unspoken decision, they realized this dead thing at their feet was one of the endless string of enemies of Rollie Finnegan, a good man, one of them.

And so this man at their feet was their enemy, too. That didn't mean they were not petrified by the sort of folks Rollie attracted to their little mountain town.

Nosey and Pops found Rollie kneeling at the edge, at the spot where the self-proclaimed world-renown actor had moments before dangled.

An ascot, thought Rollie, of all the things to see in Boar Gulch, an ascot, a red silk ascot. Closer now he saw a delicate, lacey design woven through it. If he hadn't seen it on a man, he would have sworn it was something a woman would have worn, a woman long ago, regal, beautiful, too beautiful for this world.

How did it get down there? He leaned out farther. Maybe I can reach it, he thought. And he held one hand outward, far out over the edge, his fingers felt the rush of a quick breeze out there just before him, in nothing but dim daylight. The grayness of a storm that was, or was about to be. He leaned farther, then the lean became a thing of its own and turned into a slow fall forward into nothing but air.

"Ho, there, Rollie!"

Strong, gripping hands, too hard, pinched him like clamps, pulled him from behind. His arms, shoulders, his neck, something tightened around his neck and tugged him backward. Then the pain began. Hot pain as familiar and as unwelcome as anything can be in life.

Pain from a wound through which you either lived or you died. He didn't care anymore which.

"He's been stabbed," said a voice. It sounded like that old man he knew . . . Wolfbait. "It's that bastard's sword."

"Keep him on his knees while I shuck my shirt. Going to need bandages, a whole lot of them. Wolfbait, go see if that fellow who used to be a field medic in the war is still down below. And if he is there, I hope he isn't drunk yet."

"I could shout down. Should I shout down? Have someone fetch him up here?"

"No! Just go, we're bringing him down. This is no place to . . ."

"I can't do this again," Rollie heard himself mutter.

He heard a voice respond, quickly, as if it had been waiting for him to say something of the sort. It was Pops, good old Pops. "'Course you can. You ain't got a choice, Rollie. You think I'm going to pour all those drinks on my own?"

Another voice—Nosey, that crazy kid—close by his

other side, said something, but it was not to Rollie. "Have to take it out, Pops. We'll never get him down with that thing wagging."

"Okay, but we've got to stopper him in front and back, he'll leak out any good sense he has left."

From somewhere deep inside himself, Rollie "Stoneface" Finnegan pulled a ragged scrap of strength, and in a wheezing whisper, said, "I heard that."

The last thing Rollie heard before he slipped into blackness was Pops Tennyson and Nosey Parker chuckling. Tight, grim laughs, but man alive, at least they were laughs.

The end.

Stoneface Finnegan, Pops, Nosey, and Wolfbait will return in:

Thick as Blood: A Stoneface Finnegan Western (#3)

Keep reading for a special excerpt. . . .

**NATIONAL BESTSELLING AUTHORS
WILLIAM W. JOHNSTONE
and J.A. Johnstone**

GUNS OF THE VIGILANTES

Johnstone Country. Vigilante Justice.

Introducing the newest good guys in the bad Old West. A ragtag team of misfit avengers who don't wear badges, don't follow rules, and won't stop shooting—till justice is served . . .

GUNS OF THE VIGILANTES

It begins with a massacre. A crime so brutal and bloody, the local sheriff refuses to solve it. But when young deputy Dan Caine sees the slaughter for himself—an entire family murdered—he can't let it go. Especially when the eldest daughter is missing. Right there and then, Caine makes a fateful decision: throw away his badge, form a vigilante team, and go after the killers . . .

There's one problem: Who would be crazy enough to join him? First up is a grizzled old tinpan named Fish Lee, who discovered the bodies. Then there's the Kiowa, an Indian scout with a grudge; Clint Cooley, a washed-up gambler; Mortimer Cornelius Massey, a whiskey-soaked newsman; and Holt Peters, a half-grown stock boy. Sure, they might be crazy. They might be inexperienced. But one thing is certain: be it from heaven above or hell below . . . *vengeance is coming.*

Live Free. Read Hard.
www.williamjohnstone.net

Look for* GUNS OF THE VIGILANTES *on sale now.

Prologue

On a bright, clear, West Texas morning in the late summer of 1888, when across the prairie blue mistflowers were in bloom and lark buntings sang, lawman and vigilante Dan Caine shot beautiful Susan Stanton right between the eyes.

The killing haunted historians for generations and even London's *Strand Magazine,* of Sherlock Holmes fame, was intrigued enough to publish an article about the incident under the headline, *The Medusa Mystery,* so-called since to look into the woman's face meant death.

But there was no mystery about Susan Stanton's demise. She was said to be a temptress, a witch, the most beautiful and dangerous woman on the Frontier, fast with a gun and a demon with a knife, and the tale of her downfall begins, as it inevitably must, with a bloody massacre . . .

In all his born days, old tinpan Fish Lee had never seen the like . . . the entire Calthrop family massacred . . . and it was white men that had done it.

Fish looked around him wide-eyed, everything sharply delineated by the glaring sun.

Big, laughing Tom Calthrop had been shot several times. Nancy, his plump, pretty wife died of knife wounds and unspeakable abuse. Their ten-year-old twins Grace and Rose and sons Jacob, fifteen and Esau, thirteen, had been shot and Grace, possessed of long, flowing yellow hair, had been scalped. There was no sign of sixteen-year-old Jenny Calthrop, and Fish reckoned she'd been taken.

The family dog, a friendly mutt named Ranger, lay dead in the front yard and only Sadie, the cat, had escaped the slaughter, but now mewing in piteous distress, the little animal twined and untwined itself around Fish's boots like a calico snake.

All the bodies, sprawled in grotesque death poses, lay in the main room of the cabin.

The dusty, white-bearded prospector picked up the cat and held her close in one arm as he looked around him again. Part of the cabin had been scorched by a fire that had burned for a while and then gone out, and the smell of smoke still hung in the air. There was blood everywhere and amidst it all the six Calthrops lay like marble statues. It was a wonder to Fish how still were the dead . . . perfectly unmoving, their open eyes staring into infinity. The china clock on the mantel tick . . . tick . . . ticked . . . dropping small sounds into the cabin with clockwork dedication as though nothing untoward had happened.

The walls closing in on him, Fish Lee pulled down Mrs. Calthrop's skirt so that others would not see her nakedness as he had and then stepped out of the cabin. He lingered on the shady porch for a few moments and then walked into the hot, West Texas sun. The calico cat wanted down and ran back inside, tail up, where the people she loved would no longer make a fuss over her.

Fish lit his pipe and then took a pint bottle of whiskey from his burro's backpack. The little animal turned her head and stared an accusation at him.

"I know, Sophie," he said. "But this is strictly medicinal. I seen things this day that no Christian man should ever see." Around him were the tracks of horses and high-heeled boots, most of them clustered near the well, and Fish figured six or seven horses and riders, though he didn't have enough Injun in him to make an accurate count. Tom Calthrop's bay riding mare still stood in the corral in back of the ranch house, so horse theft was not the raiders' motive. But the cabin had been ransacked, so they'd been after something. But what? Cash money probably . . . what little the family had. Fish took a swig of rye and then another and pondered that answer. He shook his head. Yeah, it was most likely money, but damned if he knew. Going back two decades, Fish Lee visited the Calthrops once or twice a year and was always given a friendly welcome and dinner and a bed for the night. He knew that in recent years with cattle prices low, Tom barely scraped by as a rancher, and money was always tight. He bred good Herefords, but they were few in number because he could no longer buy additional stock and hire punchers to work them. The boys helped and did what they could, but neither of them were really interested in ranching. Fish remembered Nancy telling him, "Jacob and Esau are readers, and readers aren't much help come roundup." At the time, she'd smiled, but he'd seen bittersweet concern in her eyes.

Damn, that had been only six months ago. And now the Calthrops were all dead and the young boys being readers and not riders no longer amounted to a hill of beans.

Fish Lee was short and wiry, dressed in worn-out colorless clothes that he'd had for a long time. His battered top hat looked as though someone had stepped on it, a pair of goggles on the brim for protection against blowing sand. He had a shovel in his pack but didn't have the strength to bury six people. He had a Bible but couldn't read the verses, and he had a Henry rifle but no enemy in sight. In other words, as he stood in afternoon sunlight beside his uncaring burro he felt as useless as tits on a boar hog.

"Sophie, we'll head for Thunder Creek and let the law into what's happened here," he said. "Sheriff Chance Hurd will know what to do." He read doubt in the burro's dark eyes and said, "He will. You'll see."

After one last, lingering look at the cabin where shadows angled across the porch where the ollas hung, Fish shook his head and said, "Oh dear Lord in Heaven, what a terrible business."

He then led Sophie west toward town, walking through the bright light of day under the flawless blue arch of the Texas sky.

Chapter One

"I send you out to investigate a murder and you bring me back a cat," Sheriff Chance Hurd said.

"With all the rats we get in here, we need a cat," Deputy Sheriff Dan Caine said.

"Rodent or human?"

"Both, but mainly rodent. I saw one in the cell the other day that if you whittled down to middlin' size would still be as big as a hound dog."

"Well, I guess the cat is kinda cute at that," Hurd said, eyeing the calico that sat on his desk and studied him with fixed, glowing attention. The lawman sighed. "You feed it. Now, put the Kiowa back in his cell and make your report. The coffee is on the bile."

"We'll need the Kiowa when we go after Jenny Calthrop and the men who murdered her family," Caine said.

"The Indian is a drunk," Hurd said.

"Drunk or sober, he can follow a cold trail best I ever seen," Caine said.

"Dan, we ain't following no trails, cold or otherwise,"

Hurd said. He was a big man with a comfortably round belly and heavy bags under wide open, expressive and cold blue eyes that gave him a basilisk stare. He pointed a thick forefinger at his deputy. "We're city. The Calthrop spread is Concho County and always was."

Hurd's chair scraped across the jailhouse's rough pine floor as he rose and stepped to the stove. He took a couple of cups down from a shelf and poured steaming coffee into both. He handed one to Caine. "Fish says seven riders."

"He thinks there were that many. He isn't sure," Caine said. "I saw the tracks, and I'm not sure either."

"What did the Kiowa say?"

"He says seven, maybe eight."

"Too many," Hurd said.

"The Kiowa says that judging by her tracks, one of them was a woman, but I'm not sure of that either. But I read a dodger that said Clay Kyle runs with a woman," Caine said.

"Black-Eyed Susan. Yeah, I know," Hurd said. "She's named for the prairie wildflower, or so they say. And she kills like a teased rattlesnake. I heard that too. But it wasn't Clay Kyle done this crime. Get that out of your head. It's too far west for him."

"No matter. The sooner we form a posse the better," Caine said. "So why the hell are we sitting here drinking coffee?"

"Like I said, we're not going after them killers," Hurd snapped. "And, like I already told you, it ain't Clay Kyle an' them, because he never, and I say never, rides west of the Brazos. Everybody knows that."

"That's not what old Fish Lee thinks," Dan said. "Fish gets around, he talks to people, some of them lawman and Rangers. He says there's stories about a crazy man by the name of Loco Garrett who scalps women with long, blonde hair. He makes a pastime of it, you might say, and there's a ten-thousand-dollar price on his head, dead or alive. Grace Calthrop was scalped . . . and Garrett runs with Clay Kyle."

"There's plenty of big windies told about Clay Kyle and his boys," Hurd said. "Don't believe all you hear." The sheriff studied Dan Caine for a few moments and then said, "The county sheriff is living up Paint Rock way and I already sent him a wire. It's his responsibility. Me and you, we got enough to contend with when the punchers come in on Friday nights." He smiled. "Fright night, I call it."

"Lucas Ward is nearly seventy years old," Caine said. "He delivers warrants during the day and at night pulls padlocks on locked store doors. He's not about to ride out after seven killers on a chase that could last weeks."

"And that's exactly why we're staying put," Hurd said. "If you and me was away from Main Street for weeks, Thunder Creek would become a wide-open town, and wide-open towns attract outlaws, gunmen, gamblers, fancy women, and all kinds of rannies on the make. The damned burg would fall into lawlessness and come apart at the seams."

The sheriff's statement was so absurd, so palpably false, that Caine smiled, his teeth white under his sweeping dragoon moustache. "Chance, look out the window, what do you see?"

"A town," Hurd said. He was an inch taller than Caine's lanky six feet, a heavy, joyless man with rough-cut black hair, long sideburns that flanked a spade-shaped beard and a nose that had been broken several times, a relic of his wild, outlaw youth. He dressed like a respectable law clerk in a charcoal gray ditto suit and a wing collared shirt and blue tie. But he had none of a clerk's sallowness, his weathered face being as dark and coppery and heavy-boned as that of a Cheyenne dog soldier. On those few social occasions when he had to deal with out-of-town rowdies, he wore twin Colts carried in crossed gunbelts. It was not an affectation, but the mark of a shootist, a man to be reckoned with.

"Look at Main Street," Caine said, turning in his chair to glance out the fly-specked window. "Three fair-sized frame houses, built in a rickety hodgepodge style, but painted white and shaded by wild oaks. The houses are surrounded by outbuildings and behind them two dozen tarpaper shacks that could fold up and blow away in a good wind. There's Doan's General Store that doubles as a saloon. Ma Lester's Guest House and Restaurant for Respectable Christian Gentlemen and Mike Sweet's blacksmith shop with its steam hammer that he claims is the eighth wonder of the world. What else? Oh yeah, a rotting church with a spire and a cross on top but no preacher, a livery barn and corral, and a windmill with iron blades bitten into by rust. And all of this overlooking a scrubby, gravelly street throwing off clouds of dust that gets into everything. Oh, I forgot the Patterson stage that brings the mail. It visits once a month . . . if we're lucky."

Caine swung back and stared at Hurd. "After the law

rides out of town, do you really think all those gunmen, outlaws, gamblers and fancy women of yours are going to beat their feet in the direction of Thunder Creek, population 97? Hell, Chance, even the town's name is a lie. It seldom thunders here, there ain't even a creek, and half the folks are as poor as lizard-eating cats."

"Poor but proud. There's enough money out there to pay your twenty-a-month," Hurd said.

"That's three months in arrears," Caine said. He waited to let that sink in, and then said, "Did I tell you about Nancy Calthrop's wedding ring?"

Hurd rose, poured himself more coffee and sat again. "No, you didn't."

"She was very proud of it. Showed it to me one time. She said it was a rose color made from a nugget of Black Hills gold that Tom bought from a Sioux Indian one time and inside the band it said, *Forever.*"

"I'm glad she liked it . . . it being a wedding ring that was rose gold and said Forever and all," Hurd said.

"Somebody cut off Nancy's finger to get that ring, and I bet right now he's wearing it," Caine said.

"Why are you telling me this?" Hurd said.

"Because I want to go after the feller who's wearing that ring and hang him," Caine said. "And I want the animal that scalped Grace Calthrop. And I want to rescue her sister Jenny. And, Chance. I want you to authorize a posse and I want you to do it right now. Time is a-wasting."

Chance Hurd sat in silence and studied the younger man. Caine was brown-eyed, broad-shouldered, and in his early thirties. He was a good-looking man with jet black hair and eyebrows that were slightly too heavy for his lean face. He had a wide, expressive mouth and good teeth, and women, respectable and otherwise, liked him just fine. Dan Caine looked a man right in the eye, holding nothing back, and most times he had a stillness about him, a calm, but of the uncertain sort that had the brooding potential to suddenly burst into a moment of hellfire action. He seldom talked about himself, but Hurd knew that the young man had served three years in Huntsville for an attempted train robbery. He'd spent the first four months of his sentence in the penitentiary's infirmary for a bullet wound to the chest he'd taken during the holdup. At some point during that time, probably in the spring of 1880 according to most historians, he was befriended by John Wesley Hardin. Prison life had tempered Hardin's wild ways and Wes convinced the young Caine to quit the outlaw trail and live by the law. Released early in the summer of 1882, Dan Caine drifted for a couple of years, doing whatever work he could find. He arrived in Montana in January 1884, the year the citizenry, irritated by the amount of crime in the Territory, appointed hundreds of vigilantes to enforce the law. Hard-eyed hemp posses dutifully strung up thirty-five cattle and horse thieves and an even dozen of just plain nuisances. Dan didn't think Montana a good place to loiter, and in the fall of 1885 owning only his horse, saddle, rifle, Colt revolver, and the clothes he stood up in, he rode into Thunder Creek, missing his last six meals. Chance Hurd liked the tough, confident look of the young man and gave him a job as a twenty-a-month deputy sheriff. Caine made no secret of his past, but, having ridden the owlhoot trail himself a time or three, Hurd was willing to let bygones be bygones. That was three years ago, and now it looked as though their association was about to come to an end.

"Dan, you're willing to go this alone, I can tell," Hurd said. "Why?"

"Because I liked the Calthrops," Caine said. "They were good people, kind, generous people, full of laughter and of life and the living of it. They didn't deserve to be slaughtered the way they were and their oldest daughter taken. Now they lie in cold graves, all of them, and their killers run free, warm in the sunshine."

"How the hell are you going to find a posse in Thunder Creek?" Hurd said. "You think about that?"

"Holt Peters and Frank Halder helped me bury the dead," Caine said. "They're willing to ride after the killers."

Hurd made a strange, exasperated sound in his throat, then, "Peters is an orphan stock boy at the general store and Halder is a momma's brat who wears spectacles because he can't see worth a damn. As far as I know, neither of them have shot a gun in their lives." The sheriff smiled. "That's two. Go on . . ."

"Fish Lee says he'll go, if he can find a horse," Caine said.

"An old man with the rheumatisms who's half-crazy with the gold fever," Hurd said. "That's three. Go on . . ."

Caine glanced at the railroad clock on the wall. "It's gone two-thirty. Clint Cooley will be getting out of bed soon. He owes me a favor or two."

"A washed-up gambler who drinks too much and is trying to outrun a losing streak," Hurd said. "He's in

Thunder Creek because his back is to the wall, and he has nowhere else to run. Maybe that's four, maybe it's not. Go on . . ."

"Cooley is good with a gun," Caine said. "That's a point in his favor."

"Sure, because he carries them fancy foreign revolvers, we heard that he's been in a dozen shooting scrapes and killed five men," Hurd said. "Only problem with that is that nobody can say where and when the killings happened. Me, I don't think he's gunned anybody. He just ain't the type."

Caine didn't push it. Cooley was a man with his own dark secrets, and he'd never heard of him boast of killings. Wild talk always grew around lonely, unforthcoming men and meant nothing. This much Dan Caine did know . . . the ivory-handled, .44 caliber British Bulldog revolvers the gambler carried in a twin shoulder holster were worn from use. But how and when he'd used the pistols was a matter for speculation, as Hurd had just noted.

"The Kiowa makes five," Caine said. "Yeah, I know he's a drunk, and we believe he's the one who killed Lem Jones behind the saloon that time, but he's a tracker."

"I never could pin that shooting on the Kiowa," Hurd said. "It doesn't take much evidence to hang an Indian, but it was like good ol' Lem was shot by a damned ghost. No tracks, nothing."

Caine smiled. "Now the son of a bitch is dead, he's good ol' Lem. When he was alive, he was a mean, sorry, wife-beating excuse for a man. He needed killing and hell, I sometimes took the notion to gun him myself."

The sheriff sighed. "Lem cheated at cards and he was

hell on blacks and Indians. Hated them both." Then, "All right, round up your posse, Dan, but leave your badge right there on the desk. You ain't going after them killers as a deputy sheriff of Thunder Creek."

"Why?"

"Because what you're doing is not authorized. Now put the badge on the desk like I said."

Caine removed the nickel silver shield from his dark blue shirtfront and laid it in front of Hurd. "Now what am I?" he said.

"Now what are you? As of this moment, Dan, you're no longer a lawman but a vigilante . . . and until a few minutes ago I'd have thought that as likely as hearing the word love in a Wichita whorehouse. A man can sure be wrong about some things, huh?"

Caine stepped across the floor to a shelf that held a number of Texas law books, three novels by Mr. Dickens, an unthumbed Bible and two quarto volumes of *Webster's Dictionary of the English Language,* the late property of a preacher who'd taken over the church and died a week later of apoplexy.

Caine flicked his way through the pages until he reached V, flicked some more and then said, "Vigilante. It says what I am right here."

"Read it."

"A member of a self-appointed group of citizens who undertake law enforcement in their community without legal authority," Caine said. He paused and then said, "This part is important because it explains why folks like me do what we do. It says here, '. . . without legal authority . . .'"—then louder—"'typically because the legal agencies are thought to be inadequate.'"

Hurd nodded. "Now you know what you are and what I am." He picked up the badge, opened his desk drawer, dropped it inside and then slammed the drawer shut. "Good luck, Mr. Caine," he said. "And thanks for the cat."

Connect with **Us**

Visit us online at
KensingtonBooks.com
to read more from your favorite authors, see books
by series, view reading group guides, and more.

Join us on social media
for sneak peeks, chances to win books and prize packs,
and to share your thoughts with other readers.

facebook.com/kensingtonpublishing
twitter.com/kensingtonbooks

Tell us what you think!

To share your thoughts, submit a review,
or sign up for our eNewsletters, please visit:
KensingtonBooks.com/TellUs.